To
ANNETTE

Love
DARYL

All stories teach us something, and promise us something, whether they're true or invented, legend or fact.

— Stewart O'Nan

drunkcow **land**mines

by **daryl**meakes

ISBN 0-7414-2257-3

Published by:

PUBLISHING.COM

1094 New De Haven Street, Suite 100
West Conshohocken, PA 19428-2713
Info@buybooksontheweb.com
www.buybooksontheweb.com
Toll-free (877) BUY BOOK
Local Phone (610) 941-9999
Fax (610) 941-9959

Printed in the United States of America
Printed on Recycled Paper
Published November 2004

I dedicate this my first book, to my first love --
Joey (atleast, I think that was her name)

chapterindex

introduction

Drunkcow landmines can be best described as a grab bag of moralistic tales, wickedly unusual news stories, false-but-oddly-believable reports, and fractured facts that have been passed along by someone who believes the story to have happened to someone he knows or to an acquaintance of a friend or family member.

These tales are set against the backdrop of contemporary times -- the stories take place in shopping malls and coed dormitories and feature such up-to-date bogeyman as Disease and President George W. Bush. Though some of these tales go back a century or more, the details of them are continually being updated to keep them current with our times; the horse and buggy of yester-year becomes the BMW of today, and the cakes and ale of long ago are the pepsi and hamburgers of the now.

Drunkcow landmines will reflect current societal concerns and fears as well as confirm our world views. These cautionary tales warn us against engaging in risky behaviors by pointing out what has supposedly happened to others who did what we might be tempted to try. Whereas, others confirm our belief that it's a big bad world out there -- one awash with crazed killers, drug addicts, unscrupulous companies, a government that could care less about the people, who are just out to make a buck at any cost, and ex-girlfriends.

Legends of this genre are passed along in oral and written form. You'll hear them over coffee and find them forwarded to you in your e-mail or pinned to the bulletin board in your local church. Consequently, the details shift depending on who tells it. These details, of course, change with every telling, and tend to localize, with the provision that the event took place in a nearby town. By definition, these stories usually involve a cast of characters and a plotline. Complicating matters further, many humorous legends also exist as jokes or funny stories -- the snippet of gossip about the town mechanic in one village will be presented as a boldfaced joke not about anyone in particular in another.

A common mistake is the equation that rumors and legends are false (i.e., "Oh, that's just a rumor."). Though the vast majority of such tales are pure invention, a tiny handful do turn out to be based on real incidents. Remember: "All ficiton is based on some form of the truth."

What moves tales of this type out of the world of news and into the genre of contemporary lore is the blurring of details and multiplicity of claims that it happened locally. These alterations that take place as the story is passed through countless hands. Though there might indeed have been an original actual event, it clearly did not happen to as many people, or in as many places as the various recountings would have one believe.

Despite our being heartily mistrustful of anything found in the newspaper, the vast majority of us tend to unquestionably believe rumors and legends. Why? Because invariably it's either a dear friend or someone we look up to doing the telling. Furthermore, that person swears a friend of hers knows the actual person it happened to. As such, it's practically first-hand news. Because it rides in on the back of someone we trust, and it skirts past our usual skepticism.

However, legends make good telling, and who doesn't like being in the spotlight and looked up to as the one who knows all the really great stories. It's almost guaranteed these tales will outlive us all.

The odd, the unusual, and the offbeat have all found their way into the following pages and now await your presence to come back to life, to again enthrall the imagination. Read them. You may be surprised; you may be shocked; and you may even learn a thing or two, so plan to spend the weekend.

chapterone

*"My dream is to one day have a puppy,
or at least have the ability to hold a puppy,
and when I grow up I want to play baseball,
but right now it looks like I may only get to be a base."*

--The Burlap Baby

bestmedicine

The old adage says, "Laughter is the best medicine." But often our best humor comes from medicine itself.

. . . .

"I'm sorry sir, I don't know, I'm on the white team."

Why is it doctors develop a God complex? Is it because we worship them for their medical knowledge, and take to heart anything a physician utters? Or is it their power over life and death? God complex or not, sometimes even our idols have feet of clay.

Bang The Head Resuscitation

In Kansas City, a dentist was horrified to discover that a patient of his had died in the chair while he was giving him a filling. Worried about the consequences to his business, the dentist lifted the man over his shoulder, carried him downstairs and left him in the mens room. Ten minutes later, the dentist was stunned to see the man walk into his surgery complaining about a headache. It turned out that the bumping motion of carrying the man down the stairs had been the equivalent of cardiopulmonary resuscitation and the dentist had inadvertently revived the man.

Flashy Examination

A woman on holiday visiting a friend ended up sleeping with a guy after a night out on the town. A few days later she developed a curious rash around her genitals. Concerned, her girlfriend recommended that she visit her gynaecologist. As any woman might feel on being seen by a friend's gynaecologist, she wanted to smell as fresh as possible, so she used her friend's deodorant spray. She arrived at the doctors office, and somewhat nervously, waited to be seen. Eventually, the gynaecologist called her name and she entered his consulting room. She followed the doctor's instructions to put on a gown and lie on the examination table, where he began to examine her. Almost immediately he looked up and said, "Well, aren't we flashy. Have you got something special on tonight?" Completely embarrassed and extremely puzzled, the woman looked down, and seeing lots of sparkly stuff, realised she had mistaken her friend s glitter hairspray for vaginal deodorant.

The Colour System

A hospital in Pittsburgh, Pennsylvania, had a simple system to cope with organising the huge number of people working there. It designated people to three teams; the red team, the blue team and the white team, which were the colours of the American flag. Everything seemed to run smoothly, however, one day a black patient innocently asked a passing nurse when a doctor could next have a look at him. Without realising what she was saying, the nurse replied, "I'm sorry sir, I don't know, I'm on the white team." Soon after, the hospital changed its system to incorporate colours that could not be misconstrued in any sentence; the purple team, the turquoise team and the violet team.

Live and Unplugged

Despite the advances in modern medicine, bizarre, and freakish accidents can happen to anyone, including us.

Ambulance Mishap

One evening, an ambulance was called out to pick up a man, reported to be in need of medical attention, from the side of a road. The ambulance driver drove down the road slowly, looking for the man on the shoulder, when suddenly, there was a bump. The ambulance appeared to run over something. In an attempt to work out what it was, the driver reversed back, only to run over the same thing again. It slowly dawned on the ambulance driver what he had just done...twice. Back at the hospital, doctors were mystified why a man coming in with a bad heart condition had two broken legs.

Compromising Position

In Stamford, Connecticut an elderly man was in the hospital for a routine operation. A nurse had given the man a bath and she was drying him, when she found her necklace had somehow become entangled in the man's pubic hair, and the clasp of the necklace was also entangled. She was unable to take the necklace off and no amount of pulling or wiggling would free it. It was at this point that the old man's wife walked in. Before either of them could explain what looked to be a very compromising position, the wife started hitting the nurse and her husband with her handbag. Eventually, other nurses managed to calm the wife down and disentangle the nurse from the old man's genitals. As a consequence, the nurse was told to remove all jewellery while she bathed patients.

Deadly Gas

A terrible diet and room with no ventilation are being blamed for the death of a man who was killed by his own farts. There was no mark on his body but an autopsy showed large amounts of methane gas in his system. His diet had consisted primarily of beans and cabbage. It was just the right combination of foods to create this deadly gas. It appears that the man died in his sleep from breathing the poisonous cloud that was hanging over his bed. Had he been outside or had his windows been opened, it wouldn't have been fatal, but the man was shut up in his near airtight bedroom.

According to reporters, "He was a big man with a huge capacity for creating 'this deadly gas."

Three of the rescuers got sick and one was hospitalized.

Did you know? *Eleven people were taken to hospital for treatment after an elderly woman at a unit for sufferers of senile dementia passed round a box of mothballs thinking that they were breathmints.*

Fastened and Framed

A few friends gathered together in Bill's basement rec room for an evening of drinking and dancing. With the party in full swing, one of the girls excused herself to go to the john. This room, it seems, had been newly painted in a charming pastel blue; it was supposed to be a fast-drying enamel, but it hadn't dried fast enough, and the young lady found herself stuck. Her shrieks brought Bill's girlfriend, who, unable to do anything about the situation herself, summoned Bill. After several minutes of uncontrolled laughter, Bill managed to produce a screw driver and detach the thing, permitting the girl to stand up. But still unable to remove it, they called a doctor.

"Did you ever see anything like this before, doctor?" the girl asked in embarrassment when the M.D. arrived.

"Well, yes," the doctor replied truthfully, "but I believe this is the first time I've ever seen one framed."

I Love You So Much I Have Trouble Breathing...

A man from Pennsylvania whose wife weighed twice as much as he did was squashed to death when she sat on him during a domestic quarrel.

Kathy Geddes, 38, sat on her husband Wayne, 40, for over ten minutes in their rural home in nearby Harrisburg, Pennsylvania.

Dr. Wallace Bradley, whose office conducted an autopsy and investigation said, "The massive amount of pressure on his chest rendered him unable to breathe, and because of that, he suffocated."

State trooper Dan Bloodworth, who investigated the case reported that Mrs. Geddes weighed about 320 pounds and the woman's husband was a "very small, very thin" frail man, weighing between 125 and 135 pounds.

"Mrs. Geddes was not in custody and will probably not be charged", the trooper said. "She was trying to restrain her husband, and there was no indication of foul play intended."

"Mr. Geddes came home drunk and in a bad mood at about 4pm", stated officer Bloodworth. "He soon went out again to go drinking and returned about 10pm after running his truck into a ditch. Upon threatened to shoot his wife, their two children and burn the house down, Mrs. Geddes attempted to subdue him while their son was sent to get the state police."

Bloodworth commented, "Weaver's drinking may have contributed to his death."

Live and Unplugged

There was a case in one hospital's Intensive Care unit where patients always seemed to die in the same bed, every Sunday morning at 11am, regardless of their medical condition. This puzzled the doctors and some even thought that it had something to do with the supernatural. No one could solve the mystery as to why the deaths occurred around 11am on a Sunday.

A Worldwide team of experts was assembled to investigate the cause of the incidents. The following

Sunday morning, a few minutes before 11am, all the doctors and nurses nervously waited outside the ward to see for themselves what the terrible phenomenon was all about. Some were holding wooden crosses, prayer books and other holy objects to ward off potential evil spirits.

Just when the clock struck 11am, Lupa Morales, the part-time Sunday sweeper, entered the ward, unplugged the life support system, and plugged in the vacuum cleaner.

Did you know? *An operation at a hospital in Chicago ended prematurely when the patient exploded. The casualty, an 87-year-old woman, was undergoing electrosurgery for cancer. The blast was attributed to an unusual build-up of stomach gas ignited by the sparks.*

Rubber Nose

After years of sleepless nights, a woman finally persuaded her husband to see the doctor about his snoring problem, which his wife explained, sounded like an elephant's fart. The doctor gave the man a thorough examination and was surprised to find a rubber stuck up his nose.

"My God," exclaimed the man, "a bully shoved that up my nose at school 20 years ago! I must've been so distressed that I forgot all about it." The wife was delighted, and finally got a good nights sleep, commenting, "Now he snores just like a purring kitten."

The Burlap Baby

In Atlantic City, New Jersey, lives a very sick little boy. He was born with only lungs and a heart, no body. It doesn't hurt him, except when he goes to sleep. The doctors gave him an artificial body. Unfortunately the body is made of a burlap bag filled with leaves.

The doctors said that was the best they could do on account that the mother has no money or insurance. He would like to have a body transplant, but they need more money. His mother doesn't work because she said, "Employers don't hire crying people."

Even though his mother is allergic to burlap and it chafes her really bad, she always gives him hugs.

If you want to help "The Burlap Baby" you can contact Dr. Johan Deitrich who is teaming up with Bill Gates and AOL to do a survey with NASA. The astronauts are collecting prayers from school children all over the world and taking them up to space so that the angels can hear them better. Then they will go to the Pope, and ask that he take up a collection in church and send the money to the doctors. That way doctors could then help him more effeciently.

His dream is too one day have a puppy, or at least have the ability to hold a puppy, and when he grows up he wants to play baseball, but right now it looks like he may only get to be a base. Time is the essence, he needs a body before the leaves rot.

To Smart For Your Own Good

Doctors are blaming a rare electrical imbalance in the brain for the bizarre death of a chess player whose head literally exploded in the middle of a championship game!

No one else was hurt in the fatal explosion, but four players and three officials at the Moscow Candidate Masters' Chess Championships were sprayed with blood and brain matter when Boris Nikolai's head suddenly blew apart. Experts say he suffered from a condition called "Hyper-Cerebral Electrosis" or HCE.

"He was deep in concentration with his eyes focused on the board," said Nikolai's opponent, Vladimir

Korloff. "All of a sudden his hands flew to his temples and he screamed in pain. Everyone looked up from their games, startled by the noise. Then, as if someone had put a bomb in his cranium, his head popped like a zit."

Incredibly, Nikolai is not the first case in which a person's head has spontaneously exploded. Five people died of HCE in the last 10 years. The most recent death occurred just last year, when psychic Sylvia Gendron skull burst. Miss Gendron''s story was reported by newspapers worldwide.

"HCE is an extremely rare physical imbalance," said Dr. Basil Cormier, famed neurologist and expert on the human brain who did the autopsy on the brilliant chess expert. "It is a condition in which the circuits of the brain become overloaded by the body's own electricity. The explosions happen during periods of intense mental activity when lots of currents are surging through the brain. Victims are highly intelligent people with great powers of concentration. Both Miss Gendron and Mr. Nikolai were intense people who tended to keep those cerebral circuits overloaded. In a way it could be said they were literally too smart for their own good."

Although Dr. Cormeir says there are probably many undiagnosed cases, he hastens to add that very few people will die from HCE. "Most people who have it will never know. At this point, medical science still doesn't know much about HCE. And since fatalities are so rare it will probably be years before research money becomes available."

In the meantime, the doctor recommends people to take it easy and not think too hard for long periods of time, and be sure to take frequent relaxation breaks when you're doing things that take lots of mental focus.

Ogling over women's breasts is good for a man's health and can add years to his life.

Medicine protects us from harm and saves us from illness, but we fear them anyway. Even the most helpful treatment can still be harmful, and put a fearsome power into the hands of the ill-intentioned. There's always the occasional "bad" medicine that slips through the checking process and reaches the market anyway.

Bowel Movements

A woman who had lost control of her bowel movements was diagnosed as having a rare condition. Fortunately, technology had the answer, and a device was surgically implanted in her backside. In order to go to the bathroom all she had to do was pass a magnet over a sensor in her abdomen to open her bowels. The device worked superbly and the woman began to enjoy a new lease of life. In fact, she was so delighted with the freedom the device gave her, that she quit her job and decided to travel around the world for a year. However, she realised that she might have made a mistake as she boarded the first of her flights and settled into her seat. The airport security X-ray machine had triggered off the device, delivering an unpleasant mess into her pants.

Fellatio may significantly decrease the risk of breast cancer in women

A North Carolina State University study found that women who perform the act of fellatio on a regular basis, one to two times a week, may reduce their risk of breast cancer by up to 40 percent.

Doctors had never suspected a link between the act of fellatio and breast cancer, but new research being performed at North Carolina State University is starting to suggest that there could be an important link between the two.

In a study of over 15,000 women suspected of having performed regular fellatio over the past ten years, the researchers found that those actually having performed the act regularly, one to two times a week, had a lower occurance of breast cancer than those who had not. There was no increased risk for those who did not regularly perform.

"I think it removes the last shade of doubt that fellatio is actually a healthy act," said Dr. Haywood Jablowme of Johns Hopkins School of Medicine, who was not involved in the research. "I am surprised by these findings, but am also excited that the researchers may have discovered a relatively easy way to lower the occurance of breast cancer in women."

The University researchers stressed that, though breast cancer is relatively uncommon, any steps taken to reduce the risk would be a wise decision.

"Only with regular performance will your chances be reduced, so I encourage all women out there to make fellatio an important part of their daily routine," said Dr. Anita Dyck, one of the researchers at the University. "Since the emergence of the research, I try to fellate at least once every other night to reduce my chances."

The study can be found in the archives of the Journal of Medical Research.

Reported by the National Cancer Institute, "In 1991, ober 43,000 women died of breast cancer."

Dr. B.J Sooner, deputy chief medical officer for the American Cancer Society said, "Women should not overlook or "play down" these findings. This will hopefully change women's practice and patterns, resulting in a severe drop in the future number of cases."

Sooner also explained that the research shows no increase in the risk of breast cancer in those who are, for whatever reason, not able to fellate regularly.

"There's definitely fertile ground for more research. Many have stepped forward to volunteer for related research now in the planning stages," he said.

Almost every woman is, at some point, going to perform the act of fellatio, but it is the frequency at which this event occurs that makes the difference, say researchers.

The reasearch consisted of two groups, 6,546 women between the of ages 25 to 45 who had performed fellatio on a regular basis over the past five to ten years, and 9,782 women who had not. The group of women who had performed fellatio had a breast cancer rate of 1.9 percent and the group who had not, had a breast cancer rate of 10.4 percent.

"The findings do suggest that there are other causes for breast cancer besides the absence of regular fellatio," Sooner said. "It's a cause, not the cause."

Did You Know? *The main ingredient in ladies Viagra is lemon gin.*

Great news for girl watchers

Medical experts have discovered that ogling over women's breasts is good for a man's health and can add years to his life.

According to the New England Journal of Medicine, "Just 10 minutes of staring at the charms of a well-endowed female is roughly equivalent to a 30-minute aerobics work-out" declared gerontologist Dr. Phil Memelons.

Dr. Memelons and fellow researchers at three hospitals in Frankfurt, Germany, reached the startling conclusion after comparing the health of 200 male outpatients -- half of whom were instructed to look at busty females daily, while the other half were told to refrain from doing so.

The study revealed that after five years, the chest-watchers had lower blood pressure, slower resting pulse rates and fewer instances of coronary artery disease.

"Sexual excitement gets the heart pumping and improves blood circulation," explained Dr. Memelons. "There's no question that gazing at breasts makes men healthier. Our study indicates that engaging in this activity a few minutes daily cuts the risk of stroke and heart attack in half. We believe that by doing so consistently, the average man can extend his life four to five years."

The conference players test came back saying he was pregnant.

Staggering numbers of couples engage in sex everyday, and ultimately have children. We believe strange things about the manner in which babies are conceived! Woman have been known to become pregnant simply by swimming or being hit by a bullet.

Baby Boom

A researcher from the Board of Health became curious about a small town in Southern Saskatchewan, Canada, after coming across an alarmingly large increase in the number of births being reported. Eager to investigate this phenomenon, the researcher decided to spend a weekend in the town.

The researcher stayed in a friendly bed and breakfast, but after a day scrutinising the town's records, he still couldn't understand what could be causing the residents to have so many children.

At about 5am on Monday morning, the researcher was suddenly woken by a loud rumbling, that felt like the whole building was shaking. Worried that it might be an earthquake, the researcher ran downstairs and started banging on the landlady's door.

The landlady eventually managed to calm him down and told him that the rumbling was due to a freight train that passed by every weekday morning at about the same time. She went on to explain that the town had been a victim to the train's rumblings since the tracks were strengthened over a year ago. The researcher, understanding the effects on couples being woken up early in the morning, realised what was causing the mysterious population explosion.

Did you know? *A Quarterback at UCLA bragged to his teammates that he got past drug testing by smuggling in his girlfriends urine. Unfortunately the conference players test came back saying he was pregnant.*

Brother Dad

A spotty teenage youth from Spokane, Washington was enjoying a long languid bath.

After having soaped and scoured himself, he begun to get quite aroused.

Needless to say, he decided to relieve himself while still soaking. So he leant on his arm until his hand went dead, that way he could pretend someone else was doing it, and finished the job.

But just as he climaxed, his mother knocked forcefully on the door and told him to hurry up. She wanted to use the same bath to save water (Don't ask me why, maybe there was a shortage, and she was in a rush).

Appalled that his mom would see conspicuous floating evidence of his vice, the young man spent a frenzied two minutes stalling her while he fished out the flotsam.

When he'd finished, he rushed out and let her in.

Happily, there was not a peep from his mom. But nine months later, the boy had mixed feelings about his mother giving birth too his new baby brother.

Congratulations, It's A Hippy!

Back in the early Seventies, a young hippy woman was in the maternity wing of south London's Saint Thomas Hospital. When it was time, the pink-mohican was taken into the delivery room and attended to by her doctor. The woman was screaming in pain, so the nurse told her to calm down while the doctor had a look.

The doctor was mildly amused to see that the woman had dyed her pubic triangle green. He also noticed that she had a tattoo just above, but because of her pregnant state the writing was all distorted.

Curious and trying to make small talk to calm her down, the doctor asked her what it said.

The woman stopped screaming, stared at him and then said gruffly, "It says 'Keep off the grass'!"

Soon after, the woman gave birth to a healthy, hippy baby boy.

Did you know? *During the Civil War, May 12, 1863, to be exact, a young Virginia farm girl was standing on her front porch while a battle was raging nearby. A stray bullet passed through the scrotum of a young Union cavalryman, then lodged in the reproductive tract of the young woman, who became pregnant by a man she had not been within 100 feet of, and nine months later she gave birth to a healthy baby soldier!*

"I want an Indian baby."

My best friend's fiancée was the Administrative Assistant for a gynecologist. One day, he received the wife of an Indian chief, who desperately wanted children but had been unsuccessful over the years of her marriage.

The gynecologist asked her a number of questions, while taking copious notes.

Then indicating a screen in the corner of the consulting room, he asked, "Would you go over there please, take off all your clothes, and lie on the table?"

"Oh, no!" she wailed. "I want an *Indian* baby."

So Many Names

A woman had just given birth to her daughter, and she was discussing the choice of name with her roommate, who was equally clueless.

Mulling over the possibilities, she considered a word that she'd recently heard on the obstetric ward. "Vagina, that be a nice name . . . hmm, I think I'll call her 'Vagina.'"

Admittedly an euphonious word, the two women agreed that "Vagina" would indeed be a nice name for a girl.

When the time came to relay the name choice to one of the hospital's personnel, the shocked worker exclaimed, "Uh, you can't name her 'Vagina'!"

To which the Mom replied, "I be her mother, and I can name her whatever I wants to!"

This prompted the worker to explain just what a vagina was, but the Mom was skeptical simply stating, "That ain't a vagina — that's a cootchie!"

The couch's family was very happy that the remote was found.

The emergency room of the hospital is a place of utmost seriousness, but it also features in some of the more amusing medical anecdotes.

A light that surpasseth all understanding.

Several years ago a friend of a friend was awaiting treatment for an allergic reaction at New York's Saint Vincent's Hospital emergency room. The hospital is located on the border of New York's Chelsea and Greenwich Village.

He was told to sit in a large room divided into many identical cubicles by curtains behind which each patient could have privacy during examination, at least in theory. Obviously you could hear something of what was going on in the next cubicle.

He became aware of a man in the next cubicle fearfully explaining to the young doctor examining him that he was experiencing pain in his rectum. The doctor positioned the man for examination, when suddenly, he heard the doctor loudly exclaim in shock, "Oh my God! What the hell is .....! I'll be right back!" before he heard the doctor rush out.

Obviously, the examining doctor discovered something rare and very serious, and needed to consult a more experienced physician.

About two minutes later the footsteps of several excited doctors where heard rushing in. There must have been a dozen doctors crammed in the small cubicle.

"Take a look." The examining doctor said with excitement.

Then he heard one of the other doctors loudly exclaim, "He's lit up like a Christmas tree! What the hell is that?"

Through close shameless evesdropping it soon became obvious to my friend what this patient's problem was. The poor embarrassed man had a flashlight stuck up his ass and the light was in the "on" position and pointing outward.

Just imagine the doctors shocked expression when he separated the man's cheeks and low and behold ....this bright light shining up into his face.

Self-Castration

A man entered the ER frantically asking to see a doctor. When a doctor finally came, the man removed his pants. The doctor noticed that the man's scrotum was wrapped in soiled linen and was swollen to the size of a grapefruit. Since the man didn't want to disclose what happened, the doctor proceeded with X-rays only to find that there were staples in the man's scrotum. The doctor confronted the man demanding to know what happened.

The man was a wood-worker. One day, he decided to use his stationery belt sander for some sexual gratification. Since he had done this many times before, without incident, he wasn't worried.

This time, however, he slipped and fell onto the belt sander while it was operating at full speed. The man was hurled a good six feet forward into the wall, tearing open his scrotum. Despite the pain, he decided to staple his scrotum together before going to the doctor. Unfortunately, the staples were neither sterile nor rust-proof. His scrotum became infected and forced him to eventually go to the doctor.

The doctor cleaned the wound and fixed the man the best he could. However, the accident caused the man's testicles to rip free from his scrotum and had been lost. Due to all the blood and pain, the man never noticed. By the time he visited the doctor, it was too late. He was castrated by the belt sander.

The Human Couch

A mordibly obese woman was brought into the Emergency Room on a tarp dragged by six firemen after suffering from shortness of breath . After positioning two gurneys side by side, the medical staff and firemen somehow managed to lift her up. She was in respiratory failure due to her weight, which was estimated to be approximately five hundred pounds.

Attempting to undress her, the doctors lifted her arms and pulled her very large blouse over her head. To their surprise, an asthma inhaler fell out from under her right armpit. It had been enveloped in the folds of her skin.

Reviewing her chest X ray, doctors discovered a round density in the left chest. With the help of an assistant, they lifted up her massive left breast to find a shiny dime. No telling how long it had been there.

Finally, a nurse and two technicians attempted to place a Foley catheter in her bladder. After spreading apart one tree-trunk leg at a time, they found a handful of industrial paper towels, apparently being used as a sanitary napkin. They also found an even larger surprise in her crotch -- a TV remote control.

When the medical examiner gave his report about the patient to the unhappy admitting physician, he tried to cheer him up by reminding him that if he did a thorough exam, he too could find buried treasure. They nicknamed their patient "The Human Couch".

Did you know? *A man staggered into the emergency room of County Hospital in Chicago with a wind-up turtle attached to his testicles, explaining that his young son had dropped the toy into his bath. A nurse said, "The mechanical joint was connected to his tender bits, and jammed solid."*

Vaginal Garden

An elderly female came to the Emergency Room complaining, "I got green vines in my virginny."

The patient reported a two-week history of a vine growing from her vagina. On physical examination it was discovered that she did indeed have a vine growing out of her vagina, and it was about six inches in length.

A pelvic exam revealed a mass, which was easily removed from the vaginal vault, with the vine still attached. Upon extraction, the patient reported that her uterus had been falling out, so she "put a potato in there to hold it up" and subsequently forgot about it.

chaptertwo

"The Bank of Hong Kong are Friggin' Bastards."

--Mr. Bastards

businessbabble

Corporate America — they're run by people who cheat the public, abuse their customers, commit astounding marketing blunders, and mistranslate their own product advertisements. It seems like they can't do anything right. But never under estimate the power of really stupid people in large groups; the business world are the whipping boys of unbelievable rumors, and the bigger they are, the harder they get whipped.

. . . .

A $1 charge for marking the wall with an X, and $9,999 for knowing where to put it.

These are tales of ingenuity, one-upmanship, and just plain business savvy.

A Bookeeper In A Whorehouse

A country lad went to the big city to seek his fortune, but had no luck finding a job. One day, wandering through the red light district, he spotted a Help Wanted sign in a window.

They were looking for a bookkeeper, but after the madam quizzed the boy about his education she discovered that he could neither read nor write, so she turned him away.

Feeling sorry for him, she gave him two big red apples as he left. A few blocks down the street, he placed the apples on top of a garbage can while tying his shoe, and a stranger came along and offered to buy them.

The boy took the money to a produce market and bought a dozen more apples, which he sold quickly. Eventually he parlayed his fruit sales into a grocery store, then a string of supermarkets. Eventually he became the wealthiest man in the state.

Finally, after years of success and prestige, he was named "Man of the Year". During an interview a a journalist discovered that his subject could neither read nor write.

13

"Good Lord!" he said, "What do you suppose you would have become if you had ever learned to read and write?"

"Well," he answered, "I guess I would have been a bookkeeper in a whorehouse."

Dead Donkey

A city boy moved to the country and bought a donkey from an old farmer for $100. The farmer even agreed to deliver the donkey the next day.

The next day the farmer drove up and said, "Sorry son, but I have some bad news. Your donkey died."

The boy replied, "Well then, just give me my money back."

The farmer said, "Can't do that. I went and spent it already."

"Okay," said the boy, "Then just unload the donkey."

The farmer asked, "What ya gonna do with him?"

The boy replied, "I'm going to raffle him off."

"You can't raffle off a dead donkey," said the farmer.

"Sure I can," said the boy. "Watch me. I just won't tell anybody he is dead."

A month later the farmer met up with the boy again and asked, "What ever happened with that dead donkey?"

"I raffled him off," said the boy. "I sold 500 tickets at $2 a piece and made a profit of $998.00."

"Didn't anyone complain?" asked the farmer.

"No!" the boy said, "Just the guy who won. So I gave him his $2 back."

That boy grew up and eventually became the chairman of Enron!

My Chimney Has The Flue

A mason built a new fireplace for a wealthy man. When the mason finished the job, he asked for his money, but the wealthy client said he couldn't pay just now, because he didn't have the correct amount.

"That's all right", the mason said. But if I have to wait, then so will you."

The wealthy man agreed that he wouldn't build a fire in his new chimney until he's paid the mason.

The mason went home. But just an hour or so later, his wealthy client appeared at the door yelling, "My house is full of smoke, goddammit!"

"I told you not to use that chimney until you paid me," said the mason. "When you pay me, I'll fix it."

So the client took out his wallet, which was full of money after all, and the mason returned to the wealthy man's house. The mason brought a brick with him, carried it up a ladder to the roof and dropped it down the chimney, smashing out the pane of glass he had placed across the flue.

Problem Area

An electrician was visiting the new Ford plant, which was having difficulty with its electrical wiring.. Henry Ford asked the electrician if he could help identify the problem area. The man walked up to a wall of boilerplate and made a small X in chalk on one of the plates. Ford was thrilled, and told him to send an invoice. The bill arrived, for $10,000. Ford asked for a breakdown. The electrician sent another invoice, indicating a $1 charge for marking the wall with an X, and $9,999 for knowing where to put it.

The Evian Secret

What tickles my funny bone is when I consider how much a bottle of water costs and ponder what any sensible person is thinking when paying for it. In my home I have a device that gives me all the water I want for free, it's called a "tap", maybe you heard of these contraptions, they are very handy.

In a society where tap water can be had for free, those who don't purchase bottled water, or those who buy one of the many cheaper brands, are amused by the millions of folks who are willing — nay, frantic — to pay a couple of bucks for a bottle of water.

The Evian bottle water company has a good chuckle over this phenomenon. Afterall, Evian is "naive" spelled backwards. Evian, like all bottled water is nothing more than water drawn from a lake.

"I am so glad I do not work for quality control at the Johnson and Johnson Company."

The folks in the business world who create the things we buy, tell us how to use their products, and manage large amounts of moolah don't always know what they are doing. Foolishly we expect them to, but that's just a bunch of "business babble".

Smoking Can Cause Firing

A top executive of a big American management consultant company entered a lift to find a man openly smoking. The executive told the man that smoking was not permitted anywhere in the building and instructed him to extinguish his cigarette immediately.

Instead of doing anything, the smoker just shrugged, mentioned that there were no ashtrays and continued smoking.

Furious, the executive grabbed the man's cigarette, threw it on the floor and stamped it out with his shoe, only to see the man casually light another one and continue smoking.

Incensed, the executive asked the man what his monthly salary was.

The man replied, "About $1500."

The executive wrote a check to the man for $1500 and handed it to the man saying, "There's a month's salary. Consider yourself dismissed with immediate effect."

The man stepped out of the lift, smiled and said, "Hey, thanks. Actually, I don't work for you, I just came in to use the bathroom."

"Special" Milk

A woman just returning from maternity leave circulated a chiding memo after someone helped themselves to the "special" milk she left in the office refrigerator.

"Whoever used the milk in the small plastic container that was in the refrigerator yesterday, please do not own up to it. I would find it forever difficult to meet your gaze across a cafeteria table while having a discussion about Java applets or brand identity. Just be aware that the milk was expressly for my son, if you know what I mean. I will label these things from now on, but if you found your coffee tasted just a little bit special, you might think about calling your mom and telling her you love her."

The "I Hate My Job!" Therapy

A friend of a friend told me that her boyfriend absolutely hates his job. So on his way home from the end of a hectic work week, he always stops at a pharmacy, goes to the thermometer section, where he purchases a rectal thermometer made by Johnson and Johnson. When he gets home, he locks his doors, draws his drapes, and disconnects the phone so he will not be disturbed during his therapy. He changes to a more comfortable clothing, usually a sweatsuit, and lies down on his bed. Then he opens the package and removes the thermometer, carefully placing it on the bedside table so that it will not become chipped or broken. He takes out the material that comes with the thermometer and begins to read it.

He always reads the small print that states, "Every rectal thermometer made by Johnson and Johnson is personally tested."

At this point, he closes his eyes and repeats out loud ten times, "I am so glad I do not work for quality control at the Johnson and Johnson Company... I am so glad I do not work for quality control at the Johnson and Johnson Company...I am so glad I do not work for quality control at the Johnson and Johnson Company..."

Moral of the story: There is always someone with a worse job than yours.

"This job will be the death of me."

The CEO of a publishing firm is trying to work out why no-one noticed that one of their employees had been sitting dead at his desk for five days before anyone asked if he was feeling okay.

Arthur Classy, 58, who had been employed as a proof-reader at a New York Publishing firm for 30 years, suffered a heart attack in the open-plan office he shared with 25 other workers.

He quietly passed away on a Monday, but nobody noticed until the following Saturday morning when an office cleaner asked why he was still working during the weekend.

His boss George Elliot said, "Arthur was always the first guy in each morning and always the last to leave at night, so no-one found it unusual that he was in the same position all that time and didn't say anything. He was always absorbed in his work and kept much to himself."

A post mortem examination revealed that he had been dead for five days after suffering a coronary.

Ironically, Arthur was proof-reading manuscripts of medical textbooks when he died.

VIP

A coworker was sitting in the VIP lounge of the airport en route to Seattle, when he noticed Bill Gates sitting on the chesterfield enjoying a cognac.

The coworker was meeting a very important client who was also flying to Seattle with him but she was running a bit late. Being a forward type of guy, he approached Mr. Gates and introduced myself. He explained to Mr. Gates that he was conducting some very important business and how he would appreciate it if he could throw a quick "Hello Johnson" at him when he was with his client. Gates agreed.

Ten minutes later while he was in mid-conversation with his client, he felt a tap on his shoulder. It was Bill Gates. He turned around and looked up at him.

Mr. Gates, as a man of his word said, "Hi Johnson, how have you been?"

To which the man replied, "Fuck off Gates, I'm in a meeting."

"Pepsi Brings Your Ancestors Back From the Dead."

It has been more than a century since the creation of soft drinks, and we're still as much in love with them as our great-grandparents were. Soft drink companies such as Coca Cola and Pepsi are the most successful companies the world has ever known; so nothing can be that big and popular, or as much a part of everyday life, without having legends spring up around it. Soft drinks have a unique and influential position in our culture, which has led to a special set of tales I call "SodaPopLore": a collection of tall tales sure to refresh even the most informationally-parched reader.

"Come Alive! You're In The Pepsi Generation"

"Come Alive! You're In The Pepsi Generation" was Pepsi's battlecry as the company sought to expand its market share by convincing young people that this beverage belonged to them, hence the famous "Pepsi Generation".

However, thanks to "The Pepsi Generation," the drink was now reaching a new market of cash-empowered youth. When the ads were ported to China, Pepsi sales dropped precipitously because the Chinese interpreted this bit as a promise that "Pepsi Brings Your Ancestors Back From the Dead."

"Harrier Fighter: 7,000,000 Pepsi Points"

In 1996 Pepsi ran a promotion through which consumers who collected empty Pepsi containers could earn "Pepsi Points" that could be redeemed for hats, jackets, bikes and other such merchandise. To gain a "Pepsi Points" T-shirt, for instance, took 80 points, or the equivalent of 40 two-liter Pepsi bottles.

Kicking off the "Buy Pepsi, Get Stuff" campaign was a playful television commercial showcasing a number of the items being offered. This controversial ad showed a suburban teen preparing for school and wearing a number of Pepsi items, such as a T-shirt, a leather jacket, and sunglasses. As the items were depicted, words at the bottom of the screen revealed how many "Pepsi Points" they cost. The commercial concludes with the teen landing a Harrier jet near a bike rack at his school while the plane's searing jet stream strips a teacher to his underwear. The smug teen then says, "Sure beats the bus," before the words "Harrier Fighter: 7,000,000 Pepsi Points" appeared on the bottom of the television screen.

Well, Jared Hannah, a 21-year-old business student, upon seeing that commercial and discovering he could purchase individual Pepsi points from the company for 10¢ each, he set about to get himself a Harrier Jet at an unbelievable bargain rate. On March 26, 1996, Jared forked over 15 original points plus a check for $700,008.50 raised from five investors for the remaining 6,999,985 points "plus shipping and handling" and demanded his jet.

"ko-ka-ko-la."

When Coca-Cola first entered the Chinese market in 1928, they had no official representation of their name in Mandarin. They needed to find four Chinese characters whose pronunciations approximated the sounds "ko-ka-ko-la" without producing a nonsensical or adverse meaning when strung together as a written phrase.

Written Chinese employs about 40,000 different characters, 200 of which are pronounced with sounds that could be used in forming the name "ko-ka-ko-la."

While Coca-Cola was searching for a satisfactory combination of symbols to represent their name, Chinese shopkeepers created signs that combined characters whose pronunciations formed the string "ko-ka-ko-la," but they did so with no regard for the meanings of the written phrases they formed in doing so.

The character for wax, pronounced "la," was used in many of these signs, resulting in strings that sounded like "ko-ka-ko-la" when pronounced, it conveyed a nonsensical meaning, which translated to "bite the wax tadpole".

Old Coke vs. New Coke

Common commodities such as honey, sodium bicarbonate, acidic fruit juices and oils have been used through history as spermicides.

Dr. Charlotte Pierre, a Harvard researcher notes that Coca-Cola is said to be favored for this purpose in some developing countries and in years gone by was touted as a contraceptive aid. No documentation of the soft drink's spermicidal capabilities was found, so Dr. Pierre and two colleagues decided to test Coke in some of its various formulations in their lab.

They found that Diet Coke and original Coke was a most effective spermicide also five times more effective than the reformulated "new" Coke. "

Although not recommended for postcoital contraception, partly because sperm can be found in the oviducts within minutes after intercourse, Coca-Cola products do appear to have a spermicidal effect," Dr. Pierre said in a letter to the *New England Journal of Medicine*. "Furthermore, our data indicates that at least in the area of spermicidal effect, 'Classic' Coke is it."

powergenitalia.com

The history of business has included some examples of colossal "marketing blunders".

"Carnation Milk is best of all..."

A lady from North Carolina worked in and around family dairy farms since she was old enough to walk, with hours of hard work and little compensation. When canned Carnation Milk became available in grocery stores in the early 50's she read an advertisement offering $5,000 for the best slogan or rhyme beginning with "Carnation Milk is best of all . . ."

She knew all about milk and dairy farms and figured it was somehting she could attempt.

She sent in her entry and about a week later, a black limo drove up in front of her house. A man got out and said, "Carnation loved your entry so much, we are here to award you $1000, even though we will not be able to use it."

They were unable to use it due to it's controversial content.

Carnation milk is best of all,

No tits to pull, no shit to haul;

No buckets to wash, no hay to pitch,

Just poke a hole in the son-of-a-bitch!

Did You Know? *There are two kinds of Alaska salmon: white and pink. A cannery stuck with unmarketable white salmon turned this handicap around by boldly labeling the roduct as "Guaranteed not to turn pink in the can!" Not to be outdone, the pink-salmon folks countered advertising their pink salmon as "Guaranteed: No bleach used in processing!"*

Made In The Usa

In the years after World War II, Japan, whose manufacturing capabilities had been almost completely wiped out by Allied bombing, attempted to rebuild both their economy and their industrial base by producing large quantities of inexpensive goods and exporting them to America and other countries. Since the US emerged from the war with a robust economy and had no damaged infrastructure to rebuild, the USA was the primary market, leaving the phrase "Made in Japan" to symbolize cheap, shoddy goods to Americans.

Eventually, Japan sought to avoid this stigma by deviously renaming one of its towns "Usa" so it could identify its products as being "Made in USA."

Did You Know? *Powergen is an electric company starting up in Italy. They wanted to publicise their services, so they launched a website. Now bear in mind that this was created by Italian developers for an English company. They chose the internet address powergenitalia.com (Powergen Italia).*

"Send this guy the standard bug apology letter."

One of the fundamental tenets of good business ethics is customer relations; always treat your customers with respect. However, slip-ups are bound to occur from time to time, as well as the occasional mischievous prank.

"Dear Rich Bastard"

The National Bank in England admitted that it kept personal information about its customers; such as their political affiliation, on computer. But *Computer Weekly* revealed that a financial institution, sadly unnamed, had gone one better and moved into the realm of personal abuse.

The institution decided to mass-mail 2000 of its richest customers, inviting them to buy extra services. One of its computer programmers wrote a program to search through the databases and select its customers automatically. He tested the program with an imaginary customer called "Rich Bastard".

Unfortunately, an error resulted in all 2000 letters being addressed, "Dear Rich Bastard".

Follow the Instructions

It is sad that the litigiousness of our society has compelled manufacturers to place the most obvious of warning messages and instructions on their product packaging. At least they've created one more outlet for humor, so read the following instructions, and repeat after me: Duh!

Do not use while sleeping: Sears hair dryer
You could be a winner! No purchase necessary. Details inside: Bag of Fritos
Use like regular soap: Dial soap
Serving suggestion: Defrost: Swann frozen dinner
Fits one head: Shower cap box
Do not iron clothes on body: Rowenta iron
Do not drive car or operate machinery: Boot's children's cough medicine
Warning: May cause drowsiness: Nytol
Warning: Keep out of children: Korean kitchen knife
For indoor or outdoor use only: Christmas lights
Not to be used for the other use: Japanese food processor
Warning: Contains nuts: Sainsbury's peanuts
Instructions: Open packet, eat nuts: American Airlines peanut packet

Do not attempt to stop chain with your hands: Swedish chainsaw

Home Sweet Home Depot

A friend of a friend of mine works for Home Depot. One afternoon we were out for lunch, and I happened to notice that he brought his Employee Manual with him. I asked if I could take a quick ponder at it. At which point he flipped through a few pages to show me the latest policy entered in the manual.

It stated that if a customer comes to the checkout area toting a toilet auger, a pair of knee-high rubber boots, a mop, two gallons of bleach, elbow-length neoprene rubber gloves, a scoop shovel, and a gallon of industrial-strength deodorizer, it is not neccesary to ask him or her, "So, how are you doing today?" Nobody really wants to know.

After the said customer tenders cash for his/her purchase, the employees are required to use an antibacterial hand sanitizer.

Just The Fax

A company found it was receiving so much junk mail via the fax that its fax machine was continually tied up, making it impossible for employees to use it.

Realising that just one marketing company was responsible for these faxes, the manager phoned the company and told the person who answered to remove his company's fax number from their database.

However, a week went by and the faxes had not stopped coming, so the manager came up with the bright idea to print a page with the word "Virus" written in large letters on it, and a second page with a picture of a skull and crossbones.

He waited for a space between incoming faxes, placed the first page in the fax and then taped the second page to it to form a continuous loop. He then sent the everlasting fax to the marketing company and left the office for the weekend.

The marketing company employees returned on Monday to find its offices knee-deep in faxed messages and acted very quickly to remove the aggrieved company's fax number from its database. Details were later transferred to their email list.

Pizza Hut of the Next Century

What do you think ordering a pizza will be liike in the future? Probably like the follwoing telephone conversation.

Operator: "Thank you for calling Pizza Hut. May I have your national ID number?"

Customer: "Hi, I'd like to place an order."

Operator: "May I have your NIDN first, sir?"

Customer: "My National ID Number, yeah, hold on, eh, it's 6102049998-45-54610."

Operator: "Thank you, Mr. Shandling. I see you live at 172 Meadowlake Drive, and the phone number's 555-2366. Your office number over at Peak Insurance is 555-2302, and your cell number's 555-2566. Which number are you calling from, sir?"

Customer: "Huh? I'm at home. Where d'ya get all this information?"

Operator: "We're wired into the system, sir."

Customer: (Sighs) "Oh, well, I'd like to order a couple of your All-Meat Special pizzas."

Operator: "I don't think that's a good idea, sir."

Customer: "Whaddya mean?"

Operator: "Sir, your medical records indicate that you've got very high blood pressure and extremely high cholesterol. Your National Health Care provider won't allow such an unhealthy choice."

Customer: "Damn. What do you recommend, then?"

Operator: "You might try our low-fat Soybean Pizza. I'm sure you'll like it."

Customer: "What makes you think I'd like something like that?"

Operator: "Well, you checked out 'Gourmet Soybean Recipes' from your local library last week, sir. That's why I made the suggestion."

Customer: "All right, all right . Give me two family-sized ones, then."

Operator: "That should be plenty for you, your wife and your four kids, sir. Your total is $49.99."

Customer: "Lemme give you my credit card number."

Operator: "I'm sorry sir, but I'm afraid you'll have to pay in cash. Your credit card balance is over its limit."
Customer: "I'll run over to the ATM and get some cash before your driver gets here."

Operator: "That won't work either, sir. Your checking account's overdrawn."

Customer: "Never mind. Just send the pizzas. I'll have the cash ready. How long will it take?"

Operator: "We're running a little behind, sir. It'll be about 45 minutes, sir. If you're in a hurry you might want to pick 'em up while you're out getting the cash, but carrying pizzas on a motorcycle can be a little awkward."

Customer: "How the hell do you know I'm riding a bike?"

Operator: "It says here you're in arrears on your car payments, so your car got repo'ed. But your Harley's paid up.
Customer: "@#%/$@&?#!&?#!"

Operator: "I'd advise watching your language, sir. You've already got a July 2046 conviction for cussing out a cop. Will there be anything else, sir?"

Customer: "Yes, I have a coupon for a free 2 liter of Coke."

Operator: "I'm sorry sir, but our ad's exclusionary clause prevents us from offering free soda to diabetics."

Standard Grovel

A wealthy gentleman was badly bitten by bugs while riding on a certain railway line.

Arriving at his destination, he wrote the company an indignant letter and received a prompt reply.

The company replied saying, that was the first complaint the company had ever had of this nature, and although an inquiry had failed to reveal any explanation for this unprecedented occurrence, a number of new precautions were being taken to make absolutely certain such an unfortunate incident never happened again. The letter was signed by an official of the railway.

The gentleman was satisfied with this reply and was returning it to the envelope when a slip of paper fell out onto the floor.

The hastily scribbled post-it note read, "Send this guy the standard bug apology letter."

State-of-the-art Cup Holder

t turns out, technical support departments around the world regularly receive calls like this one, placed by a company executive.

The top executive of an advertising firm recently had a new multimedia computer installed on his desk. He had it for a week, as he explained during a call, and was getting on fine, but couldn't work out one thing, which was the reason why he was now calling technical support for help.

The problem, the executive explained, lay with the cup-holder on the front of his computer.

A bit puzzled by this, the representative asked him to describe this unusual accessory.

"Well, it comes out of the front of my computer when I press its button," explained the executive, "but every time I try to put my cup of coffee in it, it goes back in again and won't come out."

Patiently, the technical support guy explained the function of a CD-ROM drive to a man in a suit who earned five times his salary.

"Too Stupid To Own A Computer"

My co-workers college buddy got a job as a support specialist for Word Perfect programs. He told me about one incident were he got so fed up with a particularly frustrating customer that he told the guy he was "too stupid to own a computer."

Tech Support: "Word Perfect Technical support; may I help you?"

Customer: "Yes, I'm having trouble with WordPerfect.I was just typing along, and all of a sudden the words went away."

Tech Support: "Went away? Hmm, so what does your screen look like now?"

Customer: "Nothing.It's blank; it won't accept anything when I type."

Tech Support: "Are you still in WordPerfect, or did you get out?"

Customer: "How do I tell?"

Tech Support: "Can you see the C:\ prompt on the screen?"

Customer: "What's a sea-prompt?"

Tech support: "Never mind. Can you move the cursor around on the screen?"

Customer: "There isn't any cursor. I told you, it won't accept anything I type."

Tech Support: "Does your monitor have a power indicator?"

Customer: "What's a monitor?"

Tech Support: "It's the thing with the screen on it that looks like a TV. Does it have a little light that tells you when it's on?"

Customer: "I don't know."

Tech Support: "Well, then look on the back of the monitor and find where the power cord goes into it. Can you see that?"

Customer: "I think so."

Tech Support: "Great! Follow the cord to the plug, and tell me if it's plugged into the wall."

Customer: "Yes, it is."

Tech Support: "When you were behind the monitor, did you notice two cables plugged into the back of it, not just one? If not, I need you to look back there again and find the other cable."

Customer: "Okay, here it is."

Tech Support: "Follow it for me, and tell me if it's plugged securely into the back of your computer." *Customer:* "I can't reach it."

Tech Support: "Well, can you see if it is?"

Customer: "No."

Tech Support: "Put your knee on something and lean way over?"

Customer: "Oh, it's not because I don't have the right angle-it's because it's dark. The office light is off, and the only light I have is coming in from the window."

Tech Support: "Well, turn on the office light then."

Customer: "I can't."

Tech Support: "No? Why not?"

Customer: "Because there's a power outage."

Tech Support: "A power outage? Ha! Okay, we've got it licked now. Do you still have the boxes and manuals and packing stuff your computer came in?"

Customer: "Yes. I keep them in the closet."

Tech Support: "Good! Go get them and unplug your system and pack it up just like it was when you got it. Then take it back to the store you bought it from."

Customer: "Really! Is it that bad?"

Tech Support: "Yes, I'm afraid it is."

Customer: "All right then. But what do I tell them?"

Tech Support: "Tell them you're too stupid to own a computer."

"The Bank of Hong Kong are Friggin' Bastards."

Banks are the symbol of money, usually money we don't have, and when they make a mistake, rarely are they in our favour. Banks are the businesses we love to hate. So here are a few tales you can "bank on" to tickle your funny bone.

Charges Still Apply

My co-workers Aunt died this past February. CitiBank billed her for March and April for their monthly service charge on her credit card, and then added late fees and interest on the monthly charge. The balance had been $0.00... now was somewhere around $60.00.

So he placed a phone call to CitiBank informing them that she died in February. CitiBank informed him that the account was never closed and the late fees and charges still apply.

"Maybe, you should turn it over to collections," he said.

"Since it is two months past due, it already has been," said Citi Bank.

"So, what will they do when they find out she is dead?" he asked.

CitiBank replied, "Either report her account to the frauds division, or report her to the credit bureau...maybe both!"

Sarcastically he asked,"Do you think God will be mad at her?"

"Excuse me?" said Citi Bank.

"Did you just get what I was telling you," he said. "The part about her being dead?"

CitiBank said, "Sir, you'll have to speak to my supervisor!"

When the Supervisor gets on the phone he explains, "I'm calling to tell you, she died in January."

"The account was never closed," said the supervisor. "The late fees and charges still apply."

"You mean you want to collect from her estate? he asks."

The supervisor stammers for a second then replies, "Are you her lawyer?"

"No! he says, "I'm her great nephew."

The supervisor gives him the fax number to fax a certificate of death and states,"Our system just isn't set up for death. I don't know what more I can do to help."

"Well," said the Nephew, "If you figure it out, great! If not, you could just keep billing her, I am pretty sure she won't care."

"Well, the late fees and charges do still apply." said the supervisor.

"Would you like her new billing address?" the Nephew asked.

The supervisor exclaims,"That might help."

"Okay, its Odessa Memorial Cemetery #3332 Hwy 125, plot number 744." he said.

"Sir, said the supervisor, "That's a cemetery!"

"Yeah," he replied. "What do you do with dead people on your planet?"

Final Payment

A young man who, obviously knew something about the ways of computers, applied for and received a twelve-month installment loan from the bank. Together with the loan, he received the book of computer-coded coupons he was supposed to send with his monthly payments, so he tore out the final payment coupon in the book instead of the first and sent it in to the bank along with one month's payment. He then received a computer-generated letter from the bank thanking him for effectively paying off his loan so promptly, and assured him of his excellent credit standing.

"Paid In Full"

A friend of a friend racked up credit card debt and student loans totaling $100,000. Not securely employed, she had been planning on continuing her dinners out, lavish shopping trips, a car purchase and vacations, figuring it would all get wiped out soon enough.

She said she was working with a lawyer who advised her to write $10 checks to all her creditors, with a note saying "paid in full" on the check.

Personal Account

A man walked into a bank and pocketed a sheaf of the deposit slips, then returned to his apartment, and using press-on numerals matching the type face on the bank forms, he filled in the blank on each slip with his own account number.

The following morning, he returned to the bank and just as stealthily put the sheaf of deposit slips back into a slot atop a stack of others. Four days later he returned to the bank and made a $250 deposit.

"By the way, what's my balance, please?" he asked the teller. "I forgot to enter some checks I wrote this week."

The teller obligingly said, "Your balance, including this deposit, it $56,7856.76."

Just before the bank closed, he returned and withdrew $40,000 in a cashier's check, explaining he was buying a home. He didn't, of course, but he sure did feather his nest.

Did You Know? *After being charged 20 dollars for a 10 dollar overdraft, 35-year old Fredrick Lamb changed his name to "The Bank of Hong Kong are Friggin' Bastards." The Bank has now asked him to close his account, and Mr. The Bank of Hong Kong Are Friggin' Bastards has asked them to repay the balance by cheque, made out in his new name.*

Zero Balance

In June 1999 a man living in Boston, Massachusetts received a bill for his, as yet, unused credit card stating that he owed $0.00. He ignored it and threw it away.

In April he received another and threw that one away as well. The following month the credit card company sent him a very nasty note stating they were going to cancel his card if he didn't send them $0.00 by return of post. He called them, and they informed him it was a computer error and told him they'd take care of it.

The following month he decided that it was about time that he tried out the troublesome credit card figuring that if there were purchases on his account it would put an end to his ridiculous predicament. However, in the first store that he produced his credit card in payment for his purchases he found that his card had been cancelled. He called the credit card company who apologized for the computer error once again and said that they would take care of it.

The next day he got a bill for $0.00 stating that payment was now overdue.

Assuming that having spoken to the credit card company only the previous day the latest bill was yet another mistake, so he ignored it, trusting that the company would be as good as their word and sort the problem out.

The next month he got a bill for $0.00 stating that he had 10 days to pay his account or the company would have to take steps to recover the debt.

Finally giving in, he thought he would play the company at their own game and mailed them a check for $0.00. The computer duly processed his account and returned a statement to the effect that he now owed the credit card company nothing at all.

A week later, the man's bank called him asking him what he was doing writing a check for $0.00. After a lengthy explanation the bank replied that the $0.00 check had caused their check processing software to fail. The bank could not process any checks from any of their customers that day because the check for $0.00 was causing their computers to crash.

The following month the man received a letter from the credit card company claiming that his check had bounced and that he now owed them $0.00 and unless he sent a check by return of post they would be taking steps to recover the debt.

The man, who had been considering buying his wife a computer for her birthday, bought her a typewriter instead.

The duct tape holding the two dimes and the nickel together keeps jamming the coin-operated devices.

Money is the prime target for unusual fodder. Afterall, it's the symbol of economic strength and viability of the entire planet.

Cownomics

Traditional cownomics says:

You have two cows. You sell one and buy a bull. Your herd multiplies and the economy grows. You retire on the income.

Native economics says:

You have two cows. You worship them.

Pakistan ecomonomics says:

You don't have any cows. You claim that the Indian cows belong to you. You ask the US for financial aid, China for military aid, British for Warplanes, Italy for machines, Germany for technology, French for submarines, Switzerland for loans, Russia for drugs and Japan for equipment. You buy the cows with all this and claim of exploitation by the world.

Dying To Try The New ATM

A deceased cattle rancher from Bozeman, Montana, took care of his heirs by installing an automatic teller machine in his tombstone.

Cattle rancher Chester Grove died earlier this year at the age of 82. However, before he cashed in, he installed an ATM at his tombstone and gave ten heirs debit cards, and told them they were allowed to withdraw $300 per week from the grave. Mr. Grove apparently figured the tombstone ATM was the best way to make sure his grave had regular visitors.

"It seems to be working," said Jason Flushing, who helped create the "cashing-out" machines. "And one of Chesters granddaughters recently gave up a promising acting career in Los Angeles in order to cash in on Grandpa's money-making tombstone.

Although Chester's grave is currently the only one with an ATM, Flushing thinks others will be dying to try it soon.

The Arkansas Coin

If you have any of the new State of Arkansas quarters, hold on to them because they may be worth much more than 25 cents.

The U.S. Treasury announced that it is recalling all of the Arkansas quarters that are part of its program featuring quarters commemorating each state joining the union.

"We are recalling all the new Arkansas quarters that were recently issued," Treasury Undersecretary Jack Shackleford said . "This action is being taken after numerous reports that new quarters will not work in parking meters, toll booths, vending machines, pay phones, or other coin-operated devices".

These quarters were issued in the order in which the various states joined the U.S. and have been a tremendous success among coin collectors worldwide.

Shackleford said, "The problem lies in the unique design of the Arkansas quarter, which was created by a graduate at the University of Arkansas. Apparently, the duct tape holding the two dimes and the nickel together keeps jamming the coin-operated devices."

chapterthree

chromechariots

They're big, expensive, and breath-taking marvels of engineering, but you will miss their essence if you view automobiles merely as transportation.

Automobiles are both a means of getting from one place to another, and a place in themselves. Automobiles are as much about private inviolate space as they are about transportation.

Cars are the first true freedom for the adolescent. We do things in automobiles, we dare not do at home. Such as, sing along to the radio, have our first passionate encounter, and when all other resting places fail, we sleep in them.

Throughout our adult years automobiles continue to represent escape, giving us the ability to speed away from responsibilities and cares.

The importance automobiles have in our lives secures their place in the lore of our times. They are practical, whimsical, and reliable, while at the same time frightening, mundane and exciting, necessary and exotic, commonplace and mysterious. If you think about it, automobiles are the mechanical expression of humanity.

· · · · · · · · · · · · · · · · · · ·

"A good car thief."

The long arm of the law doesn't always reach the hoodlums who make off with our prized jalopies. We know what should happen in a more just world, but sometimes those miscreants are just too clever, as the following stories of grand theft auto remind us.

Dead Grandmother

A family from New York was traveling cross country, when the grandmother died of natural causes in the backseat of the car with her two grandchildren next to her. The parents didn't know what to do, so they decided to find a phone to call for assistance. But the children became freaked out with their now deceased grandmother still in the backseat with them, and since there wasn't enough room in the front seat for all of them, the father wrapped the grandmother up in a blanket and put her up on the luggage rack on top of the car. They finally reached a gas station, and the parents got out to make the call, leaving the keys in the ignition. The children got out to wander around and stretch their legs. When they all returned, they found that their car had been stolen, including all their possessions, passports... and Grandmother.

Good Car Thief

A man from Milan, Italy, was extremely proud of his classic Ferrari sports car. It took him years to restore it to mint condition, and he was very precious about it, only taking it out on special occasions. Wary of its attraction to thieves, the man kept it locked up in his garage using heavy chains around its frame, which were secured with impenetrable locks to pins in the wall. Every night, he left the car facing into the garage, all locked up and covered with a tarpaulin. One especially beautiful morning, the man decided to take his prize possession out for a spin, and went into the garage. He removed the tarpaulin and discovered the car all locked up, but facing in the other direction.

On the windshield was a note, "We can have this car any time we want it."

It was signed, "A good car thief."

"Snooker"

Police in a small fishing town north of England were puzzled by the number of car thefts reported on one single day. While there is nothing unusual about car theft, the number of cars involved, especially the number of red cars involved, gave them cause for concern. The police decided to set a trap in order to catch the thieves. The police left a red car apparently unlocked and unattended in a car park known to be popular with car thieves, and then went off to lie in wait. They hadn't waited long before someone took the bait and attempted to drive the car away. The police grabbed the villain and tried to find out from him what had been going on. It emerged that the reason so many cars, especially red cars, were being stolen that day was that rival gangs were indulging in a game of "snooker". This involves stealing a red car, then picking a colour from the set of snooker balls before stealing another red car, and so on until they finished off 'potting' a black car.

Squad Car Thief

A man was pulled over by local law enforcement because of erratic driving. He was obviously drunk, and failed all the tests: the Breathalyzer, the walk-the-straight-line, etc. He even managed to trip and fall flat on his face.

The officer sighed and said, "I'm afraid I'm going to have to place you under arrest."

But as soon as the words came out of his mouth, a horrible accident took place on the other side of the road. The officer ran across the street to investigate, and soon became preoccupied with the messy accident. The drunken man, seeing that the officer was busy, figured the officer had lost interest in him, and decided to just drive off.

However, the next day, the same officer arrived at the man's house. Scared that the officer was there to arrest him, the man pleaded, saying, "I promise not to do it ever again, but please don't arrest me, my wife will kill me."

The officer smiled slightly and said, "I promise not to arrest you, if you'll just take me out to your garage."

Confused but grateful, the man took the officer to his garage, and there, with the motor still running, and the dome light spinning and flashing, was the officer's squad car.

Car-Crossed Lovers

Perhaps our love affair with the car starts with our love affair in the car. Cars are often commonplace for our early sexual experience. So I dedicate the following tales of auto-erotica to the young persons that discover that the family honda puts miles between them and the parent, and provides a safe refuge of privacy when parked in a dark, desolate area with that special someone.

Car-Crossed Lovers

A man and a woman were giving vent to their faired passions in a Fiat Uno, which is one of the smallest cars in the world. Suddenly, the man screamed out in pain. Due to the confined space, he had strained his back, and as a result, couldn't move. His partner was trapped beneath him. However, the woman did eventually manage to stretch out her hand and start honking the horn. A passing police officer stopped, but realised there was nothing he could do on his own, so he called out the fire department. The firemen solved the problem, but had to cut the roof off the car to free the couple. After the injured man was taken to hospital, the woman started to cry. The policeman tried to reassure her, telling her that her boyfriend would be fine. But she refused to be comforted.

"Boyfriend, nothing," she screamed, "My husband will kill me when he sees what has happened to his car!"

Good Vibrations

A woman, driving alone through the countryside, was involved in an accident. When it came time to fill in the insurance forms, it emerged that she had been alone at the time and that no other cars were involved. She stated on her accident claim form that she had been driving within the speed limit. Police reports confirmed that driving conditions were near perfect on the day of the accident, so they were boggled with what could have been the cause of the accident. The insurance company decided to investigate further, and found the woman to be very vague on many of the points put to her. Eventually they contacted the ambulance service and discovered why the woman had been reluctant to answer some of their questions.

Apparently, she had crashed the car because she had been using a vibrator at the time of the accident.

Love In Park

A couple of car-crossed lovers is suing an insurance company for damages, claiming an unplanned pregnancy resulted from an automobile accident in Tucson

Arizona newspapers reported that the claim involved an accident involving a hatch-back and a Firefly. The accident occurred in a park that attracted nightly scores of couples who make love in their cars.

The young man claimed he and his girlfriend were engaged in amorous activity in their small car when the large car hit it from behind. The impact momentarily made them lose control, resulting in the pregnancy.

The case came to light when an agent of the insurance company decided to publicize the claim to illustrate the absurdity of some bids to win compensation.

The suit demands compensation for the cost of repairing the Firefly and the cost of the wedding the couple decided to have after discovering the woman was pregnant.

Service The Car

A lady came home from the grocery store one afternoon to find her husband working under the car. All that was exposed were his legs, so in passing she reached down, unzipped his zipper, chuckled to herself, and "serviced" him. Then she went into the house, and was horrified to see her husband sitting in the easy chair reading the newspaper. She cried, "Who is that under the car?" and her husband replied, "My mechanic." She told her husband what she'd done, and they went outside to find the mechanic lying unconscious, in a pool of blood, because when the lady unzipped his pants he was so startled he sat up and clobbered his head under the car.

Wife-less and Car-less

A young couple moved into a quiet suburban enclave, and their neighbours invited them over for dinner along with several other couples who lived nearby. As the night wore on, and drinks were consumed, the new couple learned that all the guests indulged in wife-swapping, and they were asked if they wanted to join in. Although hesitant at first, they agreed. Each husband threw his car keys into a hat and a wife would blindly pick out a key and go off with the owner. The young husband threw the key to his Mercedes into the hat with the others, and the choosing began. Each wife took turns and eventually, his wife was paired off. Her husband was upset to see how excited his wife was, but didn't say anything, instead hoping that he would be pleased with his partner. However, one of the wives said she felt ill and left, leaving him the odd man without a partner. The young man sulked all the way home and was infuriated to see that his Mercedes had gone. Wife-less and car-less, the man crashed out. The next morning, he was pleased to see that his car had been returned, but distressed to find in it a note from his wife telling him that she was leaving him.

"I'm in no condition to spank my son even if I wanted to. Actually, I don't think I need to. He knows his thoughtlessness almost killed daddy."

Our best laid plans sprinkled with our finest intentions can still go horribly wrong. And when you toss a few thousand pounds of automobile into the mix you get a recipe for motoring mishaps.

Abandoned Wife

A couple on an RV holiday in France spent a few days in Bordeaux before going to their final destination near La Rochelle. Wanting to arrive in La Rochelle before dark, the husband left early in the morning leaving his wife to continue sleeping in the motorhome. After an hour of driving, the husband pulled into a small gas station to refuel. Unknown to him, his wife took the opportunity to freshen up in the garage bathroom. Meanwhile the husband paid the bill, and still thinking his wife was asleep in the motorhome, drove off to La Rochelle, where he realised his error. The abandoned wife, dressed only in a skimpy negligee and penniless, was fortunate enough to come across a helpful young biker. The biker put her on the pillion seat and roared after the husband. The husband was astounded to see the biker pull up alongside him, together with his half-dressed wife.

Better To Be Safe Than Sorry

A middle-aged woman was thought to be one of the safest drivers in the state of Washington, but this was due more to being very careful than to her expertise. On one occasion, the woman had just been to town to do some shopping and was emerging from the car park, when she came to a busy junction. The cars kept coming in both directions and every time she went to turn left, another flurry of traffic would prevent her. Six hours later, the traffic began to slow, but the woman had fallen asleep, and by the time she woke up, it was morning rush hour. After about an hour of morning traffic, the woman plucked up her courage and went for it, only to crash straight into the side of a police car.

Cross Country Roller Skating

In Chicago, a boy had been learning the art of roller-skating, when he noticed a lace had come undone. He rested the skate on the bumper of a truck and tighten it up, but the truck suddenly started up, and unable to wrench his skate free, the boy was pulled behind. Unfortunately, the truck was bound for New York and the poor boy was dragged for over 250 miles on the highway before the driver decided to stop at a raodside pit stop for a cup of coffee. The boy finally managed to break free form the truck's bumper, but now found himself without any money to get home. So he did the obvious thing - crossed over the highway and latched himself on to another truck going back to Chicago. The boy went on to become one of the fastest roller-skaters in the world.

Death By Car Wash

A 42-year-old woman died recently while attempting to wash her car. She went out to her garage to wash the vehicle but decided that it would be best to move the car on to her driveway where it would be easier to get at. Having first put the car into neutral, she pushed from the front, and eventually it began to roll backwards. It soon became obvious that the vehicle was no longer under her control, so as quickly as she could, she rushed to the rear of the car and attempted to stop it with her own body weight. Unfortunately the car had now gathered momentum, and despite her best efforts, continued to roll backwards. In her desperation to stop the vehicle, she ignored her own safety and was run over for her troubles. Having flattened its owner, the car then carried on across the road before running up a neighbour's driveway and colliding with the front of his house.

Ferry Good Parking Space

A senile old couple from Iowa City, Iowa went on vacation to California, while in Los Angeles, they stopped to visit a newly-opened National Museum. The museum was very popular so the couple found it difficult to find a parking place, but eventually they discovered a multi-storey parking garage about three blocks away. They spent a few enjoyable hours exploring the museum, but when they left, they couldn't find the car park. They went up and down the streets, but the car park had vanished. Thinking that they may have fallen victim to some massive car-stealing scheme, the couple reported it to the police. When the couple showed the policeman where they thought they had left the car, he immediately knew what had happened. Trying to keep a straight face, he told them that what they had taken to be a multi-storey parking garage was in fact a ferry. Three hours later, the ferry returned and the couple picked up their car and headed to their next destination.

Killing Daddy

A 33-year-old roofer was jerked to the ground and dragged almost 200 feet when his wife drove away in the family car with his safety rope tied to the bumper.

Willis St. Jerome was hospitalized with a broken leg, cracked ribs, concussion and numerous bumps and bruises after the bizarre accident.

He told reporters that he's lucky to be around to talk about his close call.

"One second I was hammering the roof and the next I was plowing up tomato plants in the garden," he continued. "Everything happened so fast it was like a dream. But I was in so much pain I knew what was happening was real."

St. Jerome said the drama unfolded a few minutes after he climbed onto the roof of his house to replace some weather-beaten shingles. He tied one end of a safety rope to the chimney and pulled the loose end through the belt loop in his pants. He then dropped the rope down to his 8-year-old son and told him to attach it "to something secure." The dutiful child promptly tied the rope to the bumper of their car and scampered off to a nearby park to play.

"My wife and I spoke to each other as she got into the car to go shopping," said St. Jerome. "But neither of us noticed that the rope was tied to the bumper. So I turned around and started hammering on a shingle just as she pulled away. I hit the ground hard and shot right through the garden fence. I figured I was dragged about 200 feet through the grass before the rope finally broke."

St. Jerome's wife Cindy didn't realize what happened and drove off into the distance. A neighbor found St. Jerome writhing in his front yard and called an ambulance.

"I'm in no condition to spank my son even if I wanted to," St. Jerome said. "Actually, I don't think I need to. He knows his thoughtlessness almost killed daddy."

Restrictive Clothing

A boy from Seattle, Washington had just passed his test to drive a motorbike. His parents, as a reward, bought him a new 250cc motorbike. The boy always dreamed of becoming a biker, and used his savings to buy all the gear; boots, helmet, leather jacket, leather trousers and gloves. Unfortunately, none of the shops had his size in leather trousers, but unable to wait, he bought a larger pair with the idea that he could shrink them. When he got home, he ran a bath and still wearing the trousers, got in. However, he fell asleep, and when he woke up, he was in agony. The leather trousers had shrunk so much, that they had restricted the boy's blood circulation. His mother took him to hospital where they cut the leather trousers away, and finding that the prolonged restriction of blood supply had caused permanent damage, they had to amputate his legs. The boy's dream of being a cool biker was not meant to be, but he did have fun racing around in his wheelchair.

The Hills Are Alive

A man was driving around the hilly streets of San Francisco hopelessly lost and quite late for a job interview. Passing a telephone booth, he stopped the car and telephoned the company he had the interview with. As he was explaining his predicament to the secretary, he realised he'd forgotten to put his handbrake on, and was shocked to see his car rolling down the hill towards him. Before he could do anything, the car rammed into the phone booth, jamming him inside. Hearing him cursing, the sensitive secretary must have taken it personally because she slammed the phone down on him. He waved to passers-by, but they just waved back. It wasn't until an hour later that it occurred to him to use the phone to contact the emergency services, which promptly rescued him. Afterwards the man developed a sudden loathing for hills and left San Francisco for the much flatter Iowa.

Urine Need Of Assistance

It was a brisk and cold winter morning when a van driver passed a motorcyclist who had broken down. It was snowing, and although the bike rider was well wrapped up in leathers and helmet, the van driver decided he had better stop and offer his assistance.

There was very little wrong with the motorbike. It just ran out of gas, and although the driver had a spare can of fuel, unfortunately, the gas cap was frozen stuck. Being a resourceful and brave man, he unbuttoned his fly and peed over the cap to thaw it out. He refilled the tank and the bike rider, still wrapped up against the cold, mumbled a thank you and they both went their separate ways.

A few days later the van driver was called into the office at work and the boss showed him a letter he had received from a local minister praising his helpfulness and expressed gratitude for the assistance he had given his *daughter* when she had broken down.

"I thought you could have the front wheels, and I could have the rear wheels."

Highway Hazards lurk at every turn. Whether we're out on the highway or refueling at a gas station, vigilance must be maintained, lest the bad guys get us.

Car-Stripping

A man was driving home from work one evening and suffered a blow-out on the highway, so he pulled over to change the tires. The man had just started jacking up the front of his car, when another car pulled over, and a young man got out and offered to help him. The man was happy to get any help he could and readily accepted the young man's offer. However, he was surprised, when instead of grabbing the spare tire on the ground, the young man took a jack out of his car and began jacking up the rear of the car. So he asked the young man to explain what he was up to.

"Well," said the so-called good samaritan, "I thought you could have the front wheels, and I could have the rear wheels."

Unknowingly, the driver had innocently pulled over on a road notorious for car thefts and car-stripping.

Champion Roadblock

A young woman from Austin, Texas, had an experience learning to drive that would put anyone off ever driving again. Her father thought he would take her out for a spin in the country and let her drive along the quiet country lanes. Just ouside Austin, he stopped the car, let his daughter take the wheel, and after a few false starts, she was driving smoothly. Quickly, she started to gain confidence, even putting her foot down on the pedal, then slowing down and shifting to second gear as she approached a bend in the road. Unfortunately, as she turned the corner, a giant bull was standing right in the middle of the road. She slammed her foot on the brakes, but it was too late, and she ran right into the poor beast. On discovering that the bull was dead, the young woman burst into tears. It didn't help when a distressed farmer pulled up and asked them if they had seen, Ole' Blue, his champion bull.

Detour

A young lady was driving home in her new 4 x 4 from an evening out. As she approached a set of traffic lights in a deserted area, she noticed the body of a man lying in the middle of the junction. Realising that hi-jackers often use this ruse to lure their unsuspecting victims out of their cars, the young lady droveoff the road and into the grassy field to skirt around the junction and the prostrate roadblock. She drove to the local police station to report the incident just in case the lifeless form was genuine. The police escorted her back to the scene where there was no sign of a man lying in the road. However, after further investigation the police discover the dead bodies of four armed men in the veld where they had been lying in wait for her to stop the vehicle. She had ridden over them when she took her detour around the "body".

Foggy Follower

An elderly gentleman was driving home after a day in the countryside, when a blanket of fog suddenly descended over the area. The fog was so thick, that the man could hardly see 20 feet in front of him. He was about to pull over and wait until it lifted, when he spotted a car ahead, and thinking the driver must know where he was going, latched on to the car's tail lights. After driving several miles, the car proceeded to make a series of turns before suddenly stopping. The old man saw his opportunity, got out of his car and asked the other driver where he was.

The driver coldly replied, "This is my driveway. Now, get lost!"

Leaving the old man standing there in shock, he vanished into his house.

In Two The Light

Three friends from New Hampshire were riding their motorbikes one night on an open highway. One of them decided to accelerate away from the other two. About one mile down the road, he turned around, and as he saw their headlights in the distance, he decided to give his friends a scare by riding in-between them. He sped up and went to drive through them, but didn't realise until it was too late, that the headlights belonged to a truck that had overtaken his friends. He died instantly.

Picnic Spot

In the Rocky Mountains, there are hairpin bends on the major mountain roads which are notorious accident blackspots, especially for truck drivers. So on most of these bends, uphill safety ramps have been placed for trucks with failed brakes to make an emergency stop.

One day, a truck driver with a particularly heavy load was driving along the mountain road. He had managed the ascent fine, but as the truck sped downhill, the driver realised he had lost his brakes. As the truck careered down the busy road, the driver flashed his lights and honked his horn, swerving all over the road to avoid the other cars. The driver was relieved when he eventually saw a sign stating that there was a safety ramp just around the corner, and successfully he manoeuvred the speeding truck around the tight corner. However, as he went up the ramp, he ran right into a family of Asian tourists having a picnic, killing them all instantly.

Pig Warning

In Pennsylvania, a man was driving along a country road, and up ahead he spotted an attractive woman drive around the corner towards him.

As the woman passed, he smiled at her, but the woman just shouted at him, "Pig!"

The man quickly replied, "Bitch!" and sped off.

However, when he turned the corner, there, standing in the middle of his lane, staring right at him, was a large pig. The man managed to swerve out of the way, but ended up in a ditch.

Speeding Mustang

A man was driving along a stretch of highway late one night and decided it was time he pushed his new Mustang to the limits. Putting his foot down and hurding down the deserted highway at 160 mph, the man suddenly lost control and crashed into the central barriers and turned over. The driver miraculously escaped unharmed. Although rather shakey, he managed to pull himself up, and cross the road to phone the emergency services.

Unfortunately, as he crossed over, a speeding Mustang came around the corner and hit him.

"Lift? I thought you had taken me hostage!"

Beware of the "passenger pigeon". He's not always who he seems.

Hitchhiker Day Off

A lawyer was driving to his home in Aurora, Illinois from a conference in Chicago, when he spotted a hitchhiker by the side of the road. Feeling like some company, he stopped and picked the man up. A few miles down the road, the lawyer began to worry. The hitchhiker had an evil look to him and talked in a menacing voice. The lawyer then realised that he was completely unprepared if the hitchhiker were to threaten him, so he was relieved when he spotted another hitchhiker. He stopped to pick up the second man, who was wearing a suit and appeared friendly. However, not long after driving off, the second hitchhiker produced a knife and told the lawyer to pull over and get out. Somehow, as everybody got out of the car, the first hitchhiker managed to grab the knife off the second one and knocked him out.

The first hitchhiker, gruffly remarking, "Amateur", then proceeded to take the unconscious man's wallet, offering half the contents to the aghast lawyer, who refused the money. Reading the lawyer's thoughts, the hitchhiker explained that it was his day off and he was just visiting his mother in Chicago.

Hostage Situation

A man studying at UCLA decided to save money by hitchhiking home to Bend, Oregon for Christmas. The student wasn't having much luck, due to his unwashed, unshaven and unkempt appearance, but eventually a car stopped and he jumped in. The old woman driving asked where he was going, but she wouldn't be drawn into conversation after that, so the student passed the time by counting the number of cars that overtook them. On reaching Bend, Oregon the student was surprised when the old lady asked him directions to his house. Pleased to be saving yet more money by not having to take the bus, the student directed her to his house. On reaching his house, he thanked the woman for the lift, whereupon she replied, "Lift? I thought you had taken me hostage!"

Moving Car

A guy named Cliff was on the side of the road hitchhiking on a very dark night in the middle of a storm. The night was rolling and no cars were in sight. The storm was so strong he could hardly see ten feet infront of him. Suddenly he spotted a car coming towards him and stopped. The guy without thinking about it got in the car closed the door to realise there was nobody behind the wheel. The car started to slowly move, so Cliff looked at the road and saw a curve coming his way, scared he started to pray begging for his life. He was still in shock, when just before he hit the curve, a hand appeared through the window and moved the wheel. Cliff, paralyzed in terror, watched as the hand appeared every time before rolling into a curve. Cliff gathered the strength to get out of the car and run to the nearest town.

Wet and in shock he stumbled into a cantina and asked for two shots of tequila, and started telling everybody about the religious experience he went through. A silence enveloped everybody when they realise the guy was not some crazy drunk.

About half an hour later two guys walked into the same cantina and one said to the other. "Look Esai, that's the asshole that got in the car when we were pushing it."

Unaware Passenger

A young man got completely drunk at a friends party and ended up passing out in what he thought was the bedroom. A few hours later, he woke up to see buildings and street lights flying past on either side at an alarming rate. At first he thought he was still drunk and his head was just spinning, but when he looked down, he realised he was on the roof of his friends car. It seemed that in his seriously inebriated state, he had mistaken the garage for a bedroom, and the car for a bed. The driver became aware of the extra passenger's existence when his hitchhiker was sick all over his windshield.

"No Ma'am, Highway patrolmen don't have balls."

Laws govern and dictate how we drive. If we fail to follow the rules, penalties are handed out. Though we all agree these laws are necessary to protect us from the irresponsible actions of others, we hate to see them applied to us. These stories speak to our desire to outrun John Law, either by escaping his clutches at a traffic stop or by beating the system through a technicality or clever ruse.

International Driver's License

You can avoid paying for traffic tickets or establish a new identity by obtaining an International Driver's License.

At a Convention on International Road Traffic of September 19, 1949 and World Court Decision, in The Hague, Netherlands, January 21, 1958, The United Nations gave you the privilege to drive freely throughout the world!

You now have the rights to order a valid International Driver's License that can never be suspended or revoked.

So if you need a new driver's license, or have too many points or other trouble and you want a license that can never be suspended or revoked, you should get an International Drivers License.

Not only can you use it as ID for nightclubs or hotel check-in. But you can avoid tickets, fines, and mandatory driver's education, at the same time protecting your privacy, and hide your identity.

Invisible Car

A highway patrol officer was close to signing himself into a mental institution after a series of freak readings on his speed detector. For several weeks he had been on the night shift, parking in his usual concealed spot off the main road. Several times he had just been drifting off to sleep to be suddenly woken up by his radar beeping wildly and displaying speeds of over 150 mph. Following in hot pursuit, the officer was mystified when he couldn't find any vehicles on the road. Communications with his colleague a few miles down the road also revealed nothing. After a few nights of high readings from seemingly invisible vehicles, he began to think he was losing his mind. However, the mystery was solved a few nights later when a car was found smashed by the side of the road. The dead driver was wearing infrared night-vision goggles and several kilos of cocaine were found in the panels of the car. The officer realized he wasn't mad after all, and that his nightly apparitions were actually the drug-trafficker speeding by him with his lights off and using infrared goggles to see.

Lawful Parking

A young man had just passed his driving test and was returning home to tell his friends and family the good news. On his way, he decided to stop at a liquor store to buy a celebratory bottle of champagne. He couldn't find a parking place anywhere, so he parked halfway on to the pavement, rushed into the store, bought a bottle of champagne and rushed out again. However, on returning to his car, he was concerned to see a policeman standing by the vehicle. Sheepishly, the boy approached the policeman and told him he'd only just parked it there.

The policeman replied, gritting his teeth, "I know. You parked on my friggin' foot!"

Microwave Camera

An elderly woman was driving down a country road on her way back to Houston, Texas, when she noticed what looked like a microwave oven abandoned on the side of the road. The woman stopped to pick it up hoping that her son, who just so happened to be an electrician, could repair it. The woman was so excited with her find that she tried to get home as fast as she could. She didn't notice that she was speeding, and was inevitably pulled over by the police. The police officer noticed, on the backseat of her car, the object that the woman had picked up. It was not a microwave, but a speed-monitoring camera. Despite the old woman's protests, the police arrested her and charged her with theft of government property.

"No Ma'am, Highway patrolmen don't have balls."

A woman got pulled over for speeding by a California Highway Patrolman.

When he walked up to her window and opened his ticket book she said, "I bet you're going to ask me to the Highway Patrolman Ball."

"No, Ma'am," he replied. "Highway patrolmen don't have balls."

After a moment of silence he realized what he had said, and without saying another word, he closed his book, got back onto his motorcycle and left.

No Plate

Ralph Joseph, a long time resident of Los Angeles sent in an application to the Department of Motor Vehicles requesting personalized license plates for his car. The DMV form asked applicants to list three choices in case one or two of their desired selections had already been assigned. Joseph, a sailing enthusiast, wrote down "Sailing" and "Boating" as his first two choices; when he couldn't think of a third option, he wrote "No plate," meaning that if neither of his two choices was available, he did not want personalized plates. Unfortunately, "Boating" and "Sailing" had indeed already been assigned, and the DMV, following instructions literally, send Joseph a license plate reading "No plate." Joseph was not thrilled that the DMV had misunderstood his intent, but he eventually opted to keep the plates because of their uniqueness.

Four weeks later, he received his first notice for an overdue parking fine from San Francisco, and started to receive dozens of overdue notices from all over the state. It turns out, when law enforcement officers ticketed illegally parked cars that bore no license plates, they had been writing "No Plates" in the license plate field. Now that Joseph had plates bearing that phrase, the DMV computers were matching every unpaid citation issued to a car with missing plates to him.

Joseph received over 2,000 notices over the next several months. He alerted the DMV to the problem, and they responded in a typical bureaucratic way by instructing him to change his license plates. But Joseph had grown fond of his plates, instead he began mailing out a form letter in response to each citation. That method usually worked, although occasionally he had to appear before a judge and demonstrate that the car described on the citation was not his.

A couple of years later, the DMV finally caught on and sent a notice to law enforcement agencies requesting that they use the word "None" rather than "No plate" to indicate a cited vehicle was missing its plates. This change slowed the flow of overdue notices Joseph received to a trickle, about five or six a month, but it also had an unintended side effect: Officers sometimes wrote "Missing" instead of "None" to indicate cars with missing license plates, and suddenly a man named Ray Marion in Pasadena, California started receiving parking tickets from places *he* hadn't visited either. Marion, of course, was the owner of a car with personalized plates reading "Missing."

Photo Fine

Here's one to make you think twice when trying to elude the law.

A man from Chicago was taking his prized Porsche out for a spin, when he was caught speeding by a roadside camera. The resulting penalty notice arrived in the post. It included a photograph of the car, the date, and speed of the offence. The notice demanded payment of a fine within seven days. The motorist chuckled to himself and decided to play a little practical joke on the police. He duly sent a photograph of a cheque to the unsuspecting police. A few days later, he received a letter from the police. Inside was a big glossy photograph of a prison cell. Sure enough, the speeding motorist got the hint and paid the fine.

Speeding Groom

A policeman from a small town in Virginia pulled over a motorist for speeding. The man tried to explain why he was in a hurry, but the cop, not in a good mood, arrested him for obstruction. Still protesting, the man was taken to the police station and thrown into the jail.

The bad-tempered cop then growled at him, "The Chief will sort you out, ya whiner. He's at his daughter's wedding but he should be back soon."

"I wouldn't bet on it, you moron," said the man through gritted teeth, "Seeing that I'm the groom."

Stressed Out

An honest man was being tailgated by a stressed-out woman on a busy boulevard. Suddenly, the light turned yellow, just in front of him. He did the honest thing, and stopped at the crosswalk, even though he could have beaten the red light by accelerating through the intersection.

The tailgating woman hit the roof, and the horn, screaming in frustration as she missed her chance to get through the intersection with him.

Still in mid-rant, she heard a tap on her window and looked up into the face of a very serious police officer. The officer ordered her to exit her car with her hands up. He took her to the police station where she was searched, fingerprinted, photographed, and placed in a cell.

After a couple of hours, a policeman approached the cell and opened the door. She was escorted back to the booking desk where the arresting officer was waiting with her personal effects.

He said, "I'm very sorry for this mistake. I pulled up behind your car while you were blowing your horn, flipping the guy off in front of you, and cussing a blue streak at him. Then I noticed the *'Choose Life'* license plate holder, the *'What Would Jesus Do'* bumper sticker, the *'Follow Me to Sunday School'* bumper sticker, and the chrome plated Christian fish emblem on the trunk. Naturally, I assumed you had stolen the car."

That's One Fast Parked Car

Three youths from Newcastle, Australia pulled off a trick of breathtaking bravado in order to gain revenge on a mobile speed camera van operating in the area.

Two of the group approached the van and distracted the operator's attention by asking a series of questions about how the equipment worked and how many cars the operator could catch in a day. Meanwhile, the third musketeer snuck to the front of the van and unscrewed its license plate.

After bidding the van operator goodbye, the friends returned home, fixed the license plate to their car and drove through the camera's radar at high speeds - 17 times. As a result, the automated billing system issued 17 speeding tickets to itself.

"Why? Don't ye believe me?"

Late one Friday night a policeman spotted a man driving very erratically through the streets of Dublin. They pulled the man over and asked him if he had been drinking that evening.

"Aye, so I have." explained the man. "Tis Friday, you know, so me and the lads stopped by the pub where I had six or seven pints. And then there was something called "Happy Hour" and they served these mar-gar-itos which are quite good. I had four or five o' those. Then I had to drive me friend Mike O'Malley home and O' course I had to go in for a couple of Guiness - couldn't be rude, ye know. Then I stopped on the way home to get another bottle for later .."

And the man fumbled around in his coat until he located his bottle of whiskey, which he held up for inspection.

The officer sighed, and said, "Sir, I'm afraid I'll need you to step out of the car and take a breathalyzer test."

Indignantly, the man said, "Why? Don't ye believe me?"

You Have No Evidence Except my License Plate

A woman from Queens, New York drove to a party in Manhattan with the intent of getting a taxi home if she drank too much. However, a few drinks later, and ignoring her friends wise advice, the woman decided she was in a fit state to drive home. After struggling to drive out of a tight parking spot and ignoring the fact that she'd bumped the car behind, the woman drove away, and eventually, with a few hazy close shaves, she made it home.

She struggled into the house and immediately blacked out on her sofa. She was woken in the early hours of the morning by someone persistently ringing her door bell. On opening her front door, she was startled to see an annoyed policeman, who proceeded to question her about her activities on the previous night. He told her that she would be prosecuted for drunken driving and hit and run damage to another car. Curious, the shaken woman asked the policeman how he could be so sure it was her.

The policeman smiled and held up the woman's licence plate, "This was found embedded in the other car, ma'am."

You have nothing to loose but the points on your license.

If you get a speeding ticket or went through a red light or whatever the case may be, and you are going to get points on your license, there is a method to ensure that you do not get any points. When you get your fine, send in the check to pay for it and if the fine is lets say $79, then make the check out for $82 or some small amount above the fine.

The system will then have to send you back a check for the difference, but here is the trick! -- Do not cash the check. Throw it away. Points are not assessed to your license until all the financial transactions are complete. If you do not cash the check, then the transactions are not complete. However the system has gotten its money so it is happy and will not bother you any more.

Zig Zag

A policeman was directing traffic on a highway in Los Angeles after a serious car accident.

At one point, an old lady in a beaten-up Volvo slowed down and asked the policeman, "Is there anything I can do to help? I was a nurse in the war."

The policeman thanked her for the generous offer, but said, "Ma'am! The best thing you can do is drive off around those cones ahead."

Moments later, the officer was astonished to see the old lady drive off, and ever so slowly zig-zag around each and every cone before she disappeared over the horizon.

Prized Possession

We have tender feelings for our automobiles, so they leave us vulnerable to acts of retribution-- a type of Coupe de grace, if it were--meaning those looking to get revenge know that by damaging our beloved chariots, they damage us.

Cement Love

One day a cement truck driver was driving through his own neighborhood on his way to deliver a load of ready-mix wet cement. As he passed his house, he noticed a brand-new shiny convertible in his driveway. He decided to check it out, and after stopping his truck, got out and peered into the kitchen window of his house, only to spy his wife talking to a strange man inside.

A very jealous man, he immediately suspected his wife of cheating on him and decided to exact revenge. So he backed up his truck to the convertible, and dumped the entire load of the wet cement into it.

He came home later that evening, smug, and expecting his wife to be waiting to beg for his forgiveness. Instead, he found his wife crying hysterically as the convertible, now solid concrete, was being towed away. She explained through her tears that she had been saving for over a year to surprise him with his dream car for his birthday, and just as the dealer had come to drop it off this morning, some lunatic had come by and dumped wet cement onto the car.

I'd Buy That For A Dollar!

One morning a young college student was looking through the classifieds for a used car, when his eye caught on one that stupefied him: "Porsche For Sale. Convertible. Mint condition. Loaded. Black, Leather Interior. Stereo. Asking price, One Dollar."

He couldn't believe it, and thought it had to be a misprint. But he decided to give it a shot and called the number. A woman answered, and after learning that the car was still for sale, he clarified the price, and then asked if he could check it out.

He drove out to the address she gave him, and found himself at a very large, landscaped home with a swimming pool and tennis courts. After ringing the doorbell, an attractive blond woman answered. She took him out to the garage, and the sight of the car made his heart stop. It was shiny, beautiful, and in perfect condition – the stereo, the convertible hood, the purring engine.

Once again he clarified, "The price is still one dollar?"

"Yes," she answered firmly.

He hastily wrote out the check, still not quite believing his luck. But he had to ask her. "Miss, if you don't mind my asking, why are you selling the car for this price? Nobody would sell it for a dollar."

She hesitated a bit, but then smiled slightly and said, "Well, I guess I can tell you. A few years ago, I met the perfect man. He was tall and good-looking and had a great job making over $200,000 a year. We got married, and everything was going very well. But then, a beautiful, sexy, young woman moved into the neighborhood a little while back, and she and my husband ran off together last week."

She paused, smiling again as the young man listened expectantly. "Well, he called me this week saying I handled the situation maturely, and knows he did me wrong and that I deserve much better, apologizing over and over again. Then he asked me to sell the Porsche and send him half the money."

Non-Smoking Biker

A California biker entered a roadside cafe, carrying his helmet and gloves. He ordered some food and a drink, then sat down in the non-smoking area. Just after his food arrived, a man at the next table lit up a cigarette. The biker politely pointed out that they were sitting in a non-smoking area and asked the man to either move or put out the cigarette. The smoker angrily grunted, but stood up and left. However, as he walked past the biker, he noticed his helmet, and concluding that the Harley in the parking lot must be his, pushed it over. Unfortunately for the man, the Harley actually belonged to the cafe's cook, a large, hairy, leather-clad guy, who saw what was done to his prize possession, and went after the man with a meat cleaver. Meanwhile, the biker finished his meal, grabbed his helmet and gloves, walked round the side of the building to his Harley, and rode away.

"Sorry about the dent.
I would leave my name and address,
but my insurance premium is high enough as it
is. Merry Christmas."

The financial blow of damage to our vehicles can only be cushioned by our auto insurance. But in the world of lore, it also provides an opportunity for humor.

Nice Note

In Flint, Michigan, a young woman had just returned to her car after doing some last-minute Christmas shopping. She got into the car, but as she reversed out of her parking place she knocked into the car behind, causing a huge noticeable dent in the front bumper. The driver of the other car was not around, but several people had witnessed the incident, so the woman wrote a note and left it under the windscreen wiper.

When the driver of the other car returned, he noticed the dented bumper and found the note, stating, "Sorry about the dent. I would leave my name and address, but my insurance premium is high enough as it is. Merry Christmas."

Young vs. Old

In Pittsburgh, Pennsylvania a woman in a Mercedes had been waiting patiently for a parking place to open up at a crowded shopping mall. She finally located a man who was heading to his car. Finally he got into his car and backed out of the stall. But before the woman in the Mercedes could drive into the parking space, a young man in a Ford truck zipped around her and pulled into the empty space.

"Hey," shouted the woman, "I've been waiting for that parking space."

The young man replied, "Sorry, lady. That's how it is when you are young and quick."

At that moment she put her Mercedes in gear, floored it, and rammed her car into the right rear fender, and corner panel of the Ford.

The young man shouted, "You can't do that!"

The lady shruggled and simply replied, "That's how it is when you're old and rich."

"So, you finally found the rattle, you rich son-of-a-bitch."

The most confusing and complex part of vehicle ownership is the technology behind what powers them. It's this uneasy relationship with what goes under the hood that sparks the following set of stories.

Bullet Fuse

Two miners from Sudbury, Ontario, Canada were out for a weekend hunting trip in the wilds of the northern tundra. As they were returning to their cabin that evening, their old car suddenly stopped and all the lights railed. The driver worked out that a fuse had blown, and with the aid of a torch, tried to find a temporary replacement.

After half an hour of fruitless searching, his companion got impatient and shouted out, "It's okay. Let me fix it."

He placed something in the fuse holder and the car spluttered into action. About a mile down the road, suddenly there was a loud explosion and the car died again.

The driver, somewhat pale, asked his buddy, "What did you put in there?"

His friend answered, "I just used a bullet from the gun, why?"

Painfully, the driver explained, "Because I have just been shot," and pointed to his groin.

Crazy, Not Stupid!

A friend of a friend's automobile suddenly developed a flat tire one night, outside the strong iron fence that walled off the local mental institution.

Annoyed but resigned, he jacked up the car and prepared to replace the wheel. He took off the hubcap, unscrewed the bolts, placed them in the hubcap, which happened to be resting in the road, and placed the spare tire with its hub onto the axle.

He was about to reach for the hubcap when a speeding car raced by, and even as he jumped back for dear life, it ran over the hubcap, sending it spinning for two blocks, with the bolts flying in all directions.

There was no possible way of finding the bolts in the dark, and helplessly, he realized he was standing there with a wheel on the axle, unbolted and useless.

Wondering what to do, a man from the other side of the fence shouted, "Hey, mister."

He looked up, surprised, and noticed he had attracted the attention of one of the mental inmates, who had been watching the procedures by the light of the street lamps.

He replied cautiously, "Yes? Is there something you want?"

"I just want to give you some advice. Take off the other hubcaps and remove one bolt from each wheel and use them for that spare tire you have. The other wheels will be held by four bolts apiece and your spare by three. That will hold you till you get to the nearest repair shop, where you can get additional bolts and an additional hubcap."

"Great," he said. "You're perfectly right. Now why didn't I think of that?"

Then, embarrassed, he said, "It's really amazing that, under the circumstances — uh — you could —."

"Because I'm in here?" said the inmate contemptuously. "That just means I'm crazy. It doesn't mean I'm stupid."

It Only Rattles When I Drive It

A man went to a car dealership after inheriting a great deal of money. After looking around the lot, he picked out the nicest, newest, fanciest, most expensive car he could find. He paid cash up front and drove out of the dealership in his new car.

On his way home, he started hearing a rattling sound, and figured something was wrong, so he turned around and headed back to the dealer. The dealer was of course very sorry, and offered to either fix the car or let the man take a different one while they ordered a replacement. The man really wanted the car he picked, so he just had the guy fix it.

Two hours later, the mechanics gave the car back, saying they couldn't find a thing wrong with it. The man was a bit wary, but he drove home. Whatever the rattle was, it stopped.

However, a day later, the rattle started again. Once again he took it to the dealership, and they still couldn't find anything wrong with it. This routine continued for a number of weeks. Sometimes the rattling went away on its own, but after nearly two months of this, the dealer grew very upset and concerned because he didnt want to get a bad reputation. So he ordered a replacement and exchanged it with the man for the malfunctioning car.

Then he ordered the mechanics in the shop to do a complete tear-down to figure out the problem. They began taking the car apart, piece by piece, but still didn't find anything -- until they took apart the door. Inside, they found a piece of metal pipe, along with a note.

Written on the note, in a scrawling worker's hand writing was, "So, you finally found the rattle, you rich son-of-a-bitch."

"I wish I had your faith."

A venerable old minister, was driving through the Pennsylvania countryside when his car sputtered and conked out.

The padre was distraught because he had a wedding to officiate in an hour and now he'd run out of gas. Then remembering that he'd passed a garage a short while back, he praised the Lord, and gathering his cassock, he set off.

Upon reaching the garage, he enquired whether there was a receptacle into which he might put a gallon or so to alleviate his predicament. A pump attendant shook his head glumly, then pointed to a scrapheap out the back.

The vicar scrambled about on the scrapheap, but the only thing he could lay his hands on was a child's enamel potty. Filling it to the brim, he set off back to his stranded vehicle. As he stumbled along the lane, the vicar built up quite a sweat, especially when he realised that the *yellowy* liquid was rapidly evaporating from his open receptacle.

He reached the car with but a little left, and was just pouring the dregs into the gas tank when a gleaming Bentley purred up. A dowager in the back, all wrapped up in mink, saw the red-faced clergyman administering the saffron-coloured fluid from the potty and wound her window down.

"Oh Reverend," she sighed, "I wish I had your faith."

Push Start

A man from Gary, Indiana had a very old car. It was always breaking down and constantly needed to a push-start. However, the man loved the car and refused to trade it in for a new one. One day, he was in

town, and as usual, the car stalled. He waved down a passing motorist and asked the teenage driver if he would be prepared to push-start the old car with the front end of his. The teenager said that he would be happy to help. The man warned the teenager that the old car had an automatic transmission, and he would need to get up to at least 35 mph or it wouldn't work. Unfortunately, the teenager took the man literally and before the man knew it, the teenager had reversed his car half a block away and accelerated to 35 mph as he drove towards him. His clapped out motor was a write-off and the man had to walk home.

"Sorry, My Car Doesn't Take Vanilla."

A woman from Kansas City, took her car to the garage and told the mechanic that it was behaving strangely. She explained that every time she went to the local grocery store to buy vanilla ice cream, the car would fail to start on her return. She continued that if she bought any other flavour other than vanilla, the car started fine. The mechanic thought the woman was insane, but agreed to try to repair the car. However, on examining the engine, he could find nothing wrong, so he decided to go buy some ice cream himself to test the woman's theory. The mechanic drove the car to the grocery store and bought a large tub of vanilla ice cream, and like the woman had told him, the car refused to start. Eventually, the mechanic worked out that it took longer to get vanilla ice cream than any other flavour because it was the only one that wasn't pre-packaged. It seemed the car didn't start because it remained idle for the amount of time it took to buy vanilla ice cream.

Speedometer Surprise

A man had nothing but mechanical trouble and breakdown after breakdown in the two years that he owned his car. Fed up, he decided to try and sell it. He gave it a good clean and polish, tuned up the engine as best as he could and put an advertisement in the local paper. The advert described the car as a good runner with one careful owner. The man realised that the 500,000 miles on the clock might not look so good and decided to fix it at a more appealing level.

On opening up the speedometer, the man was surprised, and somewhat peeved to find a note wedged into the back that read, "Oh no, not again. Shouldn't I be consigned to the scrap heap by now?"

The Introduction of The V8-Powered Car Created A Mob Scene

Our love of driving is equal to the auto industry's love of our money. These following stories focus on the business side of the auto world: how cars are named, marketed, and what factory secrets they contain.

"Doesn't Go"

General Motors learned the pitfalls of doing business in foreign countries when they introduced their Chevrolet Nova model of automobile into a Spanish-speaking market. They scratched their heads in puzzlement when it sold poorly. GM executives were baffled until someone finally pointed out to them that "nova" translates as "doesn't go" in Spanish. The embarrassed automobile giant changed the model name to the Caribe, and sales of the car took off.

On One Condition

It was a sweltering August day in 1937 when the Cohen brothers entered the posh Dearborn, Michigan offices of car maker, Henry Ford.

"Mr. Ford," announced Norman Cohen, the eldest of the three. "We have a remarkable invention that will revolutionize the automobile industry."

Ford looked skeptical, but their threat to offer it to the competition kept his interest piqued. "We would like to demonstrate it to you in person."

After a little cajoling, they brought Mr. Ford outside and asked him to enter a black automobile parked in front of the building.

Hyman Cohen, the middle brother, opened the door of the car.

"Please step inside, Mr. Ford."

"What!" shouted the tycoon, "Are you crazy? It must be two hundred degrees in that car!"

"It is," smiled the youngest brother, Max, "but sit down Mr. Ford, and push the white button."

Intrigued, Ford pushed the button. All of a sudden a whoosh of freezing air started blowing from vents all around the car, and within seconds the automobile was not only comfortable, it was quite cool.

"This is amazing!" exclaimed Ford. "How much do you want for the patent?"

Norman spoke up, "The price is one million dollars." Then he paused. "And there is something else: The name 'Cohen Brothers Air-Conditioning' must be stamped right next to the Ford logo!"

"Money is no problem," retorted Ford, "but no way will I have a Jewish name next to my logo on my cars!'

They haggled back and forth for a while and finally they settled. Five million dollars, but the Cohens' name would be left off. However, the first names of the Cohen brothers would be forever emblazoned upon the console of every Ford air conditioning system.

And that is why, even today, whenever you enter a Ford vehicle, you will see those three names clearly printed on the air conditioning control panel: NORM, HI and MAX.

The Introduction of The V8-Powered Car Created A Mob Scene

Americas first affordable V8-powered car was an automobile introduced in 1932 by the Ford Motor Company, one which quickly grew tremendously popular and received effusive praise from motorists. Of those enthusiastic drivers, was none other than famous "Goodfella" Clyde Barrow. He was quoted saying to Henry Ford on April 10, 1934:

"While I still got breath in my lungs I will tell you what a dandy car you make. I have drove Fords exclusively when I could get away with one. For sustained speed and freedom from trouble the Ford has got every other car skinned, and even if my business hasn't been strickly legal, it don't hurt anything to tell you what a fine car you got in the V8."

"There must be some mistake! There is no such thing as a broken spring on a Rolls-Royce!"

Dream machines; we lust after them. Whether it be for there extra power, their inherent sexiness, or the cahet imparted by previous celebrated owners. Thoughts of these machines cruise our daydreams.

A Spring In Your Jaunt

A London politician was driving his new Rolls-Royce over the Swiss Alps when he heard a disquieting "twang." His front spring had broken.

He called the Rolls plant in London by long distance, and, in what seemed like no time flat, three gentlemen arrived by plane with a new spring, and off went the politician on his interrupted jaunt.

After six months the politician received no bill from the Rolls people. Finally he appeared at the plant in person and asked that the records be checked for "the repair of a broken spring in Switzerland."

After a brief delay, the manager of the plant appeared in person, gazed at him rather reproachfully, and announced, "There must be some mistake! There is no such *thing* as a broken spring on a Rolls-Royce!"

Deal Of The Century

Back in 1963, a young man bought a brand new 1963 Corvette Split Window Coupe: a very collectible one-year-only model. He drove it around for a year before he was drafted into the Army. He carefully prepped the car for storage, went to Vietnam, and was promptly killed. Years later when the car had achieved a rare collectible status, his mother decided she was tired of looking at his car up on blocks and decided to sell it. She put an ad in the newspaper that stated "'63 Chevy for sale. $50. As is." Of course, the first person to call on her bought it and got the deal of the century.

The Rocket Car

The Arizona Highway Patrol was mystified when they came upon a pile of smoldering wreckage embedded in the side of a cliff rising above the road at the apex of a curve. The metal debris resembled the site of an airplane crash, but it turned out to be the vaporized remains of an automobile. The make of the vehicle was unidentifiable at the scene.

The folks in the lab finally figured out it was a 1967 Chevy Impala, and pieced together the events that led up to its demise.

It seems that a former Air Force sergeant had somehow got hold of a Jet Assisted Take-Off unit (JATO). JATO units are solid fuel rockets used to give heavy military transport airplanes an extra push for take-off from short airfields.

Dried desert lakebeds are the location of choice for breaking the world ground vehicle speed record. The sergeant took the JATO unit into the Arizona desert and found a long, straight stretch of road, attached the JATO unit to his car, jumped in, accelerated to a high speed, and fired off the rocket.

He ignited the JATO unit on the Chevy Impala approximately 4 miles from the crash site. This was established by the location of a prominently scorched and melted strip of asphalt. The vehicle quickly reached a speed of between 300 and 350 mph and continued at that speed, under full power, for an additional 25-30 seconds. The soon-to-be pilot experienced G-forces usually reserved for dog-fighting F-14 jocks under full afterburners.

The Chevy remained on the straight highway for approximately 2.6 miles, or 15-20 seconds before the driver applied the brakes, completely melting them, blowing the tires, and leaving thick rubber marks on the road surface. The vehicle then became airborne for an additional 1.3 miles, impacted the cliff face at a height of 125 feet, and left a blackened crater 3 feet deep in the rock.

Most of the driver's remains were not recovered. However, small fragments of bone, teeth, and hair were extracted from the crater, and fingernail and bone shards were removed from a piece of debris believed to be a portion of the steering wheel.

"To Elvis, Love Priscilla"

A friend of a friend of my co-worker was riding along a back road, when he spotted an old motorcycle for sale. It was a 1950's Harley for $600. But he bought the bike although it needed work.

He couldn't get parts because the bike was so old. So he called Harley headquarters in Milwaukee. He described the Harley, but kept getting transferred from person to person. Each time, they asked what the Harley looked like.

Finally, the CEO of Harley came on the line. He asked the guy to describe the Harley again. Then he told him to go out and check under the rear fender. That's where he found an inscription saying, "To Elvis, Love Priscilla".

It was Elvis' Harley-Davidson, a gift from Priscilla. Harley offered him $4 million for it.

There was no sign of the driver, but a pile of human excrement was found in the driver's seat.

Traffic accidents are horrifying and deadly. However, human error combined with relentless mechanical power can often prove potential for hilarity, as these stories demonstrate.

Headless Motorist

A motorcyclist was riding behind a truck that was carrying a load of thin steel plates. He decided to overtake the truck, but as he moved out towards the centre of the road, one of the steel sheets became dislodged and decapitated him. However, his momentum carried him alongside the truck. When the truck driver glanced from his window, he saw the headless motorcyclist passing, had a heart attack, ran off the road and was killed.

Did You Know? *A totally wrecked cream-coloured Ford Escort was found at the bottom of a 100 foot cliff face near Aberdeen in Washington on the early morning of July 3, 2003. It was thought to have left the road at a sharp bend. There was no sign of the driver, but a pile of human excrement was found in the driver's seat.*

Stunt Rental Car Driver

A group of American tourists had just been on the infamous Shotover Jet in Queenstown, New Zealand, and were driving back to their hotel. The driver was going over every detail of the apparently nail-biting experience. He went on about how close the jet-boat driver got to the canyon walls and how fast he was going. However, when he went on to describe how the jet-boat driver put his hand in the air to signal that he was going to spin the boat around, the American couldn't help but try out the manoeuvre himself in their rental car. To the surprise of his friends, the driver put his hand in the air and slammed on the handbrake. Unfortunately, the driver had somehow forgotten that he was not in the middle of a quiet river but on a very busy road. Luckily, there were no fatalities in the resultant 15 car pile up.

Ripped Along The Highway

Are you one of those drivers out there who think it's cool to hang their arm out of the car window while cruising around? Well, this story may cure you of that habit.

A man was driving in his convertible along a California highway one sunny day, with his shades on, the stereo blasting, and his arm hanging languidly out of the window. He was so caught up in the relaxing drive, the young man failed to notice a shovel protruding from a flat-bed truck coming the opposite direction. As they passed, the shovel struck his arm and ripped it out of the socket. With barely a swerve, the man continued driving seemingly unfazed. He drove for another ten miles until he stopped at a gas station, shocking other customers as they spotted his bleeding shoulder. It wasn't until he attempted to unscrew the gas cap on his car that he looked down and realised his arm was missing. He told doctors at the hospital that he had no memory of the accident.

49

"Well, I was doing the reverse parking, and I was waiting for the examiner to pinch me, but he didn't, so I crashed into the car behind."

Each of us has faced the rigors of becoming licenced drivers. We wrestle with impersonal bureaucracy followed by a harrowing examination of our driving skills, during which, often as not, glaring shortcomings in our abilities come to light. It's natural for some of those feelings of resentment to be transferred to the person orchestrating the test. Driving exams are occasions fraught with opportunities for things to go terribly wrong. Most mishaps that happen during driving examinations are of the minor variety, but every examiner has his or her war stories to tell.

Celebratory Drinking and Driving

A young man just passed his driving test, and celebrated with his family over a bottle of champagne. He then went to the bar to join his friends for a few more celebratory drinks, foolishly taking his car. After one too many, the boy staggered to his car, and went to reverse out of his parking place, when suddenly, there was a crunch. The boy had reversed straight into the side of a passing car. Blurry-eyed, the boy was more than surprised to discover that the driver of the passing car was none other than the driving test examiner who had passed him earlier that day. The young man was subsequently banned from driving for 12 months.

Motorbike Test

A boy from Annapolis, Maryland was taking his motorcycle driving test. Everything was going well and he was confident he was going to pass. The examiner wanted to test his emergency stop and told the boy to drive around the block, and when the examiner jumped out in front of him, he was to stop immediately. The boy sped off on his motorbike and drove around the streets the examiner had told him too. But after 15 minutes the examiner had still not appeared, and the boy was getting concerned. He drove around for another 10 minutes before finally giving up and returning to the testing centre. At the centre, the boy found out about the examiners whereabouts. It seemed the examiner heard the sound of an approaching motorbike and stepped out, only for it to be the wrong motorbike, which then hit him head on. The poor examiner was treated in the hospital for several injuries, while the boy was allowed to pass his test.

Pinch Test

In Oakland, California, a driving instructor was so exasperated with a student who had failed his driving test 12 times, that he concluded extreme measures were called for. In subsequent driving lessons, whenever the student made a mistake, the instructor pinched him hard on the leg. The instructor was so surprised by the student's improved performance, that he entered him for another test within two weeks. Unfortunately the student failed again.

When the instructor asked the student what had gone wrong the student replied, "Well, I was doing the reverse parking, and I was waiting for the examiner to pinch me, but he didn't, so I crashed into the car behind."

You Passed With Farting Colors

A 17-year-old boy from Dayton, Ohio was taking his driving test and everything was going smoothly, so he felt confident that he would pass. However, when it came time to do a three-point turn in the road, as he was about to reverse, the examiner farted loudly, causing the youngster to stall the car. The examiner made a mark on his pad and told the boy to drive on. Although a little annoyed, the boy continued, only to have the same thing happen when he was attempting to reverse park. The furious boy got out of the car and stormed off in disgust. The examiner was about to tell him that it didn't matter and that he had passed the test anyway, when a truck driving past smashed the open car door off its hinges. Needless to say, the examiner reversed his decision and failed the sensitive teenager.

"Yes, it's a Guttoe. It says right here on the grill: G-T-O. 'Guttoe'."

Automobiles are well into their second century, and people still can't grasp its American technology or culture. The automobile is one of the most ubiquitous pieces of machinery to infiltrate our daily lives. As such, it's bound to give rise to stereotypical tales about those who should probably hand in their pink slip.

Comes With New Driver Side Handbags

A young lady bought a brand new car, but she kept on returning to the dealer complaining that the engine was over heating, and was high on fuel consumption.

This baffled the dealer, because his mechanics repeatedly examined the car but could not find anything wrong with it.

The young lady insisted that there was something wrong with the car.

"It always happens when I drive it!" she informed the dealer.

In desperation, the dealer asked the young lady to drive the car in his presence. So he sat in the passenger's seat, she got the car keys out of her handbag, pulled the choke lever out to its full position, hung her handbag on the choke lever, started the car, and proceeded to drive it.

Crusin'

An American couple travelling around New Zealand decided to rent a campervan to get the best experience out of their trip. They drove through Auckland and ended up on a long stretch of road. An hour or so into their journey, the wife told her husband she was going to lie down for a while. The husband continued driving, but shortly after, realised he desperately needed to go to the bathroom. The husband, not wanting to stop, noticed that there was a "Cruise" option on the gears, and assumed that it must be the equivalent of an auto-pilot. He quickly put the campervan into cruise mode, and ran back to the toilet. Naturally, before he had even unzipped his fly, the campervan careered off the road, and straight into a river before hitting a rock and coming to a sudden halt.

My Boat Came With A Trailer?

On Lake Isabella, located in the high desert, about an hour east of Bakersfield, California, a blonde, new to boating was having problems. No matter how hard she tried, she just couldn't get her brand new 22-ft. Bayliner to perform. It was very sluggish in almost every maneuver, no matter how much power she applied.

After about an hour of trying to make it go, she putted over to a nearby marina, hoping that someone could tell her what was wrong. A thorough topside inspection revealed everything was in perfect working order. The engine ran fine, the outboard motor went up and down, and the prop was the correct size and pitch. So, one of the marina guys decided to jump in the water to check underneath. He came up choking on water, because he was laughing so hard. Under the boat, still strapped securely in place was the trailer.

"R" stands for "Stupidity"

For anyone else who doesn't already know, the R on an automatic stands for reverse.

A boy from Oakland, California, was given a brand-new, automatic transmission car for his eighteenth birthday. Eager to show off the car to his buddies, he thanked his parents and drove off. He found his friends in a deserted parking lot, where one of them challenged him to a race. Seeing it as an opportunity to test his new car, the boy agreed. The two boys lined their cars up, revved their engines, and waited for another boy to signal the start. As the flag dropped the challenger pulled away fast, and try as he could, the boy was ubable to keep up with him. Desperate to win, he spotted "R" on the choice of gears, and in a moment of stupidity, thought it stood for "race". The accelerating car suddenly spun out of control, and crashed into a post.

Skid Marks

A bored driver travelling alone decided, for reasons known only to himself, to make the journey a little more interesting. While still driving along, he dropped his pants, stuck his butt out of the window and began to "moon". The drivers who were travelling in the opposite direction. All went well until he decided to get a bit more ambitious, or rather get a bit more of his backside out of the widow. Having jammed the accelerator pedal down with his car jack, he hung right out of the window. He probably would have carried on baring his behind for the rest of the afternoon had he not lost his grip and fallen backwards on to the road. He landed relatively unhurt, apart from some very unusual skid marks, but was forced to watch as his car carried on down the road, with his trousers attached, until it came to rest into the back of a police car.

The Guttoe

My mechanic friend told me that he answered the phone in the Automotive Shop one morning and talked to a woman who was calling because her husband's car wouldn't start.

He set out to get the information for the work order, and when he asked the model of the car, she told him it was a "Guttoe".

"A Guttoe?" he asked.

"Yes, it's a Guttoe," she replied. It says right here on the grill: G-T-O. 'Guttoe'."

chapterfour

"Beam me up, Scotty. There's no intelligent life here."

--Captain James T. Kirk; USS Starship Enterprise

criminalintent

A good many rumors fall within a category encompassing crime and criminals. Many legends deal with our fears, worries and concerns about others preying on us and our property, but we also laugh at the fool-hardy ones that get caught, and we cheer the police that outwit them.

· · · · · · · · · · · · · · · · · · ·

A bid for freedom.

"If you can't do the crime, don't do the time." Here are a few captive-ating tales about great escapes.

Life In Prison

A convicted bank robber, sentenced to life in prison, came up with a plan to escape. He had noticed that when a prisoner died, the body was placed in a coffin that was then nailed shut by the caretaker and transported to a local cemetery. The prisoner promised the caretaker a hefty slice of his buried loot if he helped him to escape. The caretaker agreed. The plan was that the caretaker wouldn't nail the coffin shut until morning, and then after the funeral, he would dig him up. On the agreed night the prisoner, equipped with snacks and a flashlight, snuck into the mortuary, squeezed into the coffin next to the dead body and pulled the lid closed. With a few hours till morning, the prisoner fell asleep. He awoke to hear the coffin being nailed shut and then felt the coffin being carried, put down and then transported. After about half an hour, the van stopped, and the coffin was then carried and lowered into a grave. He could just about hear the priests last rites. When that was over, he waited a few minutes more before pulling out his flashlight and eating his snacks. Wondering how long it would be before the caretaker came to dig him up, curiosity got the better of him and he decided to have a look at who he was sharing the coffin with. He shone the flashlight on to the dead man's face, but was horrified to see that it was the caretaker himself.

Did You Know? *It costs forty-thousand dollars a year to house each prisoner. If you live in Los Angeles the government will pay you forty-thousand bucks apiece for taking a few prisoners into your home. Most homes in LA already have bars on the windows. These criminals will not be*

53

given free room and board. They are required to run twelve hours a day on a treadmill and generate electricity. And if they don't want to run, they can rest in the chair that's hooked up to the generator.

Sentenced To Life In Reading

In Washington, D.C., a man was sentenced to four months community service. However, he managed to extend his sentence to a 15 year imprisonment. The man, convicted of simple embezzlement, drew the authority's wrath after writing letter after letter to several politicians, and judges. There is nothing wrong with that, however, each letter attacked the recipients sexuality and sometimes even resorted to death threats. The man was then refused access to a pen and paper, and was told to spend his remaining time in reading.

Sticky Escape

Putting Superglue to the test in a bid for freedom.

Two prisoners managed to escape from a high security prison in Arizona by using Superglue. When their jailer came to close their cell door, the prisoners each grabbed a hand. At first, the jailer expected them to overpower him and escape, but when he tried to shake free of them, he discovered they had glued themselves to him. Attempts to remove the prisoners with alcohol proved fruitless and the three of them were taken to the local hospital for surgical removal. As soon as the surgeon had performed the task, the prisoners escaped. All arts and crafts activities have since been banned inside the prison.

Did You Know? *A neighborhood friend told me of a condemned man who was soon to meet his fate in the electric chair. He began "feeding" himself electricity in his prison cell in order to build up a tolerance to it, and when the day of his execution arrived, his preparations allowed him to survive the first jolt in the electric chair. According to the law, it a condemned man survives his jolt in the electric chair, he is allowed to live. However, the executioner "illegally" pulled the switch for a second time and finished him off.*

The Sentence Sticks

A prisoner at a high security prison in Washington doused his overalls in Superglue and stuck himself to the side of the laundry van as it left the prison. A few miles down the road, the van stopped at a red light and the prisoner saw his opportunity. However, when he tried unzipping himself from the overalls as planned, he found that the zipper had stuck fast, and no amount of squirming or wiggling helped. Four hours later, the prisoner was apprehended when the laundry van returned to the prison with clean linen.

Bored, the kids though it'd be fun to try to squish the "Ant looking things on the foot path below."

Every year the FBI, is asked to investigate over 36,000 serious crimes including Murder/Homicides. Every year the Homicide Investigations Unit puts out its "Top 20 Homicides of the Year".

20. Max Wyman, 34 years old, is killed by his wife, armed with a 20" long vibrator. Mrs. Wyman had enough of her husbands strange sex practices, and one night during a prolonged being of "fun" she snapped, pushing all 20" inches of the vibrator into Max Wyman's anus until it ruptured several internal organs and caused severe bleeding.

19. Millie-Newton, 99 years old, was killed as she crossed the road. She was to turn 100 the next day, but crossing the road with her daughter to go to her own birthday party her wheel chair was hit by the truck delivering her birthday cake.

18. Stan Peters, 45 years old, is murdered by his 8 year old daughter, who he had just sent to her room with no dinner. Young Stephanie Peters felt that if she couldn't have dinner no one should, and she promptly inserted 72 rat poison tablets into her fathers coffee as he prepared dinner. The victim took one sip and promptly collapsed. (Stephanie Stone was given a suspended sentence as the judge felt she didn't realize what she was doing, until she tried to poison her mother using the same method one month later.

17. Danny Johnson, 18 years old, was killed by his girlfriend after he attempted to "have his way with her". His unwelcome advance was met with a prompt kick in the chest and then 4 shots from a doubled barrelled shot gun the girlfriends' father had given to her an hour before the date started, just in case.

16. Hanson Vilmer, 35 years old, was killed by his landlord for failing to pay his rent for 8 years. The landlord, Karl Eastman, clubbed the victim to death with a toilet seat after he realized just how long it had been since Mr. Vilmer paid his rent.

15. Leah Carol, 13 years old, was killed by her 1 year old sister who climbed on top of her while she was sleeping, suffocating her.

14. Mary Freeman, 45 years old, is killed by 14 state troopers after she wandered onto a live firing, fake town simulation. Seeing the troopers all walking slow down the street Mary Freeman jumped out in front of them and yelled. "Boo!" The troopers, thinking she was a pop up target fired 67 shots between them, over 40 of them hitting their target. "She just looked like a very real looking target." One of the troopers stated in his report.

13. Robin Fry, 17 years old, was killed by a "Hit Man" hired by her ex boyfriend after she broke off their relationship. The "Hit Man" was promised to be paid $500,000 for the task. The "Hit Man" killed the boyfriend after he found out that the 16 year old high school student, whose father was in jail for rape, and mother worked as an ironing lady didn't have access to $500,000.

12. Gerald Goza, 71 years old, was killed as he prepared to drive to work. His wife Nellie Goza, had been plotting to kill him for over a year, and had cut the brakes on his car 4 times previously. On this attempt Nellie was just about to cut the brakes again when Gerald snuck up behind her, grabbed her and spun her around, as he did she lost her footing and stumbled into him, stabbing him in the lower ventrical of the heart, killing him instantly.

11. Ahmed Raffi, 24 years old, was killed by an unknown member of the Russian Mafia, after he accidentally took away the gangsters drink too soon at the nightclub he worked in. The gangster was so upset he forced the waiter to drink over 27 litres of 'coca cola' (the drink he had taken away) until Ahmed drowned.

10. June Sweeney, 21 years old, was killed by her brother David because she talked on the phone too long, David clubbed his sister to death with a cordless phone, then stabbed her several times with the broken aerial.

9. Helena Simms, Wife to the famous American Nuclear Scientist Harold Simms was killed by her husband after she had an affair with the neighbour. Over a period of 3 months Harold subsituted Helena's eye shadow with a Uranium composite that was highly radioactive, until she died of radiation poisoning. Although she suffered many symptoms, including total hair loss, skin welts, blindness, extreme nausea and even had an ear lobe drop off the victim never attended a doctors surgery or hospital for a check up.

8. Military Lieutenant John Whitaker killed his "two timing wife" by loading her car with Trintynitrate explosive (similar to C4) the Ford Taurus she was driving was filled with 750 kgs of explosive, forming a force twice as powerful as the Oklahoma Bombing. The explosion was witnessed by several persons, some up to 14

kilometres away. No trace of the car or the victim were ever found. Only a 55 metre deep crater, and 500m of missing road.

7. Patricia Spring, 37 years old, was killed by her neighbour in the early hours of a sunday morning. Her neighbour, Peter Hume, for years had a mounted F6 phantom jet engine in his rear yard. He would fire the jet engine, aimed at a empty block at the back of his property. Patricia Spring would constantly complain to the local sheriff's officers about the noise and the potential risk of fire. Mr. Hume was served with a notice to remove the engine immediately. Not liking this he invited Miss Spring over "for a cup of coffee and a chat" about the whole situation. What Spring didn't know was that he had changed the position of the engine, as she walked into the yard he activated it, hitting her with a blast of 5000 degrees, killing her instantly, and forever burning her outline into the driveway.

6. Bruce Michaels, angry at his gay boyfriend used the movie, "Die Hard, With a Vengeance" as inspiration. He drugged his white boyfriend, Lance Lewis, into an almost catatonic state, then dressed him only in a double sided whiteboard that read "Death to all Niggers!" on one side, and "God love the KKK." on the other. Lance then drove the victim to down town Harlem and dropped him off. Two minutes later he was deceased.

5. Newton Davies was killed after a co worker at Sea World Florida dropped a 20 tonne killer whale on him. The whale had been hoisted out of his tank by a Master Tonne Crane, when the victim swam underneath to inspect the harness his colleague, Brianne Hart released the whale, crushing the victim instantly, and emptying ¼ the water from the pool.

4. Denny Sinter, 36 years old, by a fellow worker trying to prove a point. The worker, San Amote Pet, disconnected the internal landing gear settings on a Boeing 747 test plane, and the plane's gear automatically retracted after take off. But come landing time wouldn't re-engage, the helpless Denny Sinter couldn't do a thing as the plane ran out of fuel, in an attempt at an emergency landing the 747 exploded. Denny Sinter was killed instantly.

3. Heather Ridely, JoeHolmes and Gaven Wood were killed as they walked past a New York apartment building. Kenneth Bilk, 7 years old, and his 6 year old sister were left alone in their 27th floor hotel room by their parents as they went to the hotel's gaming room. Bored, the kids though it'd be fun to try to squish the "Ant looking things on the foot path below." (people) They started by throwing fruit, then quickly graduated to chairs, televisions, even the drawers from the bedroom dresser.

2. Colin Lipton, 26 years old, was killed by his twin brother Cameron after a disagreement over who should take the family home after their parents passed away. Colin had a nasal problem, and had no sense of smell. After the argument Cameron stormed out of the house, then snuck back later, and turned on the 3 gas taps in the house, filling it with gas. Then left out a box of cigars, a lighter and a note saying, "Sorry for the spree, have a puff on me, Cameron". Colin promptly light a cigar, destroying the house, and himself in the process.

1. Whitney Brooks, 24 years old, was killed by her Zoo keeper Boyfriend Matt Kelly after she refused sex. He 'invited her' to the zoo to see the lion feeding, and at feeding time lead her into a room that had a large slide away panel, He explained to her that it was a large glass viewing window to watch the lions devour their prey. He ducked out for a quick smoke and locked her in the room. Suddenly the slide away panel opened to reveal many persons staring at her, she was just about to yell and tell them that they were on the wrong side of the glass when she realised that it was her on the wrong side. Another panel opened and 3 hungry lions were let into the pen. Whitney survived for 2 days in the hospital before dying of massive internal injuries.

Brush Twice A Day To Prevent An Anal Cavity!

We may despise those who break the law, but nonetheless, we also enjoy the occasional chuckle over the imaginative means crooks employ in doing so.

Brush Twice A Day To Prevent An Anal Cavity!

A family returned from their holidays to find that their house had been burglarized, and all of their possessions, except for their toothbrushes and a camera, had been taken. The family informed the police, filed the usual insurance claims, and went about their daily lives. However, a couple of days later they took their holiday photographs to be developed, along with the film that was in the one remaining camera. When the prints were returned they discovered that the film from the camera featured photographs of their toothbrushes, stuffed up the burglars backsides.

Burglar Homework

A couple woke up one morning only to discover that their car had been stolen, and reported the robbery to the police. However, the following day upon returning from work the car was sitting in their driveway, cleaned and waxed, with an envelope on the driver's seat.

There were two tickets to a concert, and a note inside the envelope that explained, "I am really sorry for taking your car, but my mother suffered a stroke, and had to be taken to the hospital. As a thank you, here are two tickets to the 'Cher' tonight."

Surprised and delighted by this turn of events, the couple went to the concert where they enjoyed a very pleasant evening's entertainment. But when they returned home, they discovered that their house had been thoroughly burglarized, and all their valuables had been stolen. A week later, the police informed them that their car had been used in a major bank robbery staged during the day it was missing.

Designated Decoy

A police officer was staking out a well-known bar to bust some potential DUI-ers. As it neared last call, an extremely intoxicated man stumbled out of the bar and spent 30 minutes looking for his car. When all the other drivers had left, the drunk finally located his vehicle. He spent another 20 minutes fumbling for his keys and trying to unlock his car. Finally, he got in and eventually managed to start his car. As soon as he pulled away, the police officer went after him and pulled him over, giving him the breathalizer test. It came up negative.

"How is this possible?" the officer sputtered. "I saw you! You were falling all over the place!"

The driver grinned and said, "Tonight I'm the Designated Decoy."

Goodbye Mom

A young man went into a supermarket to buy a quart of milk, a dozen eggs, and toilet paper. As he looked for the milk, he noticed a middle-aged woman staring at him with sad, forlorn eyes. He turned away, grabbed the quart of milk and went in search of the eggs. When he found the eggs, he turned around only to see the same woman staring at him. Somewhat disturbed, he hurried towards the cashier, but remembered that he still needed the toilet paper, so he returned to the main part of the store to find some. Arriving back at the cashier, he noticed that the woman in front of him in the line had a cart full almost to the brim.

The old lady finally said to the young man, "I'm sorry for staring, but you look just like my son who died only a few weeks ago."

She sniffled and added, "You have the same hair and eyes. Just like him."

As she packed her groceries, she whispered to the young man, "Could you do a grief-stricken mother a favour? Could you just say 'Goodbye Mom', as I leave?"

The man agreed, and as she left the store, struggling with four heavy bags of shopping, he shouted out,

"Goodbye Mom."

However, his feeling of worthiness was short-lived when the cashier told him the bill was $194 dollars.

"There must be a mistake," he exclaimed pointing to his three items.

But the cashier replied, "Your mother said you'd take care of her shopping too."

Did You Know? *Police in France are looking for a man who robbed banks dressed as a giant aubergine. During the armed robbery in Marseilles, he was asked by the manager, "Are you serious?", to which he replied, "No, I am an aubergine," and fired a shot. The man escaped with the cash leaving a real aubergine on the counter.*

Hollywood Heist

The residents of a small town in Virginia were very excited, when a popular police TV show chose the area as a good place to film an episode. The film crew went round talking to residents and researching locations. While in town they visited a jewellery shop. The owner was not surprised when a young man with a clipboard came in and asked if they could film a scene in his shop. The owner, thinking it would be great for business, readily agreed, and a few hours later the young man returned with a video camera and three men wearing masks of various American presidents and carrying shotguns. The young man told the owner that he was going to film the men coming in, filling their bags full of jewels, then running out into a waiting car and driving off. The owners job was to look surprised and put his hands up. Everything went smoothly, the men filled their bags, ran out and the young man followed them with the camera. However, when no-one had returned after 30 minutes, the owner realised he'd been duped and called the police.

Night Deposit

A smartly dressed man entered a bank asking to use their washroom, with no one questioning his status. Within fifteen minutes he walked out with a complete guard's outfit: hat, tie, trousers and a shirt, with the bank name emblazoned over the breast pocket and on the right shoulder of the shirt.

At 11:00 pm he was standing at attention in front of the night-deposit box of the bank's airport branch, and a beautifully lettered sign adorned the safe's depository, "Night deposit vault out of order. Please make deposits with security officer."

There was an upright dolly, with a large mail bag bulking open, in front of the depository. At least thirty-five people dropped bags or envelopes into the container. Not one of them said more than "Good evening" or "Good night."

Stuffed Ham

A friend of a friend saw two large black women come into a Walmart wearing large overcoats. The women rushed through the store and proceeded to stuff their coats with everything in sight: chips, cookies, cans of soup, bottles of pop, etc. One of them even stuffed a large carving ham in her coat, and as she was rushing through the store, the ham slipped out onto the floor.

She glared around suspiciously, and defensively said to anyone who might hear, "Who trew dat ham at me?"

The Last Straw

There was a man who worked at a factory for twenty years, and every night when he left the plant, he would always push a wheelbarrel full of straw to the guard at the gate.

The guard would look through the straw, and find nothing and pass the man through. On the day of his retirement the man came to the guard as usual but without the wheelbarrow.

Having become good friends over the years, the guard asked him, "Gerald, I've seen you walk out of here every night for twenty years. I know you've been stealing something. Now that you're retired, tell me what it is. It's driving me crazy."

Gerald simply smiled and replied, "Okay! Wheelbarrels!"

What Do You Tip A Bank Robber?

The Japanese are well known for their politeness but this example of gratitude is more mocking than respectful.

Two weeks after the biggest bank robbery in Japan's history, the bank manager received a letter postmarked Rio de Janeiro, Brazil.

The letter had been typewritten and read, "Thank you for the bonus. It may interest you to know that rather than the 50.5 million yen stated in newspapers, the amount was in fact 76 million yen, thank you for the generous tip."

The criminals are presumably still living it up in South America.

You Do The Crime, You Do The...Inmates?

A prostitute in New York found herself on the wrong side of the law once too often, and ended up receiving a two-year sentence to be served in the women's penitentiary. Taking advantage of the courses and workshops it offered, she seemed to get on well with the other inmates and the months flew by. She was released on good behaviour after serving 18 months, and found a job in a department store. A couple of months later, the prison authorities were puzzled that a large number of women inmates at the penitentiary had become pregnant, especially since most of them had been inside for more than nine months. Investigating the matter, law enforcement became puzzled by the fact that the former prostitute frequently came to visit the pregnant women, and always brought presents. Delving into her past, they discovered a startling fact that solved their mystery, she was not in fact a female, but a very convincing male transvestite.

"Dis iz a stickup."

Some criminals get caught in the dumbest of fashions, which proves that not all crooks are criminal masterminds.

Automatic Robbery Machine

A not-too-clever man from Minot, North Dakota wanted to rob a bank, but seeing that it was a Sunday, he opted to rob a bank's automatic teller machine instead. The man scribbled a note that stated, "Give me all your money or I'll blow you sky-high," and fed the piece of paper into the deposit slot. After three tries without result, the man started smashing the machine with a hammer, when a police patrol spotted and arrested the foolish man.

Beware Of Eagle

A burglar in Vancouver, BC., Canada, broke into a house and filled his bag with jewellery, cd's, and liquor, when he suddenly felt a pair of eyes on him. Looking up, he noticed an eagle staring right at him with cold, merciless eyes. Initially the burglar was too petrified to move, but after ten minutes he tried creeping towards the door, however, the eyes just followed him, so he stayed rooted to the one spot. Eventually, the homeowners turned up and found the thief motionless in their lounge. Once the homeowner had turned on the light, the thief could see that the eagle was stuffed, but it was too late and the man was arrested.

The homeowner commented, "That stuffed eagle sure is better than any watchdog."

Bloody Passenger

In New York, a man boarded a subway with blood dripping from his jacket pocket. Other passengers, obviously thinking the man had been injured, offered to help, but the man just ignored them. At the next station, two policemen boarded the train, and an old woman, thinking she was being helpful, pointed out the blood on the man. The policemen detained the man for questioning, and eventually discovered that the man was hiding a woman's cut-off finger with a diamond ring attached to it. The man tried to explain that he had found the finger while walking in Central Park, but the policemen were unconvinced and arrested him.

"Catch The Bus"

Three students who shared an apartment while attending community college in Detroit, went on a pub crawl one Friday night, and got completely inebriated, missing their last bus home. The cheapskate students that they were, began to walk the few miles home. However, on passing the bus depot, the students had an idea to sneak inside and steal their own transportation. They found their bus, the 201, parked by the gate, so they started her up and drove themselves home, leaving the bus at the nearest bus stop. Delighted by their new-found free transportation, it became a regular weekend routine. A few weekends after that, they tried again, but this time they took their time and the police caught them. The police confirmed that the students fingerprints matched those found in the previous weeks thefts.

Asked why they took so long this time, one student replied sadly, "The bus company must've been on to us, because they'd parked the 201 right at the back and we had to move five other buses to get it out!"

Did You Know? *Police arrived quickly, to find a man hanging by his fingertips from a back wall. He had run out of the house when the owner, Phil Derrow, returned home unexpectedly and spotted the intruder in the garden, who had been "visiting" Mrs. Derrow. Hearing the front door open, the visitor climbed out of the rear window. But the back wall was 8 feet high and the man had been unable to get his leg over.*

Celebrated Chip

An Arabic man held up a 7'11 at gunpoint, shouting at customers to lie down on the floor with their hands over their heads. As he went from one customer to another, emptying their pockets and taking their valuables, he came across one woman who had been eating chips at the time. Unable to resist the intoxicating smell, the man grabbed a handful of chips and stuffed them into his mouth. Satisfied with his ill-gotten gains, the man went to leave, when he suddenly slipped on a chip that he had dropped, and knocked himself out.

The arresting police officer commented, "Many a robber has been caught because they succumbed to the temptation of our celebrated chip."

Chicken Thief

A woman from Springfield, Massachusetts was out shopping, but didn't have enough money for a frozen chicken she needed for a very special dinner that evening. Desperate, the woman hid the frozen chicken under her hat and joined the line to pay for the vegetables she'd picked up. The line seemed to take longer than expected, and the woman began to shiver with cold. As it came to her turn, the woman fainted from the cold, and the frozen chicken rolled out from under her hat and came to rest at the store manager's feet.

"Forget Fingerprints, We Have His Finger!"

A thief broke into a house in the middle of the night, and disturbed its occupants by smashing a window as he climbed in. Soon lights began to come on, and he heard the noises of the householders upstairs. In his rush to escape, he left more than a few fingerprints behind. As he climbed back out though the broken window, he managed to slice his finger off, leaving it behind as evidence. After the police arrived, they put out an appeal on local radio requesting that the burglar go to the local hospital where surgeons were waiting to reattach his severed finger. Faced with the prospect of a short prison term or the rest of his life being "digit deficient" (that's the politically correct term), the man had little choice but to turn up at the hospital and get stitched up in every respect.

Did You Know? *In May 1999, suspected drug dealer Almont Adams tried to evade capture in Virginia, by running into the woods. The police had no trouble following him because he was wearing a pair of 'Light Gear' trainers, with battery powered lights that flashed when the heel was pressed.*

"Freeze! This Is A Stink Up!"

A bank robber was in the middle of holding up a bank, when the chicken curry he'd eaten earlier started to make itself known. With the bank employees cowering on the floor, the robber demanded that the bank manager take him to the bathroom. The manager obliged, and led him to a door behind the counter. The robber told everyone to stay where they were, and leaving the door slightly ajar, proceeded to use the facilities. Scared that the robber could still see them, the employees and customers didn't move. The robber eventually escaped with his loot, but to add insult to injury, he didn't flush the toilet and left an awful smell that lingered in the bank for days.

In Thin Air

The NYPD were baffled by the disappearance of a thief who ran out of the back door of a jewellery store he had just robbed, as officers of the law charged in through the front door. The rear of the store opened out on to a deserted, high-walled alleyway, and the street to which the alleyway led was also deserted. They searched for the robber for over an hour but were unable to find him. For the next five days the officers involved in the incident were puzzled over the whereabouts of the man. There were no obvious hiding places, so it seemed that the thief had simply disappeared into thin air. Eventually the man's whereabouts became known to the police after they heard banging coming from the boot of their patrol car. The officers pulled over and opened the boot to investigate the noise and discovered, to their great surprise, that the thief had been hiding in there afraid to come out for the previous five days.

It's For My Cataracts!

A grandmother from Yonkers, New York was babysitting for her daughter one night and got the scare of her life when half a dozen men burst into the apartment, shouting and pointing submachine guns at her. It seems that the drug-busting brigade had misheard a communication from headquarters. They had been told to search the furthest apartment on the left, not the first apartment. Still, the police justified their over-the-top action when they found a few joints in the ashtray and a gram of skunk on the grandmother.

Did You Know? *When a crook decided to steal the central heating system from an empty house, he removed a pipe connected to the gas supply, then lit a match so that he could see. Although the house exploded, he continued with the job and even returned the next day, only to be arrested.*

Midget Thief

A midget thief in New Brunswick, New Jersey was in the process of robbing a post office when he heard police sirens approaching. Realising he had been set up, the thief ran out the back. The police stormed the building and the post office clerk told them where to find the thief.

The Inspector smiled, "We have the place surrounded, he won't get away!"

However, they looked all over the building, both inside and out, but they couldn't find the thief anywhere. The inspector sighed cluelessly as to how the thief might have escaped, and went to use the post office toilet. As he undid his trousers, he noticed a huge mass of toilet paper in the toilet bowl, but thought nothing of it. He began to relieve himself, but was startled to see the mass of toilet paper move. Staring up at him amongst the toilet paper was a pair of eyes. The inspector flushed the toilet and arrested the choking, besodden midget thief.

Pick A Bank And Stick-Up With It.

A desperate man from Toronto, Ontario, Canada decided to rob a bank, so he went into a branch of The Royal Bank, and like all polite bank robbers, joined the line.

In order to be discrete when making his demands, he took one of the counterfoils and wrote on it, "Dis iz a stickup. Put all the money in the bag."

However, worried that he might have been spotted writing the note, he panicked and left the bank. Spotting a branch of the rival bank CIBC across the road, he decided to try his luck there. Again, he joined the line, and eventually handed his note to the teller. The teller read the note and although alarmed, realised from the bad spelling that the man obviously wasn't very bright.

She returned the note to him, saying sternly, "Sir, I'm afraid we can't accept this, it's written on a Royal Bank counterfoil."

Unsure of himself, the man left CIBC, returning to The Royal Bank branch, where he was waiting patiently in the line when the police, alerted by the CIBC teller, arrived to arrest him.

Pickled Burglar

A professional burglar's career was cut short when he picked the house of a pickle enthusiast.

Trouble started when he broke in through the kitchen window and promptly fell headfirst into a very large jar of home-made lime pickles. Unable to remove the jar, the man tried to smash it against the wall, but was overcome by the pickle's potent fumes. The homeowner returned from his night out to find the burglar unconscious on the kitchen floor.

He later told police, "He might not have survived if he'd landed in my mango chutney."

Did You Know? *Police in Detroit, Michigan were called to arrest a naked man waiting at a bus* *terminal, but was released after their suspect produced a valid bus ticket.*

Say, Cheese

An elderly woman entered a photo booth to get a picture for her Senior Citizens' Pass and was just about to put her best toothless grin on when a callow youth stuck his head into the booth and attempted to steal her purse. As he got a grip on the handle, so did she and in the resulting struggle the little thug was pulled into the booth. At that very moment the first of four pictures was taken. The resulting flash startled them both for a second, but the woman quickly coming to her senses, and resumed pulling on the bag. Once again the youth was pulled into the booth, and again there was a flash, but this time the young man realised that he met his match and made a break for it, with the old lady in tow. Tracking down the would-be thief was easy because the police had his picture, and evidence of his crime from the old lady's attempts to get a photograph for her bus pass.

Studio Time

A couple of ambitious youths broke into an exclusive Los Angeles recording studio in hopes of making a demo of a song they had written. On the third take of their song, they spotted a police car driving up the driveway, so quick as a flash, they turned out all the lights and hid inside a cupboard. The policemen had come to investigate after neighbouring merchants reported suspicious characters loitering outside the entrance earlier. As they approached the studio room, they heard two voices whispering. At first police were puzzled where the voices were coming from, but soon realised they were coming from the speakers. One of the boys had unwittingly taken the microphone inside with him.

The police were amused to hear one boy cursing the other for standing on his toe, before revealing their whereabouts with, "They'll never find us in this cupboard."

Suicidal Manslaughter

A man, living in Hong Kong was convicted of manslaughter after a failed suicide went horribly wrong. Following several other failed attempts, the man put his head in an oven and tried to gas himself. Unfortunately, a concerned neighbour popped around for a surprise visit with a lit cigarette in tow, causing a huge explosion, which destroyed the whole apartment block, killing nine people. Miraculously, the man survived with minor burns, apparently because the oven shielded him from the collapsing building.

Did You Know? *A sign was put up in a Police station in New York that read, "Will the person who took a slice of cake from the Commissioner's Office return it immediately. It is needed as evidence in a poisoning case."*

That'll Teacher

A young teacher and her friends were enjoying a particularly noisy evening at home getting drunk and annoying their neighbours in a quiet and painfully dull Los Angeles suburb. Despite repeated requests to keep the noise down, the household took no notice, and carried on partying into the night. When the drinks began to run out a person was nominated to go out and get more beer, while the rest remained behind in order to study the effects of marijuana on people over thirty. No sooner had the person left that there was a knock at the door. Assuming that the beer-getter had forgotten the money, one of the party animals went to answer the door, first having put a wastepaper basket on his head.

"Come on in you moron," he shouted, and led his friend back into the living room just moments after the young teacher had been handed a joint.

Unfortunately for all concerned, the party animal with the shade on his head, had in fact, led the police into the living room, where they conveyed the neighbours' concerns about the noise before leading the poor teacher off to the police station.

What's The Number To 911?

Just after midnight on October 3, 1987, in Charelston, South Carolina, three policemen followed up on a mysterious 911 call. The emergency dispatcher had given them the address they traced by computer, but was unable to describe the problem because the caller hung up as soon as the 911 operator had answered the phone. The dispatcher though it might be a hostage taking, or a medical emergency. The policemen dispatched to the scene had no idea what they might be walking into.

However, at the address they'd been sent to investigate, the officers found 1.25 lbs. of cocaine, more than 500 grams of crack, two pistols, and more than $12,000 in cash, as well as three very surprised crooks. Though the three people in the apartment fled, two of them were later caught and charged with possession of cocaine.

What had happened to bring the police to the criminals' door? Well, the ring leader of this operation called the cops on themselves. One of them had tried to dial 921, the first few digits of their leader's phone number, but miss dialed, and instead reached the police emergency number.

Work After Death

A woman was charged with harbouring a dead body when she made her husband continue working after he died of a heart attack. The woman, who ran a bar in Brooklyn, New York discovered that her husband had suffered and died of a heart attack while she was out shopping. Worried that without her husband customers would stop coming to their bar, so she propped him up in a rocking chair in the corner and told any concerned customer that he was just tired. For nearly two weeks the woman got away with it until one customer got suspicious when her husband wouldn't join in a conversation about football.

As police led her away, the woman was heard yelling, "He's not dead. His heart just stopped beating, that's all."

"I believe you have a basketball under your dress."

Not all crime-related legends involve crime -- sometimes they are humorous tales about people who mistakenly believe they have been victimized.

A Kodak Moment

An old man from Baton Rouge, Louisiana, took a roll of a film into a one hour photo. Later that afternoon, the man returned to pick up his photos, only to be greeted by several policemen and arrested. The photo developer had reported the man to the police after discovering that the film contained photos of little children in the nude. However, it turned out the developer had jumped to the wrong conclusion when it was found that the children in the photos were the man's grandchildren, who, without the man's knowledge, had taken the camera and photographed each other in the bath.

Ball or Girl?

A woman from Albuquerue, New Mexico, who was seven-months pregnant, was out shopping for a toy for her two-year-old daughter. She came across the perfect doll and paid for it, but as she was about to leave, a security guard pulled her aside and asked her to follow him. The security guard took the woman and her daughter to a room in the back.

The guard said, "I believe you have a basketball under your dress."

The woman began to protest, but the guard paid no mind and just replied, "Don't give me any of that pregnant stuff, I've heard it all before."

The woman had to take her dress off before the security guard was convinced of her pregnancy.

She later won a libel suit against the store for putting her through such an experience.

Believable Costume

A petrified resident frantically called police after a man dressed in ski goggles and a mechanics uniform turned up on his doorstep with a roaring chainsaw.

Fearing he was about to be taken apart limb by limb, the desperate "victim" dashed to the phone to alert officers of the impending bloodbath. But police who raced to the address arrived to find the chainsaw-wielding offender gone.

It later transpired that the menacing character waving the 3ft-long power tool had in fact got the wrong address for a fancy costume party.

Police said he had been intent on making a dramatic entrance to the party and was dressed as legendary movie monster Jason Voohries from the "Friday The 13th" films.Upon realising his mistake he skulked off into the night, chainsaw in tow.

A police spokesman said, "The poor occupant was clearly frightened out of his skin when the guy turned up at the door with the chainsaw running looking terrifying."

"Luckily he had simply gone to the wrong door." exclaimed the officer, "It must have been rather embarrassing for him."

Drug Dealers

In Las Vegas, a blackjack dealer lost his job when he tested positive for cocaine after a random drugs test. The dealer denied the charge, and an industrial tribunal took up his case. After several weeks of investigations and talks, it was soon discovered that most of the dealers in the casino tested positive in the drug test. It turned out that the dealers weren't using cocaine at all, but customers who abused the substance were using $20 bills to snort the powder, and then losing the money at the casino, whereupon the dealers handled the bills.

Hit and Run

A woman was driving home when suddenly a little girl ran out in front of her car. Although the woman slammed on her brakes, it was too late and she hit the girl. Petrified, the woman drove off. When she got home, she packed her bags and moved to Europe. After a year, the woman had settled in Paris, but wracked with guilt and missing her friends and family, she turned herself in. However, the police found no reports of a hit and run incident involving a little girl on that day. However, they did report that a pig had been run over. It seems that the pig had escaped a cider festival where it had been dressed up in a dress and bonnet.

How to call the Police...

James Church of Ann Arbour, Michigan was going up to bed when his wife told him that he'd left the light on in the garden shed, which she noticed from the bedroom window. James opened the back door to go turn off the light, when he noticed a group of miscreants in the shed stealing things.

He phoned the police, who asked, "Is someone in your house?"

When James said no. The dispatcher said that all patrols were busy, and that he should lock his door until an officer was available.

James replied with a friendly, "Okay!"

He hung up the phone, counted to 30, phoned the police again and said, "Hello. I just called you a few seconds ago because there were people in my shed. Well, you don't have to worry about them now cause I've just shot them all." Then he hung up.

Five minutes later, four squad cars, an Armed Response unit, and an ambulance showed up at the Church residence. Of course, the police caught the burglars red-handed.

When one of the policemen said to James, "I thought you said that you'd shot them!"

James simply replied, "I thought you said there was nobody available!"

Pillsbury Dough Boys In The Hood

There was a sweet older lady who often went grocery shopping for the infirm and elderly in her church. One hot, summer afternoon a lady asked her to pick up a few things and bring them by her house, which happened to be in a dangerous part of Los Angeles. The sweet old lady was wary but didn't like to say no, even though she was terrified of driving in the part of the city that often had shoot-outs and other gang-related violence. So the sweet old lady went on her way, picked up the groceries and proceeded to the lady's house.

As she entered the lady's neighborhood she noticed a group of young hoodlums gathering on every street corner. Although she had no air conditioning in the car, as a safety precaution, she rolled the windows up tightly and suffered in the 90+ degree heat.

She drove ahead until suddenly she heard a loud "pop" and felt a jolt to the back of her head. She reached to feel the back of her head and came back with a wet oozing mess that she was sure was part of her brain.

Knowing that she had been shot, the woman turned around and raced to a nearby hospital.

Miraculously, she made it to the emergency room and had the strength to walk right in. She told the attendant that she had been shot. Immediately the sweet old lady was rushed back to an examining room. Doctors whirled around and asked where she had been shot, especially since they saw no blood.

She replied, "The back of my head."The doctors found a mass of the oozing white substance the woman had first noticed.

Upon inspection the doctors realised that the white substance wasn't part of her brain but instead a lump of biscuit dough (the kind in a can) that had exploded from the heat of her car!

Snack Attack

An elderly woman, traveling by bus, had a layover during her journey. So she purchased a package of Oreo cookies from a vending machine in the bus terminal and sat at a table. She placed her cookies on the table, sat down, and proceeded to read the newspaper.

She was joined by a young man, who, to her surprise, opened the package of Oreo cookies and began to eat them. The woman, saying nothing, but giving him an icy stare, grabbed a cookie. The young man, with a funny look on his face, ate another cookie. The woman again glared and grabbed another cookie. The young man finished the third cookie and offered the last to the woman.

Completely appalled, she grabbed the cookie and the young man left. Outraged, the woman threw down her paper only to find her unopened Oreos on the table in front of her.

Super Granny

An elderly Florida lady was out shopping, and upon returning to her car, found four males in the act of leaving with her vehicle. She dropped her shopping bags and drew her handgun, proceeding to scream at the top of her voice, "I have a gun, and I know how to use it! Get out of my car!"

The four men didn't wait for a second invitation. They got out and ran like mad, but "grambo", somewhat shaken, proceeded to load her shopping bags into the back of the car and get into the driver's seat. She was so shaken that she could barely get her key into the ignition. She tried and tried, and then it dawned on her why. A few minutes later she found her own car parked four or five spaces farther down. She loaded her bags into the car and then drove to the police station. The sergeant to whom she told the story nearly tore himself in two with laughter. He pointed to the other end of the counter, where four pale men were reporting a car jacking by a mad, elderly woman described as white, less than five feet tall, glasses, curly white hair, and carrying a large handgun. No charges were filled.

The Watch

A man was in New York on a business trip, and after being out for dinner one evening, he decided to travel back to his hotel on the subway. He was just settling into his seat when he realised that his gold watch was missing.

On the platform stood a young man who was grinning at him, and jumping to the conclusion that this was the thief, the business man leapt up and tried to get off the subway before the doors closed.

Unfortunately, he didn't quite make it. Nevertheless, he managed to grab hold of the man's lapel only to rip them clean off his suit as the train moved away. When he got back to his hotel the first thing he did was phone the police and reported the theft. Then he phoned his wife to tell her of the loss.

Before he could say anything she said, "Oh! I'm so glad you called. I've been trying to get hold of you. Did you know you left your watch behind on the dresser this morning?"

Unaware Pick-Pocket

Just after getting bumped by a passerby, a man walking down the street discovered his wallet was missing. The man, thinking he had been pick-pocketed, spotted the man who bumped him, and ran back. Furious, he took the man down an alley, and beat him up. Believing that the man must have ditched his wallet, took out the money, as well as all the cash the man had on him. However, when the man returned home, he found his wallet on the kitchen table where he had left it that morning.

"If you think it's bad now, wait until November."

There is nothing more satisfying than seeing clever criminals get tripped up by police who outsmart them.

Copsicle

A Rhode Island Highway patrolman decided to stop a speeding driver late one harsh winter night. Pulling in behind the driver, he climbed out of his patrol car to have a word with the offender. The night air was extremely cold, so he left the engine of the patrol car running. He had a word with the driver, took his licence and walked back to the police car to run a check on the documents, but was unable to get back into his vehicle. Deciding to pretend to be a nice guy, he walked back to the motorist, delivered a short sermon and sent him on his way with a warning never to speed again. Looking around, he noticed that there was nobody around. His radio was in the car and there was not a pay phone in sight. However, before too long another police car turned up to find out why he wasn't answering his radio. Just as he was about to talk to his colleague, an urgent call came through, and the brother officer had to speed off.

"Get in the trunk to keep warm," he said to the freezing policeman, "I'll come back and pick you up later."

Realising that this was the only way he was going to survive the cold, he did just that, only to find himself locked in until his colleague returned five hours later, with a large audience in tow.

"If you think it's bad now, wait until November."

Apparently there doesn't seem to be a lot of marijuana available right now, which is something only important to a select few. However, signs are popping up along US highways, supposedly put up by the DEA that read something along the lines of:

"If you think it's bad now, wait until November."

This, of course, implies that the DEA have somehow finally found a way to choke off a huge percentage of marijuana traffic, and they're rubbing it in the drug users' faces.

Joint Venture

A police officer was lecturing to an elementary school class on the dangers of drugs in the community. The officer took out a real marijuana joint and passed it round on a dish, so the children could see and smell it. He warned the children not to remove it, pointing out that he had to take the joint back to the evidence room, and if it was not there when the dish came back, he would have to search them all. However, when the dish returned, the officer was surprised to see that not only was the joint still there, but it had been joined by two more joints, three wraps of speed and a rock of crack.

Shoe Thief

In Orlando, Florida, police were quite concerned with a spate of thefts from public toilets. There had been several reports from embarrassed gentlemen, who said that while they were using the bathroom, they suddenly saw a pair of hands dart under the door and grab their feet. The mysterious assailant would then make off with their shoes. Surveillance of various public toilets failed to catch the thief, so a policeman was sent in undercover. The policeman caught a number of drug dealers and sex offenders before finally nabbing the shoe thief. The officer wore a pair of 18-hole army boots, and the unfortunate thief took so long trying to untie the laces that the policeman had quietly radioed for backup and had him arrested.

The Lie Detector Photocpy Machine

A man was taken into custody of a small police department in Bucks County for suspicion of a crime. He kept repeating that he was innocent of any wrong doing, and the arresting officers, convinced of his guilt, asked him if he would be willing to take a lie detector test. He agreed, and the officers took him to the Xerox machine. In this copy machine, the police had already placed a typewritten card in it that read, "He's lying."

Then they sat the man next to the machine and on his head, placed a metal colander that had been fashioned with wires and alligator clamps. During his interrogation, whenever he gave an answer the officers didn't like, or thought was a lie, they pushed the "Start" button on the copy machine, and the copy of the "He's lying" message would come out.

The man finally decided that he couldn't beat the machine, and made a full confession, including crimes the police never knew about.

"It's 120 degrees in Iraq and the soldiers are living in tents and they didn't commit any crimes, so shut your mouths."

Satisfying tales of criminals who get nabbed by the long arm of poetic justice.

A Piece To Remember Him By

A driver was approaching the highway around dusk, and noticed ahead of him in the half light, two hitchhikers. Because it was raining he decided to stop and pick them up. However, when he got closer and slowed down, he noticed these hitchhikers were two very large, ill-dressed men. Not liking the look of these men he quickly changed his mind. As he accelerated to drive away, one of the men lashed out at the car with a large chain he had hidden. Terrified, and not at this point caring about any damage to the car, the driver sped off down the highway as fast as he could.

It was only when he stopped at a service station that he had an opportunity to inspect the car for damage and, to his surprise, he discovered the assailant's chain wrapped around the rear bumper. When he was removing the offensive weapon, to his horror, he also found, tightly fastened in a knot in the other end of the chain, two fingers torn from the hand of the hitchhiker.

"Gimme The Money, Or I'll Sneeze!"

A man in Little Rock, Arkansas, desperate for money, decided to rob a bank. Unable to find a real gun, he used a toy pistol. He planned to threaten the cashier with the fake gun, take the money and leave taking a customer with him as a hostage. Like most plans, it failed as soon as it began. The man entered the bank, and joined the line. When it was his turn, brandishing the toy gun, he ordered the teller to hand him all the money. However, the man's nose, which was particularly large, made the teller laugh. A little embarrassed, the man was determined to keep his authority, so in his most assertive voice demanded that she hand him the money, but this just made her laugh all the harder. Pretty soon, the whole bank was in hysterics, and as a result the poor man fled in tears.

Hot Pink

In Phoenix, Arizona, About 2,200 inmates living in a barbed-wire-surrounded tent encampment at the Maricopa County Jail have been given permission to strip down to their government-issued pink boxer shorts.

These men wearing pink boxers were either curled up on their bunk beds or chatted in the tents, which reached 138 degrees inside the week before. Many were also swathed in wet, pink towels as sweat collected on their chests and dripped down to their pink socks.

"It feels like you are in a furnace," said one inmate who has lived in the tents for two years. "It's inhumane."

Sheriff Bill Chrome who created the tent city and long ago started making his prisoners wear pink undies, was not sympathetic.

He informed the inmates, "It's 120 degrees in Iraq and the soldiers are living in tents and they didn't commit any crimes, so shut your mouths."

Did You Know? *Ray Kimpton, a resident of Dayton, Ohio was known for his habit of flashing women in cars at red lights, but had somehow evaded arrest. However, one day he opened his overcoat on an innocent woman driver who instantly reacted by closing her electric window on the old man's member. To the delight of passers-by, the woman slowly drove the offensive man to the nearest police station and had him arrested.*

Insured For Smoking

A Charlotte, North Carolina man, having purchased a case of rare, very expensive cigars, insured them against fire.

Within a month, having smoked his entire stockpile of fabulous cigars, and having yet to make a single premium payment on the policy, the man filed a claim against the insurance company.

In his claim, the man stated that he had lost the cigars "in a series of small fires." The insurance company refused to pay, citing the obvious reason that the man had consumed the cigars in a normal fashion. However, the man sued -- and won.

In delivering.his ruling, the judge stated that since the man held a policy from the company in which it had warranted that the cigars were insurable and also guaranteed that the cigars would be insured against fire, without defining what it considered to be unacceptable fire, it was obligated to compensate the insured for his loss.

Rather than endure a lengthy and costly appeal process, the insurance company grudgingly accepted the judge's ruling and paid the man $25,000 for the rare cigars he lost in the fires. But, after the man cashed his check, the insurance company had him arrested on 24 counts of arson. With his own insurance claim and testimony from the previous case being used as evidence against him, the man was convicted of intentionally burning the rare cigars and sentenced to 24 consecutive one-year terms.

Remember kids; don't piss off your insurance company!

I've Been Robbed!

In Chicago, Illinois, a man went to drown his sorrows in a local bar after a disastrous day. He lost his job, his wife left him, and his gambling debts were being called in by the local Mafia. The man got so drunk that on the way home, he broke into a house, via the back garden, and filled a suitcase full of valuables. To cover any trace of the crime, the inebriated man set fire to the curtains and left the same way he had come in. However, on turning the corner to his road, dragging the heavily-laden suitcase behind, he was shocked to see fire engines arriving outside his house. In his drunken state, the man had burglarized and burnt down his own house.

No Sex For The Wicked

This story demonstrates that crime really doesn't pay.

A young man desperate to impress his girlfriend in the belief that impressing her would improve his chances of getting her into bed, came across a magazine article on aphrodisiac foods and decided that an elaborate meal might be the answer. He worked out a menu and went out to do some shoplifting. The oysters, asparagus and strawberries proved easy enough to steal, but lobster was going to be a problem, until the young man passed by a fish restaurant. Seeing a tank full of live lobsters, he entered the restaurant, and when no one was looking, he reached into the tank, pulled out a wriggling lobster, and dropped it down his pants. As he walked out of the restaurant, a sudden thought surfaced in the mind of the not-too-clever thief, but before he could act on it, he was doubled up on the floor in agony. The lobster, in its panic, seized the nearest "appendage" with its large claws, and as a result the thief was in no fit state to make his date that night. He remained incapable of having sex for five years and the wound never fully healed.

Did You Know? *Iraqi terrorist, Ahmed Rahnajet, didn't pay enough postage on a letter bomb, so it came back with "return to sender" stamped on it. Forgetting it was the bomb, he opened it and was blown to bits.*

Pound for Pound

This story might shine some light on why most truck drivers are so big.

A 250 pound truck driver from Detroit was delivering a load to Flint, Michigan when he spotted a man on the side of the road waving frantically. Obviously thinking the man's car had broken down, the truck driver pulled up. However, as the truck driver went to get out, the man ran up to him, pointing a gun, and demanded that the truck driver get out. When the truck driver took his time, the impatient man pulled on his arm, only to pull too hard. The 250 pound truck driver fell right on top of the man, breaking both his arms and causing several other unpleasant injuries. Since the event the driver has gained another twenty pounds just in case he comes across a more resilient road bandit in the future.

Quake Getaway

In San Francisco, a father and son had gone to a baseball game at Candlestick Park. The father had driven there in his new BMW, but on leaving the game, they were unable to find the car where they'd parked it, and after searching everywhere, they concluded that it had been stolen. The father reported the theft to the police and caught a taxi home with his son. Just as they arrived home, there was a huge earthquake, that affected the entire Bay Area. The next day, the father received a phone call from the police. His car had been found flattened by a landslide caused by the earthquake. The car thief was also found in the car, crushed to death.

The Trio Of Streakers

Just before daybreak on January 14, 2004, three men in only shoes and hats entered a Denny's restaurant in Spokane, Washington. The trio of streakers had left their 1988 Mazda running in the frigid parking lot for a quick escape, but after sprinting nude through the 24-hour eatery, one of the restaurant's patrons left the group he was dining with and made off with the waiting car.

The streakers looked out during their high-spirited dash to see their Mazda, which contained their clothes, driving away. They gave pursuit, charging into the chill of the 20°F weather in their birthday suits.

They were unsuccessful in gaining back their car. The naked young men huddled behind vehicles in an adjacent parking lot until police arrived to claim them.

I Want To Donate My Eyes To Blind Justice.

The love-hate relationship we have with the law is a complex one. Although we expect it to protect our interests, we don't want to see ourselves held accountable to it. So we cheer for the wrongdoers who put one over on the law, while we "boo" the real crooks who slip away.

"Beam Me Up Scotty!"

An amateur pilot was arressted after flying a small aircraft under the Golden Gate Bridge. When contacted by the Air Traffic Controllers he identified himself as Captain James T. Kirk of the Starship Enterprise.

When he was asked if he wanted to say anything on his own behalf before the judge passed sentence, he stood up, flipped open his wallet as if it were a Star Trek communicator, whistled, and said "Beam me up, Scotty. There's no intelligent life here."

The judge found him in contempt of court and increased the fine.

Beyond Reasonable Doubt

The Defense counsel was giving his summation in a case involving a client who had been charged with murdering his wife, even though her body had never been found. He tried to the best of his ability to sow the minds of the jurors with the seeds of reasonable doubt, dramatically proclaiming that nobody could demonstrate that the alleged victim was even dead.

The defense thundered, "Why, she might walk through those doors any second now!"

Every eye in the courtroom gazed in the direction indicated by his outstretched arm as he pointed to the doors at the back of the courtroom. It was a masterful technique. When the jurors realized that they themselves had been expecting the supposedly dead woman to burst through the courtroom doors just then, how could they possibly maintain they were sure beyond a reasonable doubt that the defendant had killed her?

The prosecutor was undaunted. Slowly rising from his seat behind the table, he too gestured towards the courtroom doors.

But his voice was calm as he looked the jurors in the eye and began to speak, "Every head in this courtroom turned toward that door just now -- every head except one, that of the defendant. He didn't bother to look because he knows she's not going to walk through that door, because he killed her."

I Want To Donate My Eyes To Blind Justice

Six real lawsuits that showcase the need for tort reform.

On June 1997, 20-year old Kelvin Thomas of Pasadena, California won $75,000.00 and medical expenses when his neighbor ran his hand over with a Honda Accord. Mr. Thomas apparently didn't notice someone was at the wheel of the car whose hubcap he was trying to steal.

On December 1997, Penny Dalton of Morris, Minnesota successfully sued the owner of a night club in Minneapolis when she fell from the bathroom window to the floor and knocked out her two front teeth. This occurred while Ms. Dalton was trying to sneak through the window in the ladies room to avoid paying the $3.50 cover charge. She was awarded $15,000.00 and dental expenses.

On October 1998, Dick Ferr of Pittsburgh Pennsylvania was exiting a house he finished robbing by way of the garage. He was unable to get the garage door open, because the automatic door opener was malfunctioning. He couldn't re-enter the house because the door connecting the house and garage locked when he pulled it shut. The family was on vacation, so Mr. Ferr found himself locked in the garage for eight days. He survived on a case of Pepsi and a large bag of dry dog food. This upset robber sued the homeowner's insurance claiming the situation caused him undue mental anguish. The jury agreed to the tune of half a million dollars and change.

On November 1999, Maury Florence of Little Rock Arkansas was awarded $15,000.00 and medical expenses after being bitten on the buttocks by his next door neighbor's beagle. The beagle was on a chain in its owner's fenced-in yard, as was Mr. Florence. The award was less than sought after because the jury felt the dog may have been provoked by Mr. Florence who, at the time, was shooting it repeatedly with a pellet gun.

On January 2000, in Austin, Texas, Roberta Baker was awarded $780,000.00 by a jury of her peers after breaking her ankle tripping over a toddler who was running amuck inside a furniture store. The owners of the store were understandably surprised at the verdict, considering the misbehaving tyke was Mrs. Baker's son.

On May 2000, a restaurant in Philadelphia was ordered to pay Carla Dell of Allentown, Pennsylvania $114,000.00 after she slipped on a spilled soft drink and broke her pelvis. The beverage was on the floor because Ms. Dell threw it at her boyfriend 30 seconds earlier during an argument.

Did You Know? *The defence in an Italian murder trial hung on whether the accused, Anthony Bravo, could draw a gun from his pocket without shooting himself. Demonstrating in court, his lawyer shot his own foot, and died 12 hours later. Bravo, however, was acquitted.*

Lack of Evidence

A judge in New Mexico was forced to dismiss a case against a man accused of murdering and robbing a market trader. The man had been caught red-handed with a bag of wheat he had snatched from the trader after allegedly hitting him over the head with a rock. The man was arrested and the bag of wheat was taken into evidence. However, when the case came to court, rats had completely consumed the bag of wheat, and with no witnesses of the event, the judge dismissed the case due to lack of evidence.

Passing Notes

A victim of a rape was testifying in court against her attacker. The prosecutor asked the woman to describe what the attacker had done to her, but she became quite upset, so the judge suggested that she write her answer down for the jury to read, rather than say it out loud in open court. The written statement was handed to the jury and each member read it in turn. When one of the jurors, a pretty young woman, finished reading it she nudged the male juror next to her, who had fallen asleep, and passed him the statement. The puzzled juror read it, looked at the woman who passed it to him, turned a bright shade of red, and hastily put the note in his shirt pocket. The man looked around and suddenly realised that everybody in the courtroom was staring at him. After a few moments of embarrassed silence, the judge told the man to pass the note to the next juror.

The startled juror responded, "Please your honor, this is private. You really wouldn't be interested."

Peanut Butter and Contraceptive Jelly

A Los Angeles woman is suing the pharmacy that sold her a popular contraceptive jelly, because she ate the stuff on toast and got pregnant anyway. Incredibly, many legal experts are saying she's got an excellent chance of collecting.

"The woman is a complete idiot," said one attorney who asked that we not use his name. "How bright can you be if you think eating a vaginal gel will prevent conception? But certain aspects of the case involve truth in labeling and false advertising issues. She may not collect, but she'll make a lot of noise and trouble. People are down on lawyers anyway. They think we waste time and money on frivolous lawsuits. This isn't going to help our public relations any."

A spokesman for the unnamed family owned drugstore says he's shocked and angry that such a case could ever be taken seriously.

"All she has to do is open the box and read the directions," says the spokesman. "Next thing you know someone will come after us because they couldn't stick things together with their toothpaste. I can just imagine some moron saying, It's paste, isn't it? Why can't I glue these papers onto my bulletin board?"

But attorneys for the lady say she was swindled and lied to by implication and they intend to make the pharmacy pay $500,000 for the hardship the woman will have to endure.

"It says 'jelly' right on the box," said the so-called victim, a former model who was once a cheerleader for a popular professional basketball team.

"And they kept it on the shelf just two aisles from the food section. I know now, that the directions say it should be used vaginally with a condom. But who has time to sit around reading directions these days, especially when you're sexually aroused. The company should call it something else and the pharmacy shouldn't sell it without telling each and every customer who buys it that eating it won't prevent you from getting pregnant."

As bizarre as it sounds, the pharmacy could wind up losing the lawsuit. "It's hard for businesses to avoid troublesome lawsuits," said the attorney representing the mom and pop drugstore. "With the courts bending over backwards to please consumer groups, the temper of the times is perfect for these crackpots to bring legal action against businesses - even a moronic legal action like this."

Prized Collection

After finishing high school, Travis Bateman of Chicago, Illinois, went back-packing through Europe for a year. After many exciting adventures, he was ready to return home. He was disconcerted to find that his room had been rented out to a university student, and that all his belongings had been stored in the attic.

When he asked his mother about his pride and joy- a collection of comics that resulted from countless years of time-consuming research, his mother turned to him and remarked casually, "Oh, those childish things, I threw them out with all those old stamps and records."

When sentencing Mr. Bateman, the judge stated that although he could understand the boy's anger at his mother's disregard for his possessions, and even if they were valued at over $100,000 dollars, he could not condone killing her by forcing her to eat her recipe collection.

Sleepmurdering

The courts can expect a surge in cases of crimes committed while sleepwalking after this story.

An American man on trial for the murder of his wife, had the most unusual defence. He claimed he was sleepwalking, and had no knowledge of his actions. However, when the jury heard the case against him, they thought his game was up. His wife had been stabbed 40 times, and when he was found he had even managed to bandage several cuts on his hands and dispose of his clothes. He had also been seen by several witnesses attempting to drown his wife in the swimming pool in the back garden. The man's lawyer calmly called to the stand an expert on sleepwalking. On hearing the evidence, the expert stated simply that this was all possible while sleepwalking.

Sleepstreaking

Sleepwalking can be an embarrassing experience for anyone, especially for Rod Bartel, a middle-aged man from Los Angeles. On several occasions, Mr. Bartel had woken up to find himself walking down the street or climbing up a tree in his garden. In an effort to put a stop to these nightly jaunts he tried tying himself to his bedpost, but discovered he was quite an expert at untying knots while asleep. Events came to a head, when the man awoke to find himself strolling down Sunset Boulevard totally naked with hundreds of tourists gawking at him. Red-faced, the man grabbed a newspaper off a passer-by and ran into some public toilets where he hid for a few hours, only to be arrested for soliciting by the insensitive LAPD. He finally conquered his sleepwalking by handcuffing himself to his bedpost and giving his neighbour the key.

The Shit Literally Hit The Fan

When someone says "the shit hit the fan", they are not usually talking about a rapid interaction between shit and a twirly cooling system. However, for the occupants of a court in New Mexico, the term for once was very close to the truth.

During the trial of a man accused of the disappointingly mundane crime of stealing boxes from his employer, the accused kept trying to draw the judge's attention to the brutal treatment he had received at the hands of the police. As is usually the case in these situations, the judge refused to believe that police were capable of such acts. Having failed to get the judge to take him seriously, the defendant pulled out a shit-filled plastic bag and attempted to throw it at a group of police officers who were sitting in the court. Unfortunately, he missed, and the resulting shit hit the fan showering the entire courtroom in inadmissible evidence, and the case had to be delayed. The defendant was later charged with insulting the dignity of the court.

"The Twinkie Defense"

In November of 1978, Former San Francisco city supervisor, Dan White who resigned his position, entered San Francisco's city hall by climbing through a basement window and then shot and killed both mayor George Moscone and supervisor Harvey Milk. During White's trial for the murders, Defense council represented White saying he was not responsibile for his murderous actions, claiming that some external force beyond his control had caused him to act the way he did, and it arose from the successful defense mounted by White's legal team that White's eating of Twinkies had diminished his mental capacity.

The Defense even had swarn testimony from doctors who suggested excessive sugar could have aggravated a chemical imbalance in White's brain, but that comment was offered only as a parenthetical remark during testimony about White's depression. That strategy was dubbed by the media "the Twinkie defense."

The Twinkie defense was successful and White was convicted of the lesser charge of voluntary manslaughter claiming that, "Twinkies made him do it."

You've Been Served

An interesting lawsuit was brought against a Canadian tourist by a hotel owner in Kansas City. The hotel owner sued for damages, alleging that the man's actions had caused several other hotel guests to leave.

In his defence, the Canadian stated that his actions were a direct result of eating the food served in the hotel.

As it came out in court, the tourist had been lounging in the hotel swimming pool when he suffered a bout of stomach cramps. Unable to get out of the pool in time, he lost control of his bodily functions while he was still in the water. Before he knew it, a young girl spotted the brown slick circling him, and alerted the other guests. It didn't take long for the pool to empty. Eventually, the red-faced Canadian escaped into the toilets and cleaned himself up. He emerged only to face the wrath of the hotel owner. The incident had caused several guests to check out. The man blamed the sudden bowel movement on the mussels he'd had for lunch in the hotel restaurant.

Pimpin' Ain't Easy

A humorous look at the means employed by crooks to perpetrate their crimes.

Feng Shui Burglars

A recent series of burglaries in Portland, Oregon, had police puzzled because these break-ins showed a more altruistic approach to the crime. A man came back from a weekend break to find that his house had been broken into, and his TV and DVD player stolen, but the burglars had completely redecorated the house. The man told police he was delighted with their choice of colour scheme and their work was worth his TV and DVD player. Another woman came back from a two-week holiday to find burglars had renovated her garden and added a pond in return for a set of silver candlesticks.

"Better than any landscape gardening I've seen," quipped the woman.

Detectives are offering up their houses to catch the burglars after finding out that some burglaries have involved improving the feng shui of residences.

Ice Money

A couple living in Manchester, England consistently missed paying their electricity bill on time, and as a result were eventually forced by the power company to install a slot meter in their flat. The woman was a specialist at making moulds, so she made a set of moulds from a fifty cent piece, the coin used in the meter. By filling the moulds with water and placing them in the freezer, the couple found that within a few hours, they could make pieces of ice that would be accepted as valid coins by the meter. The plan worked successfully for a couple of months, but came to an end when a representative from the electricity company arrived to empty the meter only to find that it was full of water.

It's The Swedish Way

The Swedes are a curious people. They seem to combine a talent for beauty and a love of peace with a morbid fascination with death. One could be forgiven for believing that suicide is almost a way of life in Sweden.

A classic example of a Swedish-style suicide concerns the sad case of a man and his girlfriend who made a pact to die together after they discovered that ABBA were not planning to re-form in the near future. Having found a pleasant location in which to die, near a popular tourist spot, the man, by agreement, strangled his girlfriend and then set about strangling himself. He discovered to his horror that this was not going to kill him, and so he went looking for other means to end it all. Unfortunately, he soon lost the courage to take his own life, and instead, handed himself over to the police. They had little choice but to charge him with murder, for which he eventually received an eight-year prison sentence. He appealed against it on the grounds that it was too lenient.

Minor Robbery

In Chicago, an eight-year-old boy was convicted of armed bank robbery. The boy took to crime after his mother refused to buy him Masters of the Universe action figures. Bitter and twisted, the boy took his fathers shotgun and went straight to the city bank and ordered the teller to give him the equivalent of $100, so that he could buy the whole collection of Action heroes. Thinking it was a joke, the teller laughed and told him not to be silly and to go home before his mother began to worry. However, after the boy fired the gun into the ceiling, the teller took him seriously and quickly handed him the money. Soon after, the police caught the boy at Toys R' Us, trying to decide which Masters of the Universe action figure he wanted, because he had underestimated the cost of the whole collection.

Pimpin' Ain't Easy

A 13-year-old boy was convicted of attempting to organise a prostitution ring in a small town in Ohio. The boy, far from defending himself, bragged about how he had convinced girls in his class to work for him. Several boys in his school had each paid between $5 to $15 for intimate encounters with his "employees", although there was no evidence of sexual relations. The 13-year-old pimp told the court that so far he made over a $100 out of the "business", which he had already spent on a trendy pair of Nike shoes.

Religious Freak

A woman had lived in a rent control apartment building in Burbank, California most of her adult life, but her landlord was determined to get rid of her in order to increase the rent. One day, the woman noticed a new tenant moving in next door to her and she invited him over for a drink. However, the man told her he belonged to a religious sect which forbid him to be alone with a woman, and closed the door on her. The woman gave the matter no more thought, until strange things began to happen.

Every night at around 2:30am, she heard what sounded like someone being tortured and the sound of a man chanting. Occasionally she would spot the man carrying a heavy, black bag upstairs.

One morning, she noticed that the bag was leaking what looked like blood, and somewhat scared, she called the police. The police told her there was nothing they could do, at which point the woman began thinking about moving out. However, one day a letter to her neighbour was delivered to her by mistake. Hoping for evidence, the woman steamed open the envelope. She was shocked to find a cheque for $500 for the man's "portrayal of a religious freak" and immediately realised that the landlord had hired an actor in an attempt to drive her out of her apartment. The woman confronted her landlord and threatened to report him if he didn't reduce her rent, which he duly did.

Silver Dollar Cowboy Boots

A blackjack dealer in a casino in Atlantic City, New Jersey, had the habit of wearing cowboy boots to work. One evening while he was raking in the gamblers' chips, one of the silver dollars accidentally slipped off the table and down into his boot without anyone seeming to notice. The dealer decided that this was a good way to make some extra money, and he began to collect at least $20 a night using this method, until, stupidly, he got greedy and began shoving more and more dollars down his boots. One night he got so carried away that, when it came to the end of his shift and he tried to take a step, he couldn't move because of the weight of all the silver dollars in his boot. With everyone around watching, the dealer heaved as hard as he could, but eventually fell over. Dollars spilled out all over the place and the dealer was fired.

The Profanity Cycle

A rich old lady purchased a new washing machine and had it delivered to her house after her old one broke down. Over the next few hours, she kept hearing the sound of someone sneezing and muttering, but when she turned around there was no-one there. She began to think she was going mad when she used her washing machine for the first time, because during the spin cycle the washing machine uttered very abusive profanities. A superstitious person, the old lady asked her local priest to exorcise the machine, but to no avail. Finally, she called an engineer, who took the washing machine apart to find a midget trapped beneath the drum. Apparently, the midget planned to emerge from the washing machine and rob the old lady's house, but he had got wedged inside.

"Sorry we snorted your sister. No hard feelings. Have a nice day."

Here is a collection of tales regarding thieves who found their stolen loot wasn't quite what they bargained for.

Bogus Blow

When David Morin's house was burglarized, the thieves left his TV, his VCR, and even his rolex watch. What they did take was "a generic white cardboard box filled with greyish-white powder."

A spokesman for the LAPD said, "The powder looks similar to cocaine and the burglars probably thought they'd hit the big time."

Then David stood in front of the TV cameras and pleaded with the burglars, "Please return the cremated remains of my sister, Lisa. She died three years ago."

The next morning, the cardborad box was found on David's doorstep, accompanied by the bullet-riddled corpse of a drug dealer known as Tony Two Tone. But only about half of Lisa's ashes remained, with a note that said, "Two Tone sold us the bogus blow, so we wasted him. Sorry we snorted your sister. No hard feelings. Have a nice day."

Crime Doesn't Pay...Well!

A boy from San Diego, fresh out of High School, landed a job as a department store security guard. Full of enthusiasm, he was eager to catch as many shoplifters as he could. One afternoon, he noticed a suspicious-looking man wandering around. The man had been in the store for over an hour, picking up items, looking around and putting them back again. The young security guard watched as the man eventually approached the cash register with a children's colouring book. As the man handed a $10 dollar bill to the cashier, he leaned over, grabbed the register tray and ran out of the store. The detective was about to give chase when the cashier shouted to him not to bother.

Waving the $10 dollars at the young guard, the cashier smiled and said, "There was only $2.25 in the till. We made a profit!"

Dead Loot

An elderly woman was heartbroken when her cat developed cancer and had to be put down. The woman told the nurse at the veterinary hospital that she would like to bury the cat in her garden, so the nurse wrapped it in a box for the woman to carry home. On the way home, she passed a department store and decided to buy some flowers and a plaque to put on the cat's grave. She put the box down beside her and was telling the sales assistant what she wanted, when she noticed that the box had disappeared. The sales assistant told security staff, and they started to search the store for the box. It wasn't long before a security guard spotted the box in a telephone booth. The box had been opened and the dead cat was poking out of it. On the floor of the booth, a young boy was lying unconscious. It turned out that the boy was a shoplifter who took the well-wrapped box, thinking it contained something valuable, and fainted when he glimpsed the dead cat.

Did You Know? *If the garbage workers in your community ever go on strike, do what the wise New Yorkers do to dispose of their refuse for the days the sanitation workers are off the job. Each day they wrap their garbage in gift paper. Then put it in a shopping bag. When you park your car, leave the bag on the front seat with the window open. When you get back to the car the garbage always gets "collected".*

Full Tank

A man travelling through British Columbia, Canada ran out of gas in the middle of nowhere. It was late at night and there were no gas stations marked on his map for miles. However, he noticed on his map that a few miles down the road was a campsite. Hoping to find gas there, he took a gas can and walked to the campsite. When he got there, he was delighted to see that there were a few motorhome's parked. However, there were no signs of life, and the man not wanting to wake anybody up at this late hour, decided his only option was to try to siphon out gas from one of the motorhome's. He got a tube, opened the tank, and as quietly as possible, he began sucking out the contents. He expected the gas would taste nasty, but the stuff he was siphoning out was extremely foul. It was only when he spit it out that he realised he had opened the motorhome's septic tank by mistake. After vomiting up the entire contents of his stomach, the man decided to leave it until the morning, and returned to his car to try and get some sleep.

Good Exchange

A New York woman, in a hurry to get to her dentist appointment, decided to risk a shortcut through Central Park, which was known for its criminal element. Suddenly, the woman felt her necklace being snapped off, and before the attacker could run off, she turned around sharply, grabbed his neck chain and snapped that off. Both ran away in opposite directions. When safely out of the park the woman examined the neck chain, and impressed by the look of it, took it to a jeweller for appraisal. The woman was delighted by the exchange when she found out the attackers neck chain was 22-carat gold. Whereas, her necklace had just been a gold-plated fake.

Has Anyone Seen My Radioactive Material?

Police in Washinton D.C. were deeply alarmed to discover that someone had broken into the National Radiation Laboratory and stole a container of radioactive material. The radioactive material was lethal, and at first, police were concerned that the break-in might have been the work of terrorists. However, they took a different view when they were informed that the radioactive material was being stored in a lead container weighing over 500 pounds. From that moment on, they went searching the local scrap yards trying to find someone who had brought in a large quantity of dodgy lead, but to no avail. Eventually, they received a phone call from the mother of a couple small boys who said that she had found her sons trying to make lead weights for fishing from a large block that had been dumped in her garden some time in the night.

Urine For A Surprise

A man from Columbus, Georgia, was shocked to find that his car had been broken into while he popped into the off licence to grab a bottle of wine. However, he was slightly amused to find that his car stereo was untouched, and the only thing missing was a used wine bottle that contained a urine sample, which he was intending to drop off at his doctor's office.

Vanilla Loot

Inside the bank shortly after midnight, three bank robbers efforts at disabling the internal security system got underway immediately.

The robbers, expected to find one or two large safes filled with cash and valuables, but were surprised to see hundreds of smaller safes scattered throughout the bank. The robbers cracked the first safe's combination, and inside all they found was a bowl of vanilla pudding.

As recorded on the bank's audio tape system, one robber was heard saying, "At least we'll have something to eat."

The robbers opened up a second safe, and it also contained nothing but vanilla pudding. The process continued until all the safes were opened.

They found not one dollar, a diamond, or an ounce of gold. Instead, all the safes contained covered bowls of pudding.

Disappointed, the robbers made a quiet exit, each leaving with nothing more than a queasy, uncomfortably full stomach.

The next day the newspaper headline read: "Ireland's Largest Sperm Bank Robbed Early This Morning."

"Thank God, you showed up. There's no telling what those 'preppies' would've done."

In crime-related legends gangs have become a prominent feature.

Mafia Ties

A married couple moved into a wealthy neighborhood in the suburb of Chicago, right next door to a very nice, quiet Italian family, who were rumored to have ties to the Mafia. One weekend, the couple went away on a short trip, and on their return, found that they had been robbed. Shocked and upset, they went through everything and assessed the damage. Immediately after doing so, they went to their neighbors to ask if they had seen anything suspicious during the weekend. The neighbors replied that they hadn't, but also asked about the stolen property. Strangely, after telling their neighbors everything, they were told to just go to bed and not to call the police that night. The neighbors would make a few calls to see if they could find out more. The next morning, the couple woke up and found all their missing property placed neatly on their front porch.

Unsuspecting Criminals

In Arizona, a group of leather-clad, rough-looking bikers pulled into a gas station and entered the confectionary. The clerk was worried that the bikers would cause trouble, so when a group of smartly-dressed kids showed up, he was noticeably relieved. The bikers grabbed what they wanted, paid for it, and left without a word.

The shop assistant turned to the group of kids and said, "Thank God, you showed up. There's no telling what those bikers would've done!"

80

At which point, one of the kids pulled out a shotgun and ordered the clerk to hand over all the money in the till. The shop assistant vowed never to give into stereotyping again.

The Wrinkled Avenger

Sometimes we can't depend upon the law to enforce justice, so we take it into our own hands.

Assault With A Deadly Granny

Charges were dropped against Dorothy "Grambo" Ruth, an 89-year-old wheelchair-bound grandmother, who was originally charged with assault and battery, and assault with a deadly weapon, because an altercation she had with six airport security guards, that left all six hospitalized.

"Justice has been served," said the 95-pound (when wet) mother of six and grandmother of eight, as she sat in her wheelchair, aided in her breathing by an oxygen bottle. "Now I'm going to sue every fool in the federal government for ignorance, stupidity, and just plain general incompetence. I'm an American, and I won't be treated like this."

The Wrinkled Avenger

Gun-toting granny Estelle Tracy, 86, was so ticked-off when her 18-year old granddaughter was carjacked and raped by two knife-wielding creeps in a section of town bordering on skid row that the vigilante granny tracked the unsuspecting ex-cons down and shot off their testicles.

"When I saw the look on my granddaughters face that night in the hospital, I decided I was going to go out and get those bastards myself 'cause I figured the police would go easy on them," recalled the retired librarian."And I wasn't scared of them, neither -- because I've got me a gun and I've been shootin' it all my life."

Using a police artist's sketch of the suspects and her granddaughter's description of the rapists car, tough-as-nails Estelle spent days prowling the wino-infested neighborhood where the crime took place until she spotted the suspects entering their flophouse hotel, and that's were she took revenge on them in her own special way," said admiring Mississippi police investigator Dean Humer.

"So I went to their hotel, found their room and knocked on the door -- and the minute the big one, Raymond, opened the door, I shot 'em! I got 'em right square between the legs, right where it would really hurt 'em most, you know. Then I went down to the police station and turned myself in," recalled the ornery oldster.

Cops say convicted rapist and robber Huey Raymond, 34, lost both his penis and his testicles when outraged Estelle opened fire with a 9-mm pistol in the seedy hotel room where he and former prison cellmate Larry Russ, 30, were holed up.

"Grambo" also blew Russ' testicles to kingdom come, but doctors managed to save his mangled penis, police said.

"The one guy, Russ, didn't lose his manhood, but the doctor said he won't be using it the way he used to," Detective Humer told reporters. "Both men are still in pretty bad shape, but I think they're just happy to be alive after what they've been through."

Now, baffled lawmen are tying to figure out how to deal with the vigilante granny.

"What she did was wrong, but you can't really throw an 86-year-old woman in prison." said Detective Humer, "Especially when all 3 million people in the city want to nominate her for sainthood."

chapterfive

"I had no idea cows were mean drunks.
I will have to teach them to hold their alcohol better."

-- a stupid farmer

crittercountry

There is a fair share of rumors that highlight the lighter side of the animal kingdom. However, rarely does anything good happen to them in this realm.

If these creatures aren't the object of some unfortunate mishap, they are being treated cruely, causing a calamity, or being unceremoniously disposed of. And when the animal becomes the star of the story, it's usually because he's attacked some unsuspecting human being.

The following tales will provide the reader with all the "creature comforts" of home, and give our friendly critters their due.

. . . .

"...and you wonder why the ocean is so salty.

Critters are mysterious to us, and because they are so different, we tend to believe the wild tales that depend for their plausibility upon some misunderstanding of what a particular animal will or will not due. The wild inaccuracies we exchange about them reflects our sense of wonder and puzzlement for the animal kingdom.

Bonsai Kittens

In New York there is a Japanese Pet store that breeds and sells bonsai-kittens. They are used as original and exclusive souvenirs. These are the latest trends in New York, China, Indonesia and New Zealand .

Sound cute? Not really! If you are not familiar with the Bonsai Cat, let me expalin; these kittens are fed muscle relaxant, and then squeezed into bottles where their urine and feces are removed through probes. They are fed only chemicals through a tube to keep their bones soft and flexible so the kittens grow and form into the shape of the bottle. The animals will stay their for all nine of their lives. They can't walk or move or wash themselves.

It's illegal to hunt camels in the state of Arizona

This sounds like the looniest of them all. Why would Arizona ban the hunting of an animal not native to the area in the first place. And privately-owned camels, such as those held by zoos or circuses or other tourist attractions would already be protected under property laws. So what could lawmakers have been trying to prevent by banning camel hunting?

Actually, Arizona, along with Texas and Nevada were once home to some small herds of these creatures. In 1856 and 1857, the U.S. Army imported camels with the intent of forming a Camel Corps to move freight and men across the desert. Early forays were a success, but the Civil War put the Corps out of business.

Western entrepreneurs took up the cause and used the beasts to supply remote mining camps. The California and Utah Camel Association bought army surplus camels and sold them in Nevada.

A San Francisco merchant imported camels from China to establish an express to Great Salt Lake City, but gave up in 1862, and the camels he left in Nevada created such a stir that the state legislature banned them from public roads in 1875. One private herd was turned loose near Indianola, Texas.

In other areas, some of the camels managed to get loose on their own.

Arizona declared camels extinct in 1913, but hunters reported seeing them in the desert around Yuma in the 1950s.

Penguin Dominos

A Mexican newspaper reported that bored Royal Air Force pilots stationed on the Falkland Islands have devised what they consider a marvelous new game. Noting that the local penguins are fascinated by airplanes, the pilots search out a beach where the birds gather and fly slowly along the water's edge. The tens of thousands of penguins turn their heads in unison watching the planes go by, and when the pilots turn around and fly back, the birds turn their heads in the opposite direction, like spectators at a slow-motion tennis match.

The paper reported, "The pilots fly out to sea and directly to the penguin colony and overfly it. Heads go up, up, up, and ten thousand penguins fall over gently onto their backs."

Did You Know? *The average blue whale produces over 400 gallons of sperm when it ejaculates, but only 10% of that actually makes it into his mate. So 360 gallons are spilled into the ocean every time one unloads, and you wonder why the ocean is so salty.*

The Anaconda Survival Tip

If you are ever attacked by an anaconda, do not run. The snake is faster than you are. Just lie flat on the ground, put your arms tight against your sides, your legs tight against one another, and tuck your chin in. The snake will come and begin to nudge and climb over your body. But do not panic. After the snake has examined you, it will begin to swallow you from the feet and, always from that end. Permit the snake to swallow your feet and ankles. But do not panic. The snake will begin to suck your legs into its body. You must lie perfectly still. This will take a while. When the snake has reached your kneck slowly and with as little movement as possible, reach down, take your knife and very gently slide it into the side of the snake's mouth between the edge of its mouth and your leg. then suddenly rip upwards, severing the snake's head. Be sure you have your knife, and be sure your knife is sharp.

The Endangered Naugas

A friend of a friend was on a telephone reference shift when a woman, sounding a bit agitated, called to ask if he could give her specific information about Naugas, their gestation period, and their status on the endangered species list. After a bit of cursory searching, he enlisted a few colleagues, who also had not heard of such an animal. Fifteen minutes later, they still had no answers, so he got back on the phone and told the patron she could help narrow their search if she could at least tell them in which phylum or class naugas resided.

She replied with a heavy sigh, "Oh, you know. They're the animals they use to make naugahyde couches."

Don't Step In The Poodle!

As humans we all deal with the potential for things to go wrong, and when you factor an animal into the equation, that potential grows. If you fail to properly assess the situation, understand how things work, or plan for the eventualities, it could result in a series of hilarious beastly mishaps that victimize the hapless critters roped into the fray.

Air Kitty

A woman who just moved to Fresno, California decided to get a pet kitten. Some weeks later, the woman was doing some gardening, when she heard the kitten meowing. She saw that it had climbed into the highest branch of a tree and no manner of coaxing could persuade it to climb down. The woman tried looping a rope around the end of the branch, hoping to pull it down so that she could reach the kitten.

Unfortunately, as she pulled on the rope, it snapped, and the branch sprang back, launching the meowing kitten into the air. The distraught woman spent days searching all over the place and knocking on peoples' doors in the area, until one morning, an old man answered her knock. The woman explained what had happened to her kitten and asked if the man had seen it.

The man snickered and said, "So that's where the little bugger came from. I was minding my own business, sitting in the back garden, when this kitten dropped out of the sky and into my lap. Gave me the fright of my life!"

The man went back into his house and returned with the meowing kitten.

Choke'n Curry

Donna Gibson of St. Louis, Missouri invited some friends around for dinner one night. She had intended to cook chicken curry, but was worried that the chicken breast might have gone bad. As a test, she gave a little piece to her cat to see if he would touch it. She was relieved to see him gobble it down without hesitation, so she went on to make the curry. Later on, her friends were complimenting her on how good her chicken curry was. Pleased, the woman went into the kitchen to prepare the dessert, only to find her cat choking in the corner. The woman hurried back to tell her friends what happened and advised them to go to the hospital to have their stomachs pumped.

She took her cat to the vet for emergency treatment, and upon examining the cat, the vet said, "Your cat is perfectly fine. He just had a hairball in his throat."

Does My Insurance Cover Doggy Damage?

A man bought a brand new Jeep Grand Cherokee for $30,000, with $400.00 monthly payments. He decided to christen his new car with a duck-hunting trip. So with a friend, he took his dog to the lake. But the guys needed a natural landing area for the ducks and the decoys to float on, and the lakes were completely frozen. In order to make a hole large enough to look "casual" enough for a wandering duck to just land on, they decided an ice-hole drill won't be good enough. So out came a stick of dynamite with a short, 40-second fuse.

The guys realised the risk of slipping while running away from the lit dynamite, so instead, they decided to throw it as far as they could, but the dog was an exceptionally trained lab, and when they threw the lit dynamite, he ran to retrieve it. As he ran back, the two men shouted and yelled, waving their arms, but the dog, cheered on, and kept running. One of the guys decided that a dead dog was better than their own deaths, so he grabbed a gun and shot the dog. But the bullets meant for duck hunting weren't enough to take down a lab, it only slowed him down. Confused, the dog kept running, so the man took another shot at the dog. Now, the dog was even more confused, and getting scared, so instead of coming toward his owner, he decided to find cover, and did so under the Jeep. "Boom!" went the dog and the brand new car into the bottom of the lake.

The insurance company didn't cover a sunken vehicle in a lake by illegal use of explosives, and the man had to pay for the first of his $400.00 monthly payments.

Don't Step In The Poodle!

A friend of a friend had a grandmother who was a little bit "ecentric." One day, the Grandma had just finished bathing her miniature poodle, Kiwi, and was about to towel-dry him when the phone rang. It was her daughter, reminding her they had arranged to meet for lunch a half hour earlier. The Grandma apologized for being late and said she'd be there as quickly as she could.

As she began towel-drying Kiwi, it dawned on her that there was a quicker way to do it: the microwave. So she put her beloved pet inside the oven, set the dial to "defrost" and switched it on.

About 30 seconds later, as Grandma was donning her coat to leave, she heard a muffled explosion in the kitchen.

Kiwi the poodle was no more.

Elderly Cat

In Charleston, South Carolina, a missionary paid a visit to an elderly woman who was a regular at his church. The old woman told him to sit down in the livingroom and then brought him tea and biscuits. The missionary told the woman about his recent missionary work in South America, but he was getting increasingly annoyed with the woman's cat, which kept pulling and chewing on his robe cords. At one point, the woman had gone to make some more tea, so the man kicked the cat away. However, he didn't realize how old the cat was and the kick killed it. Hearing the woman coming back in, the missionary panicked and picked up the cat and put it on his lap and began stroking it. The old woman didn't seem to notice and they continued their conversation. The missionary finished his cup of tea and wished the old lady good health and left. That following Sunday, the old lady turned up at the church and took the missionary aside. With a tear in her eye she said, "I hate to tell you this because you seemed to be getting on so well, but my cat passed away soon after you left."

Flat Cat

In Salt Lake City, Utah, an old lady called the fire department when her cat got stuck up a tall tree and wouldn't come down. Unfortunately, there was a strike on at the time, so a group of volunteers turned up in the fire engine. Although this was the first cat they had to rescue, they managed it without mishap and the old lady made them all a cup of ice tea as a thank you. However, when the volunteers went to drive off, they didn't see the cat under the wheels of the fire truck, and they ran over the poor pussy.

Flying With Him Could Be A Cat-astrophe!

A woman was planning to take her cat with her on an airplane trip. During a Veterinarian appointment she asked her doctor if there was anything she could give her cat to keep it calm on the trip. After a moment's thought, the doctor took a tranquilizer pill, broke off a portion that seemed about cat-dosage size, and told her to give it to the cat about an hour before takeoff.

Sometime later the doctor related this to a veterinarian associate, and the vet said, "You didn't really do that, did you? On a cat that drug has the opposite effect as on a human. That cat will be a clawing wreck!"

Later the doctor saw the lady again, and she told him, "I took your advice and gave my cat the pill, and on the plane he was out of control, about to jump out of his skin. It was all we could do to restrain him."

The doctor didn't know what to say, but luckily the woman continued, "I can't thank you enough for that pill, doctor. I just can't imagine how the cat would have behaved without it."

High Rise Doggy Door

A man from Kentucky had to relocate to New York City because of his job. Unfortunately, he could only find an apartment in a high rise in Upper Manhattan. He loathed to leave his faithful dog behind so he took her with him, vowing to take her for long walks through the park at least twice a day. The man moved in with his dog and everything seemed to work for the first few weeks. So much so, that the man invited his brothers family for a weekend visit. The brother brought his wife and their five-year-old daugher, who was particularly fond of the dog. The girl played with the dog in the apartment, but got a little over-enthusiastic while throwing the tennis ball because it ricocheted off the wall and straight out the window. The dog, probably not used to its new city life, trotted eagerly after the ball following it out the window and down some 32 floors.

His Ringing Is Worse Than His Bite

Gord James of Phoenix, Arizona became frantic when he couldn't find his mobile phone anywhere in his house. He looked everywhere and even phoned the number from his house phone in the hope of hearing the mobile ringing somewhere. Soon after he'd tried phoning the mobile, his wife returned home from walking their dog, looking very concerned. She'd been playing fetch with Bruiser, their 200 pound St Bernard, when she heard a strange, muffled ringing sound coming from somewhere nearby. After realising that the ringing became louder when Brusier approached her, she put her head to the dog's stomach and discovered the ringing was coming from the dog. Worried, she returned straight home. The man was delighted that the phone had been found, but a little bemused as to how to retrieve it, and like his wife, was concerned for Brusiers health and well-being. He called the veterinary surgeon who told him the best thing to do was to wait for time, and the phone to pass. They took the dog for another walk and sure enough, half an hour later, the phone popped out.

Innocent Doggy Bystandered

In Allentown, Pennsylvania, a teenage boy took his father's car without permission and crashed it. For some months the father's mother had been asking her grandson if he could paint her livingroom, so the father saw this as an appropriate punishment for his son. Consequently, the following weekend the father left his son at the grandmother's house with a can of yellow paint and a paintbrush. The son went about the task with an enthusiastic attitude and finished quite quickly. He stepped back to admire the work, but accidently kicked the can of paint all over a priceless Persian rug.

The boy knew he would be in an enormous amount of trouble, but just then he heard the yapping of his grandmother's poodle, so he grabbed the dog and dropped her in the middle of the spilt paint while shouting loudly, "Oh, no! You bad, bad dog!"

The boy got away with the deed, but the grandmother punished her dog by not feeding it for three days.

Innocent Kitty Bystandered

A lady from Lincoln, Nebraska, baked a blueberry pie and set it on the table to cool, when her two sons came home from school. The mother told them she was just going to visit the woman next door and they were not to touch the pie because it was for dessert later. The boys helped themselves to a cold drink and were about to go outside and play, when the lure of the freshly-baked blueberry pie called them back. They decided to risk a small bite. However, one small bite led to several and soon they had consumed half of the pie. When they heard their mother returning, they had to think quickly, and spotting the cat drinking its milk in the corner, they grabbed it, plonked its face into the middle of the pie and ran out of the kitchen. The mother entered the kitchen, saw the cat on the table with its whiskered covered in crumbs and blueberries, and in an outburst of anger, picked the cat up and threw it out of the window. The unfortunate cat landed in the road right in front of a passing school bus.

Just Lucky I Guess!

"We will not have Lucky put down. He is basically a damn good guide dog," Walter Holmes, a dog trainer from Boston told reporters. "He just needs a little brush-up on some elementary skills, that's all."

Holmes admitted to the press conference that Lucky, a German shepherd guide-dog for the blind, had so far been responsible for the deaths of all four of his previous owners.

"I admit it's not an impressive record on paper." said Holmes, "He led his first owner in front of a bus, and the second off the end of a pier. He actually pushed his third owner off a railway platform just as the the train was approaching and he walked his fourth owner into heavy traffic, before abandoning him and running away to safety. But, apart from epileptic fits, he has a lovely temperament. And guide dogs are difficult to train these days."

When asked if Lucky's fifth owner would be told about his previous record, Holmes replied, "No. It would make them nervous, and it would make Lucky nervous. And when Lucky gets nervous he's liable to do something stupid."

Kitty Makeover

A woman was driving home from work late one night when a cat ran out into the middle of the road. The woman tried to avoid the foolish cat, but when she felt a bump she realised she'd hit it. She got out and found the cat behind her front wheel. Picking it up, she noticed the cat's tag had a phone number on it and decided the least she could do was call the owner. Finding a nearby telephone, the woman called the number and an old lady answered. The woman told the old lady what had happened. The old lady then asked the woman to describe the cat.

"Well," the woman hesitantly replied, "it's mottled brown, rather bloody and flat as a pancake."

The old lady said, "Oh no, you must be mistaken, my cat doesn't look anything like that", and hung up.

Last Taste Of Freedom

My co-worker was asked by her grandmother to look after her pet budgie "Sweetie", so she could keep her usual Saturday-afternoon appointment with the hairdresser.

The young woman decided to bird-sit with her new boyfriend, and as they waved the grandmother off, the boyfriend came up with the idea to give the bird a treat, reasoning that it must have been ages since it had been allowed to fly around.

After checking that all the doors and windows were closed and that the cat was out of the room, he opened the cage door and encouraged the bird to stretch its wings. The timid thing took some enticing, so long ago had it last tasted freedom, but it gathered itself, waddled over to the door, and burst upwards, flying and flapping around in a small feathery frenzy.

However, its over-enthusiasm, combined with a novice's grasp of aerobatics, proved costly. For in a crazed bid for even greater liberty, it flew head-on into the large double-glazed patio doors, smashing the glass and tumbling to the floor.

Luckily, Sweetie was still alive, though its leg was clearly broken.

"What would Granny say!" the young couple thought.

To resolve the issue they applied first-aid and agreed to come clean with her.

Ingeniously, the boyfriend produced a box of matches from his pocket, and taking a reel of cotton, delicately bound one stick around the distraught budgie's damaged leg making a splint. Then he gently lowered the bird back inside its cage.

Tragically, the boyfriend had not known that the floor of the cage was lined with sandpaper, and as the poor budgie shuffled over to nibble its dried cuttlefish, the match struck, and the poor thing was engulfed in flames.

Lifecycle of the Salmon

A wildlife television crew had been commissioned to document the lifecycle of a salmon. The project was to follow the salmon's progress over a period of six months. They caught a salmon in the sea and without harming it, attached a radio transmitter so they could track it up river where it would lay its eggs. After two months of tracking and filming the salmon's movements, the crew was excited because the fish was about to make its amazing trip upriver. However, they were startled when the signal suddenly veered away from the river and through a forest. Thinking they had discovered a freak tributary of the river, the crew set about following the signal. After an hour, they stumbled across a campsite and a fire surrounded by a group of boy scouts. On the fire being barbecued to perfection was their precious salmon.

Oh Deer!

General Electric received a call from a customer complaining that his power went out, and when they come to fix it be sure to bring a truck with a tall enough bucket to remove the deer.

The customer service representative prudently trying to gather helpful information to help diagnose the problem asked, "What deer?"

The customer replied, "There is a deer on top of one of the electric poles."

The customer service rep, trying desperately to pull herself together and not laugh in front of the customer said, "We will dispatch someone right way to investigate the power outage. Thank you for the call."

Upon completion of the call, the customer service rep proceeded to share the story with her coworkers in the office and they all had a good laugh.

Well, low and behold, the serviceman who repaired the problem stopped by the customer service office the following day and said, "A poor deer was hit by a train and landed on top of a distribution feeder pole!"

Plight Of The Horse

A friend of a friend pulled up to a set of automatic railway level-crossing gates that were in the down position. In front of him was a horse and carriage, and in front of that was another car. All three were waiting for the train to come, when a man walked past with his dog. The dog, for some reason, took a disliking to the horse and nipped it on the leg. The horse did not relish this kind of treatment and kicked out at the dog, but missed and kicked the dog's owner instead. He in turn was furious. So, he tied his dog with a leash to the automatic gates, and before the carriage driver could prevent him, he gave the horse a hefty kick.

In some consternation, the horse reared and kicked the boot of the car in front. In panic, it backed the carriage into the front of my friend of a friend's car. While all this was going on, the dog owner stood by and laughed at the chaos he had caused. However, while he was laughing at the plight of the horse and the various drivers, the train passed, the automatic gates rose, and his dog was hanged.

That's Bull!

A Baltimore, Maryland man decided to take a weekend break deer hunting in the country. After a few hours of driving he came across a farm and asked the farmer if he could hunt on his land. The farmer told the man he could hunt as long as steered clear of his prize winning bull, which was worth $8,000. A few hours later, the man returned to the farmer, and shaking his head nervously, told the farmer he shot his prize bull by mistake. Without another word, the man wrote out a cheque for $8,500, gave it to the farmer and left. The farmer went to look for his prize bull and was more than delighted when he found it completely undisturbed grazing in its pasture. Searching the rest of his farm, he discovered the body of a buck. The city man had been too thick to know the difference between a bull and a deer. The farmer couldn't believe his luck - $8,500 the richer and three weeks worth of venison.

The Bigger They Are The Louder They Fall

Two boys were walking in the woods when they came across an old cabin in a clearing. After discovering that it was deserted, they went to investigate and discovered an old, overgrown well. Being that curious age, they decided to find out how deep it was by picking up rocks and dropping them down the well. The first boy found a stone and dropped it down the well, and after what seemed like forever, there was a quiet splash as the stone hit the bottom. The other boy found a bigger stone and dropped it down the well - the splash was even louder this time. The boys began competing, looking for bigger and larger objects to make louder and louder splashes. Eventually, one boy found a large metal spike in the ground. He pulled it out, and with a big grin, threw it down the well. The boys then noticed that the spike was actually attached to a long chain that was now rattling through the long grass and down the well. The chain gathered momentum until suddenly, a tethered dog, scared out of its wits, burst through the bushes, whizzed past them and went hurding down the well.

The Cat Came Back...

An old man from Anchorage, Alaska, put up with his temperamental cat for long enough. He was fed up with her scratching all the furniture and peeing all over the place, so he decided to give her to a friend who lived on the other side of town, with the excuse that he was getting too old to look after her. A week later, on a particularly harsh winter's day, the old man returned home from shopping and was surprised to see the cat shivering on his doorstep. Moved by the fact the cat had found her way back from the other side of town in such cold weather, the man took the cat inside and gave her plenty of loving attention. However, the next day he ran into another friend, who asked him if he had found his cat. The old man said he had and asked what the other man knew about it.

The friend replied, "I was on the other side of town the other day, when I recognised your cat in the road, so although she was hissing and struggling all the way, I drove her home and left her on your doorstep."

The Gifts

Three sons left home, to find their own way in life, and God willing, prosper. Getting back together for a family barbecue, they discussed the gifts they were able to give their elderly mother.

The first son said, "I bought a big house for our mother, and she moves in next week."

The second son replied, "Well, I sent her a Mercedes with a driver."

The third son smiled and simply said, "I've got you both beat. You remember how mom enjoyed reading the Bible? And you know she can't see very well? So I sent her a remarkable parrot that recites the entire Bible. It took elders in the church 15 years to teach him. He's one of a kind. Mother just has to name the chapter and verse, and the parrot will recite it."

A few days later, mom phoned her three sons:

Martin," she said to the first one son, "The house you built was so huge. I live in only one room, but I have to clean the whole house."

"Richard," she said to the second son, "I am too old to travel. I stay home most of the time, so I rarely use the Mercedes. And the driver is really rude!"

"My dear Michael," she said to her third son, "You have the good sense to know what your mother likes. The chicken was delicious."

The Lion Cut

My co-workers sister-in law is from Arkansas and has a slight accent. She has a few cats and when she lived in Arkansas she always took them to the groomers and had what was called a "Line Cut". A line cut is when all of the fur hanging down below the cat's tummy is taken off because it gets matted or snarled.

When she moved to New York with her husband, one of the cats fur got all tangled up during the move so she took it in for a line cut. She was quite surprised when she heard the price because it was twice as much as it was in Arkansas.

She confirmed with the groomer that he understood what a line cut was and he said "Of course I know what a lion cut is."

It seems that her accent came out sounding like "lion" not "line" and her cat was returned to her, completely shaved, except for a big fuzzy lion mane. She cried for a week, but not as much as the cat, because it was November in New York, and the cat needed all the fur it had.

Gas in car to get to groomers $6.00

Cat car carrier $39.99

Grooming fee $69.00

Getting the look from one seriously pissed off cat ... Priceless!

The Lump

A carpet-layer just finished off putting a new carpet in an old woman's lounge, when he noticed a curious lump in the middle. Reluctant to start all over again and remove all the nails, the carpet-layer took his hammer and attempted to flatten the lump. After a few good hits with the hammer and a few stomps with his boot, the carpet looked as good as ever and the carpet-layer packed up his tools.

As he was about to leave, the old woman emerged from the kitchen and asked the man, "Young man, before you go could you help me find my pet hamster?"

The carpet-layer mumbled an excuse about being late for another appointment and rushed out the door.

The Ninth Life Cut Short

A wealthy woman, living in Beverly Hills, had a cat that was very precious to her. The cat was getting old and the woman decided that the least she could do was move out to the country for the final years of the cats life, so he could enjoy the space, fresh air, and tranquillity away from the noise and smog of the city. Eventually, the woman moved into a small farmhouse in a small town just outside of Los Angeles. After unpacking, the woman put the cat on the grass to soak up the sun, and while she talked to him, she prepared his dinner in the kitchen. Suddenly she was alarmed to hear the cat squeal in pain, and immediately ran outside just in time to see a falcon fly off with her beloved cat in its claws.

"Those Stupid Americans"

During a long drive to a distant campground in an area of Ontario popular with hunters, my grandfather pointed to the cattle grazing in a nearby field and informed me that local farmers took to writing "Cow" in big letters on the side of these beasties every fall because of "those stupid Americans".

Apparently, a large number of hunters from the US traveled to Canada for Deer Hunting Season, and shot cows mistaking them for a deer. Then they tagged the cows and loaded them onto their trucks. To this day a Game Warden has a post at the border crossing. His job is to simply spot these misguided hunters and inform them they have shot a cow, not a deer.

Unwelcome Guest

In Tulsa, Oklahoma, a local priest was making the usual rounds of his congregation. A family had just moved into the area and the priest was eager to make a good first impression to welcome them. As the priest approached the family's house, he noticed a large, playful dog in the front garden and gave it a friendly pat. When the woman of the house invited the priest inside, the dog followed. The priest was shown into the livingroom where the father and their three children were sitting. The priest attempted to make polite conversation, but was thwarted by the dog's antics. The dog smelled like it hadn't been washed in months, tracked mud all over the carpet and furniture and gobbled up all the biscuits that the mother had thoughtfully provided. The priest decided it might be best to leave before the dog became even more embarrassing.

As he headed towards the door, the mother remarked coldly, "Don't forget your dog, Father."

"My dog?" the priest exclaimed, "Isn't he yours?"

It's Raining Blubber....Hallelujiah!

The passing of a beloved pet can be painful, and the grim task of disposing of the remains of our animal companions makes the ordeal even more unpleasant. However, our grief has to be interrupted for the mundane concern of nature very few of us plan for ahead of time.

A goldfish can easily be flushed, but what about a dead dog? Or what if the problem was larger; say the carcass of a rotting whale?

The following tales are attempts to be rid of the corspe of a deceased animal. Perhaps the humor in these dubious disposals will reflect our unease at the thought of dealing with anything dead.

Dead Luggage

At Charles de Gaulle Airport in Paris, a baggage handler was horrified to discover a dead poodle in a crate bound for New York. Worried that he would be blamed for neglecting the animal, the baggage handler frantically rushed around the city hunting through the pet shops, until he finally found, and bought, an identical poodle. The relieved baggage handler put the poodle in a crate on the next flight to New York. The poodles owner was an old

Italian woman, who became very annoyed when she was informed that her poodle had been put on the next flight by mistake. However, when the crate finally arrived a few hours later, the old lady fainted as the lively poodle yapped at her. It seems that her own poodle had died while on holiday in Paris and she was shipping it back to New York for burial.

Fetch the Stick...of Dynamite

A farmer in the Australian outback realised that his 15-year-old dog was painfully sick and would have to be put down. Unable to bring himself to shoot the poor animal, he decided to tie the dog up to a small tree and put a lit stick of dynamite in its mouth. Tears welled up in his eyes as he backed away from the dog, and unable to watch anymore, he retreated into his farmhouse. Thirty seconds later, as the man was helping himself to a beer, he heard the all too familiar ail whining at the front door. It was the dog still holding the lit stick of dynamite.

Gone Today, Hare Tomorrow

A man living in the suburban outskirts of Los Angeles was used to his dog digging up old bones and objects and bringing them into the house, but he was most upset when his dog brought home the neighbour's pet rabbit looking very limp, and as it turned out, very dead. His neighbours had gone on holiday for a week, and not feeling able to face the prospect of confessing his dog's misdemeanour, he snuck into their back garden and placed the lifeless rabbit back in its hutch. A few days after the neighbours returned, he bumped into the husband, and discreetly asked about their rabbit.

"Funny thing," said his neighbour. "Our rabbit died just before we went away and we buried it in the garden, but when we got back some sick joker dug it up and put it back in its hutch!"

It's Raining Blubber....Hallelujiah!

An eight-ton, 50-foot sperm whale that had been dead for some time, washed up on a Pacific Ocean beach in California. At first, it was a curiosity for local residents and visitors, but soon the foul smell of rotting whale pervaded the area and it became unbearable. The authorities thought if they buried the carcass the tide would just uncovered it. So after much discussion it was decided to blast the blubber to bits using dynamite. Unfortunately, the explosives experts miscalculated the amount of dynamite needed and the resulting explosion sent pieces of blubber raining down over a stunned crowd of curious spectators that had gathered. The authorities were forced to organise a task force to comb the area. It took two weeks to collect all the pieces of blubber and burn the lot.

Kitty Bag To Go

Two elderly women were coming out of a mall when they spotted a dead cat in the parking lot. Being cat lovers, they couldn't bear the thought of leaving the poor dead kitty there, so they decided to take it home and give it a decent burial. They went back into the store and got a shopping bag. They wrapped the dead kitty in one sack and then put it in another, hoping to contain the odor. It was lunch time so their next stop was a local restaurant. Since it was a warm day, they were reluctant to leave the dead kitty closed up in the car. So they placed the bag beside the car and went in to eat. As it happened, their car was visible through the window where they were sitting in the restaurant. They watched as a lady walked by their car, stopped, looked around, walked back and picked up the bag, before heading into the restaurant. The lady was then seated next to the two elderly cat lovers. The lady ordered her lunch and curiosity getting the better of her, opened the shopping bag. She peeked inside, screamed, and in trying to get out of her chair, fell and hit her head. An ambulance was called to take the poor woman away.

As they were taking her away, one the elderly cat lovers placed the shopping bag on the gur— think this belongs to her."

"Look at this, I've caught the fish that swallowed your bloody teeth!"

People like to put one over on their friends whenever possible, and they are not above employing animals in their dastardily scenarios. These trusting critters unwittingly become the accomplices to whatever scheme or brute farce these pranksters can induce them to participating in. But in some cases the critter turns the table, unwittingly making the human the object of fun by simply behaving like...well, an animal.

Bird Calling For Dummies

The moisture dripped from the eucalyptus trees, the skies were gray, and the ground was damp as 15 college students crouched down with their attention focused on the professor of a bird-study class who, at regular intervals, was hooting like an owl in an attempt to attract the elusive bird. In the distance came an answering hoot, and the bird-study class moved cautiously, stopped, and their instructor hooted again.

For about 20 minutes the hooting and creeping forward continued while the answering hoots grew louder and louder. Quietly the class rounded a small hill. Instead of sighting their quarry they came upon a young man, hooting mournfully. Behind him stood another group of cold, damp, eager students.

Do Not Intoxicate The Animals!

A friend of my colleague had just bought a brand new Jeep Grand Cherokee, complete with sunroof and all the trimmings. He and a group of friends decided to go on a weekend road trip to Florida with a group of friends. The gang, being the partying sort, bought liquor and beer to supply them for the trip.

While on their trip, they decided to visit a safari park where you drive through in your own car. At the entrance to the park, as well as all through the park, there were signs reminding patrons that the animals in the park are wild and that all windows must remain rolled up at all times. But it was a smoldering hot day, and the guy's friends had been drinking a good deal of beer, so everyone decided they would leave the sunroof open, but keep the windows closed.

The group drove on through the park, drinking and blasting the stereo. Suddenly, a giraffe took notice and started to move toward them. Thinking it was cool, they stopped the vehicle to watch to see what the beast would do.

Curious, the giraffe approached them. One guy decided to entice the animal with one of the beers that they had by holding it out the sunroof. This really got the beast's attention and he came running up to the car and started licking the beer that was being poured onto the roof.

It was at this point that the animal decided to peek in to see if there was any more of that delicious liquid and before they could get the beer in and close the sunroof, the giraffe had his head all the way in the car and was looking for more beer. Terrified, the driver pushed the button for the sunroof to close, effectively putting the animal's neck in a vice grip, whereupon the animal panicked and vomited repeatedly.

When park officials arrived, they were able to get the giraffe unstuck, and invited the travelers to leave the park and never return.

Unable to find a place to clean the car and their belongings, the group decided to head back home. Of course, during their drive home, they were stopped by the highway patrol. He became suspicious of the young men and searched the vehicle, finding of course more than the legal limit of open alcohol. The officer charged them with fines and duties for the offense.

Fancy Meeting You Hare

A Frenchman was late for a fancy costume party, so he took a shortcut through the forest. The only thing wrong with that was the man was dressed up as a giant rabbit, complete with floppy ears. However, unbeknown to him, the forest was popular for weekend hunters. One such hunter was astounded to see a giant rabbit hobbling on the other side of the field from him, and thinking it would feed his family for a year, took a shot at it. The hunter was even more astounded when he saw the giant rabbit jump up and start charging towards him, cursing loudly. After a somewhat bizarre confrontation, the man dressed as a rabbit and the hunter teamed up and won first prize in the fancy costume party competition.

Fish Teeth

Two old men were out fishing, but weren't having much luck and were about to turn back when the weather turned nasty. Their boat was getting tossed every which way. Before long one of the old fellows felt ill and began vomiting over the side. Much to the amusement of his companion, the old timer retched so hard that he lost his false teeth along with the contents of his stomach. The storm soon passed and the men decided to have another try at fishing. Eventually, one of them hooked a large fish and brought it in. But before announcing his catch, he decided to play a trick on his friend. He slit open the fish, took out his own false teeth and put them inside the fish.

Calling over his companion, he said, "Look at this, I've caught the fish that swallowed your bloody teeth!"

The other fellow grabbed the set from the fish and put them in his mouth.

After trying to adjust them, he took them out again and said, "Don't fit. They're not mine," as he threw them overboard.

Giant Squid

The New Zealand coast guard reported sightings of a rare giant squid off the coast of Kaikoura on the South Island. Hundreds of scientists, wildlife photographers and fishermen went out in search of the elusive creature. Eventually, one fisherman spotted the squid and chased it for miles before finally netting it.

The proud fisherman was looking forward to a life of fame and fortune, when he was shocked to hear the giant squid say, "Hey, you stupid moron, get me out of this bloody net!"

The "squid" was, in fact, an amateur photographer who made and put on a giant squid suit in a bid to attract the attentions of the real creature, which he was convinced lived in the area.

Have A Pheasant Day

Frank Carter, an intrepid hunter from Duluth, Minnesota was particularly pleased after bagging an enormous pheasant. To celebrate he went down to his local pub to show off his prize winning bird. After a few drinks, the proud hunter took his buddies out to his truck and showed them his catch. However, the man, a bit worse for wear from all the alcohol he consumed, stumbled and lost his grip on the dead pheasant. The pheasant knocked over the man's gun resting on the side of the truck, causing it to shoot the man in the foot. Forced to report the incident, the man not only lost his job because of his incapacitated foot, but he was also fined for shooting pheasant out of season. The pheasants had the last laugh that weekend.

Kanga-Rude Awakening

A group of Amercian tourists were driving a jeep through the Australian countryside, and after driving what seemed like miles through the desolate outback, they decided to turn around. Just then, a kangaroo hopped onto the road directly in front of them. They struck the poor creature, which then landed with a bone-crunching thud on the pavement.

The Americans had never seen a kangaroo before, and didn't seem all that sorry that they had killed it in the process. In fact, as it lay motionless in the road, they decided it would be a great photo opportunity. The animal stood about six feet tall and would really impress their pals back home. So the intrepid tourists propped up the Roo, and to add insult to injury, one of the group members put his red Roots jacket on the unfortunate beast.

However, when another member of the group went to focus the camera, at that moment, the kangaroo leaped straight into the air and bounced off into the distance, wearing the jacket. It turns out, he was only stunned. It might not have been so bad, had the left breast pocket not contain the keys to the jeep, a wallet and a passport.

Manhunt

Frustrated by a recent series of fox hunts and thwarted by hunt saboteurs, an English country squire decided to do the next hunt without a fox. He engaged a young local man to make a trail of aniseed through the fields and forests. The young man was hired to make an elaborate trail for the fox hounds to follow. After completing the trail the young man retired to the local pub to spend the money the squire had given him. A few pints later, the young man was surprised to hear the barking of fox hounds drawing closer, especially since he made the aniseed trail lead back to the squire's estate, a few miles away. As he ventured out to investigate, it slowly dawned on him why the fox hounds were coming his way: he stank of aniseed. The man ran for his life, but the hounds soon caught up with him, and subsequently licked him to death. The country squire's weekly sport of man-hunting has since proven to be an extremely popular activity with fellow red coats.

Rhino-sore-ass

Drew Ronald, a California native, found himself in a difficult position while touring the Eagle's Rock African Safari Zoo with a group of thespians from St. Petersburg, Russia. Mr. Ronald went to extremes to demonstrate the power of Crazy Glue, one of America's many marvels, to the Russians.

To prove the effectiveness of Crazy Glue, he rubbed several ounces of the adhesive onto the palms of his hands and jokingly placed them on the buttocks of a passing rhino.

The rhinoceros, a resident of the zoo for thirteen years, was not initially startled, as it had been part of the petting exhibit since its arrival as a baby. However, once it became aware of being involuntarily stuck to Mr. Ronald, it began to panic and charge wildly about the petting area with Mr. Ronald as an unwitting passenger.

"Rambo the Rhino hadn't been feeling well. He was constipated, and had just been given a laxative when the American played his juvenile prank," said caretaker Jerry Whitaker.

During Rambo's tirade, a shed wall was gored, two fences destroyed, a number of small animals escaped, and three pygmy goats and one duck were stomped to death. During the stampede and subsequent capture, Rambo began to feel the effects of the laxative, showering Mr. Ronald repeatedly with over 30 gallons of rhinoceros diarrhea.

A team of medics and zoo caretakers were needed to remove his hands from Rambo's buttocks. "It was tricky. We had to calm him down while shielding our faces from the pelting rhino dung. I guess you could say that Mr. Ronald was in it up to his neck", said Whitaker, "Once Rambo was under control, three people with shovels were working to keep an air passage open for him. We were eventually able to tranquilize Rambo and apply a solvent to remove Mr. Ronald's hands from Rambo's rear. I don't think he'll be playing with Crazy Glue for awhile."

Meanwhile, the amused Russians were impressed with the power of the adhesive.

Vladimir Zolnikov, leader of the troupe commented, "I'm going to buy some for my children, but of course they can't take it to the zoo."

The Hunter Becomes The Hunted

A man from Ontario, Canada, went on a hunting trip in the country. Needless to say the day went badly, spotting only a few deer, and missing each one. When it started to get dark, the man decided to call it a day and drove home. On the way home, the man was delighted when he hit a deer that ran into the road in front of him. Although illegal, the man put the deer in his back seat and continued to drive home. However, a few miles down the road, the deer recovered and began thrashing around. The man grabbed a hammer from under his seat and swung at the deer, still steering his car. Unfortunately, he caught his faithful hunting dog in mid-swing and the dog bit him in retaliation. The man brought the car to a halt, leapt out and ran down the road, with his angry dog in hot pursuit. The man came across a telephone booth and shutting himself inside, he dialed the emergency services. He explained to the operator that he was trapped inside a telephone booth by a ferocious dog while a deer was smashing his car. He begged the operator to send a policeman to shoot the animals and save him. The police rescued the man without having to resort to killing the animals, but the man never went hunting again.

Which One Is The Turkey?

A hunter, frustrated at not bagging any deer, illegally shot a wild turkey instead. He cleaned the bird, took it home and packed the carcass into his freezer. However, he failed to notice a tiny radio receiver that had been implanted under the turkey's wing by wildlife researchers. A few days later, officials of the Department of Natural Resources came straight to the hunter's house, walked to the freezer, took out the dead turkey and arrested the live one.

Wild Suitcase

My co-worker and his buddy were doing a little trapping in Montana, and caught a genuine full-grown wildcat. For some reason, they decided to put the thing into an old suitcase.

They told a couple of other friends about it, then the four took the suitcase containing the live bobcat out to a country road and carefully set it on the shoulder, and proceeded to hide in a nearby clump of bushes.

A few minutes later a vehicle with six passengers came rattling down the gravel road past the suitcase, stopped, and backed up. A door swung open and the suitcase was grabbed and tossed into the back seat.

About a quarter-mile down the road, the car came to a sudden hault, all four doors flew open, and six grown men plus an angry bobcat came flying out.

Mutant Marsupials Take Up Arms Against Australian Air Force.

From time to time our furry, feathered, and slithering friends have been known to scamper across the front page of the daily newspaper, captured in all their newsworthy glory!

Cows Are Mean Drunks

A herd of cows created havoc in a small town in Louisiana when they broke out of their paddock. The towns people were stunned to see the cows staggering down the road, mooing loudly, urinating against walls and flirting with local bulls. Eventually, the cows were rounded up, and it came to light that the cows were heavily intoxicated. It seems the cows had been fed on beer waste from a local brewery. The farmer explained that beer contained vital nutrients, and was an excellent supplement to their diet. However, the farmer had not anticipated the effect of alcohol on his herd.

"I had no idea cows were mean drunks," said the farmer. "I will have to teach them to hold their alcohol better."

It Just Wooden Work Between Us

One winter, a wooden deer, used for target practice near a village in Alaskan attracted the attention of a wild bull moose. Undeterred by the pockmarks in the life-sized model, the bull made several passionate passes as amused hunters watched from a safe distance. The brief affair ended when the bull's advances became increasingly physical. The bull didn't seem to notice when the deer's antlers broke off, but when its head fell off, he stopped abruptly and dismounted the decapitated deer. The frustrated bull moose looked down at the broken head, snorted and trotted off back into the woods...just like a man!

Love At First Trunk

To help with their logging activities the people in a small village on the edge of the jungle of southern India domesticated a female elephant. The elephant was named Savita and when she wasn't working, she was chained to a tree. Although it's unusual for wild elephants to be attracted to domesticated elephants, for one three-ton bull elephant it was love at first sight and refused to leave Savita's side. At first, the villagers tried to lure the huge beast away with bananas, but when that failed, they tried intimidating it by shouting and throwing firecrackers, which successfully drove the animal back into the jungle, but not before it left a trail of demolished huts in its wake. Still consumed with love, the bull elephant snuck back into the village that night and freed Savita by breaking her chains, and the two lovers eloped back into the jungle.

Mutant Marsupials Take Up Arms Against Australian Air Force

The reuse of object-oriented code has caused tactical headaches for Australia's armed forces. As virtual reality simulators assume larger roles in helicopter combat training, programmers have gone to great lengths to increase the realism of the their scenarios, including detailed landscapes, and in the case of the Northern Territory's Operation Phoenix, herds of kangaroos, since groups of disturbed animals might well give away a helicopters position.

The head of the Defense Science and Technology Organization's Land Operations and Simulations Division reportedly instructed developers to model the local marsupials' movements and reaction to helicopters.

Being efficient programmers, they re-appropriated some code originally used to model infantry detachments reactions under the same stimuli, changed the mapped icon from a soldier to a kangaroo, and increased the figures' speed of movement.

Eager to demonstrate their flying skills for some visiting American pilots, the hotshot Aussies "buzzed" the virtual kangaroos in low flight during a simulation. The kangaroos scattered, as predicted, and the Americans nodded appreciatively, but did a double-take as the kangaroos reappeared from behind a hill and launched a barrage of stinger missiles at the hapless helicopter. Apparently the programmers had forgotten to remove that part of the infantry coding.

The embarrassed programmers learned to be careful when reusing object-oriented code, and the Yanks left with the utmost respect for Australian wildlife. Simulator supervisors report that pilots from that point onwards have strictly avoided kangaroos, just as they were meant to.

Reckless Endangered Species

Police investigating a hit-and-run accident arrived at the scene of the crime to find an 11-year-old boy and a middle-aged man in a state of distress. When questioned as to what had happened, both witnesses provided statements that the officers found hard to believe. Apparently, the boy had been illegally riding a moped, when a moose ran out in front of him. The frightened creature leapt into the air and came crashing back down onto the back seat of the moped, at the same time knocking the boy off. The moped, now being "driven" by the moose, carried on a little way down the road before crashing out of control into an oncoming car. The moose chose that moment to make its getaway. The driver of the car, who ended up with a damaged pelvis, and wiplash was able to confirm the boy's story, at least the bit about the moose riding the moped anyway. The police officers had little choice but to file a report detailing a hit-and-run accident involving a moped being driven in a dangerous fashion by a moose.

That's One "Elepha" Jump!

Earlier this year, the dazed crew of a Japanese trawler were plucked into the Sea of Japan clinging to the wreckage of their sunken ship. Their rescue was followed by immediate imprisonment once authorities questioned the sailors on their ship's loss. They claimed that an elephant, fell out of a clear blue sky, striking the trawler, shattering its hull and sinking the vessel within minutes.

They remained in prison for several weeks, until the Russian Air Force reluctantly informed Japanese authorities that the crew of one of its cargo planes had apparently stolen an elephant wandering at the edge of an airfield in Siberia, forced the elephant into the plane's hold and hastily taken off for home. Unprepared for live cargo, the Russian crew was ill-equipped to manage the now rampaging elephant within its hold. To save the aircraft and themselves, they shoved the animal out of the cargo hold as they crossed the Sea of Japan at an altitude of 30,000 feet.

The Car Attraction

In Budapest, Hungary, a travelling circus had set up in a large park in the old part of the city. To encourage people to come and see the circus, the owners decided to lead a parade through the streets. It was a huge procession, with jugglers, clowns, acrobats, seals on floats, lions in cages and the star attraction, Madhu the elephant. The residents were cheering and applauding until suddenly, Madhu broke free of her chains and stormed into the crowd. Apparently, she had mistaken a small red car parked by the side of the street for a stool used in the circus act, and had run over to balance on it.

Those Dam Beavers

A "tail" of bureaucracy gone mad.

Harold Baker lived by a small river in Texas. Mr. Baker informed his local authority that a dam built by beavers had caused flooding on his land. In due course, Mr. Baker received a letter telling him that the local authority was prosecuting him for unauthorised construction on the river. The baffled man wrote back, saying that it was the beavers that had built a dam, and that was what his complaint was about. Mr. Baker didn't hear anything for a month, until one morning, two bailiffs knocked on his door and asked him if he knew where a Mr. and Mrs. Beaver lived. Apparently, the local authority had fined the beavers $15,000 for unauthorised construction on the river, and another $2,000 for not showing up to court.

Worst Job In Singapore

The Singapore Zoological Gardens announced that they were setting up a bank containing sperm samples of all the wildlife under their supervision. At the same time, zoo sperm bank worker Duc Bintang won a competition for "Worst Job in Singapore".

Wildlife Reserves Singapore, which runs the Singapore Zoo, set up a bank of sperm and animal tissue in order to help preserve species.

The thankless task of collecting the sperm fell to Mr. Bintang, who starts his rounds at 4 am.

"We start so early in the morning because a lot of the animals have 'morning glory' when they wake up, and it's easier to collect the sperm." explained Bintang.

Wearing rubber gloves and carrying a cooler box filled with ice and tupperware, Mr. Bintang told reporters that he'd just graduated from Singapore Polytechnic with a diploma in life sciences. He liked nature and animals, and thought that the Singapore Zoo would be the perfect place to work.

"I never thought I'd be giving an orangatang a hand job every morning," he said somewhat ruefully. "And he is the worst. He expects to be kissed first. Each morning when I approach the orangatang enclosure, I always see the Zoo's most famous resident lying casually on his back, hands behind his head, and sporting a huge erection."

The procedure involves Bintang applying massage oil onto his gloves, outside the enclosure before entering. Then he kneels before the orange beast, and about 2 minutes' worth of squelching noises could be heard before Mr. Bintang emerges again.

Then he heads over to the tiger enclosure, were the big cats are sprawled lazily on the grass verge, in a somewhat half-hearted manner as he puts on a fresh set of gloves and enters the enclosure. He summons the randy beats with, "Here, kitty, kitty, kitty . . ."

Moments later, he emerges with several Tupperware full of viscous fluid.

One reporter asked, "Isn't it dangerous?"

"They know I'm not there as an enemy," he replied with a glazed, faraway look in his eyes.

Mr. Bintang continued to work his way round the zoo, finishing his rounds at 3 pm in the afternoon. Carrying out his duties with the rhinoceros, giraffe and the gorillas, amongst others.

"Each animal is different," he said, removing his gloves, now speckled with traces of polar bear spunk. "The chimpanzees always want to be hugged afterwards. The elephant is the trickiest of all because of the size of its thing, and sometimes I have to use both my arms to tug on it. As you can expect it's really affecting my sex life. I can't help it. Each time my wife initiates sex, these ejaculating Rhinos keep floating through my mind."

How long Mr. Bintang will continue his work is difficult to predict, but deputy assistant director Lai Jee thinks it is important to continue.

"The animals have gotten too used to Bintang coming over every morning to pull them off." Jee said, "Now many of them can't be bothered to engage in real sex."

Save Their Bacon

For those of you who love animals, when you hear of a creature being mistreated or unnecessarily put at risk, something inside of you dies. The appeal for us to protect these hapless creatures hit us right where we live, so we hope that our small action or contribution can somehow make a difference in saving the life of animals at risk. Here are some hilarious tales of crusader habitats!

Caught and Vested

As you know PETA, People for the Ethical Treatment of Animals, will do almost anything to protect animals. This year's efforts to save Ohio's deer from the annual statewide gun season has backfired. For safety's sake, hunters in Ohio are now required by law to display at least 400 square inches of hunter's blaze orange on their person when in the woods.

Capitalizing on the fact that hunters do not usually shoot orange, PETA recently bulk purchased blaze orange vests and have been affixing them to live-trapped deer. According to PETA spokesperson Sharlene Reed, a total of 405 vests were successfully put into circulation prior to this week, with additional specimens still being caught and vested.

An Ohio entrepreneur Garth Young, of Garth's Outfitter has spit in the face of PETA by offering rewards for the returned vests this week. Hunters who can successfully bag a vested deer will be paid $50 for each one.

As of today, 308 of the vests have already been recorded as bagged with most of the hunters registering for Mr. Young's contest.

"It's so easy, you can see them coming a mile away" said one hunter after checking in his first spike buck.

ODNR officials are worried that the poorly thought out plan by PETA might get somebody shot instead of saving the deer.

"Hunters have turned their plan upside down, we're just hoping that nobody gets hurt and are hoping that none of the vested animals get tangled in brush" said one ODNR official. "PETA has really outdone itself this time."

Did You Know? *The average cost to rehabilitate a seal after the Exxon Valdez oil spill in Alaska was $80,000. At a special ceremony, two of the most expensive seals saved were released back into the wild amid cheers and applause from onlookers. A minute later, in full view, they were both eaten by a killer whale.*

Penguin Wear *by Tommy Hilfeather*

When an ocean-going tanker goes down at sea, it releases crude oil into the ocean, the immediate and long-term effects on the environment are often catastrophic. Equally as dangerous is the illegal practice of passing ships' dumping fuel oil into the water rather than properly disposing of it in port. In the case of the "little penguins" who live on Phillip Island near Melbourne, Australia, such accidents and illegal activities have threatened the entire population of penguins.

Cleaning the animals by hand with warm water and a mild detergent then returning them to their natural habitat was found to be an effective means of dealing with the danger posed by oil spills, but there's a snag in the plan: Often the little penguins are far too ill to be bathed right away, and the scrubbing can be quite stressful. The solution the World Wildlife Federation came up with was to slip the oil-coated birds into wool sweaters, which will prevent them from preening themselves and possibly swallowing toxic petroleum-based oil as they regain needed strength. It will also keep them warm until their bodies are once again producing the natural oils that were removed by the cleaning, necessary to their insulation.

Did You Know? *A sanctuary for dogs is maintained on "dog island" off the coast of Florida. Over 2,500 dogs are already enjoying a better life at Dog Island. Dogs on Dog Island live a* *natural, healthy and happy life. They live with almost limitless space, and tens of thousands of rabbits, rodents and other natural prey. Surrounded by thousands of other dogs, this is the only place for them to be truly social and create healthy families. Dog Island, is operated as a sanctuary where canines can live "separated from the anxieties of urban life". Dogs at Dog Island have another chance.*

Poor Horse

A farmer in Southern Saskatchewan, Canada hit hard times. To keep things going, he decided to sell his prize stallion. The farmer was so poor even getting to the market place was a problem. He had to borrow a car from a neighbour and use a trailer that had been rotting in the corner of the stable for years. Nevertheless, he made the trailer as sturdy as he could, secured his horse inside and started off. Unfortunately for the horse, the farmers carpentry skills were not so hot. When the trailer went over a bump, the poor horse plunged through the rotten floorboards and was forced to gallop all the way to the market place. When the farmer opened the trailer, he was devastated to see his prize stallion collapsed in a heap. Not surprisingly, the farmer was unable to sell his steed, although he declined an offer from a merciless butcher.

Save Their Bacon

Two pigs about to be slaughtered, escaped from an abattoir recently. The pigs, thought to be in love, dug a hole under a fence, crept through and swam across a river to escape certain death at the hands of merciless farmers. Following a nation-wide pig hunt, widely reported in the media, an anonymous animal lover offered to buy the pigs for a thousand dollars each to "save their bacon". The pigs were eventually discovered hiding out in an abandoned church. The pig farmer, surprised at the turn of events and happy to make such a huge profit, passed the pigs on to their new benefactor.

Did You Know? *Two animal rights protesters were protesting the cruelty of sending pigs to a slaughterhouse. Suddenly, all two thousand pigs, stampeded through a broken fence and trampled the two hapless protesters to death.*

"That'll teach him. I shot two of his cows."

Man is the highest beast on the food chain. This exalted position leads some to engage in acts of callous cruelty against critters of the lowest order. Yes, we are carnivores, but we want to believe that we are civilized about it. How we view animals is such that, though we routinely consume animals for sustenance, there are those who hunt and inflict suffering simply for pleasure-- hence our social distate of those we see mistreating their prey or the domesticated creatures they come in contact with.

These tales of animal mistreatment communicate our condemnation with such practises, and contain hilarious twists leaving the bad guy holding the bag.

Cat Hater

One night, a truck driver was driving through the outskirts of Detroit to deliver his last load of the week. Suddenly, a cat ran out into the road in front of him. The driver slammed on the brakes, but he was sure it was too late. He got out of the truck and looked underneath, but it was too dark to see anything. Retrieving a flashlight from inside the cab, he spotted the cat writhing on the sidewalk. Close to tears, the man did the decent thing and ended the cat's agony with a swift blow with a hammer, then climbed back into his truck. He was about to depart when an old lady opened his cab door and began screaming at him. Thinking she must be the owner of the poor cat, he tried to explain, but she was to hysterical and started hitting him. Eventually, the woman calmed down, and told him that she saw him run over her neighbour's cat, stop the truck and then hit her own cat with a hammer.

Gopher It!!

On May 15, 2001, students from Carroll Fowler Elementary School in California brought a very much alive and healthy gopher to the janitor and two maintenance men. The three guys decided to kill the gopher and took it to a small room where the janitorial supplies were stored. They tried to off the critter by spraying it with a cleaning solvent used to remove gum from floors. Three cans were used on the condemned furball, but the product didn't seem to faze the gopher one bit.

Forgeting about all the flammable cleaning liquids, one of the men attempted to light a cigarette in the tiny enclosed space. As any sensible person would expect, there was one hell of an explosion, and all three men were injured. Sixteen kids were also hurt, but nothing all that serious.

In the aftermath of the explosion, the sprayed-down gopher was discovered unharmed and clinging to a wall. He was later released back into the wild.

That'll Teach Him

Two men were driving up to a lodge in the mountains for a weekend of deer hunting, when they realised they were lost. Spotting a farm up ahead, the driver stopped the car, telling his friend to wait while he asked for directions. At the farmhouse, he came across a distressed farmer who told the hunter that his horse was ill and needed to be put down. The farmer explained that he had become too fond of the horse to kill it himself, and on learning that the man was a hunter asked him to shoot the horse. At first, the man refused, but the farmer continued to plead with him and eventually he relented. The farmer showed the man to the horse and gave him a rifle, and the man shot the horse. The farmer thanked him and told him the way to the lodge. As he returned to the car, the man decided to play a joke on his buddy. He explained that the farmer was so rude, that he shot his horse. Instantly, his friend grabbed a rifle from the back of the car and disappeared.

After a few minutes there were two gunshots, then the friend returned, jumped in the car and said, "That'll teach him. I shot two of his cows."

The animal's gag reflex forced it to swallow.

We live among them, we dominate them, but we don't trust them. In the back of our minds lurks the realization that we will end up eaten or brutalized by a creature of a lower order. This fear plays a huge part in a number of rumors about animals. Nobody wants to be some critters dinner, and there is always a chance that the tiny streak of wild that runs through even domesticated creatures could suddenly surface, turning our trusted companion or docile pet into a rampaging beast.

Adding to our fear is our awareness that the wild kingdom carries on its everyday business merely steps from where we live, work, and play. Untamed beasts, although often unseen, still co-exsist with humans in the urban jungle, because even bustling centers of humanity prove no bar to creatures of all descriptions.

These stories of bear malice, although humorous, remind us to stay alert and exercise extreme caution when dealing with all manner of animals or when intruding upon their habitat.

Balls Aren't For Pussies

My co-workers sister came home one day to find her boyfriend lying naked and unconscious, face-down under the sink in their bathroom. Looking him over, she felt a small bump on his head and some mysterious scratches around his groin. Wondering whether she should call an ambulance, her boyfriend recovered and was able to explain what happened. He was about to take a shower when he dropped the bar of soap under the sink. Bending down to retrieve it, he suddenly felt intense pain around his groin, which startled him so much that he hit his head on the sink and knocked himself out. Examining the scratches, they both agreed that they looked like they could have been made by a cat, which puzzled them both because they didn't own one. A little later they found out their neighbours' kitten was in their house and figured the kitten must have snuck into the bathroom. When the boyfriend was bending under the sink, the kitten presumably regarded his dangling genitals as an interesting toy, and swiped at them with claws fully extended.

Bird of Prey

A man who was fond of "birds of prey" developed a ritual every time he left his local bar in the evening. He would take a small sausage out of his pocket and hold it up in the air. Before long, an owl would swoop down from the trees and grab the sausage out of his hand. One night, after one too many beers, the man staggered out of the pub, and was so drunk he forgot to take the sausage out of his pocket. Feeling a sudden need to take a leak, he went behind a tree and took his pecker out. The confused owl swooped down and grabbed the poor man's member in its talons. The man swore he'd never drink again.

Hand Clam...p

A man went on a diving holiday off the coast of Florida, and was having a wonderful time exploring the beautiful underwater scenery of the ocean. On one dive, he came across a cave, and on further investigation, spotted a giant clam inside. Realising that the clam could be worth a lot of money, the man approached it, knife in hand. However, as he went to pry the clam off the rock, it slammed shut on his other hand. He tried prying the clam open with his knife, but without success. Realising that if he didn't free himself soon, he would run out of air and drown, the man took the only option he had left. He cut his hand off with his knife and just managed to swim to the surface before his air ran out.

Did You Know? *An African circus dwarf died recently when he bounced sideways from a trampoline and was swallowed by a hippopotamus. Seven thousand people watched as little Naboo Jinstsu popped into the mouth of Boda the Hippo and the animal's gag reflex forced it to swallow. The crowd applauded wildly before other circus people realised what had happened.*

Rustling Creature

A rugged old man was out hunting in the forests of British Columibia when he heard a loud rustling in the trees above. Figuring it must be a large bird, the man let off a volley of shots into the foliage. Since nothing seemed to result from his shooting, the man moved under the tree, and when he heard yet more rustling directly overhead, he let off another volley of shots. This time, he was delighted to hear an animal cry out in pain. However, his joy quickly turned to despair, when tumbling at a fast speed towards him was a large porcupine. The spiky creature landed right on his face, causing so many lacerations, the man died.

When You Have Friends Like That, Who Needs Enema's!

Frederick Badger, an overzealous zookeeper at the Los Angeles Zoo, fed his constipated elephant Baku doses of animal laxative and more than a bushel of berries, figs and prunes before the plugged-up pachyderm finally let fly, and suffocated the zookeeper under 250 pounds of poop.

Investigators said ill-fated Badger, 38, was attempting to give the ailing elephant an olive-oil enema when the relieved beast unloaded on him like a dump truck.

"The sheer force of the elephant's unexpected defecation knocked Mr. Badger to the ground, where he struck his head on a rock and lay unconscious as the elephant continued to evacuate his bowels on top of him," said flabbergasted LAPD police detective Bruce Reisfeldt. "With no one there to help him, he laid under all that dung for at least two hours before a watchman came along, and during that time he suffocated.

It seems to be just one of those freak accidents that happen sometimes. A billion-to-one shot, at least."

The heartbreaking tale of constipation and tragedy began one June 21, 2003 when the conscientious zookeeper noticed that his prize, 8,000-pound African elephant didn't seem to be producing his usual poop aplenty.

"Badger had been concerned for several days because he knew that severe constipation could kill an elephant," recalled assistant zookeeper Eric Curtis. "He told me he was going to stay late that night to treat Baku with laxatives and possibly give him an enema. I offered to help, but he sent me on home, saying he had everything under control."

But two hours later, a horrified night watchman found Badger lying lifeless under a mound of manure, his body visible only from the knees down.

"I had never really thought about it before," Detective Reisfeldt said. "But obviously, giving an elephant an enema can be a very dangerous activity, and not something that should be attempted alone."

The catfish were so large that one of the divers was sucked into the giant bottom-feeders mouth, only to be spat out.

When animals are invited into our world, we can control them: they are our pets, a form of domesticated livestock if you will. We keep them in cages, thinking they can't hurt us...wrong! Even mice have been known to upset the best laid plans of men. There is only one clear division between parts of the planet inhabited by man and the part that form the domains of lethal lurkers: we stay in our world; they stay in theirs.

Family Pet

A couple in New Jersey gave the staff of an animal rescue centre in the city great cause for concern when they rang to say that they felt they could no longer look after their 13-year-old pet, "Mitsie". The animal rescuers, who are often called upon to deal with such cases, requested that the couple bring the pet in to the centre, and they would try to find a new home for it. The couple refused, but gave their address. So the rescuers climbed into a van and drove over to the couple's house in order to pick up the unwanted pet. Despite frosty looks all round, they were shown in and taken to the room where the pet was being kept, only to discover that "Mitsie" was in fact a crocodile.

The couple appeared to have no idea that the crocodile was dangerous, and even allowed it to sleep in the same room as them.

Helpful Passerby's

A woman got in her car for a nice relaxing drive in the countryside, but before long she felt something tickling her ankle. She looked down, and of all things, she saw a snake sticking out of the bottom of her pants leg.

Terrified by the snake, which was creeping rapidly up her leg, the woman pulled the car over, leaped out and began to kick in an effort to dislodge the snake. However, the snake crept further up her pant leg, so she dropped to the ground and rolled around, hoping the snake would slither out.

A man driving by saw her contortions and though, "Oh, my God! That poor woman is having a seizure!"

So he stopped his car and ran over to help her.

Another man driving by saw the first man bent over the kicking, screaming woman and thought, "Oh, my God! That guy's attacking her!"

He stopped his car, ran over and punched the first man in the face.

Did You Know? *Skin Divers, while cleaning out the intake to the power plant, had to be rescued from the murky depths by EMS crews. Found floating and unconscious, one of divers was in a coma for several days. It was reported that the catfish were so large that one of the divers was sucked into the giant bottom-feeders mouth, only to be spat out.*

Once A Snake, Always A Snake!

In the middle of winter, a young girl found a snake almost frozen to death.

So the girl said cutely, "Don't bite me Mr. Snake", then put the snake in her jacket to keep it warm and she continued on her walk. Suddenly, she felt a sharp pain in her side, the snake dropped out and began to slither away.

The girl yelled, "Why would you do that to me? I took care of you!"

To her astonishment the snake simply replied, "You knew what I was when you found me."

Snake In The Couch

A couple in Phoenix, Arizona had a lot of potted plants, and during a recent cold spell, the wife brought them indoors to protect them from a possible freeze. It turned out that a little green garden grass snake was hidden in one of the plants and when it warmed up, it slithered out. When the wife spotted it slither under the sofa she let out a blood-curdling scream. The husband, who was taking a shower, ran out into the living room naked to see what the problem was. She told him there was a snake under the sofa. He got down on his hands and knees to look for it. About that time the family dog came and cold-nosed him on the leg. He thought the snake had bitten him and he fainted. His wife thought he'd had a heart attack, so she called an ambulance. The attendants rushed in and loaded him on the stretcher and started carrying him out.

At which time the snake came out from under the sofa and the Emergency Medical Technician saw it, and surprised he dropped his end of the stretcher. That's when the man broke his leg. The wife still had the problem of the snake in the house, so she called on a neighbor man. He volunteered to capture the snake, and armed himself with a rolled-up newspaper and began poking under the couch. After a while, he decided it was probably gone and told the woman, who sat down on the sofa in relief. But in relaxing, her hand dangled in between the cushions, where she felt the snake wiggling around. She screamed and fainted. The snake rushed back under the sofa, and the neighbor man, seeing her lying there passed out tried to use CPR to revive her.

The neighbor's wife, who had just returned from shopping at the grocery store, saw her husband's mouth on the woman's mouth and slammed her husband in the back of the head with a bag of canned goods, knocking him out and cutting his scalp to a point where it would need stitches. The noise woke the woman from her dead faint and saw her neighbor lying on the floor with his wife bending over him, so she assumed he had been bitten by the snake. She went to the kitchen, brought back a small bottle of whiskey, and began pouring it down the man's throat, just in time for the police to arrive.

Law enforcement saw the unconscious man, smelled the whiskey, and assumed that a drunken fight had occurred. They were about to arrest all invloved, when the two women explained how it all happened over a little green snake. They called an ambulance, which took away the neighbor and his sobbing wife. Just then the little snake crawled out from under the couch. One of the policemen drew his gun and fired at it. But he missed the snake and hit the leg of the end table that was on one side of the sofa. The table fell over and the lamp on it shattered. The bulb broke causing a fire in the drapes. The other policeman tried to beat out the flames and fell through the window into the yard on top of the family dog. Startled, the dog jumped up and raced out into the street, where an oncoming car swerved to avoid it and smashed into the parked police car and set it on fire. Meanwhile the burning drapes had spread to the walls and the entire house was consumed by flames.

Neighbors called the fire department. The arriving fire truck started raising its ladder as they were halfway down the street. The rising ladder tore out the overhead wires and put out the electricity and disconnected the telephones in a ten-square radius of south Phoenix.

Time passed, and both men were eventually discharged from the hospital, the house was rebuilt, the police acquired a new car, and all was right with the world. However, about a year later they were watching TV and the weatherman announced a cold snap for that night. The husband asked his wife if she thought they should bring in their plants for the night. Naturally, she shot him.

chaptersix

"Rufus is pimping for three girls. If the price is $65 for each trick, how many tricks will each girl have to turn so Rufus can pay for his $800-per-day crack habit?"

-- The City of Los Angeles High School Math Proficiency Exam

higherlearning

For many of us college is our first experience living away from home so you become susceptible to the hallowed halls of urban legendry. College life is also your first encounter with tales of pranks and debauchery — some true, some not.

These tales play on the unease and fear of life in a strange new land among unfamiliar surroundings.

Students often deal with university administrators and their bewildering array of rules and regulations, and with instructors -- all of them at times frustratingly arbituary and uncaring to whom you may be nothing more than names on a roll sheet. And, of course, students are always trying to come up with new and innovating ways of cheating and outsmarting their instructors -- and sometimes vice-versa.

. . . .

"If those are his quizzies, I'd hate to see his testes."

In the devious quest to achieve good grades, students of all generations have devised inventive ways of cheating, such as switching test booklets, obtaining advance copies of examinations, and answering questions they aren't asked. However, instructors have devised equally inventive means of tormenting the unprepared student, such as including pop quizzes, trick questions, and clever means of uncovering cheaters. The struggle continues between the two sides, saved for those unfortunate few for whom the pressures of exam time are too much to endure.

"A quiz? Why, I'd climb through that transom over the door before I'd give a quiz tomorrow."

Students at Mississippi University asked the oft-repeated query at the end of their professors lecture, whether he planned to give a quiz the next day.

The professor answered nonchalantly, "A quiz? Why, I'd climb through that transom over the door before I'd give a quiz tomorrow."

A sigh of relief passed through the classroom. But the next day, after the class had assembled, there was a sudden clamor outside the door. The transom began to creak open, and to the utter amazement of the students, in climbed their professor — grinning happily and clutching a three-page quiz in his hand.

A Simple Answer

A student protested when his answer was marked wrong on a physics test.

In answer to the question, "How could you measure the height of a tall building, using a barometer?" He was expected to explain that the barometric pressures at the top and the bottom of the building are different, and by calculating, he could determine the building's height.

Instead, he answered, "I would tie the barometer to a string, lower it to the ground and measure the length of the string."

His instructor admitted that the answer was technically correct but did not demonstrate a knowledge of physics.

The student then rattled off a whole series of answers involving physics: I would drop the barometer and time its fall -- I would make a pendulum and time its frequency at the top and the bottom of the building -- I would walk down the stairs marking "barometer units" on the wall.

But not one answer used the principle in question.

When the instructor finally demanded the "simplest" answer to the question, the student replied, "I would go to the building superintendent and offer him a brand-new barometer if he will tell me the height of the building!"

A Total Disregard For Christian Virtue

Students studying for their Theology degree arrived at their final examination to find a note on the door saying that the examination would take place in a room on the other side of the campus. The students all rushed to the other room where they encountered a bedraggled fellow blocking the doorway begging for change. All the students except one barged by the man and took their seats. The one student chatted to the beggar and then gave him five dollars, before taking his seat. After the exam was over, the students discussed the questions they had been asked, and all seemed quite satisfied that they had passed, but when they received the results, they were shocked to discover that all but one of them had failed. Confronting their professor, the students were told that they failed because they had ignored the beggar at the door, and in doing so, confirmed their disregard for Christian virtue. The one student who had demonstrated Christian charity became a very popular priest. The others apparently became politicians and lawyers.

"Do you know who I am?"

An aging teacher was overseeing a chemistry examination one afternoon. When the allotted two hours was up, he told the students to put down their pens as he went down the aisles collecting their papers.

When he came to one pupil, the teacher stated, "I won't be collecting your paper because I saw you cheating."

He was about to proceed when the pupil stood up and exclaimed haughtily, "Cheating? Do you know who I am?"

The teacher, having dealt with many an arrogant pupil in his day, responded disdainfully, "No, young man, I do not, nor does it bear any consequence."

The pupil said smiling, "Oh, it does. If you don't know who I am..." and without finishing the sentence, he knocked all the papers out of the teachers hand onto the middle of the floor, then proceeded to stuff his paper in the pile, and ran out of the classroom.

"God gets and A; you get an F."

My co-workers husband is a teacher, and he loves giving lectures, but hated marking papers. He was always afraid he would have to fail someone. The head of his department, when told of his worries, was quite unsympathetic. He said failing people was his job — if they deserved it.

Of course, if the student made it easy, that was different.

A student, despairing of a certain question, stared at his blank examination booklet and finally wrote, "God only know!"

The paper came back with the notation: "God gets and A; you get an F."

Good Excuse

Two students at NYU were so confident about their psychology final examination the following Monday, that they decided to let loose and party all weekend with the intention of doing some last-minute revisions on the Sunday. However, their night out turned into a drinking marathon and they woke up Monday morning with stinking hangovers. In no mood to sit through an exam, they phoned the Dean of the University and told him that their car had a flat tire and they wouldn't be able to make it back in time. The Dean agreed to let them take the exam the next day. Relieved, they studied that night and felt confident they would pass the exam. They arrived at the college and the Dean put them in separate rooms, gave each student a surprisingly slim test booklet and told them to begin.

The first and only question in the booklet, was "Which tire?"

Needless to say, both students failed the exam and had to retake the year.

symphony written by his professor while still a grad student. He then copied it backwards, note for note and turned it in. It was returned to him with the comment, "Why did you turn in Beethoven's Fourth?"

Got The Name Right

A student working his way through college was afraid that he would not have enough time outside of work to adequately prepare for an upcoming exam. He began taking amphetamines in order to stay awake and study throughout the day while continuing to work at night. A few weeks later, he sat for his exam and left the room confident that he had done extremely well. The next day, he was summoned to the instructor's office and asked to explain why he handed in an exam consisting of nothing but sheets of paper covered with his own name.

I Blue The Exam

A student at an East Coast university entered the room for a final exam. He asked the professor for two blue books, and when the test ended, the blue books were collected. He handed in only one. In it, he had written a note on the first page and left the rest of the book blank. The note said, "Dear Mom, Just finished my Psych 101 final and wanted to tell you that I love you."

The student took the second blue book home, which was blank. There, with the help of his textbooks and class notes, he finished the exam, and promptly mailed it to his mother. When his professor called him about the mix-up, the student acted surprised and upset about the events. He then got the other blue book back from his mother, turned it in to the professor, and received an A on the exam.

It's All In The Legs!

A student's biology professor announced there would be an exam next week on birds.

"You will have to know everything about every type of bird there is," he said.

The student spent the week studying beaks, wings, and feathers of dozens of bird species.

On the day of the exam, the professor had a table with five paper bags on it. Under each bag was a model of a bird. The professor lifted the first bag to reveal only the legs, and told the class to write down the type of bird. The students groaned, because their was no way they could identify the type of bird using their feet.

When the professor got to the third bag, one of the students stood up, walked up to the table, threw her crumpled test paper onto the professors desk, and said, "This is the most ridiculous test I have ever seen, and you sir, are an idiot!"

The professor replied, "Just hold it right there, what is your name?"

The student raised her dress to the knees and said, "You tell me!"

Kings Of Isreal

The head of the department devoted to the study of comparative religions at Harvard University invariably asked the same question on every final examination: "Who, in chronological order, were the Kings of Israel?"

Students came to count on this procedure as a sacred institution and prepared accordingly. Some crabby misanthrope tattled, and one precedent-shattering spring, the professor confounded his class by changing the question to: "Who were the major prophets and who were the minor prophets?"

The class sat dumbfounded and all but the one member slunk out of the room without writing a word. The sole survivor scribbled furiously and deposited his paper with the air of a conqueror.

"Far be it from me," he had written, "to distinguish between these revered gentlemen, but it occurred to me that you might like to have a chronological list of the Kings of Israel."

Literally Following Instructions

Students ready to write their English GCSE were given three pieces of writing, each with a set of questions attached, and were asked to "Choose one of the three exercises below".

All except one student were sweating out the pages and pages of answers, instead, he simply wrote "I choose number two", and did nothing for the rest of the exam.

Since he had, technically, fulfilled the requirements of the paper, he had to be given full marks. Since then all GCSE's have the instruction "Choose and complete one of the following".

Literature You Eat Like A Meal

A young man studying for his school exams got into the habit of nibbling bits of paper while studying. He became so engrossed in this habit that he began to consume whole pages, and before long whole books. His habit turned to obsession, and as a student of Literature, he started choosing which books to eat. He found that the pages of Shakespearean plays were much tastier than Thomas Hardy novels, and ate his way through all his works from "The Tempest" to "Hamlet". However, when he discovered that the older the edition the better the taste, he landed himself in trouble. One day, the police were called into a rare book store where the owner discovered the hapless boy nibbling on a first edition copy of "Macbeth". The boy is currently in a psychiatric institution where they are trying to wean him off Shakespeare and on to modern poetry, such as Philip Larkin, in a vain hope that he will soon tire of the habit.

Did You Know? *There was a tough professor who always gave students painful quizzes, which he irritatingly called his "little quizzies." After the third or so ordeal with these "quizzies," a coed wrote a note to a fellow classmate that said, "If those are his quizzies, I'd hate to see his testes."*

Religion, Royalty, Sex, and Mystery

A creative writing professor coldly announced to his class he wanted a concise essay containing the following elements: Religion, Royalty, Sex, and Mystery.

It'll take quite some time to write an essay of this nature and smoothly incorporate all subjects, so please begin."he said.

About fifteen minutes later, a boy raised his hand and announced that he was finished.

The startled professor said, "I don't see how you can be finished with an essay of that nature in that short a time."

"Well, I have," said the smiling student.

"If you think so," replied the professor, "Read it aloud."

The student stood up and proudly read, "My God!" said the queen, "I'm pregnant. I wonder whose it is?"

Rip Off

A student stopped by the office of one of his professors to ask a question and found that the professor had stepped out for a moment, leaving an unguarded stack of the next day's final examinations on his desk. The student quickly stole one of the exams and disappeared. However, before issuing the exam, the professor counted them and noticed that one was missing, so he cut a half-inch off the bottom of every exam prior to distributing them to the class, then failed the student who turned in a test paper longer than the rest.

The LA Math Quiz

In Los Angeles, California, the LA school district barred a Grade 8 instructor from teaching for a year after she distributed a math quiz that used pimps and cocaine trafficking to illustrate questions of arithmetic.

The 10-question quiz asked how much Willie would make for stealing a number of luxury cars, the distance a thief could travel on a stolen skateboard before he gets "whacked," and how many "tricks" a day three prostitutes must turn to support their pimp's cocaine habit.

The School District suspended the veteran teacher on June 5, two days after irate parents brought the "joke" test to the district's attention. This week the district disciplined her further by assigning her to non-classroom teaching until June, 2005. The teacher has not been identified.

"I don't know where she got the idea to give this to kids. We were outraged," one student's father, who asked not to be identified, told The LA Times. The father saw the Math Proficiency Exam" after his young son brought his copy home from school.

The official City of Los Angeles High School Math Proficiency Exam:

1. Johnny has an AK-47 with an 80-round clip. If he misses 6 out of 10 shots and shoots 13 times at each drive-by shooting, how many drive-by shootings can he attempt before he has to reload?

2. Jose has 2 ounces of cocaine and he sells an 8-ball to Jackson for $320 and 2 grams to Billy for $85 per gram. What is the street value of the balance of the cocaine if he doesn't cut it?

3. Rufus is pimping for three girls. If the price is $65 for each trick, how many tricks will each girl have to turn so Rufus can pay for his $800-per-day crack habit?

4. Jarone wants to cut his 1/2 pound of heroin to make 20% more profit. How many ounces of cut will he need?

5. Willie gets $200 for stealing a BMW, $50 for a Chevy, and $100 for a 4X4. If he has stolen 2 BMWs, 3 4X4s, how many Chevies will he have to steal to make $800?

6. Raoul is in prison for 6 years for murder. He got $10,000 for the hit. If his common law wife is spending $100 per month, how much money will be left when he gets out of prison and how many years will he get for killing the bitch that spent his money?

7. If the average spray can covers 22 square feet and the average letter is 3 square feet, how many letters can a tagger spray with 3 cans of paint?

8. Hector knocked up 6 girls in his gang. There are 27 girls in the gang. What percentage of the girls in the gang has Hector knocked up?

9. Thelma can cook dinner for her 16 children for $7.50 per night. She gets $234 a month welfare for each child. If her $325 per month rent goes up 15%, how many more children should she have to keep up with her expenses?

10. Salvador was arrested for dealing crack and his bail was set at $25,000. If he pays a bail bondsman 12% and returns to Mexico, how much money will he lose by jumping bail?

Two For One

A student had to write two essays, but could only tackle one of them, so he wrote what looked like the ending of the first essay at the top of a new page, ruled it off, and then did the second. The instructor, not wanting to admit that he lost half the answer paper, marked him double on the 'second' essay. The student received top marks.

What The Hell?

A thermodynamics professor had written a take home exam for his graduate students. It had one question: "Is hell exothermic or endothermic? Support your answer with a proof."

Most of the students wrote proofs of their beliefs using Boyle's Law or some variant. However, one student, wrote: First, we postulate that if souls exist, then they must have some mass. If they do, then a mole of souls can also have a mass. So, at what rate are souls moving into hell and at what rate are souls leaving? I think that we can safely assume that once a soul gets to hell, it will not leave. Therefore, no souls are leaving.

As for souls entering hell, lets look at the different religions that exist in the world today. Some of these religions state that if you are not a member of their religion, you will go to hell. Since there are more than one of these religions and people do not belong to more than one religion, we can project that all people and all souls go to hell.

With birth and death rates as they are, we can expect the number of souls in hell to increase exponentially.

Now, we look at the rate of change in volume in hell. Boyle's Law states that in order for the temperature and pressure in hell to stay the same, the ratio of the mass of souls and volume needs to stay constant.

So, if hell is expanding at a slower rate than the rate at which souls enter hell, then the temperature and pressure in hell will increase until all hell breaks loose. Of course, if hell is expanding at a rate faster than the increase of souls in hell, than the temperature and pressure will drop until hell freezes over.

It was not revealed what grade the student got.

When Taking Finals In Britain. Do As The Brits

Finals in Britain at most universities are what 80% or more of your degree is based on. Most classes don't have mid-terms like the US. In Britain, you take six courses — three in the autumn, three in the spring — and then at the end of the whole year, do the finals.

A guy was taking his finals with about three hundred other students, and was overcome with frustration and stress. The student sat up in the middle of the exam, stuck a sharpened pencil in each nostril, threw his head back and then slammed it into the desk, thrusting the pencils into his brain. He died pretty instantaneously.

The other students were given credit for their exam. Whatever grade they obtained in other exams was used for their final degree.

"I liked it better with the whale."

It has been a long standing tradition for students to avoid doing their homework, either by making up excuses, not doing it, or by taking lazy shortcuts. This tradition continues to follow you right into college. Not only are institutions of higher learning attended by diligent students eager to put forth their best efforts on academic assignments, but they also house those who seek to succeed by pulling fast ones on their professors -- sometimes they get away with it, and sometimes they don't.

Gets Better Each Time

A professor who was notoriously tough on grading term papers, rarely gave out any grade higher than a "D", finally rewarded one student's effort with a "B-".

The student hung on to this prized paper and sold it to the highest bidder at the end of the term; the buyer submitted it to the same professor during the next term and receives a "B".

The next school year, another student submitted the same paper to the same instructor and received a "B+".

Finally, yet another student submitted the paper for a fourth time and received an "A"; the grade was accompanied by a written comment from the professor, "Ive read this paper four times now, and I like it better each time."

I always felt it richly deserved an 'A'!"

A sophomore student was asked to write an essay about Shakespeare's Hamlet. He was gratified to receive an 'A' for his effort, but then was summoned to his professor's inner sanctum.

"Son," began the professor, "you probably are not aware of the fact that I am a fraternity brother of yours, and spent my undergraduate days in the very chapter house you live in now. What's more, we used to keep a pile of old student essays on hand for consultation just as you do today. You have had the bad luck to copy word for word a paper on Hamlet that I happened to write myself."

"Now," continued the professor, "I suppose you're wondering why I gave you an 'A' on it. When I turned in the paper, the crusty professor I had only marked it `B', and I always felt it richly deserved an 'A'!"

"I liked it better with the whale."

A student in a marine biology class turned in a term paper which included a lavishly-drawn illustration of a whale and received an A. The next year a different student copied the paper, submitted it, and also received an A. However, the third student to hand in the same paper neglected to include the drawing of the whale and received only a B from the professor and a written comment, "I liked it better with the whale."

Did You Know? *A psychology student in Los Angeles rented out her spare room to a carpenter in order to nag him constantly and study his reactions. After weeks of needling, he snapped and beat her with an ax leaving her mentally retarded.*

Labour Of Love, But Your The Only One Who Cares

Those of you who have labored to obtain your Ph.D.s must sometimes wonder if anyone in the world can possibly be interested in the learned dissertation over which you have sweated, even though it is carefully filed in the library of the institution at which the degree was earned.

A scholar who, years ago, produced a dissertation that was loudly hailed as the best written and most valuable in a generation. A copy was reverently placed in the library files and the scholar, as an experiment, placed a crisp $50 bill among its pages. Every year he returned to the library and took down the dissertation, and every year, the crisp $50 fell open to the stuffed page untouched.

Problem Solved

A student arrived late to math class and found two problems written on the chalkboard. Assuming they were homework problems, he jotted them down in his notebook and worked on the equations over the next few days before turning his solutions in to the instructor. Several weeks passed, and the professor turned up at the student's door with the student's work. He informed the student that his work was written up for publication. The two problems were not a homework assignment; they were problems previously thought to be unsolvable which the instructor had used as examples in his lecture that day.

The Wind Took My Homework

A woman studying for her masters degree in History at Cambridge University had finally completed her thesis. It ran hundreds of pages and involved many months of research, so the woman thought it would be a good idea to photocopy everything. She packed her thesis into a box, put the box on the backseat of her car and drove to the college where the photocopier was. However, the woman forgot to close the back window, and the box lid blew off and years of work was blown out the window as she drove. It took three weeks for the woman to recover most of the pages, but by then, she missed her deadline and failed the course.

"I request that you bring me Cakes and Ale."

The rules and regulations administration puts in the students way are often arcane. It's tough enough for the average student to gain admission to the educational institution of their choice, to finance that education, and pass all their classes and graduate without having to deal with all the who, what, where, when and whys. It's only fair that the student poke fun at academic bureaucracy by simply making up rules themselves.

A Pressing Matter

A principal of a small middle school had a problem with a few of the older girls starting to use lipstick. When applying it in the bathroom they would then press their lips to the mirror and leave lip prints.

Before it got out of hand he thought of a way to stop it. He gathered all the girls together that wore lipstick and told them he wanted to meet with them in the ladies room at 2pm. They gathered at 2pm and found the principal and the school custodian waiting for them.

The principal explained that it was becoming a problem for the custodian to clean the mirror every night. He said he felt the ladies did not fully understand just how much of a problem it was and he wanted them to witness just how hard it was to clean.

The custodian then demonstrated, by taking a long brush on a handle out of a box, dipping the brush in the nearest toilet, moving to the mirror and proceeded to remove the lipstick.

That was the last day the girls pressed their lips on the mirror.

Automated Message

The Board of Education has voted to record a standard message on all High School telephone answering systems through Canada. This came about because they implemented a policy requiring students and parents to be responsible for their children's absences and missing homework. The school and teachers are being sued by parents who want their children's failing grades changed to passing grades even though those children were absent 15-30 times during the semester and did not complete enough school work to pass their classes. This was voted unanimously by the Board of Education as the actual answering machine message for all High Schools:

"Hello! You have reached the automated answering service of your school. In order to assist you in connecting the right staff member, please listen to all your options before making a selection":

To lie about why your child is absent, press 1

To make excuses for why your child did not do his/her work, press 2

To complain about what we do, press 3

To swear at staff members, press 4

To ask why you didn't get information that was already enclosed in your newsletter and several flyers mailed to you, press 5

If you want us to raise your child, press 6

To request another teacher for the third time this year, press 7

To complain about bus transportation, press 8

To complain about school lunches, press 9

To complain about bus transportation, press 8

If you realize this is the real world and your child must be accountable and responsible for his/her own behavior, class work, homework, and that it's not the teachers' fault for your children's lack of effort . . . hang up and have a nice day!"

Breast Stroke 101

A young lady from a wealthy home went away to university. Unfortunately while at university she drowned. So the girls wealthy father donated a grant to the school which provided all kinds of student activity funds, including chocolate ice cream served every lunch hour, the daughter's favorite desert. This grant came with one string attached. At the behest of the wealthy benefactor, the university had to implement mandatory swim tests. Meaning all students had to pass a swim test before graduation. So if students blew off their swim test, they did not graduate.

Class Is In Play

A professor at Sarah Lawrence College became so enamored at giving outside lectures that he decided to tape his weekly remarks to his seminar group. When he unexpectedly returned early because of a canceled engagement, he went right to his classroom to see how his students were getting along. As he opened the door, he heard his own voice coming out of the tape recorder — and in the students' places were 12 other tape recorders.

Dead Roomate Priviledges

Many universities offer some sort of bereavement consideration under exceptional circumstances. In the United States colleges and universities have a policy awarding a 4.0 average to a student whose roommate dies.

The type of death required to qualify a student for a 4.0 average varies. It is said that a roommate's murder, accidental death, violent death, slow drawn-out death (such as cancer), or death from any cause is covered by the regulation. Murdering one's own roommate does not qualify. But their are extra provisions, such as "death must occur in the room or with the roommate" or "death must occur during the last six weeks of term." A student who does not witness his roommate's death receives only a 3.4 average; survivors each receive a 3.5 average if the deceased had more than one roommate.

The "reward" received by the surviving roommate is not always a 4.0 average. Some universities award only a 3.0 average, or an alternate "prize" such as first choice in the next dormitory "room draw", or a dead roommate entitles one to free tuition that year.

Full Grown Student

A well-known public school in England came under investigation after the headmaster allegedly assaulted a school inspector. Several students had been caught smoking, and had been sent to the headmaster's office for punishment. While they were waiting outside, a school inspector paid an unannounced visit and waited for the headmaster at the end of the line of boys. The headmaster eventually emerged from his office, admonished each pupil in turn for smoking, and gave each of them a whack with his cane. However, when the headmaster came to the school inspector he obviously wasn't concentrating because, despite the man's moustache, he assumed that he was just an unusually tall pupil. Before the man could protest, he thrashed him three times on the hand with the cane.

"I am the John Kallam who wrote the textbook you're using."

After graduating with a BA in criminology, John Kallum entered the US Army. He served for 20 years beginning in the late 1930s. He was an investigator during the Nuremberg trials of Nazi war criminals, and stayed in Germany for many years organizing civilian police forces in the post-war era. He also wrote numerous books on criminal justice. He retired from military service in the late 1950s at the rank of full colonel.

Returning to California, he began teaching criminology at Fresno, California State University. His work was well respected, but after about ten years of service, he was called to see the president of the college. He was informed that he could no longer teach with just a bachelor's degree. Times were changing, he was told, and the school demanded that faculty members hold a graduate degree. Merely having 20 years of distinguished experience was no longer considered sufficient qualification to teach. It was explained that all new faculty were being required to hold a doctorate, and the school was actually doing him a favor by letting him keep his job by getting 'only' a master's degree. So John enrolled in a summer program at an out of state college. Three months of intensive seminars and nine months of home study would get him his masters. On the first day of class, the instructor was taking roll, but stopped when he read John's name.

"Are you related to the John Kallam who wrote the textbook we'll be using?" he asked.

"I *am* the John Kallam who wrote the textbook you're using," came the dry response.

"I request that you bring me Cakes and Ale."

At Cambridge University, during an examination, a bright young student popped up and asked his proctor to bring him Cakes and Ale.

"I beg your pardon? said the proctor.

117

"Sir," replied the student. "I request that you bring me Cakes and Ale."

"Sorry, no," the proctor said.

"Sir, I really must insist," the student exclaimed, "I request and require that you bring me Cakes and Ale."

At this point, the student produced a copy of the four hundred year old Laws of Cambridge, written in Latin and still nominally in effect, he pointed to the section which read, rough translation from the Latin, "Gentlemen sitting examinations may request and require Cakes and Ale."

Pepsi and hamburgers were judged the modern equivalent, and the student sat there, writing his examination and happily slurping away. Three weeks later the student was fined five pounds for not wearing a sword to the examination.

Mandatory Wait Times

All colleges have regulations specifying how long students must wait if an instructor fails to appear, and these wait times vary depending upon the academic rank of the instructor. The varying wait times are generally between 10 and 20 minutes, and are usually assigned according to the rank of the instructor. The shortest wait times are for graduate assistants and the longest wait times are for tenured, doctorate-holding professors. Mandatory wait times for classes led by instructors with other academic rankings, such as, non-tenured faculty, instructors with Master's degrees, and visiting professors, fall somewhere in between the two.

The Best Employee I Never Knew We Had

A school librarian was annoyed when she didn't receive her monthly salary, and contacted the office responsible. However, not only was there no employee record of her on the payroll system, the clerk also told her he couldn't find any record or even barest mention of her anywhere on file.

She protested that she had worked at the same library for over ten years, but the clerk just replied, "Sorry, we have no record of you or your employment," and hung up.

Thinking this was a temporary error, the librarian borrowed money from a friend and looked forward to being paid two months' wages at the end of the next month. When the next month came, and she still had not received any wages, the librarian was furious, so she phoned the office again, but the clerk just repeated what he had told her the previous month and hung up. Flabbergasted, the librarian went to the office in person to sort it out once and for all.

She shouted at the clerk, "Here I am. I exist. I've been working at this Library for over ten years. Here is my contract. I want my money!"

Undaunted, the clerk replied, "I'm sorry. We've found your file now."

Pointing to a rather short woman at the back, the clerk continued, "Our new assistant couldn't reach her desk, so she took a pile of files to sit on and one of them was yours."

Did You Know? *Philosophy courses are famous for asking difficult questions such as, "If you took a boat apart and rebuilt it again of the same material, would it still be the same boat?", but at least that allows room for argument. Imagine the poor students in the hellish philosophy exam where the one and only question was, "Why?", to which the only correct answer was, "Because".*

Observation in diagnosis

Medical students necessarily find themselves handling human organs, bodily fluids, skeletons, detached limbs, and cadavers, which makes them a perfect target for a plethora of grotesque medical school legends.

Di-hypnosis Murder

A group of Birmingham students were discussing the question of hypnosis. They decided to try an experiment and invited into the lecture room a laboratory assistant who was always causing them problems and getting them into trouble.

They explained to him that no one could be made to do anything under hypnosis that they would not do when fully awake. They said that a student had been hypnotized, told to execute someone and they wanted the laboratory assistant to help them prove the student would not go through with it.

They asked the assistant to kneel down with his head bent as if ready to have his head chopped off. The 'so-called hypnotised' student was then brought in and with a suitable build-up he gently dropped a wet towel across the back of the victim's neck. Unfortunately, the assistant was of a nervous disposition and the shock brought on a heart attack which killed him.

Limb-ited Knowledge of Right and Wrong.

A group of medical students at Harvard University hit upon a novel prank they could play. They managed to get hold of an arm of a cadaver and then drove off towards a bridge in the harbour. Just before they reached the toll booth over the bridge, the driver put the dead arm through the sleeve of his jacket and placed several coins in its hand. The student drove up to the toll booth and extended the arm. The poor man behind the toll booth was horrified when the car drove off, leaving him holding the limb. Unfortunately for the students, fingerprints were taken from the hand of the arm, which traced back to the cadaver at the university and the group of students were identified. The students were not expelled, but their professor failed them in anatomy because it seemed they had used a right arm instead of a left arm.

Positive Reinforcement

A psychology class had been learning about the effects of positive reinforcement on test subjects, meaning: people who are told they are doing well, consequently do well. So the students decided to try an experiment on their teacher. One half of the class smiled appreciatively at everything he said and managed to look interested throughout the entire class, while the other half of the class pretended to ignore the lesson and look bored. Within a few minutes, the teacher began to focus all of his attention on the enthusiastic group while ignoring the other half of the class. Later that day the students wrote up their observations and were rewarded with top marks.

Urine Test

A professor at a medical school was trying to convey the importance of using the sense of taste during the process of diagnosis. To demonstrate his point he conducted a diabetes test. The professor asked some of his students to provide urine samples for the test. When the students brought back the flasks of their urine, the lecturer dipped a finger into a sample and then licked it, telling his students that he could determine the sugar content by the taste. He then told the students to repeat the same test themselves. Although most of them were feeling a bit ill from the suggestion, they all feared failure if they refused to go along with the request. After the students performed the test, with looks of disgust on their faces, the professor moved on to reveal the importance of observation in diagnosis. He showed them that he had been dipping his 'index finger' in the urine samples before licking his 'middle finger'. At which point, several students ran to the classroom windows and emptied their stomachs.

Teachers Can Be Tough, I Think They Need To Relax-ative!

Every institution of higher learning has its own rich lore of legendary pranks --some true, some not. Some pranks are so infamous that they claimed to have taken place at dozens of different colleges and universities throughout the world. Here is but a small sampling of such pranks.

Animal House

A registrar, as a joke, filled an entire class with students whose last names were all animal names, such as Byrd, Lyon, Finch."

A professor came to me yesterday," said the registrar, "trying to get one of the students, a young man named Foxx."

"Why did he do that?' asked the librarian.

"Because he wants his classroom in all species of the planet, and likes them to have answerable names. He has a Lemming, a Byrd, a Bare, a Lyon, a Panda and even a Zebra, and he has longed for a foxx."

Feeding Pattern

One summer, a science student at a University in London woke up every day at dawn before anyone else was up, and went to the "Arsenal" football grounds. He always wore a black top and black shorts and he would scatter birdseed while walking up and down the field for about 20 minutes, finishing his

visit with a sharp blast from a football whistle.

In August, it was time for the first football game of the season and "Arsenal" were playing "Chelsea". The referee tossed a coin and "Arsenal" decided to kick off. However, when the referee blew his whistle, thousands of birds suddenly descended onto the field like a scene out of Alfred Hitchcock's "The Birds". The game was postponed for an hour as referee's ran around trying to clear the field of the birds.

The science student graduated on the basis of his study: *the feeding patterns of the common sparrow.*

Road Leading To Trouble

Roadwork on a highway near UCLA inspired some students to create a little mischief. They telephoned the police and claimed that some students had dressed up as road workers and were not only causing tremendous traffic disruption, but were actually digging up the road. The police said they would come out to investigate. The students then went out to the road workers and told them that some students had dressed up as policemen and were going to try to remove them as a joke. The students assured the workers that they could say or do anything to these bogus officers. The road workers said they were looking forward to a little fun. So were the students.

Teachers Can Be Tough, I Think They Need To Relax-ative

Three students were caught cutting class by their teacher, and were given a whole term's detention for their misdemeanour. Thinking the punishment was to extreme, the kids decided to exact revenge on the teacher. Early one morning, before school started, the students snuck into the teacher's staff room and emptied an entire packet of Exlax into the coffee jar. Later that afternoon, half of the school's teachers were taken to the hospital with severe abdominal pains. It seems that the children had misread the instructions on the box and gave the teachers 100 times the recommended dose.

You'll Be Happy To Know...

It has been three months since my friends sister left for college. She had been remised in writing and was very sorry for her thoughtlessness in not having written before. So she wrote a letter to her family bringing them up to date. She wrote:

Before you read on, please sit down. You are not to read any further unless you are sitting down, okay.

Well then, I am getting along pretty well now. The skull fracture and the concussion I got when I jumped out of the window of my dormitory after it caught fire are pretty well healed. I only spent two weeks in the hospital and I can almost see normally. I only get headaches once a day now.

Fortunately, the fire in the dormitory and my jump was witnessed by an attendant at the gas station near the dorm, and he was the one who called the Fire Department and the ambulance. He also visited me at the hospital and since I had nowhere to live because of the dormitory fire, he was kind enough to invite me to share his apartment with him. It's really a basement room, but it's kind of cute. He is a very fine boy and we have fallen deeply in love and are planning to get married. We haven't set the exact date yet, but it will be before my pregnancy begins to show.

I know how much you are looking forward to being grandparents and I know you will welcome the baby and give it the same love and devotion and tender care you gave me when I was a child. The reason for the delay in our marriage is that my boyfriend has some minor infection which prevents us from passing our premarital blood tests and I carelessly caught it from him. This will soon clear up with the penicillin injections I am now taking daily.

I know you will welcome him into the family with open arms. He is kind and although not well educated, he is ambitious, and although he is of a different race and religion than ours, I know that your oft-expressed tolerance will not permit you to be bothered by the fact that his skin color is somewhat darker than ours. I am sure you will love him as I do. His family background is good too, I am told his father is an important gunbearer in Iraq, from which he comes.

Now that I have brought you up to date, I want to tell you there was no dormitory fire; I did not have a concussion or a skull fracture; I was not in the hospital; I am not pregnant; I am not engaged. I do not have syphillis, and there is no terrorist in my life. However, I am getting a D in sociology and an F in science; and I wanted you to see these marks in proper perspective. Your loving daughter, Brenda.

"The next plane doesn't leave until tomorrow afternoon."

College is often our first experience in living away from home so the opportunity for supremely embarrassing ourselves under such circumstances are tremendous. Anything is bound to happen when sharing quarters with others our own age under relatively little supervision -- as the following tales dictate.

It won't kill you, but it will prevent worms

Many years ago some friends decided to have the party to end all parties. The five students sharing a house at the time decided they would move most of the furniture out, take up all the carpets, contact every DJ they knew, and turn the whole event into a night to remember. By midnight the house was shaking. The hallway became so packed that the only way to get up or down the stairs was to go outside, climb on to the kitchen roof and go in through the bathroom window. By 4am there were bodies everywhere, and people were starting to burn out. By 5am there were just a few brave souls left, and everyone started looking for somewhere to crash, well, everyone except one lonely girl in a corner. Nobody knew who she was, and the students certainly hadn't invited her, but she seemed determined to kill herself. She sat there rather forlornly taking pill after pill from a bottle she found in the bathroom. Everybody felt sorry for her, because no one had the heart to tell her that she was trying to commit suicide by taking the dog's worming tablets.

Leaving So Soon?

Annoyed by the professor of anatomy who told racy and sexist stories during class, a group of coed females decided that the next time he started to tell a joke, they would all rise and leave the room in protest.

However, the professor got wind of their scheme just before class the following day, so halfway through the lecture, he began. "They say there is quite a shortage of prostitutes in Mexico . . ."

The girls looked at one another, arose, and started for the door.

"Young ladies," said the professor, "the next plane doesn't leave until tomorrow afternoon."

Spontaneous Combustion

A young man attending UCLA shared a house off campus with three other students. They were all getting ready to go to the first big party of the year, and the young man, rushing around like a maniac, was refilling his lighter with gas when a freak spark caused it to explode in his face. Although he wasn't harmed, the ball of fire scorched his hair, so he ran to the bathroom to douse it with water. The older students had got impatient waiting for their friend, so they went up to his room to hurry him along. When they entered, all they saw was a cloud of smoke and a tuft of burnt hair on the floor. They all jumped to the conclusion that their friend had spontaneously combusted. Meanwhile, the young man had washed his hair, and when he didn't see his roomates waiting downstairs, he figured they had left without him and ran out the door after them. His roomates stayed in to mourn their friend's mysterious combustion. The young man returned later that night, very much alive and drunkenly merry.

Needless to say, when he said, "Wow, what a great party. What happened to you guys?" they lynched him.

chapterseven

"May the force be with you."

--Obi Wan Kenobi; Jedi Knight

holycrap

Urban legends and religion share a familiar aspect. Like urban legends, religion uses narratives such as parables and fables to teach moral attitudes and religious principals in a form easy to assimilate and remember. Urban legends are also narratives often used to reinforce societal morals and beliefs. Since a large chunk of our moral code derives from religion, it frequently intersects with the world of urban legendry.

Many religious folks want you to believe they are very nice and wholesome. So they use words like 'Cripes' — 'For Cripes sake.' Who would that be; Jesus Cripes? The son of 'Gosh' of the church of 'Holy Moly'? These following stories are not meant to make fun, but merely to inform. You think I wanna burn in 'Heck'?

. . . .

"Arrived safely, but it sure is hot down here."

"Tis better to reign in hell, than serve in heaven." says the old adage.

So why do people fear going to hell? It's always warm, there's work for everybody, and hell could care less about your credit rating...this is bad how?

If there is a Hell, scientists have yet to discover it. Here are a small sampling of enthralling legends that have been spun off actual events?

Evil Incarnate

A few minutes before a church service in Norfolk, Virginia began, the townspeople reported they were sitting in their pews and talking when suddenly, Satan appeared at the front of the church.

Everyone started screaming and running for the front entrance, trampling each other in a frantic effort to get away from the evil incarnate.

123

One witness stated that veryone exited the church except for one elderly gentleman who sat calmly in his pew without moving, seemingly oblivious to the fact that God's ultimate enemy was in his presence.

Satan proceeded to walked up to the old man and said, "Don't you know who I am?"

To which the man replied, "Yep, sure do."

"Aren't you afraid of me?" Satan asked.

"Nope, sure ain't." said the man.

"Don't you realize I can kill you with a word?" asked Satan.

"Don't doubt it for a minute," returned the old man, in an even tone.

"Did you know that I could cause you profound, horrifying, physical agony for all eternity?" persisted Satan.

"Yep," was the calm reply.

"And you're still not afraid?" asked Satan.

"Nope." the elderly man replied.

More than a little perturbed, Satan asked, "Well, why aren't you afraid of me?"

The man calmly replied, "Been married to your sister for over 48 years.

Safe Arrival

Mr. Johnson, a businessman from New York, was on a business trip to Louisiana. Immediately he sent an e-mail back home to his wife, Jennifer .

Unfortunately, he forgot his wife's exact e-mail address and the e-mail ended up going to a Mrs. Joanne Nagle of Wisconsin, the wife of a preacher who had just passed away. The preacher's wife took one look at the e-mail and promptly fainted.

When she was finally revived by her son, she nervously pointed to the message, which read, "Arrived safely, but it sure is hot down here."

Welcome To Hell

Geologists working in a remote and isolated area of Siberia drilled a hole some 9 miles deep when the drill bit suddenly began to rotate wildly. Mr. Azzacov, the project's manager was quoted as saying that the center of the earth was hollow, and hellishly hot.

Supposedly, the geologists measured temperatures of over 2,000 degrees in the deep hole. They lowered super sensitive microphones to the bottom of the well, and to their astonishment they heard the sounds of thousands, perhaps millions, of suffering people screaming.

The article about the experimental well in Russia's Kola Peninsula appeared in *Scientific American* under the headline, *"Scientists Discover Hell"*.

The article went into great detail about the drill well reaching 9 miles into the ground, where scientists encountered rare rock formations, flows of gas and water, temperatures up to 2000°, and the sound of suffering souls.

"Hello, This Is Heaven, The Almighty God Speaking!"

We're accustomed to hearing about folks who "get the call" from God, but previously always in terms of them being summoned to the ministry to serve Him. Were it not, one would have to wonder about the many who have died by their own hands who *didn't* receive a sign from God.

The following "God moves in mysterious ways" stories have been circulating for over a decade. There's no reason to believe they are true stories — simply chalk these up as humorous inspirational tales.

God Nailed Me

Doug Cornforth of Richmond, Virginia claimed that God drove a nail through his brain in order to save him for higher things. Mr. Cornforth, a construction worker, was messing around with his fellow workers during a lunch break when a nail gun went off, forcing a nail a little over one inch long into his skull just above his right ear.

The surgeon who removed the nail commented, "Had the nail penetrated any deeper, it would have damaged his brain and in all probability killed him.

" Mr. Cornforth had a brain scan, just to make sure that no brain damage had occurred, and during the course of the scan, doctors discovered a malignant tumor. Surgeons operated to remove the tumor and the man recovered.

Speaking about the accident, the victim said, "God put that nail in my brain, but I knew even then that he must have had a reason."

Did you know? *The most common warning in church bulletins are to inform the Congregation that the bowl at the back of the Church labeled "For The Sick", is for monetary donations only.*

"Hello, This Is Heaven, The Almighty God Speaking!"

One Saturday night, a pastor was working late, and decided to call his wife before leaving for home. It was around 10:00 pm. The pastor let it ring many times, but his wife didn't answer the phone. He thought it was odd that she didn't answer, but decided to wrap up a few things and try again in a few minutes. When he tried again she answered right away. He asked her why she hadn't answered before, and she said that it hadn't rung at their house. But, they brushed it off as a fluke and went on their merry way.

The following Monday, the pastor received a call at the church office, on the phone that he'd used that Saturday night. The man on the other end wanted to know why he'd called on Saturday night. The pastor was dumbfounded and couldn't figure out what the guy was talking about.

Then the caller said, "It rang and rang, but I didn't answer."

The pastor remembered the apparently misdirected call and apologized for disturbing the gentleman, explaining that he'd intended to call his wife.

The caller replied, "That's alright! You see, I was planning to commit suicide on Saturday night, but before I did, I prayed, 'God if you're there, and you don't want me to do this, give me a sign now.' At that point my phone started to ring. I looked at the caller ID, and it said, 'The Almighty God'. I was to afraid to answer!"

The man who had intended to commit suicide is now meeting regularly for counseling with the pastor of The Almighty God Tabernacle.

I Didn't Know The Virgin Mary Was Scottish!

A church in a small town in Scotland, gained notoriety when the statue of the Virgin Mary was reported to speak to visitors. Rumors began when a local woman praying to the statue said she heard the Virgin Mary tell her that Jesus would return to the people very soon.

In no time at all, flocks of people were turning up at the church, and every now and then the statue would talk about the return of Jesus and what the people should do to prepare for it. At one point, hundreds of people were gathered in the church, as they all waited with bated breath to hear the Virgin Mary speak.

Eventually, the statue began to speak, "Jesus will...".

Suddenly there was an ear-splitting whine and the statue continued, "Shit, I spilt my cup of tea!"

The priest turned scarlet red and the people began murmuring. It didn't take long for people to figure out that a local businessman had planted a radio transmitter in the statue, and his wife had made the pronouncements in a bid to boost tourism to the town. Funny that most people didn't question the Virgin Mary having a strong Scottish accent.

Did You Know? *A guy in Texas became a multi-millionaire by charging people admission to sit in his living room recliner - which had a mustard and ketchup stain that looked exactly like Jerry Falwell and Jesus Christ.*

I know from Lev 11:6-8 that touching the skin of a dead pig makes me unclean, but may I still play football if I wear gloves?

Religious folks do so much to educate people using the good book. But, one of the first issues we have to consider is that the Bible is thousands of years old, and the accounts it contains have come to us through many oral tellings, re-copyings, printings, and translations. We have to be very careful about presenting a specific interpretation of a single English word or phrase from one particular version of the Bible as being "what the Bible actually says."

Eternal and Unchanging

Christians do alot to educate people regarding God's Law. Especially, when someone tries to defend the homosexual lifestyle, because there is always someone there to simply remind them that Leviticus 18:22 clearly states it to be an abomination. However, people need some advice regarding some of the other specific laws and how to best follow them.

When someone burns a bull on the altar as a sacrifice, I know it creates a pleasing odor for the Lord (Lev 1:9). The problem is my neighbors claim the odor is not pleasing to them. Should I smite them?

I would like to sell my daughter into slavery, as sanctioned in Exodus 21:7. In this day and age, what do you think would be a fair price for her?

I know that I am allowed no contact with a woman while she is in her period of menstrual uncleanliness (Lev 15:19-24). The problem is, how do I tell? I have tried asking, but most women take offense.

Lev. 25:44 states that I may indeed possess slaves, both male and female, provided they are purchased from neighboring nations. A friend of a friend claims that this applies to Mexicans, but not Canadians. Can you clarify? Why can't I own Canadians?

I have a coworker who insists on working on the Sabbath. Exodus 35:2 clearly states he should be put to death. Am I morally obligated to kill him myself?

A friend of mine feels that even though eating shellfish is an Abomination (Lev 11:10), it is a lesser abomination than homosexuality. I don't agree. Can you settle this?

Lev 21:20 states that I may not approach the altar of God if I have a defect in my sight. I have to admit that I wear reading glasses. Does my vision have to be 20/20, or is there some wiggle room here?

Most of my male friends get their hair trimmed, including the hair around their temples, even though this is expressly forbidden by Lev 19:27. How should they die?

I know from Lev 11:6-8 that touching the skin of a dead pig makes me unclean, but may I still play football if I wear gloves?

My uncle has a farm. He violates Lev 19:19 by planting two different crops in the same field, as does his wife by wearing garments made of two different kinds of thread: a cotton, polyester blend. He also tends to curse and blaspheme a lot. Is it really necessary that we go to all the trouble of getting the whole town together to stone them? (Lev 24:10-16) Couldn't we just burn them to death at a private family affair like we do with people who sleep with their in-laws? (Lev. 20:14)

I am confident that the Christians out there have studied these things extensively, so I am confident you can help educate the world. Afterall, God's word is eternal and unchanging.

The Giving Bible

Idly turning the pages of the Gideon Bible on the bedside table of his hotel room, a young man was amazed to find a crisp 20-dollar bill tucked between the pages.

Clipped to the bill was a note that read, "If you opened this book because you're discouraged, read the 14th Chapter of John. If you're broke, then take this $20 bill. If you had a fight with your wife, buy her a present. If you don't need it, leave it for the next fellow." The note was signed: "Just A Wayfaring Stranger."

But the punch came with the P.S. "On second thought, maybe you ought to take it down to the Mirror Room and try their martinis. That's how I got this idea anyway!"

"May the Force be with you!"

Lets look at the different religions that exist in the world today. Some of these religions state that if you are not a member of their religion, you will go to hell. Since there are more than one of these religions and people do not belong to more than one religion, we can project that all people and all souls go to hell.

Common to human experience is the desire to bask in the sure and certain knowledge that those who adhere to different practices have it much worse than we do. Part of belonging to any group is the need to believe it's the best of its kind, and that holds true even when the groups in question are different religions, or even sects within the same religion. One needs to feel comforted that one has made the right choice and is indeed upon the right path, after all. Consequently, bits of wild misinformation about what goes on in the other camp often get circulated as truth because these tales serve to confirm the rightness of one's own choice.

An Atheist Holiday

In Orlando Florida, an atheist became outraged over the preparation for Easter and Passover holidays. So he decided to contact the local ACLU about the discrimination inflicted on atheists by the constant celebrations afforded to Christians and Jews with all their holidays, while the atheists had no holiday to celebrate.

The ACLU jumped on the opportunity to once again pick up the cause of the godless and assigned their sharpest attorneys to the case. The case was brought before a judge who, after listening to the long passionate presentation of the ACLU lawyers, promptly banged his gavel and declared, "Case dismissed!"

The lead ACLU lawyer immediately stood up and objected to the ruling and said, "Your honor, how can you possibly dismiss this case? Surely the Christians have Christmas, Easter and many other observances. And the Jews, in addition to Passover, have Yom Kippur and Hanukkah, yet my client and all other atheists have no such holiday!"

The judge leaned forward in his chair and simply said, "Obviously your client is too confused to know about, or for that matter, even celebrate the atheists' holiday!"

The ACLU lawyer pompously said, "We are aware of no such holiday for atheists. Just when might that be, Your Honor?"

The judge said, "Well, it comes every year on exactly the same date: April 1st!"

Did You Know? *A dozen people committed suicide after losing their life savings in a Casino in Reno, Nevada. Slot machines were breaking down because devout Catholics were pouring holy water into the coin slots for good luck, rusting the computer chips.*

"May the Force be with you!"

As some of you may know the government will be taking a census around the beginning of January. For those who don't know, a census is where the government collates general information about it's residents, such as the number of people living in your house, religion, etc. If there are enough people in Canada or any country for that matter who put down a religion that isn't mentioned on the census form it

becomes a fully recognised and legal religion. It usually takes about 10,000 people to nominate the same religion.

It is for this reason that it has been suggested that anyone who does not have a dominant religion, to put "Jedi" as their religion.

"Star Wars" enthusiasts may be thrilled, but government officials in Australia and England have already started balking at a campaign encouraging fans to declare "Jedi" — as in "Jedi Knights," the zen-like warriors of the film series, as their religion on census forms.

If you are a member of the Jedi religion then you are by default a 'Jedi Knight'.

So if this has been your dream since you were 4 years old, then do it because you love Star Wars. If not, then just do it to annoy people and your government.

"May the Force be with you!"

Did You Know? *There are only three religious truths. Jews do not recognize Jesus as the Messiah; Protestants do not recognize the Pope as the leader of the Christian faith; and Baptists do not recognize each other in the liquor store or at bars.*

"We're just glad our daughter had Jesus in her heart when she died."

Jesus is coming, everyone look busy.

"A Mistaken Rapture"

A Little Rock woman was killed after leaping through her moving car's sun roof during an incident best described as "a mistaken rapture" by dozens of eye witnesses. Thirteen other people were also injured after a twenty-car pile up resulted from people trying to avoid hitting the woman who was apparently convinced that the rapture was occurring when she noticed twelve people floating up into the air, and then passed a man on the side of the road who she claimed was Jesus.

"She started screaming, "He's back! He's back!" and climbed right out of the sunroof and jumped off the roof of the car," said Gerald McCree, husband of 52-year-old Mary Beth McCree who was pronounced dead at the scene. "I was slowing down but she wouldn't wait till I stopped."

Mr. McCree went on to say, "She thought the rapture was happening and was convinced that Jesus was gonna lift her up into the sky."

This is the strangest thing I've seen since joining the force," said Gary Morin, the first officer on the scene.

Officer Morin questioned the man who looked like Jesus and discovered that he was dressed up as Jesus and was on his way to a toga costume party when the tarp covering the bed of his pickup truck came loose and released twelve blow up sex dolls filled with helium, which floated up into the air.

Troy Reno, 32, of Jonesboro, Arkansas, who's been told by several of his friends that he looks like the Messiah, pulled over and lifted his arms into the air in frustration, and yelled, "Come back here," just as the McCrees' car passed him.

Mrs. McCree was sure that it was Jesus lifting people up into the sky as they passed by him, according to her husband, who says his wife loved Jesus more than anything else.

When asked for comments about the twelve sex dolls, Reno replied, "This is all just too weird for me. I never expected anything like this to happen."

The Plastic of The Christ

An Ohio teenager was killed when her plastic Jesus dashboard figure was driven into her chest by her car's airbag, which inflated during an accident involving two other vehicles.

16-year-old Darla Pulpit of Cincinnati was apparently holding her Jesus figure close to her chest when she ran through a red light and collided with two other vehicles in a busy intersection.

"The air bag inflated and pushed the head of Jesus straight through her heart," said Allan Lancaster, medical examiner at the scene of the accident. "If it wasn't for the plastic Jesus, Ms. Pulpit would still be alive today."

"Air bags have saved thousands of lives, but in this case it actually took a life, thanks to Jesus," said police officer Garry Kent, first officer at the scene.

Russell Pulpit, Darla's father and devout Christian man said, "It was just our daughter's time to go, and we can't question the actions of God. My daughter loved Jesus and worshipped Him, and I think she's probably talking to Him in heaven right now."

"We gave our daughter the dashboard Jesus for her birthday last year, and she really liked it," said Marg Pulpit, the victims mother. "It's too bad that Jesus ended up killing her, but we believe she's in heaven now, and we're happy for her, and hope to re-unite with her when we get to heaven."

"We're just glad our daughter had Jesus in her heart when she died," said Mr. and Mrs. Pulpit.

Did You Know? *Modern People News has revealed plans for the filming of a movie based on the sex life of Jesus Christ, in which Jesus and his disciples are portrayed as swinging homosexuals. This film will be shot in the US later this year unless the public outcry is great. A French Prostitute has already been cast to play the part of Mary Magdalene, with who Christ has a blatant affair. The film has already been banned from Europe.*

The Secong Coming Project

There is a not-for-profit organization devoted to bringing about the Second Coming of Our Lord, Jesus Christ, as prophesied in the Bible, in time for the 2,000th anniversary of his birth. The Second Coming Project's intention was to clone Jesus, utilizing modern cloning technologies pioneered at the Roslin Institute in Scotland.

The procedure enables scientists to clone any large mammal - including humans - using just a single cell from an adult specimen, and throughout the Christian world there are churches that contain Holy Relics of Jesus' body, such as, his blood, his hair, his foreskin.

Unless every single one of these preserved relics is a fake, this means that cells from Jesus' body still survive to this day.

The Second Coming Organization made preparations to obtain a portion of these relics and remove incorrupt cells from one of these many Holy Relics of Jesus' blood and body.

The DNA is then be inserted into an unfertilized oocyte, or human egg, through the now-proven biological process called nuclear transfer. The fertilized egg, now the zygote of Jesus Christ, is implanted into the womb of a young virginal woman, who volunteers of her own accord, and will then bring the baby Jesus to term in a second Virgin Birth.

If all went according to plan, the birth took place on December 25, 2001, thus making Anno Domini 2001 into Anno Domini Novi 1, and all calendrical calculations would begin anew.

No longer can you rely on hope and prayer, waiting around futilely for Jesus to return. We have the technology to bring him back right now. There is no reason: moral, legal or Biblical, not to take advantage of it.

chaptereight

"Those people eat cow, rabbit and mice, squirrel and frog and every thing else,
but still give us trouble. But dog is good food. Dog is good medicine, make sick people strong,
make old people young, make penis hard, make sex good again."

--Ki So Joo; President Kea So Joo Food, Inc.

incredibleedibles

The most dominant activity in the lives of animals is the hunt for food. For thousands of years the collection, growing and hunting of food was our primary occupation. The preparation, consumption, and enjoyment of food remains a significant factor in our lives. However, these days the only difference are the technological advances, meaning far fewer people take part in the production of our food.

. . . .

Endangered Produce

Food is the most important factor of our lives -- without it we would all perish. So the safety of what we eat is of the utmost concern to us. Many of the warnings we come across everyday deal with the safety of the food we eat, expressing concern about everything from the containers we cook in to the use of genetically-engineered plants and animals.

Cyanide Melons

A couple years back there was a watermelon pach owner living in Florida. Every so often kids would come by and eat the watermelons. After a while of this, the man got angry and decided to put an end to it, so the next day the man wrote a note and put it on one of the nicest, juiciest watermelon he could find.

The note said, "One of these watermelons has been injected with Cyanide."

A few days passed and his watermelons were almost ready to take to the market. As he was walking through the field he approached the watermelon with the note on it, when he bent over to take it off he noticed another note right next to it that read, "Now one more watermelon has been injected with Cyanide."

Endangered Produce

According to a report in *New Scientist*, "Bananas as we know them will not be in existence in the next decade. They have been genetically altered so much that new plants can not be grown because there are no seeds, and the existing plants are slowly being destroyed by a parasite."

Randolph Blight, Professor at the University of Florida's Tropical Research and Education Center was quoted in the article stating, "Diseases remain the major constraint to both export and subsistence production of the banana, and there is no doubt that Black Sigatoka and Panama Disease constitute the most important threats. It is very likely that these problems will cause production to decrease greatly in the next decade, and the crop will become extinct."

Long Shelf Life

The Hostess Company has not produced any new Twinkies in as many as two decades or more. Instead, the Twinkies that you buy in the store have been sitting in a Hostess warehouse for years. Twinkies are made entirely out of artificial ingredients, and contain no food products. Therefore, Twinkies have a very long shelf life, possibly decades. At some point many years ago Hostess over produced Twinkies by the billions, due to an error in market research, and could not sell all their stock. So Hostess stored the billions of excess Twinkies in a giant warehouse and waited for their distributors to place orders. However, the distributors did not place as large of orders as expected, and Hostess was forced to continue storing the Twinkies. Because of the lack of food products in Twinkies, they do not go bad for a very long time, and to this day the Twinkies that you by in the store are from the original stock.

"Grade D Beef: Fit for human consumption."

Fewer and fewer of us take part in the production and processing of the food we eat, leaving the vital task in the hands of faceless strangers and corporate monoliths who may not have our best interests at heart...or our stomachs.

Can I Order A Pizza, Hold The "P"!

A friend of a friend was stuck at home with a non-functioning car suffering from hungar pains, so he ordered a Pizza Hut pizza. He told them he'd be working in the office at the apartment complex where he also lived.

About an hour and a half later his pizza still had not arrived, so he called the Pizza Hut. They were really irate because they went to his apartment instead of the office. He tried to explain where he was, and get them to send a new pizza right away, but the manager on duty was really rude and insulting. After chewing out the manager, he demanded the original order for free.

The manager said, "Okay, we will have that order for you in about an hour." Which made the guy mad, but had no choice because he was stuck at home and starving.

Exactly one hour later, the order arrived, and he noticed the box felt damp all over. But he was so hungry he went ahead and ate the pizza, even though it tasted "funny". The next morning he woke up sick to his stomach and decided to walk to the nearest clinic. On his way, however, he noticed a polaroid stuck in the Office door. He couldn't believe what it showed: Three employees in Pizza Hut uniforms urinating on a pizza he assumed was his. Needless to say, he swore off Pizza Hut! He likes his pizza without the P!

I Go Ape For Borneo!

During the winter in 1861, the conductor of a train received for transport a huge parcel addressed to a professor of the College of France. On the way to Paris, the train was held up, waiting for an express to pass. During the wait, the conductor and his assistant noticed the parcel was leaking. Naturally, he called in his mates, and they boozed on until the express had passed. Wiping their moustaches, they went on to their destination, only to be greeted by the professor who informed them that the parcel held the body of a "great ape of Borneo."

Did You Know? *There have been a number of complaints from students who work in the cafeteria system of major Universities claiming they have seen recently delivered crates of beef labelled, "Grade D Beef: Fit for human consumption."*

Toilet Seat Fit For A Meal

In Los Angeles, a customer in an international hamburger chain lost his appetite after discovering the restaurant's toilet seats being washed in its dishwasher alongside the kitchen utensils.

The local news agency reported that while visiting the toilet the man noticed all the seats in the cubicles had been removed. When he asked staff about the missing seats, an employee took them out of a dishwasher where they had been cleaned, together with trays and kitchen utensils.

According to sources, the employee of the restaurant tried to reassure the customer by saying the freshly washed toilet seat would be warm and pleasant to sit on. However, the restaurant chain now says the incident is not standard company procedure.

"I don't actually like peanuts, so I just suck the chocolate off them."

Food preparation ranges from a sumptuous banquet crafted by those who have dedicated years of their lives to perfecting the culinary arts to hastily thrown-together, barely edible, food-on-the-run. Such a wide range of activity makes for some humorous anecdotes about the efforts of the culinary-challenged.

Do As Mother...

A newly wed couple were looking forward to spending their first Christmas together. On Christmas day, to the bemusement of her husband, the wife took the turkey, and cut the bones out of the bird's legs before placing it in the oven. The husband asked her why she mutilated the bird, and she explained she was merely doing what her mother always did when preparing to roast a turkey. The couple had invited their parents for the Christmas meal, and when they were all gathered around the table, the wife took the opportunity to ask her mother why she cut the bones out of the turkey drumsticks.

The mother replied, "Oh, that's because the oven at home was so small, it was the only way I could get the big bird in."

"Leave room to rise"

A young boy wanted to impress his mother by baking her a cake for her birthday. The boy's mother returned home from work early that evening to find him hovering outside the door to the kitchen. So she asked her son what he was doing. He explained that he was just following the recipe for baking a cake.

Slightly bemused, she asked the boy what the recipe told him to do. He explained that the recipe said to fold the dough into a cake tin, which did, and then the directions instructed, "Leave room to rise", so he had left the room. He told his mother, who was straining to stop herself laughing, "I left it over two hours ago and nothing's happened!"

Peanut Surprise

An elderly man was recovering in the hospital after a major operation. A Christian boy had volunteered to visit patients who didn't get many visitors, and the old man was one such patient. The boy visited him three times a week and enjoyed their chats. The old man would always had sweets to offer the young man. One week, the old man was due to be discharged and on the eve of his departure, the boy came and sat down next to him. The old man was so excited at the prospect of going home that he'd forgotten to provide any sweets. However, he did have a bag of peanuts, and somewhat embarrassed, offered them to the boy. The boy, while munching on the peanuts, listened to the old man talk about what he'd do when he got back home.

When it was time for the boy to go, the old man, seeing that he'd finished the bag of peanuts, remarked how hungry he must be and added, "I don't actually like peanuts, so I just suck the chocolate off them."

Did You Know? *Do you know why a choice cut of beef taken from the upper hindquarter of the cow is called "sirloin". Dining with the Abbot of Reading, Henry VIII ate such a heartily loin of beef and was so delighted with his meal that King Henry knighted the meat, dubbing it "Sir Loin".*

Two Ply Angel Food Cake

A lady was suppose to bake a cake for the church ladies' group bake sale, but forgot to do it, so at the last minute she baked an angel food cake. However, when she took it out of the oven, the center had dropped flat. There was no time to bake another cake, so she looked around the house for something to build up the centre of the cake. In the bathroom she found a roll of toilet paper, plunked it in and covered it with icing. The finished product looked presentable, so she rushed it over to the church.

She then gave her daughter some money and instructions to be at the sale the minute it opened and to buy the cake and bring it home.

When the daughter arrived at the sale, the attractive cake had already been sold. The lady was beside herself.

A couple of days later the same lady was invited to a friend's home for an afternoon of playing bridge. After the game a fancy lunch was served, and to top it off, the cake in question was presented for dessert.

When the lady recognised the cake, she got off her chair to rush into the kitchen to tell her hostess all about it. But before she could get to her feet, one of the other ladies said, "What a beautiful cake!"

The first lady sat back in her chair when she heard the hostess reply, "Thank you, I baked it myself."

Wash, Boil and Serv

According to the US Department of the Interior, the inscription on the metal bands they use to tag migratory birds has been changed. The bands used to bear the address of the Washington Biological Survey, abbreviated "Wash. Biol. Surv." until the agency received a letter from an Alabama camper stating, *"While camping last week I shot one of your birds by mistake. I think it was a crow. I followed the cooking instuctions on the tag to "Wash, Boil and Serv" and I want to tell you it was terrible."*

The bands are now marked "Fish and Wildlife Service."

Did You Know? *Vegetarian is an old Indian word meaning "lousy hunter."*

Many country eat dog. Korea, China, Philippines, Japan, Thailand, Cambodia eat dog. Dog is healthy for you.

What we consider to be food, and how that food is prepared, can widely vary from culture to culture. Many cultures relish foodstuff that we consider taboo, and prepare food in ways that give us a gag reflex. Yet many of them feel the same way about our food choices.

Baby Food

In countries where many of the people are illiterate, companies use labels with pictures to depict what the package contains. This very logical practice proved to be quite perplexing to one big company when it tried to sell baby food in an African nation. By using its regular label, which showed a baby and stated the type of baby food in the jar. Unfortunately, the local population took one look at the labels and interpreted them to mean that the jars contained ground-up babies. Sales, of course, were terrible.

Doggy Soliciting

A Korean company solicited American dog shelters for excess dogs to turn into soup. This is what was written in the letter:

"Excuse my English Please, Thank You. First congratulation on all you good work with animal. We support. We would like to offer help so you company make money.

Dog shelter kill million of dog, cost money. Dog shelter cremate dog cost money. Dog shelter need money to operate. Where it get money? Hard to get money.

Many people like to eat dog. People need to eat dog. Where do they get dog? Some people they raise dog to eat. Some steal dog, make some people angry, hurt some people. That not right.

We like make proposal to your dog shelter to sell us dog. You save money, you make money. We buy all dog, regardless of size or color. We prefer big, young, strong dog but we take all dog from your dog shelter. We cook dog in America. We can dog in America and sell some dog in America in Asian market place. Lot people in America eat dog. Most dog we ship oversea. Many country eat dog. Korea, China, Philippines, Japan, Thailand,

Cambodia eat dog. Dog is healthy for you. This way your cost of business is less. You make more money, more people happy. You get cleaner air. No burn up dog. No waste dog. People pet no disappear. Everybody happy.

Cause we understand some people no like idea to eat dog. But they make trouble for people who like eat dog. Those people called two face. Those people eat cow, rabbit and mice, squirrel and frog and every thing else, but still give us trouble. But dog is good food. Dog is good medicine, make sick people strong, make old people young, make penis hard, make sex good again. Our business getting very big. Need more dog. We are prepared to offer you ten cents per pound per dog. We pick up dog every day, so you also save on feeding dog. We like very much to speak with you and make deal.

Please tell us how many dog available in your business. We have deal already to do same with dog shelter in New York, California and Ontario, Canada. We hope to be eventually in big city cross America. You can join us now, save money and continue doing your good job. We do big business together. We have big business already with many dog breeder and many dog hospital. Dog no suffer, We have quick death for dog. Looking to hear from you soon." Signed Kim So Joo; President Kea So Joo, Inc.

Family Dog Food

An American couple fled home from Hong Kong after their pet poodle, Peaches, was cooked, garnished with pepper sauce and bamboo shoots and served to them at a Chinese restaurant.

Harold and Erma, who asked the American newspaper *New York Times* not to publish their full names, said they took Peaches with them to the restaurant and asked a waiter to give her something to eat.

The waiter had trouble understanding the couple but eventually picked up the dog and carried her to the kitchen where they thought she would be fed.

Eventually the waiter returned carrying a dish. When the couple removed the silver lid they found Peaches.

Good to the last dropping

Apparently there is a brand of expensive coffee from Indonesia called Kopi Luak, which is harvested from half-digested coffee beans picked from the turds of a small weasel-like animal.

Guests of an East Java plantation will almost certainly be offered Kopi Luak for breakfast. The secret of this delicious blend of coffee, usually explained only after the guest have drained their mugs to the last drop, lies in the bean selection, which is performed by a luak, a species of civet cat endemic to Java. The luak will eat only the choicest, most perfectly matured beans which it then excretes, partially digested, a few hours later. Plantation workers then retrieve the beans from the ground, ready for immediate roasting.

The aroma is rich and strong, and the coffee is incredibly full bodied, almost syrupy. It's thick with a hint of chocolate, and lingers on the tongue with a long, clean aftertaste. It's the most interesting, unusual, and expensive cup of coffee in the world.

"When A Tea Bag Comes A Long, You Must Dip it....Dip It Good!"

The packaging of consumer products is a convenience familiar to Americans, but can be baffling to a foreign visitor. A friend of a friend was lunching in the college cafeteria one afternoon with a young student from India. Noticing that he had torn open his tea bag and emptied its contents into his cup, he explained that the bag itself was meant to be unopened, and dipped into the water.

A bit surprised, he thanked my friend graciously for correcting him -- and then confidently dropped an unopened sugar packet into his tea.

Phlemonade

We can never really be sure what is in the products we eat, since very few of us grow or prepare our own food. Here is buffet of legends dealing with ordinary foods that may contain some rather extraordinary ingredients.

Dog Food

A man particularly fond of steak pies couldn't resist an offer on *The Ultimate Prime Steak Pie* at a marked-down price in his local supermarket. That evening, excited about digging into the huge pie, he warmed it up, cooked some vegetables and got out a few beers. Sitting down to eat, he licked his lips, took his time and savoured every mouthful, only pausing now and then to take a swig of beer. He nearly ate the entire pie, when his fork hit something metallic.

He choked on his beer when he pulled out a dog tag with the inscription, "If you find our darling Princess, please call this number".

After that night, the man gave up eating meat and became a dedicated vegetarian.

Phlemonade

A young boy went to stay at his grandparents' house for the weekend. He awoke in the middle of the night with a terrible thirst, so he went downstairs to the kitchen. Still half-asleep, his eyes lit on what he took to be a bottle of homemade lemonade, a particular treat for him, because his grandmother was known for making a mean lemonade. It was only when he opened the bottle and took a deep swig that he realised his error. The bottle was actually his grandfather's phlegm jar, in which the old man would relieve a particularly nasty lung infection. Still, as the boy picked a long, stringy piece of crouton-like phlegm from his mouth, at least we can be certain that the midnight thirst was not the main thing bothering him any more.

chapternine

*"I was planning to blow the 'chit' out of the plane.
I wanted to kill all the 'Ahmedicans' (americans) and Jews
to show that we are a peace loving pipple."*

--Convicted Terrorist;
Mohammed Rahim Apu Ali Baba Mafai Kajaffe Ahmed Sharif Opdahl Rajpal Anupma Smith

jeeperscreepers

Creepy tales are one of folklore's richest veins. They are often a means of expressing our fears about the dangers that flow beneath the surface of what we see as a calm and untroubled world. We fear terrible accidents we're powerless to prevent, and we are terrified of the malicious madmen who choose victims at random. We worry that we will be unable to protect ourselves from the onslaught of insects who invade our homes and bodies, and the contaminants that lurk in our food. We fear for our childrens' safety in a world infested with drugs, kidnappers, and poisons. We never know what gruesome discovery may be waiting around the next corner. And even if we somehow escape all of these horrors, even our own vanities may do us in.

. . . .

A rare case of spinach poisoning.

How horrible is it to contemplate losing our lives to something unforseeable and unpreventable, such as an accidental poisoning. There's very little defense against a deliberate random poisoning. But we want to believe we're masters of our own fate, and tales of accidental or deliberate poisoning give lie to that notion. We're vulnerable, and that vulnerability frightens us.

Ban Dihydrogen Monoxide

Dihydrogen monoxide is colorless, odorless, tasteless, and kills an uncounted thousands of people each year. Most of these deaths are caused by accidental inhalation of DHMO, but the dangers of dihydrogen monoxide do not end there.

Prolonged exposure to its solid form causes severe tissue damage. Symptoms of DHMO ingestion can include excessive sweating and urination, and possibly a bloated feeling, nausea, vomiting and body electrolyte imbalance. For those who have become dependent, DHMO withdrawal means certain death.

Dihydrogen monoxide is also known as hydroxl acid, and is the major component of acid rain. It contributes to the "greenhouse effect", and may cause severe burns. It contributes to the erosion of our natural landscape. It accelerates corrosion and rusting of many metals, and may cause electrical failures and decreased effectiveness of automobile brakes. It has been found in excised tumors of terminal cancer patients.

Contamination is reaching epidemic proportions!

Quantities of dihydrogen monoxide have been found in every stream, lake, and reservoir in North America today. But the pollution is global, and the contaminant has even been found in Antarctic ice. DHMO has caused millions of dollars of property damage in the midwest, and recently California.

Despite the danger, dihydrogen monoxide is often used as an industrial solvent and coolant, in nuclear power plants, and in the production of styrofoam. It's used as a fire retardant, and is used in many forms of cruel animal research. DHMO is found in the distribution of pesticides, and as an additive in certain "junk-foods" and other food products. Even after washing, produce remains contaminated by this chemical.

Companies dump waste DHMO into rivers and the ocean, and nothing can be done to stop them because this practice is legal. The impact on wildlife is extreme, and we cannot afford to ignore it any longer!

The American government has refused to ban the production, distribution, or use of this damaging chemical due to its "importance to the economic health of this nation." In fact, the navy and other military organizations are conducting experiments with DHMO, and are currently designing multi-billion dollar devices to control and utilize it during warfare situations. Hundreds of military research facilities receive tons of it through a highly sophisticated underground distribution network. Many store large quantities for later use.

I Came To A Finish, Cause I Eat Me Spinach...

An 11-year-old boy from Warsaw, Poland, was overjoyed when his father brought home a second-hand television set. Everyday he would come home from school and watch cartoons for hours. The boy was particularly taken by the cartoon, "Popeye" and demanded that his mother cook spinach for him every night, so he could be big and strong like Popeye. Of course, the mother was delighted that her son suddenly wanted to eat such a healthy diet. This went on for weeks, but the boy was disappointed to find that the spinach had no effect on his stature. Deciding that he obviously wasn't eating enough, he opened all the cans of spinach in the kitchen cupboard and consumed the lot. The boy later died in hospital in a rare case of spinach poisoning.

Tee Time

A Japanese man was on the fifth day of a golfing holiday when he suddenly collapsed and had to be taken to the hospital for treatment. The examining doctor diagnosed the man as being poisoned, and informed the police of the incident. The detective in charge of the case questioned the man, but could think of any reason why anybody would want to poison him. The detective continued to ask the man questions, and was eventually able to deduce that the man had unwittingly poisoned himself. The golfer had the habit of holding the tee between his teeth after teeing off on each hole. The golf course had been heavily sprayed with pesticide, so every time the man put the tee in his mouth, he ingested a small amount of toxic pesticide that day, eventually, poisoning himself.

Dad's Nuts Roasting On An Open Fire...

No one wants to discover a corpse, whether it be the remains of a person or a pet. Dead bodies belong in funeral homes where we have a chance to emotionally prepare for viewing them; they shouldn't turn up in our fireplace, or having fall from the sky, where their shocking appearances can send us screaming into the night. The following tales of gruesome discoveries is to remind us of our own fragile mortality, something we'd much rather not dwell on.

Air Diver

In California, Fire Authorities found a corpse in a burnt out section of the forest while assessing the damage done by a forest fire. The deceased male was dressed in a full wetsuit, complete with a dive tank, flippers and face mask. A post mortem examination revealed that the person died not from burns but from massive internal injuries. Dental records provided a positive identification. Investigators then set about determining how a fully clad scuba diver ended up in the middle of a forest fire.

It was revealed that, on the day of the fire, the person went for a diving trip off the coast, some 25 kilometers away from the forest.

The firefighters, seeking to control the fire as quickly as possible, called in a fleet of water-bombers. When these bombers dropped down onto the ocean for rapid filling, to fly to the forest fire and emptied, the diver who was making like Flipper in the Pacific, was now doing the breaststroke in a water-bomber some 300m in the air. Apparently, he extinguished exactly 1.78m of the fire.

Catopia

The body of Andy Adams, an elderly man from Houston, Texas was discovered after he had lain undiscovered for several weeks. When police arrived at the house of the pensioner to investigate reports of strange smells that had been bothering the neighbours, they discovered 15 apparently healthy and happy cats running about the place, apparently having the time of their lives. Mr. Adams was not known to be an animal lover, and the mystery of why there where so many cats running around his house was cleared up when officers discovered a broken downstairs window through which the cats had gained access to the man's house. However, upon going upstairs they discovered why his house had become such a hotbed for feline activity. He may not have fed any cats while he was alive, but Mr. Adams was now feeding all 15.

Dad's Nuts Roasting On An Open Fire...

A father from New Jersey, had always disappointed his family at Christmas by not turning up because of a business meeting or being too tired to join in the festivities. So this year, he was determined to give his wife and daughter a big surprise. He told his wife that he would not be able to make it home until Boxing Day, but on Christmas Eve, he dressed up as Santa Claus and climbed on to the roof of his house with a sack of presents. Unfortunately, as he was climbing down the chimney, he got stuck in the flue and choked to death on the soot. Later that night, the family lit the fire, as they did every Christmas Eve, and the room filled with smoke and the stench of burnt flesh. The mother called the police who discovered her roasted husband halfway up the chimney.

The Sky Is Falling

A couple came home one evening to discover a huge gaping hole in the roof, their dog dead and their furniture soaked in gallons of foul-smelling matter. Distressed and baffled by what they saw, they called

the police who duly arrived to investigate. After several phone calls, the detective was finally able to ascertain what had happened. It seems that the container holding the waste from the lavatories on a passing Boeing 737 had burst open. The contents froze in the atmosphere as it fell toward the ground, and the resulting block of ice smashed through the roof of the unlucky couples house, killing their dog before melting all over their belongings.

"Do you have Spider Leg Gum?"

Entomologists might think they are cute, but to the rest of us, bugs are creepy, multi-legged, horrid-looking monsters. The swarms of bugs are to numerous count, and they are all out to get us. Their single-minded dedication with the intent upon invasion is the most chilling of all, and they will keep coming.

Bugs out number humans by the hundreds, and during their assault thousands -- nay, millions -- of their dedicated comrades continue the onslaught until one side or the other wins. There is no negotiation in this war, and no chance to take things only so far.

Bugs are vile, unthinking, and unfeeling pests, and many of them are also venomous and nearly impossible to kill. It's one against the many, intelligence against sheer numbers; and we greatly fear that we will ultimately be the losers.

Alarming Bug

In Columbus, Mississippi, a middle-aged couple had seen the last of their children leave the nest. The couple rarely went up to the top floor of their house where their children had their rooms. One day, the mother noticed an odd chirping noise coming from the top floor, and scared it was some horrible creepy crawly creature, she went and got her husband. The husband, not the most courageous of men, crept slowly up the stairs and searched all the rooms for the source of the noise, but was unable to work out where the noise was coming from. The next day, the husband called in an exterminator. The exterminator arrived, and after some fruitless searching, suddenly worked out what was causing the noise. He went downstairs and informed the couple that the batteries in their smoke alarm needed changing.

Black Wig Spider

A California woman returning from shopping one day was unpacking her groceries when she noticed, among a bunch of bananas, what looked like a spider. Earlier that morning, the woman had heard on the radio about the risks of bringing poisonous spiders in shipments of fruit from South America. The size of the thing convinced the woman it was a bird-eating spider and she slowly backed away towards the back door, shutting it behind her. She ran to her next-door neighbour, and told her about the discovery. Her neighbour phoned the police, and not long after, the police evacuated the entire area. Firemen pumped toxic gases into the woman's house and experts from the local zoo began a thorough search of the premises. Five minutes after the team had entered the house, they emerged with angry looks on their faces. The dangerous spider turned out to be a harmless black wig that had somehow fallen into the old woman's groceries.

Crotch Flies

Live flies emerged out of a perforation in the lower part of the body of a 12-year-old boy in Florida in a bizarre — but not unknown — phenomenon.

Admitted in Florida University Hospital, Charlie Gomi stunned doctors as flies began to come out a part of his crotch to take flight. Some of these flies were caught by the boy's parents, and then studied by Scientists at the University.

The surgeon taking care of Charlie said with excitement, "This is a rare condition called "myiasis", in which a human or animal body, dead or alive, can be invaded by the larvae of particular types of flies."

Man-Made Mosquitos

The "love bug", also known as the honeymoon fly, telephone bug, double-headed bug, united bug, and March fly are a nuisance for any motorist in the Southern US. Though these bugs neither bite nor sting, at certain times of the year their sheer numbers transform these innocuous insects into airborne hordes seemingly determined to devil anyone fool enough to take to the road. The adults splatter on windshields, lights, grills, and radiators of motor vehicles, and their dried remains are near impossible to remove.

Love bugs have been known to cause overheating of motors when large numbers of them are drawn into the cooling systems of liquid-cooled engines. Unlike other bugs, something particular to them adversely affects the paint jobs on cars, pitting and etching the paint if their mortal remains are left on a vehicle for more than 48 hours.

Every May and September these sex-crazed critters become an annoyance bordering on intolerable as the air teams with mating pairs. But the "love bugs" haven't always been part of the Floridia landscape, these love bugs were accidentally released from a biological experiment station at the University of Florida.

Scientists were genetically engineering females by crossing a fly and a mosquito in an attempt to create an enemy for mosquito larva, and a mate for the male mosquito that would be sterile and produce no offspring. Unfortunately, they accidentally created a male Love Bug, and a pair somehow escaped into the wild. Sincethen, these bugs have no natural predators, so their numbers quickly exploded into the millions, and now populate the whole southern US.

It was a nice "trip"

Demonization -- the time-honored technique used to band together and fight off the danger of drugs that threatens us all. Drugs are our enemies with whom we're at war -- we create tales that show them to be evil incarnate There must be no room left for doubt in public sentiment; no amount of embellishment or outright lying is considered excessive in service of the cause. So it is with our ubiquitous tales about the horrors of illicit drug use that dangers are exaggerated off the scale, and those who traffic in drugs are portrayed as unfeeling monsters. The message that drugs are bad is deemed far too important to be presented in anything less than black and white. Improbable, illogical, or downright impossible, these well-known stories are nonetheless circulated as the truth, even by those who should know better.

Cop A Swig

A man was driving cross-country with his most prized possession, a clear glass flask containing liquid LSD, of which he partook quite frequently. A couple of days into his adventure, he was stopped for speeding. He fumbled in the glove compartment for his registration, when the flask fell out onto the seat.

"Well," intones the officer, "Is that liquor? Have you been drinking?"

"No sir, it's not alcohol," replied the man.

"I think you're drunk -- let me see that," said the officer, who picked up the flask, unscrewed the top, and took a swig. "Well, I guess it's not liquor, but I'm gonna have to write you up for speeding."

The officer went back to his car. Since the guy had out-of-state plates, he figured it'll be a long wait until the officer gets the results of the computer check. Fifteen minutes passed, then twenty, then nearly thirty. The guy finally mustered up the courage to look back at the cop, and saw him staring off into space. As quietly as possible, he started his car and drove off.

Flashback

A student attending UCLA had his final exams coming up, so he decided to have some dangerous fun before settling down to study. He went out to a party and proceeded to take LSD and have a mind-expanding experience. After recovering from the weekend, he got down to work, and the next week went to take his first exam. When the exam was over, the student felt confident he had answered the questions impressively. That was, until the professor picked up his paper and scanned it.

"What's this?" the professor said suddenly, "Where are your answers?"

The confused student looked at the paper and realised what had happened. The student had answered each question splendidly, but experiencing a flashback to the LSD, he squeezed each answer into one tiny line.

Going Nuts

An American tourist gave in to temptation while on a holiday in the Dominican Republic, and bought a whole sheet of LSD to smuggle back into the US. However, while in line at customs, "the no-holds-barred" message of the customs' advertisments on drugs smuggling worried the man, and in a panic, he consumed the whole sheet of acid. He passed through Customs unhindered, but just as he took a seat on the plane, the large dose of LSD struck. The man is now in a psychiatric unit convinced he's a squirrel. He literally went "nuts."

Going Bananas

In a similar story, a Canadian man decided to take a trip to the US. While in New York, he came across an amazing deal on acid, so he bought the dealers lot (a hundred hits). He figured that it wasn't likely they would strip search him at the border, so he taped the whole sheet to his stomach and headed back.

At the border he was ordered to get out of his car and wait in a room while they searched his car. He got so freaked out, thinking they were going to strip search him, that he started sweating. The sweat soaked the sheet taped to his body and he absorbed all hundred hits of acid through his skin. Pretty soon he started to believe he was a banana and decided to "peel" himself, so he started peeling off his clothes. To this day he's still confined to a psychiatric ward, convinced he's a banana.

It was a nice "trip", with lots of sun.

According to a spokesman for the California Ophthalmological Society, four college students suffered permanent impairment of vision as a result of staring at the sun while under the influence of LSD.

One of the youths told his doctor he was "holding a religious conversation with the sun."

Another said he was gazing at the sun "to produce unusual visual displays."

The students, all males, suffered damage to the retina, and the sensory membrane that receives the image formed by the lens.

In the same way a piece of paper will burn when bright light is beamed through a magnifying glass, a pinhead-size hole was burned into the retina of each eye of the students as sunlight passed through the lens. What this has left the students with is not total blindness, but "a blind spot" in the center of their vision. As a result, the victims have lost their reading vision completely and forever.

The ophthalmological spokesman explained, "If you wanted to read, you might see all of the corners of the page and most of the print -- except you wouldn't be able to see that one word you were directly looking at. If you were to look at a traffic stoplight, you might see the pole and trees and cars -- but you wouldn't see the stoplight itself. That little black hole always moves directly where you want to see."

"Solar burns of the retina", the spokesman said, "are not uncommon, particularly among children watching eclipses of the sun." But he knew of no previous cases which resulted from someone being under the influence of LSD.

In the cases here, the victims admitted they were users of LSD.

The spokesman said it was his impression that each of the sun-staring incidents occurred separately.

He did not know whether the students knew each other.

"The four had no awareness of pain or discomfort while the sun was burning through the eye tissue," the spokesman said. "The damage is permanent, because tissue that damaged does not regenerate itself."

"I was planning to blow the 'chit' out of the plane. I wanted to kill all the 'Ahmedicans' (americans) and Jews to show that we are a peace loving pipple."

What happens when mean spirited pranks get out of hand, and real harm is done? It's our nature to play pranks -- the appeal is that they make us feel powerful. Whether we're throwing a prank at someone we know is bound to panic, or merely engaging in mindless vandalism, we're in charge. We say how much gets destroyed or how far the prank goes. There's something deeply satisfying in leaving a big mess, then snickering behind our hands as others try to figure out who the perpetrators were. But sometimes the jokes can turn ugly.

"Butt Bomb"

An America Airlines flight enroute from Los Angeles to JFK airport in New York City was diverted to Kansas City when a passenger was noticed attempting to light a fuse protruding from his rectum. Flight Attendant Cee Cee Harding said she noticed the man seated in an aisle seat leaning forward and holding a cigarette lighter behind his legs.

"I though he was just trying to light a fart," said Harding, "like our pilots are always doing on layovers. Then I saw some string-like thing hanging from his ass, and I got scared."

Harding immediately called for assistance. Several male passengers subdued the man before he was able to light the fuse.

After landing in Kansas City, authorities found the man's intestines were stuffed with military grade C4 explosive. FBI agents stated that it would have been a complete catastrophe if the passenger had succeeded in lighting the fuse.

The passenger, Mohammed Rahim Apu Ali Baba Mafai Kajaffe Ahmed Sharif Opdahl Rajpal Anupma Smith, Age 28, was carrying fourteen passports from various countries throughout the middle east.

When asked why he had stuffed himself full of plastic explosives, Mohammed Rahim Apu Ali Baba Mafai Kajaffe Ahmed Sharif Opdahl Rajpal Anupma Smith stated, "I was planning to blow the 'chit' out of the plane. I wanted to kill all the 'Ahmedicans' (americans) and Jews to show that we are a peace loving pipple."

Airport security agents in Los Angeles remembered seeing Mohammed Rahim Apu Ali Baba Mafai Kajaffe Ahmed Sharif Opdahl Rajpal Anupma Smith as he boarded American flight 90. They were a bit concerned because his name would not fit on the front of the ticket, he was wearing a checkered tablecloth as a hat, and he was reading an Al Quaeda training manual and had on a "F*** America" T-shirt. However, according to Federal Airport Security standards, individuals cannot be profiled for additional security simply because they are young, middle-eastern men.

The security supervisor, Jack Leonard, said he was somewhat concerned with the way Mohammed Rahim Apu Ali Baba Mafai Kajaffe Ahmed Sharif Opdahl Rajpal Anupma Smith walked.

"Hell, the guy waddled like he had a stick of dynamite up his ass! Had I not been on the phone with my probation officer, I might have checked this guy out some more. But, we want and need complete diversity in our passenger screening," stated Leonard. "Plus, we think the flight crews on those planes pose more of a threat to safety than one raghead with an exploding ass. That's why you can always find one of them pilots in barefeet waiting for his shoes to be x-rayed. I love seeing the look on their faces when we make them do that."

He guffawed, adding "I just hope they don't give those guys guns, cause they might want to even the score."

Federal officials are now referring to this latest terrorist attempt as a "butt bomb". Security experts believe this could be even more difficult to detect than the primitive 'shoe bomb' used by terrorist Richard Reid.

"I'm not sure how were going to check for 'butt bombs,'" stated Leonard. "We don't have technologyto do it, but we've got to check somehow in the interest of safety," adding, "I think we should start with the Flight Attendants first."

Did You Know? *Following a drinking binge in New York, Sam Salinski passed out, so his buddies stripped him and shaved off his eyebrows as a joke. Getting no reaction, they proceeded to cut off his ear and glue it onto his forehead. Doctors managed to sew it back on.*

"Mommy, when I grow up I wanna be a Policeman-nequin."

Just outside a town in New Jersey there was a stretch of road greatly favoured by speeders. The local police couldn't afford to keep a patrolman assigned there, so they dressed a mannequin in a cop's uniform, seated it behind the wheel of an old patrol car no longer worth fixing, and positioned the car by the side of the road.

It worked ... but only after a fashion. Those breezing through from someplace else slowed down as soon as they saw the squad car lying in wait, but the locals weren't taken in by it at all. Then some of the local good ol' boys took to shooting up the car and its dummy as they drove by. Pretty soon the squad car was a wreck.

One day a carload of youths spotted the bright, shiny new squad car parked where the bullet-riddled one had been. They aimed their shotguns and blasted away, only to see a real policeman slump forward onto the steering wheel, blood gushing from his wounds. Seems the local council finally found the money to keep a patrolman assigned there.

Luckily, most of the other workers were off that day or the man might have lost all his fingers.

We fear what we don't understand, so advances in industry and technology bring with them a new set of scary legends. There is nothing less comprehensible to the average person than the flood of new-fangled machines, devices, and technology that constantly intrude our daily lives.

"Don't Pee On The Electirc Tower"

There are many transmission lines that crisscross Connecticut, which are held up by Transmission Towers of various constructions. They are called "Metal Ornamental Towers" and are most commonly installed near urban areas, and are supposedly prettier than wood towers. More often than not, adventurous folks climb these towers in order to enjoy the view and the night air. Most stay away from the wires, and when they get bored, come back down.

Apparently, a man who was distraught after a spat with his girlfriend needed some fresh air to clear his head and decided to climb a tower. He stopped for a 6 pack of beer to help clear his thoughts, went to a tower, and climbed it.

The man sat there 60 feet above the highway, drank his beer and consoled his bruised ego. After 5 beers, he needed to do what people often need to do after 5 beers, and it being such a long hike down, he unzipped and did his business right there off the tower.

Electricity is a funny thing. One doesn't need to touch a wire in order to get shocked. Depending on conditions, 115,000 volt lines, like those supported by the tower, could shock a person as far away as 6 feet.

When the man "whizzed" near the conductor, the power raced up his "stream", because urine is an excellent conductor of electricity, traveled up to his private parts, and blew him off the tower.

The guys at the power company noted a momentary outage on the line and sent repairmen to see if there was any damage. When they got to the scene of the accident, they found a very dead person, his fly down, what was left of his private parts smoking, and a single beer left on top.

Exploding Lighter

In 1983 a Burlington Northern railroad worker had his leg blown off by an exploding Bic butane lighter. It seems that the worker who had a Bic lighter in his pocket was walking by another worker who was engaged in wielding some steel. One of the sparks from the wielder landed on the pants of the Bic carrying worker. The spark burnt through the fabric of the pants and contacted the Bic lighter.

"The Bic lighter exploded with the force of a stick of dynamite," said one witness.

The worker subsequently lost his leg.

Fingered

A Polish man working in a saw mill must have had his thoughts on something else when he pushed a plank of wood too far and sliced one of his fingers off. When his colleague asked the man what had happened, he simply put another plank of wood on the saw mill and repeated what he had done, lopping off another finger. Immediatley he was rushed to the hospital, and the doctors were able to reattach the first finger he originally cut off. Luckily, most of the other workers were off that day or the man might have lost all his fingers.

Fused Lenses

A welder from Lexington, Kentucky, recently started to experience headaches and blurred vision. On his wife's advice, he went to the opticians for an eye test, and was told he was short-sighted. He told the optician he didn't want to wear glasses, so he was prescribed contact lenses. Wearing his contact lenses, the man was delighted to find he could see things in detail, and experienced a new lease of life. However, one day he was doing a particularly tricky piece of welding, and removed his goggles so he could see better. Unfortunately, the welding generated so much heat, it caused his contact lenses to fuse to his cornea.

Satellite Fire

A man in Bakersfield, California bought a satellite dish, and being rather miserly he decided to set it up himself. Climbing up his ladder, he attached the dish to the side of his house. Then, with his wife inside shouting to him when the reception was best, he adjusted it. Finally satisfied, he and his wife relaxed for a night in front of the television. The next day was a real scorcher, but still enamoured by the satellite television, the couple stayed in. That afternoon, they heard sirens and shouting outside. The man went outside to find out the cause of the commotion, and saw the house across the road on fire. The fire was put out, but the house was completely gutted. The firemen were unable to work out how the fire had started.

The man thought no more of it. However, the next day, a fire inspector was examining the charred remains when a sudden flash of sunlight caught his attention. The inspector eventually worked out that the neighbour's satellite dish had been concentrating the sun's rays on the curtains of the house and had caused the fire. The man was fined $3,000 and forced to take down his satellite dish. The next year he got cable.

Shoe Shock

An electrician who was hired by his local council to maintain and repair the boroughs street lights ended up in the hospital after a well-intentioned passer-by attempted to save him from what appeared to be certain death. While the electrician was high up a ladder trying to rewire one of the street lights, he became bothered by a stone in his shoe. Rather than taking the shoe off, he attempted to move the stone by shaking his leg vigorously. A passer-by who was out walking his dog at the time, happened to look up at the electrician shaking his leg, and immediatley assumed it was the result of a convulsion brought on by a huge shock of electricity from the street lamp. Naturally, he did what any sensible person would do, and attempted to free the victim from the source of the shock. Unfortunately, this involved kicking the ladder out from under the electrician, an action that resulted in two broken legs and several months off work.

Speed Trap

A report was revealed that two traffic patrol officers from London, England were involved in an unusual incident while checking for speeding motorists on the road between London and Edinburgh.

Last September, the officers were using a hand-held radar device to trap unwary motorists. One of the unnamed officers used the device to check the speed of an approaching vehicle, and was surprised to find that his target had registered a speed in excess of 350 miles per hour. The $15,000 machine then seized up and could not be reset by the bemused police officer's. It turns out, the radar had in fact latched on to a NATO Tornado aircraft in the North Sea, which was taking part in a simulated low-flying exercise over the Borders and Southern Scotland.

Following a complaint by Sir William Sutherland, Chief Constable of the Lothian and Borders Police force to the RAF liaison office, it was revealed that the officers had a lucky escape. The tactical computer on board the aircraft not only detected and jammed the "hostile" radar equipment, but had automatically armed a Sidewinder air-to-ground missile ready to neutralize the perceived threat. Luckily the Dutch pilot was alerted to the missile status and was able to override the automatic protection system before the missile launched.

The Police have declined to comment, although it is understood that officers will be advised to point their radar guns inland in the future.

Manbeef

There's an old saying, "You are what you eat." And in world of folklore this rings true. Though many cultures favor wildly different culinary creations, one dish taboo to everyone is the flesh of our own species. Just the thought of consuming it, inadvertently or indirectly is enough to give us the shudders. These stories are food for creepy thought. Bone appétit!

Hmmm! Juicy White Men

In June 2001, a self-ordained minister of his own Blessed Children Church left Melbourne, Australia with his wife Sherry and their daughters Paula, Anna and Lisa. The ill-fated Reverend was determined to bring religion to a tribe of satanic cannibals in New Guinea. He dragged his fearful wife and daughters into the jungles of New Guinea. His sister begged him not to risk his babies' lives like that. But he said the cannibals would love his kids, and that would make his job even easier. As it turned out the Reverend guessed right. The Tuoari tribesmen loved him and his children, they promptly ate the Reverend, his wife and their three daughters.

Concerned locals said, "We tried to tell him that Tuoaris don't want missionaries. They are perfectly happy worshiping the devil and eating any juicy white man who comes along."

"Neighboring tribes say that the preacher and his family were in the stewpot before he ever got his Bible out of his duffel bag," reported Detective Nabu Doka, "The Tuoaris ate like kings and danced all night long."

Did You Know? *For the last 20 years ManBeef has been the worlds leading human meat distributor. They have established a reputation for providing the highest quality human meat products and dedicated customer service representatives. Because they only cater to a select group of people, Manbeef tries to keep a close relationship with all of their customers. This allows them to help get their clients the best quality human meat for their budget, and ship it right to their front door.*

Well-Preserved Jamaican Rum

A number of years ago, the father of a friend of a friend of mine bought a fairly enormous house in Virginia, it was one of those Victorian style homes built on the site of an older farmhouse.

In the cellars they found half a dozen very large barrels.

"How wonderful!" said the mother, "We can cut them in half and plant orange trees in them."

Immediately they set to work cutting the barrels in half, but found that one of them was not empty, so they set it up and borrowed the necessary equipment from a local pub. The cellar filled with a rich, heady Jamaican odour.

"Good Lord!" said the father, "It's Rum!" and proceeded to take advantage of the some fifty gallons of the stuff before cutting the barrel in half.

About a year later, after gallons of rum punch had been consumed, it was getting hard to get any more rum out of the barrel, even by tipping it up with wedges. So they cut it in half, and found inside, the well-preserved body of a man.

Who's For Dinner

An Italian family received an unexpected package from an aunt who had emigrated to the USA a few years before. On discovering that the package contained a jar of dark powder, the mother decided that it must be some exotic spice, and that evening, made a pasta sauce using the powder. The family were more than pleased with the strong meaty flavour the powder gave to their pasta dishes. However, they were more than distraught the next morning when they received a letter from their aunt telling them to expect their uncles cremated remains any day.

The man pretty much psyched himself to death.

Daily life is hazardous, and no matter how imaginative our precautions, or how steadfast our vigilance, the unthinkable does happen. Sometimes even doing all the right things to prevent these freakish fatalities are nowhere near enough. Here are a few legends that speak to that fear, that all our good planning and careful thought may not protect us from these bizarre mishaps.

Bad Gas

One hot summer day, a couple had a few friends over for a barbecue. After everybody had eaten, the man of the house, who had been drinking since that morning, slipped on a piece of dropped meat and twisted his ankle. A friend immediately took the injured host to hospital.

Meanwhile, the party came to an end, the guests left, and the wife started cleaning up the mess. She noticed the can of gasoline her husband had been using to light the barbecue was virtually empty, and not wanting to contaminate the sink, she poured the contents down the guest toilet. A few minutes later, the husband returned from the hospital, and his wife fussed over him before returning to the clean up. The husband had a sudden urge for the toilet, but because of his ankle he couldn't make it upstairs so he went to the guest bathroom. As he sat down, he lit himself a cigarette. By the time he noticed the smell of gasoline, it was too late, the toilet exploded.

Cactus Landing

A man was flying his glider through the Arizona desert one day, when the wind suddenly dropped and he was forced to make a crash-landing. The man crashed into a giant cactus, and fortunately survived the landing. The pilot got out of the cockpit and began dancing wildly in the sand, overjoyed to still be alive. However, the crash dislodged the cactus, which consequently toppled over and squashed the man.

Died of Laughter

On April 22, 1975, 55-year-old bricklayer Mitch Bryant of Norfolk, England, kicked the bucket while roaring with laughter at one of his favorite British television shows, the comedy programme "The Goodies". The skit that precipitated Bryant's fatal fit of gleeg involved a kilted Scotsman's flailing away with his bagpipe at a vicious black pudding intent upon attacking him.

"Bryant was unable to stop laughing, and after twenty-five minutes of uproar he gave one last "tremendous belly laugh, slumped on the settee, and died," said his widow who witnessed his passing.

Making Mr. Bryant the first man in history to "die laughing."

Did You Know? *Police say a lawyer demonstrating the safety of windows in a downtown Toronto skyscraper crashed through a pane with his shoulder and plunged 24 floors to his death into the courtyard of the Toronto Dominion Bank Tower. He was explaining the strength of the building's windows to visiting interns.*

Emergency Call

A French man just moved into an apartment on the outskirts of Paris. The phone hadn't been connected yet, so he went to a telephone booth around the corner to phone his girlfriend and invite her over to see his new flat. While chatting to his girlfriend, a man, looking as if he'd been sleeping on the streets for years, started banging on the telephone booth. The man turned his back, ignored the bum and continued talking to his girlfriend. Finally, the tramp screamed that it was an emergency, and continued banging until the man relented, finished the conversation, and hung up. Before he could admonish him, the tramp pushed past to use the phone. The man shrugged, and returned to his apartment. However, on turning the corner, he realised why the tramp was making such a fuss, his apartment was on fire.

Fluff and Folded

A 40-year-old Charlottesville man died in a freak accident involving his washing machine. According to police reports, Randolph Strickland was doing laundry when he tried to speed up the process. Strickland apparently tried to stuff approximately 50 pounds of laundry into his washing machine by climbing on top of the washer and attempting to force the clothing into the basin. Apprently, Strickland then accidentally kicked the washing machine's ON button. When the machine turned on, Strickland lost his balance and both feet went down into the machine, where they got stuck. The machine started its cycle, and Strickland, unable to free himself, started thrashing around as the machine's agitator went into gear. Stricklands head started banging against a nearby shelf, knocking over a bottle of bleach, which poured over his face, blinding him.

Forensic reports say Strickland apparently also swallowed some of the bleach. He then vomited, but was still unable to free himself. Strickland's dog apparently came into the laundry room, at about the same time.

According to police, a large box of baking soda fell from the shelf, startling the dog, which then urinated. Urine, like vinegar, is acidic, and the chemical reaction between the urine and the baking soda resulted in "a small explosion."

However, the dog escaped unharmed, but Strickland remained stuck in the washing machine, which eventually went into its high-speed spin cycle, spinning Strickland around at about 80 miles per hour, according to forensic experts.

Strickson's head then smashed against a steel beam behind the washing machine, immediately killing him. A neighbor heard the commotion and called 911, but Strickland, a 1995 graduate of Virginia Tech, was pronounced dead at the scene.

I Can't Even Afford To Die

A social worker in Glasgow had to visit a woman who had been put through the mill due to the incompetent Tories' recession. The worst slump since the 1930s had decimated her life, and nothing was going right.

The company she worked for had sacked her, and then she went bust, so she had no redundancy money after sixteen years' service. Her husband had lost his well-paid job in the building trade and they'd fallen way behind on their mortgage.

The house was about to be repossessed, but it had plummeted in value so they owed the building society more than it was worth. The car and furniture had been taken by the bailiffs, and every letter was a final demand.

Finally, the strain of living on the breadline had wrecked their marriage and her husband had left to build a new life for himself in Austrailia.

It was the last straw; the poor woman had enough, and decided to end it all. So she opened the oven, stuck her head inside and switched the gas full on. But she awoke the next day with a stinking headache, only to find the gas supply had been cut off.

Did You Know? *A man found himself locked in one of those giant walk in freezers. He was convinced he was going to freeze to death, so he began writing a letter. His letter ended with a final passage saying he could not write anymore because his fingers were beginning to freeze. When they found him dead, not only did they find the letters but they discover that the freezer's temperature never dropped below 50 degrees. Thus, the man pretty much psyched himself to death.*

Let's Go Get Chipmunk Faced!

In Tokyo, the recent craze for hydrogen beer is the heart of a three way lawsuit between unemployed stockbroker Takashi Kyoto, the Tic-Tac-Toe karaoke bar and the Otama Beer Corporation.

Mr. Kyoto is suing the bar and the brewery for selling and distributing toxic substances and is claiming damages for grievous bodily harm leading to the loss of his job. The bar is countersuing for defamation and loss of customers.

The Otama Beer corporation brews "Asaka" brand beer, where the carbon dioxide normally used to add fizz has been replaced by the more environmentally friendly hydrogen gas. A side effect of this has made the beer extremely popular at karaoke sing-along bars and discotheques.

Hydrogen, like helium, is a gas lighter than air. Because hydrogen molecules are lighter than air, sound waves are transmitted more rapidly; individuals whose lungs are filled with the nontoxic gas can speak with an uncharacteristically high voice. Exploiting this quirk of physics, chic urbanites can now sing soprano on karaoke sing-along machines after consuming a big gulp of Asaka beer.

The flammable nature of hydrogen has also become another selling point, even though Otama has not acknowledged that this was a deliberate marketing ploy.

It has inspired a new craze of blowing flames from one's mouth using a cigarette as an ignition source. Many new karaoke videos feature singers shooting blue flames in slow motion, while flame contests take place in pubs everywhere.

"Mr. Kyoto has no-one to blame but himself. If he had not been drunk and disorderly, none of this would have happened. Our security guards undergo the most careful screening and training before they are allowed to deal with customers" said Mr. Toshira Yochama, Manager of the Tic-Tac-Toe bar.

Mr. Yochama went on to add, "Mr. Kyoto drank fifteen bottles of Asaka hydrogen beer in order to maximise the size of the flames he could belch during the contest. He catapulted balls of fire across the room that Mothra would be proud of, but this was not enough to win him first prize since the judgement is based on the quality of the flames and that of the singing, and after fifteen bottles of lager he was out of tune."

"Mr. Kyoto took exception to the result and hurled blue fireballs at the judge, setting the front of Mrs. Nomura's hair on fire, entirely removing her eyebrows, lashes, and ruining the clothes of two nearby customers. None of these people have returned to my bar. When my security staff approached, he turned his attentions to them, making it almost impossible to approach him. Our head bouncer had no choice but to hurl himself at Mr. Kyoto's knees, knocking his legs out from under him."

"The laws of physics are not to be disobeyed, and the force that propelled Mr. Kyoto's legs backwards also pivoted around his centre of gravity and moved his upper body forward with equal velocity. It was his own fault he had his mouth open for the next belch, his own fault he held a lit cigarette in front of it and it is own fault he swallowed that cigarette, and The Tic-Tac-Toe bar takes no responsibility for the subsequent internal combustion, rupture of his stomach lining, nor the third degree burns to his oesophagus, larynx and sinuses as the exploding gases forced their way out of his body. His consequential muteness and loss of employment are his own fault."

Did You Know? *Sponge Bob Square Pants is being cancelled because a four yearr old boy on a cruise ship with his parents, finished breakfast and announced he was going to see "Sponge Bob". His parents, thinking that he was going down to the cabin to watch TV agree that it was a good idea. However, the child proceeded to jump over the rail and drown in his attempt to visit Sponge Bob who "lives in a pineapple under the sea".*

Mode Of Death

On May 7, 2003 a medical examiner viewed the body of Claude Casey and concluded that he died from a gunshot wound to the head caused by a shotgun. Investigation to that point revealed that the decedent had jumped from the top of a ten story building with the intent to commit suicide, a note was found indicating his despondency. As he passed the 9th floor on the way down, his life was interrupted by a shotgun blast through a window, killing him instantly. Neither the shooter nor the decedent was aware that a safety net had been erected at the 7th floor level to protect window washers, and that the decedent would not have been able to complete his intent to commit suicide because of this.

Ordinarily, a person who starts into motion the events with an intent for suicide ultimately commits suicide even though the mechanism might be not what he intended. Because he was shot on the way to certain death nine stories below probably would not change his mode of death from suicide to homicide, but the fact that his attempt to commit suicide would not have been achieved under any circumstance caused the medical examiner to feel he had homicide on his hands.

Further investigation led to the discovery that the room on the 9th floor from where the shotgun blast emanated was occupied by an elderly man and his wife. He was threatening her with the shotgun because of an interspousal spat, and became so upset that he could not hold the shotgun straight. Therefore, when he pulled the trigger, he completely missed his wife, and the bullets went through the window, striking the decedent.

"When one intends to kill subject person A, but kills person B in the attempt, one is guilty of the murder of person B," stated the medical examiner. "The old man was confronted with this conclusion, but both he and his wife were adamant in stating that neither knew that the shotgun was loaded"

It was a longtime habit of the old man to threaten his wife with an unloaded shotgun. He had no intent to murder her; therefore, the killing of the decedent appeared then to be an accident, because the gun had been accidentally loaded.

But further investigation turned up a witness that their son was seen loading the shotgun approximately two weeks prior to the fatal accident. The investigation also showed that the mother had cut off her son's financial support, and her son, knowing the propensity of his father to use the shotgun threateningly, loaded the gun with the expectation that the father would shoot his mother. The case now became one of murder on the part of the son for the death of Claude Casey.

Further investigation revealed that the son became increasingly despondent over the failure of his attempt to get his mother murdered. This led him to jump off the ten story building on May 7, only to be killed by a shotgun blast through a 9th story window. The medical examiner closed the case as a suicide.

Did You Know? *An Indian man who decided to spend his life in a tree died after eight months. He fell out of it.*

TV Did A Much Better Job Raising Me Than My Parents!

An 11-year-old boy watched the film Poltergeist at a friend's house and was unduly influenced by its content. One night, his mother found him sitting in front of the television after transmissions had finished for the day staring at the "snow" on the screen, and any attempt to remove him from the television to put him to bed ended up with the boy in hysterics. This went on for a few nights and the parents were at their wits end, so they asked their friends for advice. One of them suggested they put a radio transmitter in the television set and try talking to him through that. The parents followed their friends advice, and putting on a ghostly voice, the father talked to the boy through the TV, and were delighted when the boy responded. When the father told his son to go to bed, they were even more delighted when he obeyed. It became a nightly ritual and the parents found life became a lot easier for them, because anything they asked of their son, he would do. He got up for school without complaint, helped make meals, did all his homework and all his chores, as long as they told him to do things through the television.

The new ones had the texture of cooked oatmeal.

There's the common burglar, the armed robber, and the criminal who cold-bloodedly kills his victims before stripping them of their valuables. However, there is a class of thief who fills the niche between these criminals: the mutilator. He may spare his victims' lives, but he's not averse to chopping off one or two of their body parts to acquire as his loot. For the "body snatcher" sometimes body parts are the valuables he seeks.

A Better Place?

Residents of a remote village on the border with North Korea seemed oddly reluctant to bury their dead. When asked to explain, many villagers replied that evil spirits came in the night and removed the bodies of their loved ones and took them away to Hell. One journalist investigating the story decided that this explanation seemed less than plausible, because the bodies were removed from above rather than below, so he set out to investigate what was happening. Having arranged for an empty coffin to be buried with the traditionl show and ceremony, he took up a hidden position and waited to see what happened. He did not have to wait long, because a small group of North Koreans crossed over the border from their country, which was in the grip of famine, and dug up what they thought was a fresh body. Apparently, the food situation had become so desperate that they had resorted to cannibalism in order to feed their families.

Thighs Does Matter

A ladies thighs were stolen from her during the night of March 23, 2003. It was just that quick. She went to sleep, and woke up with someone else's thighs.

"The new ones had the texture of cooked oatmeal," the victim told reporters. "Who could have performed such a cruel act? And whose thighs were these?"

She spent the entire summer looking for them. She searched, in vain, at pools and beaches, anywhere she might find female limbs exposed. She became obsessed. She had nightmares filled with cellulite and flesh that turned bumpy in the night. Finally, hurt and angry, she resigned herself to living out her life in jeans and Sheer Energy pantyhose.

Then, just when her guard was down, the thieves struck again. Her ass was next. She knew it was the same gang, because they took pains to match her new rear end, although badly attached at least three inches lower than the original, to the thighs they had stuck her with earlier. Now her rear complemented her legs, lump for lump. Frantic, she prayed that long skirts would stay in fashion.

Then a few months later, while fixing her hair she realized her arms had been switched. She watched, horrified but fascinated, as the flesh of her upper arms swung to and fro with the motion of the hairbrush. This was really getting scary. Her body was being replaced, cleverly and fiendishly, one section at a time. In the end, in deepening despair, she gave up T-shirts.

What could they do to her next? Age? Age had nothing to do with it. Age was supposed to creep up, unnoticed and intangible, something like maturity. No, she was being attacked, repeatedly and without warning. That's why she decided to share her story. She can't take on the medical profession by herself. Women of America, wake up and smell the coffee.

That isn't really "plastic" those surgeons are using. You know where they're getting those replacement parts, don't you? The next time you suspect someone had a face lift, look again! Was it lifted from you? Check out those tummy tucks and buttocks raisings. Look familiar? Are those your eyelids on that movie star? She did eventually find out were her nice slender thighs went... and she hopes that Cindy Crawford paid a really good price for them!

chapterten

--English Soldiers; addressing The French during the Battle of Agincourt.

laughablelore

There is a very fine line seperating joke from urban legend. The same tale can be put in either category, the only distinction is whether or not it is an obvious bit of fictional humor or related as a true story. Here for your reading enjoyment are legends with a humorous twist that could possibly circulate widely as jokes, or assorted bits of amusing lore.

. . . .

"But Mom! You said these were for special occasions!"

Whether you're grocery shopping, or just simply sitting in the comfort of your own home waiting for the repairman, the opportunities for supremely embarrassing ourselves under the simplest of human dealings are tremendous.

Always Thumbtacks

One of the funniest "most-embarrassing-moments" happened to a lady who picked up several items at a discount store. When she finally got up to the checker, she learned that one of the items had no price tag. So the checker got on the intercom and boomed out for all the store to hear, "Price check on aisle ten, Tampax, Supersize!"

That was bad enough, but somebody at the rear of the store apparently misinterpreted the word "tampax" for "thumbtacks", and in a business-like tone, a voice boomed back over the intercom, "Do you want the kind you push in with your thumb, or the kind you pound in with a hammer?"

Blind Man

In Beverly Hills, California, a woman had spent the morning working in her garden. Feeling hot, bothered and somewhat dirty, she went to have a shower. Five minutes into the shower, she heard the doorbell. She was about to put on her bathrobe, when she heard the doorbell ring again and a man shouting, "Blind man!" Assuming it was a blind man begging for money, and not wanting to soak her bathrobe, she ran downstairs and opened the door.

The man at the door just stared at the naked woman, before spluttering out, "Um, hi. I'm here to put the blinds in."

Boys Will Be Boys

A gang of boys were doing their best to show off in front of a group of girls they spotted on a street corner. Being boys, they decided that the best possible way to impress the girls was to ride their bicycles in a dangerous and reckless fashion. All went well to begin with, and the girls were even humouring the boys by pretending to be impressed, but then one junior stuntman decided to go just that little extra mile. Having got up a fair bit of speed, he climbed on to his handlebars of his bicycle and tried to ride along standing upright. For a creature who had barely learned to walk upright, this was a little over ambitious. Inevitably, the bike folded under him and he suddenly found himself with half a handle bar up his ass. This display really impressed the girls, who fell down with laughter until the ambulance took him off to the hospital.

Colors Of The Flag

The father of a family in Dublin, Ireland had just installed a new toilet seat and intended to paint it the colors of the Irish flag - green, white and orange. He painted it green and orange, but ran out of white paint, so he told his wife he was just popping out to the hardware store. However, on his way back, he decided to stop for a quick pint of Guinness in his local pub. Meanwhile, the priest made an unexpected visit, and the mother of the family was entertaining him with tea and biscuits. At one point, the priest asked if he could use the bathroom, so the mother directed him upstairs. When the priest hadn't returned after 30 minutes, the mother went to see what happened to him. The poor priest was fastened to the toilet and had been too embarrassed to shout for help. The mother averted her eyes as she helped the priest off the toilet, and vowed never to say a word about it, although she did giggle when she saw the priest's green and orange backside.

Decorative Encounter

A woman was about to take a shower, when she remembered she was supposed to unlock the back door for the decorator so he could get in to start painting the kitchen. Without thinking, the woman ran downstairs without her clothes on. Just as she opened the back door, the gardener came round the back and saw her.

Embarrassed and somewhat flustered, the woman told the gardener, "Oh, excuse me, I was just waiting for the decorator."

The wrinkled gardener responded with a lascivious wink, "Well, he should have a good time I'll bet," and continued pulling weeds.

He Suffered A Briefcase of Motion Sickness

A financial adviser who worked in downtown Toronto returned to his home in the suburbs after a few hours of drinking with his colleagues. Travelling on a train that was so full of people, he had to stand in the middle of the carriage. At one point, the effect of drinking on an empty stomach and the lurching motion of the train began to make the man feel sick. Realising that he suddenly had to vomit, and knowing he wouldn't make it to the window in time, he opened his briefcase and discretely threw up. The next morning, he woke up with a serious hangover, but suddenly remembered the events of the night before. Rushing down to stop his wife from putting his sandwiches in his briefcase, he found that the briefcase was devoid of vomit. Clearly, he had used a fellow traveller's briefcase on the train, a traveller who must have had a most unpleasant surprise.

Ice Cream When I See Famous People

In Hollywood, California, a famous actor was in an ice cream parlour, when a Canadian tourist came in to buy an ice cream. The tourist recognised the actor, but resisting the urge to swoon, stayed calm, bought her ice cream and left without saying a word. However, a few steps out of the parlour, she realised that while she had taken her change, she was missing her ice cream. Slightly embarrassed, she returned to the ice cream parlour and asked for her ice cream.

The actor stepped up to her, and with a wink, said, "Miss, you'll find your ice cream in your purse, where you put it."

My Scarf

A woman travelling on a subway in New York spotted an expensive cashmere scarf on the floor of the carriage just as a man was leaving. Quick as she could, she grabbed the scarf, threw it out of the door onto the platform, and shouted after the man as the train doors closed. Feeling good about herself, the woman resumed her seat in the carriage, but soon realised that people were staring at her. Then one of them, an elderly man said to her, "Ma'am, are you insane? That was my scarf you just threw out the door."

Phone-y Calls

A friend of a former coworker told me about an incident that recently befell his boss on a train. He was feeling chuffed at claiming a four-seat table for himself and settled down to a nice quiet journey reading his book. The whistle blew and as the train lurched away, a loud, acne'd yuppie trousered his way into the carriage, threw his bags down on the table, collapsed into the seat opposite, and immediately brandished his portable phone and began a loud, oafish conversation: "Buy! ...Sell!... Take a rain check!"

The quieter man couldn't believe his misfortune and tried to ignore the boorish city type, but he was so noisy, ringing up people and rustling papers and shouting into the phone all the time, that the man couldn't take any more and set off with his stuff for another part of the train.

He'd just sat down when an old man opposite him went pale and groaned. He was having a heart attack and collapsed on the floor. The guard arrived as passengers tried to come to the old gent's aid, and he explained that they'd have to wait 'til the next station before they could phone as the train's communication lines were down.

"I know someone with a phone!" said the man happily. "We can ring ahead and have an ambulance waiting for him at the station."

So the guard, the man and some other concerned passengers marched triumphantly back down the carriage. The yuppie was still in mid-conversation when the guard cut in to explain the emergency situation and ask him if they might have the use of his cellphone.

At first the yuppie waved them away as if he was busy, still talking down the line. But when they persisted and got increasingly agitated, he threw the phone down, went the colour of beetroot and looking down mumbled, "You can't. It's a fake phone."

Pump Up The Jam

A salesman staying in Seattle, Washinton returned to his motel a little tipsy after a few drinks in a local bar. It was only 12:30am, so he decided to have a quick dip in the pool before retiring for the night. Since no one was around, he didn't bother with swimming shorts, he just stripped down and dove in. Around 2am, the motel caretaker was roused from a deep sleep by shouts coming from the pool area. He got dressed and wandered down to investigate what sounded like desperate pleas for help. In the pool, the salesman appeared to be struggling against the wall of the swimming pool. The clerk discovered that the man's penis had become stuck in the inlet to the pump that circulated water through the pool's cleaning and filtration plant. Without daring to ask how the swimmer got himself into this predicament, the caretaker switched off the power to the pump, but the man's penis had become so swollen that he was still unable to free himself. Paramedics arrived on the scene, and after careful consideration they applied lubrication around the entry to the pump. The distressed salesman whose quick swim turned into a very painful four-hour soak was eventually released with no long-term after effects, except for a bruised ego.

Share The Love

A co-worker of a friend had one of those corny, positive messages on his answering machine, "Hi! It's a great day and I'm out enjoying it right now. I hope you are too. The thought for the day is 'Share the love.'" Beep.

Naturally, my coworker replied into the machine, "Uh, yeah, this is the VD clinic calling. Speaking of being positive, your test is back. Stop sharing the love."

Special Napkins

My friends mother taught him to read when he was four years old, which was her first mistake. One day, he was in the bathroom and noticed one of the cabinet doors was open. He read one of the boxes in the cabinet, then ran to his mother and asked, "Mother why do you keeping 'napkins' in the bathroom. Don't they belong in the kitchen?"

Not wanting to burden him with unnecessary facts, she told him those were for "special occasions."

A few months later, on Thanksgiving Day, his folks were leaving to pick up the pastor and his wife for dinner. The mom assignmented him and the siblings to set the table while she was gone.

When they returned, the pastor came in first and immediately burst into laughter. Next came his wife who gasped, then began giggling. Next came his father, who roared with laughter. Then mom entered, who almost died of embarrassment when she noticed each place setting on the table had a "special occasion" napkin accompanying each plate, with the fork carefully arranged on top. He even tucked the little tails in so they didn't hang off the edge!

His mother asked him why he used these, and of course, his response sent the other adults into further fits of laughter when he said, "But Mom! You said these were for special occasions!"

Team Player

A housewife spent the afternoon doing the laundry. Her washer and dryer were located in the basement of her family's home, so she took a basketful of dirty laundry to the basement to put in the washer, and decided to strip off her own clothing to add it to the load. She then removed a load of clean laundry from the dryer, put it in the basket, and was about to walk up the basement steps with it, when she noticed that her son left his football helmet on the steps. She picked up the helmet to take it to his room, but having no other place to put it with both arms holding the laundry basket, she plunked it on her head. At that moment the outside basement door opened. It was the meterman who had come to read the meters, also located in the basement. The housewife dropped the basket, and stood exposed in the sunlight streaming in through the open doorway.

The meterman gulped, and said, "I sure hope your team wins, lady."

'For Unlawful Carnal Knowledge'

Language -- the very tool we use to communicate to each other is it self a source of folklore The plethora of dirty words and rude phrases in use today have very interesting origins that have become obscured in the mists of time. Some of the more famous terms have attracted specious explanations of their origins which paint them as irredeemably offensive when in fact they are perfectly innocuous.

Fornication Under Consent Of The King

In ancient England a person could not have sex unless you had consent of the King, or if you were a member of the Royal Family. When anyone wanted to have a baby, they got consent of the King. The King gave them a placard that they hung on their door while they were having sex. The placard had the letter F.U.C.K on it -- menaing "Fornication Under Consent of the King". Now you know where that came from.

It has also been said that the f-word comes from colonial times, when someone would be punished for 'prostitution'. It was an acronym for the words: 'For Unlawful Carnal Knowledge'. F.U.C.K. was written on the stocks that held these criminals because officers got sick and tired of writing those 26 characters, not including spaces, so it got abbreviated to F.U.C.K. and stuck.

Pluck Yew!

During the Battle of Agincourt. The French, who were overwhelmingly favored to win the battle, threatened to cut a certain body part off of all captured English soldiers so that they could never fight again. The English won in a major upset and waved the body part in question at the French in defiance. What was this body part?

The body part which the French proposed to cut off of the English after defeating them was, of course, the middle finger, without which it is impossible to draw the renowned English longbow. This famous weapon was made of the native English yew tree, and so the act of drawing the longbow was known as "plucking yew". Thus, when the victorious English waved their middle fingers at the defeated French, they said, "See, we can still pluck yew! PLUCK YEW!"

Over the years "pluck yew" became rather difficult to say, like "pleasant mother pheasant plucker", which is who you had to go to for the feathers used on the arrows. The difficult consonant cluster at the beginning has gradually changed to a labiodental fricative 'f', and thus the words often used in conjunction with the one-finger-salute are mistakenly thought to have something to do with an intimate encounter. It is also because of the pheasant feathers on the arrows that the symbolic gesture is known as "giving the bird".

Ship In High Transit

In the 1800's, cow pie's were collected on the prairies and boxed and loaded on steam ships to burn instead of wood. Wood was not only hard to find, but heavy to move around and store.

When the boxes of cow pie's were in the sun for days on board these ships, they would begin to smell extremely bad. So when the manure was boxed up, they stamped the outside of the box, S.H.I.T....which means, 'Ship High In Transit'.

When people came aboard the ship and said,"Oh what is that smell!" They were told it was shit. That is where the saying came from...It smells like shit!

"Hello, you fat bastard."

The world has its own rich lore of legendary pranks; some true, some not. Its human nature for

159

people to enjoy putting one over on their comrades whenever possible, and they are not above employing animals, food, or strange inanimate objects, such as toilet seats or the telephone to do so. Our trusting friends become the unwitting accomplices to whatever scheme we can induce them to participate in. Here is a sample of such debauchery.

"American Resurgent, an Essay in Street Art. Please give Generously"

The primary reasons cat flaps are called cat flaps is because they are flaps specifically designed for cats, as opposed to dogs, or giraffes, or humans. All of this became abundantly clear to teenager Evan Ecks, of Aurora, Illinois, after spending two days wedged in one while using it in an attempt to get into his house because he had mislaid his keys. Unfortunately he was spotted by a group of young pranksters who removed his trousers and pants, painted his bottom bright blue, stuck a daffodil between his buttocks and erected a sign saying, "American Resurgent, an Essay in Street Art. Please give Generously".

Passers-by assumed Mr. Ecks screams were part of the act and it was only when an old woman complained to the police that he was finally freed.

"I kept calling for help," he said, "but people just said, "Very good! Very clever!" and threw coins at me."

A modern version of David and Goliath...

A young man upset the big bully in a small town in redneck Alabama, with the result that the bully threatened to tear the young man limb from limb that night if he saw him. Knowing from past experience that the bully was true to his word, but not wanting to give in to the bully's threats, the 90 pound weakling hatched a plan. Early that evening, he tip-toed by the bully's residence and put a jar of wasps in the back of his car. A little later, as the bully was driving into town, the angry buzzing wasps caused him to crash his car into a tree.

Hotel Delilah

Delilah Braun of Los Angeles, California, had a serious telephone problem. But unlike most people she did something about it.

The brand-new $100 million Los Angeles Plaza Hotel opened nearby and had acquired almost the same telephone number as Delilah.

From the moment the motel opened, Delilah was besieged by calls not for her. Since she had the same phone number for years, she felt that she had a case to persuade the hotel management to change its number. However, the management refused claiming that it could not change its stationery.

The phone company was not helpful, either. A number was a number, and just because a customer was getting someone else's calls 24 hours a day didn't make it responsible. After her pleas fell on deaf ears, Delilah decided to take matters into her own hands.

At 9 o'clock the phone rang. Someone from Austin, Texas was calling the hotel asking for a room for the following weekend. Delilah said, "No problem. How many nights?"

A few hours later Aspen, Colorado checked in. A secretary wanted a suite with two bedrooms for a week. Emboldened, Delilah said the Presidential Suite on the 18th floor was available for $1600 a night. The secretary said that she would take it and asked if the hotel wanted a deposit.

"No, that won't be necessary," Delilah said. "We trust you."

The next day was a busy one for Delilah. In the morning, she booked a Financial Planners convention for

Memorial Day weekend, a college prom and a reunion of the 82nd Airborne veterans from World War II.

During lunchtime she turned on her answering machine so she could watch "The Ellen Degeneres Show", but her biggest challenge came in the afternoon when a mother called to book the ballroom for her daughter's wedding in May.

Delilah assured the woman that it would be no problem and asked if she would be providing the flowers, or if she wanted the hotel to take care of that. The mother said that she would prefer the hotel handle the floral arrangements. Then the question of valet parking came up.

Once again Delilah was helpful. "There's no charge for valet parking, but we always recomend that the clients tip the drivers."

Within a few months, the Los Angeles Plaza Motel became a disaster area. People kept showing up for weddings, bar mitzvahs, Sweet Sixteen parties, and conventions, but were all told there were no such events.

Delilah had her final revenge when she read in the local paper that the motel might go bankrupt. Her phone rang, and an executive from Marriott said, "We're prepared to offer you $50 million for the motel."

Delilah replied. "We'll take it, but only if you change the telephone number."

Did You Know? *Phone hackers, managed to break into the telephone system of 'Weight Watchers and changed the outgoing message to "Hello, you fat bastard."*

Just Dial

I was sitting at my desk, when I remembered a phone call I had to make. I found the number and dialed it. A man answered nicely saying, "Hello?" I politely said, "This is Daryl, could I please speak to Ron Nelson?"

Suddenly the phone was slammed down on me. I couldn't believe that anyone could be that rude. So I tracked down Ron's correct number and called him. Turns out Ron transposed the last two digits. After I hung up with Ron, I noticed the wrong number still lying there on my desk. So I decided to call it again.

When the same person once more answered, I yelled "You friggin' loser!" and hung up.

Next to his phone number I wrote the word "loser," and put it in my desk drawer. Every couple of weeks, when I was paying bills, or had a really bad day, I'd call him up. He'd answer, and then I'd yell, "Loser!" It always cheered me up.

Later in the year the phone company introduced me to caller ID. This was a real disappointment for me, because I would have to stop calling "loser". Then one day I had an idea. I dialed his number, and heard him answer, "Hello."

"Yeah. This is Mark with the telephone company and I'm just calling to see if you're familiar with our caller ID program?"

He yelled, "No!" and slammed the phone down.

I quickly called him back and said, "That's because you're a friggin' loser!"

Just Redial

An old lady at the mall really took her time pulling out of the parking space. I didn't think she was ever going to leave, but finally her car began to move and she started to slowly back out of the stall. I backed up a little more to give her plenty of room to pull out.

All of a sudden this red Sunfire came flying up the parking aisle in the wrong direction and pulled into her space. I started honking the horn and yelling, "You can't just do that, you Asshole.. I was here first!"

The guy climbed out of his Sunfire completely ignoring me, and walked toward the mall as if he didn't even hear me.

I thought to myself, this guy's a friggin'' jerk". Then I noticed a For Sale sign in the back window of his car. I wrote down the number. Then hunted for another place to park.

A couple of days later, I was at home sitting at my desk writing this book. I had just gotten off the phone with "Loser!" It's really easy to call him now since I have his number on speed dial. I noticed the phone number of the guy with the red sunfire lying on the desk and thought I'd better call this guy to see how he is doing.

After a couple rings someone answered the phone and said, "Hello."

I said, "You the guy with the red Sunfire for sale?"

"Yes I am." he said.

So I asked if I could come and take a look at it.

He said "Of course, and gave me his address, "Yes live at 102 West 33rd Street. It's a blue house and the car's parked right out front."

I decided to be friendly and asked his name. He told me it was Danny Blake. "When's a good time to catch you, Danny?" I asked.

"I'm home in the evenings." he replied.

"Listen Danny, can I tell you something?" I asked.

He said "Yes."

Then I yelled, "Danny you're a friggin' jerk!" And slammed the phone down.

After I hung up I added Danny Blake's number to my speed dial.

For a while things seemed to be going really good for me. Now when I had a problem I had two jerks to call. Then after several months of calling "Jerk" and "Loser" and hanging up on them, the whole thing started to seem like an obligation. It just wasn't as enjoyable as it used to be. So I gave this problem some serious thought and came up with a solution.

First, I had my phone dial "Jerk", which was speed dial#1. A man answered nicely saying, "Hello." I yelled "Friggin' jerk!" But didn't hang up.

The jerk said, "Are you still there?"

I said, "Yeah.."

He said, "Stop calling me."

I said, "No."

He said, "What's your name, pal?"

I said, "Danny Blake."

He asked were I live, so I told him, "I live at 102 West 33rd Street. It's a blue house and my red Sunfire is parked out front, but you don't have the balls to come over you Jerk!"

The phone conversation ended with him yelling,"I'm coming over right now, Asshole! You'd better start saying your prayers," and he hung up.

Then I called "Loser", which was speed dial #2.

He answered, "Hello."

I said, "Hello? Friggin' loser!"

He yelled, "If I ever find out who you are..."

"You'll what?" I interuped.

"I'll kick your ass!" he said.

"Oh yeah? I replied, "You just wait right there. I'm coming over right now, loser!" And I hung up.

Rock Candy

Times were bad for a sweet factory that supplied rock candy to shops all over England, and the manager had been advised to lay off staff. As far as the manager was concerned, the first to go would be a young man who was always rude to other employees, and usually had a lazy approach to his work. The manager was surprised when, instead of cursing him as expected, the man worked his day's notice and departed with a warm farewell. A few days later, everything became clear when he received an angry phone call from a big customer in Brighton. The customer was fuming mad because a consignment of rock, which was supposed to read "Brighton Rock", instead read "Brighton Cock!"

Lack Of Forward Planning

Construction sites can be hazardous places. The equipment is costly, the jobs sometimes perilous, and opportunities for calamity are almost a guarantee. This is fertile ground for folklore, from the building of the pyramids to the present.

Antique Sawdust

An antiques dealer went for a walk in the countryside one Sunday. He was taking a shortcut through a farmyard, when he spotted a cabinet in the chicken shed. On closer inspection, he discovered that the cabinet was a Chippendale antique, and even though it was covered in chicken droppings, once restored, it could fetch a heafty price. The dealer approached the farmer and asked about the cabinet. In order to get a cheap price, the dealer told the farmer that the cabinet legs would be perfect for a table back home. Eventually, the farmer agreed to sell the cabinet for $100 and the dealer told him he would return in the morning with his van to pick up the cabinet. The next day, the dealer drove to the farm and the farmer greeted him.

The farmer said, "I saved you the trouble and removed the legs for you. I even chopped up the rest of it to use as fire wood. Not bad for a hundy, eh?"

The dealer fainted on the spot.

Carpenter Mishap

A carpenter from Baltimore, Maryland was severely injured after he made the most basic of errors. Having spent the day painting and decorating his house, he washed off all the dirt he had accumulated during the course of his day, and set to work removing the paint that had splattered all over his hair and skin.

Ignoring the fact that he was burning incense in several different containers placed about the bathroom, he opened a can of gasoline that he had siphoned from his car, and set about scrubbing away at the paint. For a second or two, before he knew what had happened, the gas fumes were ignited by the candle flames in the incense burners. The carpenter was then blasted out into the street. There was minimal fire damage, and two of the non-supporting walls in his bathroom were later found to be propping up the bedroom. Some people really should pay more attention in chemistry class.

Lack Of Forward Planning

When a building worker was applying for compensation after an accident he was asked to write down what, in his opinion, had been the cause of the accident.

On the form he wrote, "lack of forward planning".

His insurers were puzzled by this and contacted him for clarification. It turns out the man had been given the task of lowering a huge amount of bricks to street level after too many had been taken up to the top of a building to complete a job. Having set up a pulley system, he tied a rope around a barrel full of bricks, wound it through the pulley and dropped the rest of the rope to the ground.

His plan was to lower the barrel via the pulley, an operation he would control from the ground.

Unfortunately, as the barrel began to descend it soon became clear that even with the assistance of the pulley, he was getting lifted off the ground.

Like a true hero he held on for dear life, smashing his kneecaps as he passed the barrel on his rapid journey up the side of the building. When the barrel hit the ground it smashed open and the bricks fell out, with the result that he began to head groundwards at a remarkable speed. He hit the pavement with a thump, breaking both ankles, and when he let go of the rope, the remains of the barrel came crashing down around his ears.

Mr. Glory Days

A man decided to relive his glory days by crashing the prom party at his old high school where he had recently been overseeing some building work. Stopping off at a local bar on the way to the school, he got well and drunk before continuing on his way, and arriving just as the party was coming to an end. As is the way with alcohol, he found several like-minded students who were in the mood to party. Finding that everyone else was of a mind to go home, the man used his pass key to take his new friends into the brand new, almost finished gym.

One of the guys picked up a Frisbee, and without looking where he was going, "Mr. Glory Days" ran towards the other end of the gym shouting, "Throw it to me".

However, before he had a chance to catch the Frisbee, he fell down a hole in the flooring that he had failed to cover over in the course of his building work, and ended up spending the next six months in a wheelchair.

Voice-Activated Lift

A council housing officer from London was transferred to another district, so he spent his first week in his new job getting acquainted with the housing estates that were now under his jurisdiction. His usual approach to visiting a block of apartments was to go to the top floor and work his way down, and on his last visit of the day he followed his usual pattern.

However, entering the lift he pressed the button to take him to the top floor, but nothing happened.

Deciding that the lift must be broken, he was about to leave, when a young girl entered and shouted, "Fourth floor!"

The lift went up to the fourth floor. The housing officer was amazed that the estate had a voice-activated lift.

So he shouted, "Sixth floor!" and the lift went up to the sixth floor.

Back at the office, he asked his colleagues when the council had installed hi-tech, voice-activated lifts on their estates.

His colleagues all looked at him as if he was crazy, but one of them knew what he was talking about and laughingly explained, "The lift controls are broken, so the residents of the apartment block

are paying a man to stay on top of the lift. When people shout what floor they want, he connects the two appropriate wires and the lift goes to that floor."

My Big Bathroom Break

The big break, the hidden treasure, the easy money -- we create a great many tales expressing our optimistic fantasies that good fortune may come at any given moment. In some cases good fortune does find its way into our pockets, but we also have to be wary because reversal of fortune is just as possible. Lady Luck may be a stunning spirit, but sometimes she can be a cold-hearted bitch.

Act Of Kindness

An auto mechanic who specialized in BMWs was driving on a desolate part of the highway when he spotted a BMW on the shoulder of the road, with the driver standing beside it.

The mechanic stopped and asked if there was anything he could do to help, but the driver thanked him and explained that he had called BMW's roadside assistance line and was now just waiting for the BMW person to show up. The mechanic offered his business card and explained that he specialized in repairing BMWs, again offering to see if he could help, with no obligation. Perhaps he could save the driver a long wait. Again, he was thanked for the offer and turned down politely.

But the mechanic insisted and was finally allowed to look at the car. He found nothing more than a loose wire, reattached it, and the car ran fine.

The following week, the mechanic was in the bank making his monthly payments on his house mortgage and student loans. However, the bank manager informed the mechanic that Bill Gates came in earlier in the week, paid off all his outstanidng balances, and drove off in a BMW.

My Big Bathroom Break

A woman from Oregon went to Los Angleles on a shopping weekend, and in the middle of her trip she had an urgent need to use the bathroom. Each shop she tried didn't have a public toilet, and eventually she became so desperate, she entered a funeral home to use their facilities. Having used the toilet, the woman went to leave the building, but on the way, she passed a darkened room with a coffin containing a man's body in the centre with flower arrangements on each side. Feeling guilty about using the toilets, the woman entered the dark room and signed the guest book. Since no-one was around, the woman breathed a sigh of relief as she left the funeral home. A few weeks later, the woman received a letter from the dead man's lawyer informing her that the deceased had left $100,000 to be divided between the people attending his funeral. As she was the only person to show up, she got the whole 'kitten kaboodle".

Nothing To Lose

Stan Vilmer, of Chicago, Illinois was suffering from an inoperable and fatal brain tumor. Doctors gave him only two months to live, so Stan decided to end it sooner rather than face the pain. He wrote a suicide note and then placed the gun to his head and shot.

Later, friends found him on the floor in a pool of blood. They called the ambulance and within hours, Stan was up and walking around.

"His sense of humor was amazing, but even more amazing was his luck," remarked his doctor.

The chances of him shooting out his brain tumor are 254 million to one. The bullet missed all of the vital parts of the brain and only shot out the tumor. Friends and family have urged Stan to put his luck to good use and buy lots of lottery tickets.

Nice Tip

A New York cab driver was given a pair of tickets, as a tip, to go see an off Broadway musical, but he heard the show had been given appalling reviews and was reluctant to waste his time by going. Hating to see anything go to waste, the taxi driver left the tickets on the back seat of his cab, hoping that someone would take them and make use of them. However, at the end of the shift not only were there no takers, but someone had placed another pair of tickets on top of them.

Trainstopping

A man from the south of England had one too many drinks in a bar on the way home from work one day and lost track time. Fortunately he just managed to catch what he thought was the last train of the night out of London to his home town of Basingstoke. However, he found out that the train he boarded didn't stop at Basingstoke, it only passed through. He had climbed on an express train that went straight on to Southampton. He figured that if the train slowed down enough at Basingstoke, he could probably jump off. The train did slow down at the station, and the unlucky traveller grabbed his bag, jumped on to the platform and then began running alongside the train to reduce his speed.

As the next coach passed him, he was suddenly yanked back onto the train by another man who said, "Lucky I saw you running. Didn't you know this train never stops here?"

You Win, Loser!

A man from Rhode Island who had been buying several lottery tickets every week for the last two years was in his local bar, and as usual, he was watching the lottery numbers being drawn on television. On this occasion, it turned out the man got five of the six winning numbers and stood a good chance of winning a million dollars, so he bought everybody in the room a celebratory round of drinks and had several himself. Dreaming about how he would spend his new found wealth, the man passed his ticket around for people to inspect. However, when the ticket eventually came back to him, it wasn't the same ticket. Someone had switched it on him.

No TP For Me Bum Hole

In the early nineteenth century when news spread primarily through word of mouth, it was often difficult to verify in a timely manner, so newspapers used to print them as gossip and rumors under the headline "Important If True"-- the reason being that some of the stories might in fact be true, and if so, they were important news.

That same phenomenon still takes place but in a slightly different manner, today we have hundreds of gossip columns, and reports that use words like "alleged". Thanks to the internet we receive all types of obvious hoaxes and jokes but we forward them along as if they were real news, because they might be true, and if they are true, they're important. All of these strange stories and rumors have been sent to us more than once. So here are afew of these stories that just might be "Too Good Too Be True"!

I would like to order a pizza, hold the crazy!

The FBI conducted a "search and seizure" at a Pennsyvania Psychiatric Hospital in Pittsburgh, which was under investigation for medical insurance fraud. After hours of poring over rooms of financial records, the sixty-some FBI agents worked up quite an appetite. The case agent in charge of the investigation called a local pizza parlor with delivery service to order a quick dinner for his colleagues.

However, when the agent told the pizza guy that they were all FBI agents at the Pennsylvania Psychiatric Hospital and wanted twenty large pizzas and seventy bottles of coke to be delivered to the service entrance behind the hospital, the pizza man responded by hanging up the phone.

Did You Know? *The term "hot dog" was coined in 1906 by cartoonist T.A. "Tad" Dorgan who penned a drawing of a dachshund inside an elongated bun. Dorgan didn't know how to spell "dachshund", so he wrote the term "hot dog" instead...and the name stuck.*

Late For An Important Date

Not so long ago, a Texas oil tycoon employed a chef named Napoleon whose roasts and sauces were famous for miles around. The president of a nearby university borrowed him one day to cook an important dinner, and Napoleon proudly set forth to fill the engagement, bringing along his trusty carving knives wrapped in a piece of old newspaper.

Just barely missing the bus, and breathing heavily, he instructed the driver, "Step on the gas, mister. The president is waiting for me."

The driver looked warily at the carving knives and nodded, "You're the boss," and drove him straight to a lunatic asylum.

Thinking this must be the university, the cook unwrapped his knives and announced to the guard at the gate, "I'm Napoleon. Where's the party?"

Next thing Napoleon knew he was in a padded cell.

No TP For Me Bum Hole

Toilet paper isn't the most popular subject to discuss. However, we know by comparing disease rates in civilized countries versus countries with no flushable toilets and no toilet paper that your health and life depends on good hygene. Much of the reason people are so healthy in North America is because of running water, washing hands, and of course, toilet paper. But what if we ran out?

Remember all those wildfires in southen California last year? Well, I bet you didn't know that the Clappington Paper Products factory is one of the many business that burned down.

There are alot of brands of toilet paper, but there are only five different types of toilet paper on the market, with only a couple different types of packaging for toilet paper.

Unfortunatley, about 98 percent of the toilet paper in the US, Canada, and Mexico is manufactured in one facility: the Clappington Factory, in southern CA. The finished product is so light weight, it is easy to transport by truck. Nearly no weight at all. And the factory is so close to the border, they use a lot of illegal immigrant labor. This is an open secret — because INS knows what would happen to the nation if the one TP factory closed.

Well, after the wildfires in southern CA burned down the one factory that made the TP in the US, Mexico, and Canada, it did close. It is expected to be 6 to 8 more months before any other manufacturing facility can make adequate supplies of TP.

Governor Arnold Schwartzenegger has enough troubles and can't afford to be known as the governor who deprived the nation of toilet paper. So, he's ordered a news blackout of the story. That's why you havn't seen it on the news.

Stores have only about a 3 day supply of TP left on the shelves, that is until the word gets out, then you'll see a run on toilet paper like never before. And it's going to be 8 months at the very minimum before stores have any more.

Now is a good time to stock up, and inform everyone in your adress book. You wouldn't want your close friends to be out of something so important.

Did You Know? *In 1995, Perry Ellison of New York made an attempt on the world flagpole-sitting record. By the time he had come down, eight hours short of the 400 day record, his sponsor had gone bust, his girlfriend had left him and his phone and electricity had been cut off.*

1-800-OH-GOD

American viewers, responding to a new evangelical television programme, received a shock when they tried to make a phone donation. The evangelist in question had requested money to help him embark on a crusade to save lost souls. However, when people phoned the number he gave, all they heard was a woman panting and talking in seductive tones about all kinds of sexual practices. Apparently the evangelist had mistakenly reversed two digits of the phone number and inadvertendy given the number for an X-rated sex chatline.

Did You Know? *William Skakespeare originally penned the Hokey Pokey.*

O proud left foot, that ventures quick within
Then soon upon a backward journey lithe.
Anon, once more the gesture, then begin:
Command sinistral pedestal to writhe.
Commence thou then the fervid Hokey-Poke,
A mad gyration, hips in wanton swirl.
To spin!
A wilde release from Heavens yoke.
Blessed dervish!
Surely canst go, girl.

The Hoke, the poke--banish now thy doubt.

Verily, I say, 'tis what it's all about.

Steve

In Melbourne, 130 men, all named Steve attacked each other during a 'My Name is Steve' convention. Steve Pan of Sydney accused Steve Pallan of Sydney of not being a Steve at all, but in fact a Cletus.

"It was a lie", explained Mr. Pallan, "I'm a Steve and always will be," whereupon Steve Pallan attacked Steve Pan, whilst two other Steve's attempted to pull them apart.

Several more Steve's became involved and soon the entire convention descended into a giant fist fight. The brawl was eventually broken up by riot police, led by a man named Steve.

What's Your Sign?

The government is passing a new law requiring stupid people to wear signs that sinply say, "I'm Stupid."

Stupid People should be required to wear signs that say, "I'm Stupid!" If stupid people wore signs that said, "I'm Stupid" you wouldn't rely on them, would you? You wouldn't ask them anything. It would be like, "Excuse me...oops...never mind, didn't see your sign."

It's like before my wife and I moved. Our house was full of boxes and there was a U-Haul truck in our driveway. My neighbor comes over and says, "Hey, you moving?" "Nope. We just pack our stuff up once or twice a week to see how many boxes it takes. Here's your sign."

A couple of months ago I went fishing with a buddy of mine, we pulled his boat into the dock, I lifted up this big ol' stringer of bass and this idiot on the dock goes, "Hey, you catch all them fish?" "Nope. Talked 'em into giving up. Here's your sign."

I was watching one of those animal shows on the Discovery Channel. There was a guy inventing a shark bite suit. And there was only one way to test it. "Alright, Jimmy, you got that shark suit on, it looks good... They want you to jump into this pool of sharks, and you tell us if it hurts when they bite you." "Well, all right, but hold my sign. I don't wanna lose it."

Last time I had a flat tire, I pulled my car into a side-of-the-road gas station. The attendant walked over, looked at my car, looked at me, and said, "Tire go flat?" I couldn't resist. I said, "Nope. I was driving around and those other three just swelled right up on me. Here's your sign."

We were trying to sell our car about a year ago. A guy came over to the house and drove the car around for about 45 minutes. We get back to the house, he gets out of the car, reaches down and grabs the exhaust pipe, then says, "Darn that's hot!" See, if he'd been wearing his sign, I could have stopped him.

I learned to drive an 18-wheeler in my adventurous days. Wouldn't you know, I misjudged the height of a bridge. The truck got stuck and I couldn't get it out, no matter how I tried. I radioed in for help and eventually a local cop showed up to take the report. He went through his basic questioning. I thought for sure he was clear of needing a sign, until he asked, "So, is your truck stuck?" I couldn't help myself! I looked at him, looked back at the rig and then back to him and said, "No, I'm delivering a bridge... here's your sign."

I stayed late at work one night and a co-worker looked at me and said, "Are you still here?" I replied, "No. I left about 10 minutes ago. Here's your sign."

Anybody you know need a sign today?

The next time someone says something stupid ask them where their sign is.

The Shallow End of the Gene Pool

The following tales will titillate, horrify, and tickle your funny bone -- sometimes all at once, and prove that people do foolhardy things.

A Lethal Combination

Any story that starts with two friends and a rifle can only have a limited number of endings, but the end of this one may come as a surprise to some of you.

One night armed only with a severe lack of intellect and a loaded .22 calibre rifle - a lethal combination, two friends took to the streets of Redneck Alabama. Our boys decided to go hunting for mailboxes. Between them they made a number of holes in half the town's mailboxes before one of them decided to try a trick shot. He fired over his shoulder at one of the vicious mailboxes, and to his surprise he managed to hit the target. Not to be outdone, his friend decided to go one better. Standing with his back to the target, he bent over, pointed the gun between his legs and waved goodbye to the mailbox. Unfortunately the bullet ricocheted off the box and right back at him, making him one of the few men in history to have shot himself in the ass with his own rifle.

Bell of the Bear

Joseph Angel of Pittsburgh, Pennsylvania went to a fancy costume party as a bear and proceeded to drink like one, downing one vodka shot after another. The drunken bear was making such a commotion that the other party goers eventually kicked him out. Feeling sad and dejected, the man stumbled home. However, on passing the local church, the man had an idea to rouse the boring residents of his home town. He broke into the church and entered the bell tower where he pulled the bell rope as hard as he could. But instead of making the loud ringing sound he had hoped, the man ended up 30 feet in the air and tangled in the ropes. Restricted by his bear suit he was unable to break free, and remained hanging in the bell tower until a somewhat mystified priest found him two days later.

Fast Adhesive Relief

Its hard not to sympathise with the man from Las Vegas, Nevada who returned home and went straight to the toilet after an evening of drunken merriment rounded off by a visit to an Indian restaurant. As a regular sufferer from hemorrhoids, the man assigned the pain in his backside to his familiar problem, rather than the hot curry he had just eaten. Somewhat embarrassed by this recurring ailment, he previously hid the hemorrhoid cream in a cupboard below the bathroom sink, and as usual, he took out the tube and smeared the contents over the affected area. To his dismay, he realised that instead of relief, he found himself unable to withdraw his hand from between his buttocks. It was then that he took a look at the tube he had taken from the cupboard only to discover that he'd grabbed a tube of super-fast glue instead of his hemorrhoid cream. As a result, he had firmly stuck his buttocks together, with his hand in-between for good measure.

Did You Know? *A woman came home one afternoon to find her husband in the kitchen, shaking frantically with what looked like a wire running from his waist towards the electric kettle. Intending to jolt him away from the deadly current, she whacked him with a cast iron frying pan, breaking his arm in two places along with his walkman, that he was happily listening to at the time.*

"Here Sex!" Where Are You Sex! Good Sex!"

Everybody who has a dog usually calls him "Rover" or "Boy." Well my hypohondriac next door neighbour told me his gynecologist calls his dog "Sex."

Now, Sex has been very embarrassing to him. When he went to City Hall to renew his dog license, he told the clerk that he needed a license for Sex.

The clerk replied, "I'd like to have one too."

Then he said, "You don't understand. I've had Sex since I was nine years old."

The clerk replied, "You must have been quite a kid!"

When he got married and went on his honeymoon, he took the dog with him, and told the hotel clerk that he wanted a room for he and his wife, and a special room for Sex.

The hotel clerk said, "Every room in the place is for sex."

To which he replied, "You don't understand. Sex keeps me awake at night."

The clerk said, "Same here."

One day he entered Sex in a contest, but before the competition began, the dog ran away. Another contestant asked why he was just looking around. So he told him he planned to have Sex in the contest. The man said to him, "I should have sold tickets."

"But you don't understand," he said, "I was hoping to have Sex on T.V."

The man called him a show-off.

When he and his wife separated, they went to court to fight for custody of Sex.

He stated, "Your Honor, I had Sex before I was married."

The judge said, "Me too."

Then he told the judge that after he was married, Sex left him.

The judge exclaimed, "Me too."

Anyway, the other night Sex ran off again. He spent hours looking around town for him.

A cop came over to him and asked, "What are you doing in the alley at 4 o'clock in the morning?"

He said, "I'm looking for Sex."

His case comes up later this month.

171

Human Cannonball

In rural Pennsylvania, a group of men were drinking beer and discharging firearms from the rear deck of a home owned by 28-year old Earle Prince. The men were firing at a raccoon that was wandering by, but the beer apparently impaired their aim, and despite the estimated 40 shots the group fired, the animal escaped into a 3 foot diameter drainage pipe some 100 feet away from Mr. Prince' deck.

Determined to terminate the animal, Mr. Prince retrieved a can of gasoline and poured it down the pipe, intending to smoke the animal out. After several unsuccessful attempts to ignite the fuel, Prince

168emptied the entire 5 gallon fuel can down the pipe and tried to ignite it again, but to no avail. Not one to admit defeat by a tiny animal, the determined Mr. Prince proceeded to slide feet-first approximately 10 feet down the sloping pipe to toss the match.

The subsequent rapidly expanding fireball propelled Mr. Prince back the way he had come, though at a much higher rate of speed.

"He exited the angled pipe 'like a missile leaving a submarine'," said witness John Farley.

Mr. Prince was launched directly over his own home, right over the heads of his astonished friends, onto his front lawn. In all, he traveled over 200 feet through the air.

"There was a Doppler Effect to his scream as he flew over us," Farley reported, "Followed by a loud thud."

Amazingly, he suffered only minor injuries.

"It was actually pretty cool," Prince said, "Like when they shoot someone out of a cannon at the circus. I'd do it again if I was sure I wouldn't get hurt."

I Guess You Don't Have The Balls To Take The Bet...

Based on a bet by members of a golf threesome, Horatio Morales tried to wash his own "balls" in a ball washer at the local golf course. Proving once again that beer and testosterone are a bad mix. Morales managed to straddle the ball washer and dangle his scrotum in the machine. Much to his dismay, one of his buddies upped the ante by spinning the crank on the machine with Morales' scrotum in place, thus wedging them solidly in the mechanism. Morales, who immediately passed his threshold of pain, collapsed and tumbled from his perch.

Unfortunately for Morales, the height of the ball washer was more than a foot higher off the ground than his testicles were in a normal stance, and the scrotum was the weakest link. Morales' scrotum was ripped open during the fall, and one testicle was plucked from him forever and remained in the ball washer, while the other testicle was compressed and flattened as it was pulled between the housing of the washer, and the rotating machinery inside. To add insult to injury, Morales broke a new $300 driver that he had just purchased from the pro shop, and was using to balance himself. Morales was rushed to the hospital for surgery, and the remaining two were asked to leave the course.

James Bond 007: If Stupidity Could Kill

Two British businessmen were sent to Moscow to finalise a building contract for their company. The men had been forewarned that their Russian counterparts would do anything to jeopardise the deal, so the men were on their guard. Having watched too many James Bond spy films, they set about searching their hotel room for bugs. One man came across a curious-looking bulge in the carpet and upon lifting it, discovered a strange black box with four large screws attaching it to the floor. Thinking it must be a hi-tech bug, the two men spent a good hour removing the screws. After finally removing the last screw, they were bemused to find that the box was completely empty. The men realized they were being somewhat overzealous and went to the hotel bar for a quick drink before retiring for the night. However, on entering the bar, they were greeted by a scene reminiscent of the London Blitz. It turns out that a huge chandelier hanging in the centre of the ceiling had suddenly crashed down, smashing tables and chairs and narrowly missing the shocked patrons. The men put two and two together and made a hasty retreat back to their room to pick up their bags and check out.

Let's Constipate Our Relationship

When two young Italian lovers were refused permission to marry by their respective parents, they decided to do what any other couple in their position would do, if you believe Shakespeare anyway. They checked into a cheap hotel with the intention of committing suicide. Before doing so, they had stopped off at their local pharmacist, who knew both their families well, and asked for the strongest pills he had in his shop. The pharmacist suspected that they might be up to no good, and instead gave them the most powerful laxative he could find. This was particularly unfortunate because the room they had rented at the hotel did not come with an in-suite bathroom, and they had thrown the key to the locked door out of the sixth floor window after locking it from the inside. After making their final farewells to each other, the couple proceeded to swallow the entire contents of the bottle before settling down on the bed to die. Three days later, and after numerous screams for help, the couple were finally discovered by a maid who had come to clean the room. Unfortunately for the maid, the room needed more cleaning than she had imagined.

The manager of the hotel stated later, "The room stunk. The walls were caked and even the ceiling was splattered. You couldn't even see through the windows."

Naturally, the couple abandoned their plans to marry.

Lucky Numbers

A Detroit, Michigan man committed suicide by shooting himself in the head, because he found out he hadn't won the National Lottery. The 32-year-old man believed he had chosen all six of the numbers drawn in that weeks lottery, entitling him to a share in the grand prize of a million dollars. Then he discovered that he didn't pay for his numbers that week. His dreams shattered, the man took his own life. Police investigated the facts, and discovered that the unfortunate man had made two mistakes, rather than one. Only four of his regular numbers had been selected in the draw, not all six, so the poor man killed himself because he didn't win a hundred dollars!

Pave The Way Home

A man was walking home after a long night at his local pub. Drunkenly, he decided to take a shortcut down a side street. He soon came to a fork in the road and couldn't remember which way would take him home, so he decided to take the left fork. About half an hour later he realised he was lost. Feeling dizzy, he decided to rest a while and sat down on the pavement. However, his back soon ached, and noticed it was softer further on, so he staggered up and lay down on the softer part of the pavement. A few hours later, he woke up and discovered he couldn't move. He looked around and realised that he was lying in a patch of cement, which unfortunately set while he slept. He spent the night unable to move, and too embarrassed to shout for help. In the morning, the workmen came and chiselled him out. He was lucky it wasn't the weekend.

Rolling Tire

A poor Saskatchewan farmer's tractor was on its last legs and the threadbare tires needed patching yet again. The farmer was inside the tractor tire patching it, when it suddenly began rolling down the hill. Before he knew it, the tire was rolling at a substantial speed and the farmer became dizzy and disorientated, before blacking out completely. He ended up on a major road, rolling against traffic, causing a number of cars to swerve out of the way, but luckily avoided crashing into them. Eventually, the tire rolled into a field of wheat, slowed down and stopped. When the farmer came to, he realised he had a long walk home and it was all uphill.

The Shallow End of the Gene Pool

A family in Virginia was obviously determined to prove Darwin's theory of evolution wrong. However, despite a number of very determined attempts to remove themselves from the gene pool, the family continues to thrive.

It all began when a father and son went out to hunt squirrels. Armed to the teeth, they went in search of the bushy-tailed varmints. They were soon rewarded when the son spotted one on a low branch.

"There's one, paw!" he shouted and both father and son fired at once.

Unfortunately, they succeeded only in shooting each other.

Meanwhile, back at the ranch, the daughter of the family, who had been watching far too much television, decided that she was going to learn how to twirl a pistol around her finger the way she had seen the gunfighters do it in those spaghetti westerns. Clearly not one to do things half-ass, she used a loaded pistol with the safety latch off and managed to shoot herself in the foot on the first twirl. The second twirl sent a bullet flying through the kitchen window, narrowly missing her mother's arm and hitting her in the chest instead.

"This dish cheap but very tasty."

*"To say that something was lost in the process
is to be wildly ungrateful for all that was gained."*

--*Time* magazine

The English language is difficult enough for those of us who learned it as our native language. But putting it in the hands of an inexperienced practitioner can produce some truly risible results.

Cheap Dish

An up-and-coming fashion designer from London, England, was eating a meal in a Chinese restaurant when she noticed the Chinese characters in the menu, and decided they would make a great design on a dress. She copied out a few lines in her notebook, and a few weeks later she completed her first design incorporating the Chinese characters. The woman decided to wear the dress to a party at the community centre that weekend. As it happened, a few Chinese people from the area were also attending the party, and several started snickering and nudging one another when they noticed the designer dress. Not one to be the subject of a joke, the woman asked what they found so funny.

He explained that the characters on her dress read, "This dish cheap but very tasty."

Do You Speak Klingon?

The Department of Human Resources in Portland, Oregon, has a position available. They are looking for an Interpreter, who must be fluent in Klingon.

The language created for the "Star Trek" TV series and movies is one of about 55 needed by the office that treats mental health patients in metropolitan Multnomah County.

"We have to provide information in all the languages our clients speak," said Norman Braun, procurement specialist for the county Department of Human Services, which serves about 60,000 mental health clients.

Although created for works of fiction, Klingon was designed to have a consistent grammar, syntax and vocabulary. And now Multnomah County research has found that many people -- not just fans -- consider it a complete language.

"There are some cases where we've had mental health patients where this was all they would speak," said the county's purchasing administrator, Mariette Canton.

County officials said that obligates them to respond with a Klingon-English interpreter, putting the language of starship Enterprise officer Worf and other Klingon characters on a par with common languages such as Russian, Vietnamese, and less common tongues including Dari and Tongan.

Illegal Alien Abductions

In a small town in Florida, a mother was worried when her not-too-bright son failed to return home from work. She told the police, who organised a search party. They combed the surrounding area, but they couldn't find any trace of him. Two days later the young man turned up looking worse for wear and talking about being abducted by aliens. He told interested reporters that he had been walking back home from work when he had met the aliens, who had taken him back to a brightly-coloured room with strange loud music playing. He went on to describe how the aliens forced him to eat food that burnt the back of his throat and to drink a foul-tasting liquid before blacking out. He remembered nothing after that, until he woke up in a field with a splitting headache and made his way home. One sceptical reporter, investigating the details that the man had given him, discovered a bar full of Mexicans near the field where the man had woken up, and he realised that it was the Mexicans that had taken the man in, and plied him full of hot spicy food and tequila. The man had got drunk and passed out. On relating the story, he used the US immigration term of "alien" to apply to the Mexicans.

Lacking Character

Hilda Jackson, an amateur genealogical researcher, discovered that her great-great uncle, Remus, a fellow lacking in character, was hanged for horse stealing and train robbery in Montana in 1889. The only known photograph of Remus shows him standing on the gallows.

On the back of the picture was an inscription that said, "Remus; horse thief, sent to MontanaTerritorial Prison 1885, escaped 1887, robbed the Montana Flyer six times. Caught by Pinkerton detectives, convicted and hanged in 1889."

Hilda hired a professional image consultant to crop Remus's picture, scan it, enlarge the image, and edited it with image processing software so all that's seen is a head shot.

Accompanied with the photo was a very creative biographical sketch that stated, "Remus was a famous cowboy in the Montana Territory. His business empire grew to include acquisition of valuable equestrian assets and intimate dealings with the Montana railroad. Beginning in 1883, he devoted several years of his life to service at a government facility, finally taking leave to resume his dealings with the railroad. In 1887, he was a key player in a vital investigation run by the renowned Pinkerton Detective Agency. In 1889, Remus passed away during an important civic function held in his honor when the platform upon which he was standing collapsed."

Shamrocks and Whiskey

Nowadays the President of the Irish Republic presents a shamrock to members of the diplomatic corps and army on St Patrick's Day. The Irish Government arranges for neat bunches of shamrocks to be flown to all parts of the world so that they can be presented to heads of state and other dignitaries. Embassy receptions are also held, and guests are given bunches of shamrocks. On one such occasion in the late 70's a distinguished African diplomat was presented with a bunch of shamrocks and a glass of whiskey when he arrived to a St Patrick's Day gathering. Not knowing any better, but determined to cause no offence, he politely sipped the whiskey and ate the shamrock.

What Do You Expect From A Place That Starts With A Bang, And Ends With A "kok!"

A British diplomat lost his job when the government changed after an election. He told his wife that there finances would be scarce, and would have to be careful with money for a while. The wife was saddened to see her husband in such a state, and decided to sell some of her possessions to ease their financial plight. One item she decided to sell was very precious to her and she only wore to very special occasions. It was a bronze pendant that had been presented to her during a visit to Bangkok. There was an inscription on the pendant written in Thai, but everyone she asked said they couldn't translate it. The diplomat's wife was more than a little ashamed when she came across the item at the auction with the description, "19th Century bronze medallion with inscription in Thai, translated to 'Legalised Prostitute Number 283, Bangkok.'"

"This sort of thing is all too common these days."

Despite the noble efforts of the diligent armies of proofreagers, plenty of mistakes still find their way into print. Many of these goofs turn out to be quite amusing. Newspapers and magazines are notorious for running apocryphal stories from time to time. And then there are the stories that supposedly ran in the news but really didn't. Which ones are real, and which ones are imposters? Who cares. Why be concerned with such trifling details.

Saving Time

The *Daily Journal* recently asked its readers to save daylight during Daylight Savings Time, and has offered a prize for the person who saves the most daylight. The rules are simple:

Beginning with the first day of Daylight Savings Time, those entering the contest must begin saving daylight. Those who save the most daylight by midnight of the last day of Daylight Savings Time will be awarded a prize.

Only pure daylight is allowed. No pre-dawn light or twilight will be accepted. Daylight on cloudy days is allowable. Moonlight is strictly prohibited and any of it mixed with daylight will bring immediate disqualification.

Contestants are instructed to save their accumulated daylight in any container they wish, then bring the container to the *Daily Journal* office at the end of Daylight Savings Time -- or when they think they have saved enough daylight to win.

SBF Seeks Male Companionship

There was an add in a newspaper that read:

SBF Seeks Male companionship. Age and ethnicity unimportant. I'm a young, svelte good looking girl who loves to play. I love to take long walks, riding in pickup trucks, hunting, camping, and fishing trips. I enjoy cozy winter nights spent lying by the fire. Candlelight dinners will have me eating out of your hand. Rub me the right way and watch me respond. I'll be at the front door when you get home from work, wearing only what nature gave me. Kiss me and I'm yours. Call 555-XXXX and ask for Daisy.

Turns out the phone number was the Humane Society and the SBF was an eight week old female black

Labrador Retriever. They received 643 calls in two days.

Did You Know? *A young girl, blown out to sea on a set of inflatable teeth, was rescued by a man on an inflatable lobster. A coast-guard spokesman commented, "This sort of thing is all too common these days."*

Time Traveler Arrested For Insider Trading

In New York, On Monday, March 17, 2004 Federal investigators arrested an enigmatic Wall Street wiz on insider-trading charges -- and incredibly, he claimed to be a time-traveler from the year 2225!

Sources at the Security and Exchange Commission confirm that 45-year-old Monte Allans offered the bizarre explanation for his uncanny success in the stock market after being led off in handcuffs.

"We don't believe this guy's story -- he's either a lunatic or a pathological liar," says an SEC insider. "But the fact is, with an initial investment of only $800, in two weeks' time he had a portfolio valued at over $350 million. Every trade he made capitalized on unexpected business developments, which simply can't be pure luck. The only way he could pull it off is with illegal inside information."

He's currenlty resides in a jail cell on Rikers Island until he agrees to give up his sources."

chaptereleven

"She had a great sense of humor and I'm sure she would appreciate being my coffee table."

-- Dale Jeffereys: Tucson, Arizona

lovestinks

The range of human endeavors has provided us with plenty of urban legends, and the arena of love is the most fertile ground. Love is a very powerful emotion that provokes us to engage in unusual activities as we pursue the objects of our romantic desires. Love also leads us to heights of creativity in finding inivative ways to get back at those who betrayed us.

. . . .

"She had a great sense of humor and I'm sure she would appreciate being my coffee table."

"She had a great sense of humor and I'm sure she would appreciate being my coffee table."

Loyal lovers and spouses have inspired some truly heartwarming tales of true love. At least, they have in legend.

Accident?

Dean Angell, a Welsh man from Norfolk, Nebraska decided that the perfect present for his wife on their 25th anniversary would be if he turned up in a package in the morning post. So, the day before their anniversary, with the help of a neighbour, he packed himself in a large crate and his neighbour took him to the post office and posted him. All might have gone well had there not been a postal strike that day which resulted in a computer error shipping the crate off to Alaska. As it turned out, the husband became a wonderfully successful fisherman, and the wife eventually moved in with the neighbour.

coincidencedesign.com

Through the web site coincidencedesign.com, you can arrange to "accidentally" meet the girl of your dreams by having her habits researched so you'll know where and when to run into her and then what to say.

The website coincidencedesign.com has become extremely popular as of late through its claims to make any woman accessible for a price of $78,000. It purportedly offers a research service that will investigate and uncover all the details of a "target's" life with the goal of using this information to set up an accidental meeting between her and a deep-pocketed client.

The object is matrimony, but results are not guaranteed, and Coincidence Design considers its work done after arranging the appropriate "accidental" encounter and sending the client to it armed with all the information about the girl the client needs to make himself highly appealing to her.

Dedicated Husband

An old couple had been together for over 60 years and their lives were deeply entwined. One afternoon, the man dropped his wife off to do some shopping and told her he'd wait for her in the car. He turned on the radio and entertained himself while amusing the people-watching. Meanwhile, his wife had done her shopping, and completely forgetting about her husband, she walked home. When her husband didn't show up that evening, the wife got worried and reported him missing. He was found two days later exactly where she'd left him after a policeman noticed him asleep at the wheel.

End It All

A teenager from Tulsa was sitting along side a pond thinking to himself that the whole world had become utter darkness, and life was not worth living -- his girl "the one he thought of every waking moment, the radiant image of all his dreams," turned him down cold. Spurned by his one great passion, he decided to put an end to it all, and perhaps when she saw the look on his rigid face, she would realise her cruelty, and bring her to tears.

So he procured a bottle of carbolic acid, a rope, a pistol, and some gasoline. He rushed to a nearby river, jumped into his canoe -- first tying one end of the rope to a stout tree limb, the other end around his neck. He drank the carbolic acide, poured the gasoline over his clothes, set fire to them, and jumped from the canoe, shooting his gun at the same time. The shell missed his head, cut the rope in two, and pulled him into the river, which quenched the flame.

He swallowed so much water, in his excitement -- up came all of the carbolic acid.

"If I hadn't been a darned good swimmer," he said, "I surely would have drowned."

The best part, his lady love was waiting at the shore, yelling, "You dumbass, won't you ever learn that when a woman says 'No,' she might just be playing hard to get?"

Guess Who?

A guy walked into a post office one day to see a middle-aged, balding man standing at the counter methodically placing "Love" stamps on bright pink envelopes with hearts all over them. He then took out a perfume bottle and started spraying scent all over them.

The guys curiosity got the better of him, so he walked up to the balding man and asked him what he was doing.

The man explained, "I'm sending out 1,000 Valentine cards signed, 'Guess who?'"

"But why?" the man asked.

"I'm a divorce lawyer," the man replied.

Hollywood Romanticism

A young actor, trying to make it in Hollywood, was broken-hearted when his first love left him for a movie producer. Brought up on the sentimental romanticism of the Hollywood love story, the actor planned to kill himself by taking an overdose of sleeping pills. Before doing so, he took all the love letters from his sweetheart and proceeded to burn them. However, the burning pile soon got out of control, and before he knew it his whole apartment was consumed with flames. Overcome by smoke, the actor passed out. Fortunately, the fire department came and rescued him. Like a good Hollywood ending, the actor fell in love with the fireman that rescued him and they lived happily ever after.

Did You Know? *While at the funeral of her own mother, the daughter met a guy whom she did not know, but she thought this guy was amazing, so much so, she believed he was her dream guy, and she fell in love with him there and then. A few days later, the girl killed her own sister. Her motive in killing her sister? She was hoping that the guy would appear at the funeral again.*

My Dead Husband Has Perfect Timing

Peter Bornyk, the resident of a small town in the north of England, decided that when he died he wanted to be cremated. There was nothing unusual in that, however, he made an addition to his will at the last moment. Having carefully set aside a certain sum of money, he requested that his ashes be placed not in an urn, but in a rather elaborate egg timer, which was to be kept in his wife's kitchen after he was gone. With the help of a very skillful glassblower, his wife was able to carry out her husband's last wish, and he now sits on her kitchen table, helping her to boil eggs whenever he is required.

"She had a great sense of humor and I'm sure she would appreciate being my coffee table."

Dale Jeffereys, a 32 year old man from Tucson, Arizona, wife passed away. Due to the great pain he suffered on account of her death, did something totally out of character for a normal and sane person. He said, he could no longer take the pain that his wife's death had caused him, and was going to bring her back home.

Dale's wife, Amanda, was born with a heart condition that cut her life short at the young age of 29.

Amanda's last words to Jeff were, "We will be together again in heaven."

These words served no consolation to Dale's despair. At the funeral, in an act of desperation, Dale decided that he would not allow Amanda to leave him.

"I called the cemetery caretaker and explained my feelings," Dale said, "I spoke with the authorities and got special permission to take my wife home with me. They thought it strange, but I was allowed to take her with me. I would rather have her with me at home than seven feet under ground. Amanda had a great sense of humor and I'm sure she would appreciate being my coffee table."

Dale ordered a special glass casing that eliminates the decomposition of a dead body.

"It cost me about $8,000.00, but it was worth it," Dale stated.

Some of his friends and relatives, filled with fear, stopped visiting Dale. His true friends respected his decision and continue visiting him. Some even comment that it is a nice piece of furniture.

"The car and the house are yours. I'm sleeping with your sister."

There are very few painful moments in life that compare to the heartbreak of discovering that our affection has been betrayed by the ones we love, and sometimes the worst part of the discovery is how we find out.

Coffee is Good With Cream, But Better When It's Black!

At the University of Toronto located on a remote campus in the suburbs, there was a secretary who was engaged to be married. Both she and her fiance were Caucasian. The female friends of this soon-to-be married woman threw her a raucous bachelorette party, featuring a big black male stripper who provided "private" entertainment. Several months after the wedding, divorce proceedings were initiated after the secretary gave birth to healthy black baby.

Evidence Of Infidelity

An American woman with a rich Italian boyfriend told her husband she was visiting her aunt for her birthday, and went to Paris, where her lover bought her a mink coat. Travelling home, she realised she had to hide the evidence of her infidelity, so she parcelled it up and left it at the luggage counter before going home. She then told her husband that she had found someone's check ticket and was going to claim it. He decided to do it for her. Finding the contents of the parcel to be what it was, he gave the coat to his secretary with whom he was having an affair, and bought an umbrella, which he took home to his wife.

Laying Pipe

A man called the plumber after finding that his toilet was blocked. The plumber discovered that the U-pipe was clogged, and upon opening it, discovered the blockage was caused by almost a hundred used condoms. The plumber fixed the problem, cleaned up the mess, and on the way out, told the man that he shouldn't flush condoms down the toilet. Soon after, the man packed his bags and left the house, pausing only to leave a note to his wife, explaining that he was leaving her. He also suggested that she pass on the plumbers advice to her "idiot boyfriend".

Lottery Confession

A couple was eating out at a fancy restaurant, when the woman called the waiter aside and said, "My boyfriend is bound to ask you what numbers won the lottery today, and I wanna play a prank on him. These are the numbers he bet on. Will you tell him they won?"

The waiter agreed.

Sure enough, the boyfriend asked which numbers won.

"We've got a television in the kitchen," the waiter said, "I'll go and find out for you."

The waiter returned telling the boyfriend his numbers won.

Calmly, the man put his car keys on the table and said to his girlfriend, "The car and the house are yours. I'm sleeping with your sister."

At which point he got up and walked out of the restaurant.

Man's Best Friend

A man surprised his wife when he started taking their dog for regular evening walks to the park. He told her how much he enjoyed the fresh air and how it took his mind off any problems he was having at work. She was satisfied with this, especially when she saw how relaxed he seemed when he returned from these walks. One evening, her husband phoned to ask her to take the dog to the park because he had to work late. The wife set out with the dog, but was quite startled when, upon leaving the house, the dog dragged her in the opposite direction. The dog led her to a house just around the corner, so she knocked on the front door, and an attractive, scantily-clad young woman opened the door. Before anyone could say anything, the dog rushed in, pulling the wife with him, and there, reclining on the couch, was her half-naked husband.

Motorhome Liason

A middle-aged couple were on motorhome holiday in Colorado. They were staying at a campsite outside Denver when, early one morning, the wife decided to do some shopping while her husband slept. The shopping took a little longer than expected, and when the wife returned, she heard strange noises coming from inside the motorhome. Looking through the window, she saw her husband having sex with a young woman. Angry, the wife got into driver seat, started up the RV, and began to drive at full speed around and around the campsite, accelerating over all the bumps. Eventually she stopped the vehicle, ordered her husband and his partner to get out of the motorhome, at which point she told the battered and bruised duo that she was leaving them, and she drove off disappearing into the horizon.

When the girlfriend came back, her carpets were sprouting like a veritable urban jungle.

If love is an art, then so is the practice of finding devious ways to strike back at those who have betrayed our affection.

Fall For You

A hardworking business man was in his office when he received a surprise visit from his wife, she informed him that she was leaving him for a professional Japanese karaoke singer. Overcome by emotion, the man decided to kill himself by throwing himself out of his six floor window. It happened that he threw himself out of the window just as his wife was leaving the building, and he landed right on top of her, killing her instantly. The husband survived, but was sentenced to life imprisonment for murder.

"Post This, Bitch!"

Apparently there was a man who abandoned his wife of 15 years for a foxy little tart half his age. The wife tried to get on with her life as gracefully as possible, but it wasn't easy for her, especially since the husband was now living with his girlfriend, and the two of them were reputed to be painting the town red. In Everywhere she turned it seemed like she was getting her nose rubbed in it.

One day she received one of those diet advertisements with a cutesy post-it note affixed to it with a message reading, "Patricia, Try this, it works! Love D."

Unfortunately for all concerned, the girlfriend's initial was "D" and in the wife's mind there was no doubt that her husband's bouncy ball of fluff was the sender. Bad enough to lose her husband to a 36-24-36, but to have the smirking little bitch send her something like this disguised as "friendly advice" was "the nail in the coffin!"

So wifey marched over to the love nest, and as soon as the home wrecker answered the door, she shot twice, now there is one less cheerleader in the world.

Precious Manuscript

An Author had been sweating for years over a piece of writing, which took him ten years to research and complete. During that time the writer had neglected his wife, and ruined his social life by devoting all his time to the project. In order to safeguard the precious manuscript he gave it to his wife for her to photocopy. Unfortunately his wife, in a bizarre twist of fate, mistook the paper-shredder for the photocopying machine and every page of the manuscript ended up as scraps of paper. There was nothing the writer could due but start all over again.

Smelly Car

Back in the mid-nineties, a friend of my girlfriend had a major disagreement with her boyfriend, so she decided to get back at him. Afew months prior to the fight, he bought himself a brand new car, worth around $50,000, which was typically his pride and joy. So she had two other friends removed the passenger seat from the car, cut open the lining along the edge, inserted a fresh fish, and neatly restitched along the seam. It was fine for the first few days, until the flesh started to rot.

The boyfriend vacuumed, deodorised, pulled out the seats, and washed everything down, but didn't find the fish. When the two split up he had no luck picking up a new chick because no woman would set foot in the car. He finally gave up and sold the car: losing around $30,000 of its actual worth because of the horrible smell.

Stamped Out

A literary professor had an unusual talent for extremely small writing and could copy pages of writing on to minuscule pieces of paper. Seeking the biggest challenge for his talent, he decided to try to copy the entire works of Lenin on to a postage stamp. Every evening, he spent hours in his study copying pages on to a tiny section of the stamp. This went on month after month until, 18 months, three weeks and five days later, he finally finished. He shouted for joy and went out to celebrate at his local bar. The next morning, the man, suffering a stinking hangover, went to his study to frame his accomplishment, but couldn't find the stamp anywhere. Having searched unsuccessfully, he asked his wife if she'd seen the stamp.

"Stamp?" replied the woman nonchalantly, "Oh, yes, I needed one for a letter to my mother and found one on your desk yesterday. You didn't need it, did you?"

"That Revenge Was Off The Hook."

Just before a couple were due to go on a one-week holiday to Hawaii, the boyfriend discovered that his girlfriend had been having an affair. Since he had already paid for the holiday in full, it seemed foolish not to go, so he decided to take his sister instead of his soon-to-be-ex-girlfriend. Before leaving, he told his girlfriend in no uncertain terms that he was ending their relationship, and all of her belongings where to be out of his apartment before he returned. Arriving home after the holiday, he was pleasantly surprised to find his place in one piece, and actually remarkably tidy, with no detectable trace of his ex-girlfriend. Looking around the room, he noticed that the phone had been left off the hook. He picked up the handset to hear several men talking about sex, so he hung up. When his telephone bill arrived, it included a 200 hour phone call to an x-rated chatline, and a charge that amounted to several thousand dollars.

Did You Know? *In Omaha, Nebraska, a man discovered that his girlfriend was seeing someone else. He decided to exact revenge after she told him she was going away for a business conference. He sprinkled alfalfa seeds all over the carpets of her apartment, and sprayed them with water before packing all his things and moving out. When the girlfriend came back, her carpets were sprouting like a veritable urban jungle.*

"Where the hell is that water glass I always leave my contact lenses in overnight?"

In the arena of romance, few engagements are as precarious as the first date. "You never get a second chance to make a first impression", so we desperately strive to ensure that everything goes perfectly during the initial encounter. But sometimes things are a little less than perfect and can be disastrous.

Bathroom "Break"

This girl had been dating a rich guy from Los Angeles, and after a few months he took her to dinner at his parents mansion. During dinner she needed to use the bathroom. Not wanting to be indiscreet she asked where the "powder room" was. The parents had the butler assist her to the powder room. When she went inside it had only a vanity and sink. Not wanting to embarrass herself by asking for the toilet, instead she decided to pee in the sink. However when she sat on the sink, it pulled out of the wall, and she fell off, hitting her head on the towel rack, and knocking herself unconscious. On hearing a loud thump from above, the family rushed upstairs to find the sink broken, the girl passed out, and her skirt hiked up above her waist.

Explosive Atmosphere

A young man, wanting to propose to his girlfriend, needed a romantic setting for the special occassion. Looking in the local newspaper, he came across an advertisement for a restaurant that seemed ideal.

The advertisement read: "Romantic restaurant with panoramic views of countryside, and an atmosphere that will create an explosive reaction for lovers."

The man collected his girlfriend the next evening and they drove out to the exclusive restaurant. On parking the car and approaching the restaurant, the young man was devastated to find a mass of disgruntled people leaving.

On entering, he saw the reason why. The panoramic view of the countryside, included a nuclear power station, and all over the walls were models of weapons of mass destruction.

Realising that this particular restaurant was perhaps not the ideal place to propose marriage, he took his girlfriend home, got Chinese takeaway, and later that night proposed in the less explosive atmosphere of his bedroom.

Feeling Lucky

A young man decided to be well-prepared for his date, so he went into a pharmacy to buy some condoms.

A middle-aged man served him and noticing that the young man was a bit nervous, decided to joke with

184

him, "You think you might get some tonight, eh?"

The young man chuckled and answered, "No doubt about it". That evening, all dressed up and feeling lucky, the young man arrived at his date's house and rang the doorbell. His date opened the door and welcomed him inside, saying she just had to visit the bathroom before they left, and motioned him to sit down on the sofa.

As he sat down, he heard the girl say, "Daddy, this is Steven. We're going out tonight."

The young man turned round only to recognise his date's father as the Pharmacist he had shared a joke with earlier that day.

Freezing My Butt On

A friend of a friend told me the most embarrassing first date story that she ever had. She said it was snowing and cold, so the guy took her skiing. It was a blind date, and because they had never met before, the ski date was a day trip (no overnight).

The date went okay until they were coming back that afternoon. They were going along in the car and she had to pee real bad, but it was still about an hour or more back to civilization. Her date said she should try to hold it, which she did for a while, but it finally came to the point where she told him that he could either stop and let her pee beside the road, or in the front seat of his car. So he stopped and she went out beside the car, pulled her pants down and started to tinkle. However, not having a real good balance, she let her butt rest against the rear fender to steady herself. The guy was a real gentleman looking the other way the entire time.

When she was finished, she quickly noticed that her warm butt had stuck to the fender. Thoughts of tongues frozen to pump handle nightmares immediately came to mind and she soon realised that she had a real problem. She was thinking of every way she could to get released from his fender. Her date got a bit concerned, and finally cried out to her asking if she was alright.

With a red face, she said she was freezing her butt off, and finally had to ask for assistance. She took off her sweater and covered herself as good as she could and asked him to came around to see if he could help.

After the laughter subsided, they assessed the situation, and realised they had a real problem. They agreed that they needed something warm to melt her butt off of the fender. Thinking about the pee that she just sprinkled on the ground made her think that pee was about the only thing that they had that could get her free.

Well, after exploring every other possible solution, she looked the other way, and he proceeded to unzip his pants and pee her butt off the fender. The rest of the trip home there wasn't much conversation.

Good Fart Impression

A girl was out on a date with the man of her dreams. He was funny, good-looking and rich. He took her to dinner and then to a party where they had a great evening. They hit it off so well, she eagerly agreed when he asked her back to his place. Just as they were leaving, she suddenly felt the urge to fart, and not wanting to jeopardise her chances, she told her date that she'd meet him at the car. She found the bathroom, but unfortunately it was occupied, and she was becoming desperate, but unable to find anywhere discreet to let free the trapped wind, she decided to try her best to hold it in, and went to meet her date. Getting into the car, the girl was very relieved when her date said he'd forgotten something at the party and that he'd be back in a minute. When her date was out of sight and out of earshot, she let out a loud greasy fart, which ended with a huge sigh of relief.

Not long after, her date returned to the car and he said, "Oh, sorry, have you met Chris and Anita? I said I'd give them a lift".

Mortified, the girl turned around to see a couple sitting in the back, holding their noses.

Just The Pants

A guy living in Brooklyn, New York and attending school at NYU had been wanting to ask a certain girl out on a date for the past two years, but never had the courage. Finally, one day over the summer, he saw her at home and finally mustered up the courage to ask her out. She accepted, and they made dinner plans for the following Saturday night.

Friday night, the guy went out with all of his buddies, and drank like Prohibition was coming back. Saturday, he was in such bad shape that he could barely make it through twenty minutes without either puking or shitting. After several hours of this, he was able to stop puking, but still ran to the toilet every 20 minutes to shit. He didn't want to cancel the date, fearing he would never get this chance again. So they met at the subway terminal, and took the train to Manhattan. They got to the restaurant, but during appetizers he excused himself to use the bathroom. They enjoyed the rest of the appetizers without interruption, but he had to go back again during the entrees. They decided to get dessert, and during dessert, he felt his pants beckon, but not wanting to look like a complete bathroom freak, he held it in.

After a few minutes, the rumbling subsided, but still having a bit of gas stored up, he decided to let the little bit of gas discreetly fly right there at the table. Unfortunately, with the little bit of gas came another little surprise.

"Oh shit," he though to himself.

But instead of running to the bathroom right away, Mr. Poopy-pants immediately leaned on the arms of his chair to keep from sitting on this surprise. He maintained this yoga position for the rest of dessert, trying to figure out what to do before his tan pants started to smell, and started to show stains on the outside.

He quickly paid for dinner and walking like a cowboy, they left the restaurant. On the way to the train station, they passed "The Gap."

"Do you mind if I run in and buy a sweater that I was looking at last week?" he asked.

"No problem", she replied." I'd like to look around too," and the couple went into The Gap.

Fortunately at the Gap, men's fashions are on the right, and women's fashions are on the left, so they split up. Mr. Shit-for-gitch grabbed the first sweater within reach, and hurried back to the khakis. After selecting a pair that most closely resemble his current outfit, he brought both items to the register. His eyes were on his date, who was on the other side of the store, to make sure that she didn't see him buying the pants.

Not really needing the sweater, he said to the clerk through clenched teeth, "Just the pants."

To which the Gap girl replied, "Alrighty."

He paid for the pants and walked over to his date, then they left the store. They boarded the subway just before it left the station and found two seats in the middle of the car. Without sitting down, he excused himself and walked to the bathroom in the back of the car. He got to the bathroom as the subway departed, and quickly ripped off his pants and boxer shorts. He rolled them into a ball and threw them out the window. After cleaning himself off, he opened the Gap bag and pulled out...just the sweater.

Macho Man

A forty-year-old Casanova-type, complete with orange tan, leisure suit, hairy chest and huge medallion won the attention of an innocent young woman, so they arranged to meet at a trendy bar in town that night. The man was walking towards the bar when he passed a department store. Realising he'd forgotten to put on "scent", he went in and doused himself with the free samples. Satisfied, he continued on to the bar, and making sure his hair was greased back and his shirt wide open, he entered the room. To emphasize his macho guise, he popped a cigarette in his mouth and in one swift movement, took out his zippo lighter and lit the cigarette. But before he knew it, the flame had reacted with the heavy dousing of cologne, and he suddenly burst into flames. The man quickly picked up a pitcher of water and threw it over himself to douse the fire. His new wet look didn't go down very well with his date. She made her excuses and left.

Meet The Pet

In Hartford, Connecticut, a young man struck gold when a girl from a rich family invited him over to meet her parents. The boy dressed up in his best suit and arrived early to make a good impression. The young man could hardly contain his excitement when he saw the family's huge mansion. The door was answered by a butler, who showed him into a room, where he was told to make himself comfortable. Spotting a sumptuous leather armchair, the boy leaped into it, only to hear a loud series of cracks. The young man quickly got up to see what had made the sound. His worse fears were substantiated when he discovered that he sat on the family's pure bred Pekinese dog and broken its neck. Not knowing what else to do, the young man hid the dead dog under the leaves of a large potted plant and quickly left the premises.

Social Graces

My friend Brian was dating a girl from a very posh family. She invited him to dinner to meet her parents. Brian was not schooled in the fine art of social graces, but followed everyone's lead at the table. Everything was going well until, during the salad course, a piece of lettuce fell onto his lap. Fortunately, nobody seemed to notice. But Brian was stymied as to how to recover the lettuce. He happened to be seated at the table facing a window, with his girlfriend facing him with her back to window, and the parents at either end of the table to his left and right. Finally, he arrived at a solution.

"Wow, look at that!" Brian yelled, as he motioned toward the window.

When they all turned and looked, he picked the lettuce off his lap and returned it to his plate. The perfect crime!!

However, they continue to look out the window. So Brian stood up to look himself, and saw two dogs copulating on the well manicured lawn.

Special Gift

A young man wished to purchase a gift for his new girlfriends birthday, because they had not been dating very long, after careful consideration, he decided that a pair of gloves would strike the right note -- romantic, but not too personal.

Accompanied by his girlfriends younger sister, he bought a pair of white gloves, while the younger sister purchased a pair of panties for herself.

During the wrapping, the clerk mixed up the items and the sister got the gloves and the girlfriend got the panties.

Without checking the contents first, he sealed his package and gave it to his girlfriend along with a card that he inscribed with, "I chose these because I noticed that you are not in the habit of wearing any when we go out in the evening. If it had not been for your sister, I would have chosen the long ones with buttons, but she wears short ones that are easy to remove. These are a delicate shade, but the lady I bought them from showed me the pair she had been wearing for the past three weeks and they were hardly soiled. I had her try yours on for me and she looked really smart. I wish I were there to put them on you for the first time, because there is no doubt other hands will come in contact with them before I have a chance to see you again. When you take them off, remember to blow in them before putting them away as they will naturally be a little damp from wearing. Just think how many times I will kiss them during the coming year. I hope you will wear them for me on Friday night. The latest style is to wear them folded down with a little fur showing."

"Where the hell is that water glass I always leave my contact lenses in overnight?"

A couple on their first date became very well acquainted, and were very attracted to each other, so the decided to spend the night together in her apartment. Having had a bit too much to drink, they soon collapsed into bed and fell into a deep sleep. But the man woke up during the night with a powerfully dry throat. Luckily there was a glass full of water right there on the night table, which he downed in one gulp.

The next morning as his woman friend slowly awoken, she seemed to be fumbling around the night table for something.

"What is it, honey?" he inquired solicitously.

She continued to grope around half-blindly, muttering, "Where the hell is that water glass I always leave my contact lenses in overnight?"

Zip It Good!!

A girl invited her boyfriend home for dinner to meet her parents. The boy really liked the girl, and was very eager for the meeting to go well, so he expressed interest in the parents' respective jobs and tried to show that he genuinely cared for their daughter. The evening seemed to be going fine by the time they all sat down for dinner. The mother served dinner and told him that she had cooked lobster, which at that time of year was very expensive and extremely hard to get hold of. The boy was about to start eating, when he looked down and realised his zipper was undone. As inconspicuously as he could, he fastened up his zipper, and remembering what his mother told him about washing his hands, he asked if he could use the bathroom before eating. Unfortunately, the tablecloth had got caught in the zipper, so as he rose from the table and walked away, he took the tablecloth with him, complete with all the plates full of food, the glasses, bottles and condiments. To the boy's horror, everything smashed on the floor. There was an awkward silence before the boy fled in tears.

chaptertwelve

"If GM had kept up with the technology like the computer industry has, we would all be driving $25.00 cars that get 1,000 miles to the gallon."

--Bill Gates, CEO of Microsoftf Corporation

madscience

She blinded me with science!

. . . .

A billion hours ago our ancestors were living in the Stone Age.

A pseudoscience is a set of ideas based on theories put forth as scientific when, in fact, they are not scientific.

"Australopithecus spiff-arino."

A friend of a friend was digging out his backyard when he discovered a number of items he insisted were actual archeological finds, so he sent the findings off to the Smithsonian Institute, labeling them with scientific names.

The Paleoanthropology Division of the Smithsonian Institute replied:

Thank you for your latest submission to the Institute, labeled "211-D, layer seven, next to the clothesline post. Hominid skull."

We have given this specimen a careful and detailed examination, and regret to inform you that we disagree with your theory that it represents "conclusive proof of the presence of Early Man in Charleston County two million years ago."

Rather, it appears that what you have found is the head of a Barbie doll variety. One of our staff, who has small children, believes to be of the "Malibu Barbie" era.

It is evident that you have given a great deal of thought to the analysis of this specimen, and you may be quite certain that those of us who are familiar with your prior work in the field were loathe to come to contradiction

189

with your findings. However, we do feel that there are a number of physical attributes of the specimen which might have tipped you off to it's modern origin:

The material is molded plastic, whereas, ancient hominid remains are typically fossilized bone. The cranial capacity of the specimen is approximately 9 cubic centimeters, well below the threshold of even the earliest identified proto-hominids. The dentition pattern evident on the "skull" is more consistent with the common domesticated dog than it is with the "ravenous man-eating Pliocene clams" you speculate roamed the wetlands during that time. This latter finding is certainly one of the most intriguing hypotheses you have submitted in your history with this institution, but the evidence seems to weigh rather heavily against it. Without going into too much detail, let us say that the specimen looks like the head of a Barbie doll that a dog has chewed on, because clams don't have teeth.

It is with feelings tinged with melancholy that we must deny your request to have the specimen carbon dated. This is partially due to the heavy load our lab must bear in it's normal operation, and partly due to carbon dating's notorious inaccuracy in fossils of recent geologic record. To the best of our knowledge, no Barbie dolls were produced prior to 1956 AD, and carbon dating is likely to produce wildly inaccurate results. Sadly, we must also deny your request that we approach the National Science Foundation's Phylogeny Department with the concept of assigning your specimen the scientific name "Australopithecus spiff-arino." Speaking personally, I for one, fought tenaciously for the acceptance of your proposed taxonomy, but was ultimately voted down because the species name you selected was hyphenated, and didn't really sound like it might be Latin. However, we gladly accept your generous donation of this fascinating specimen to the museum. While it is undoubtedly not a hominid fossil, it is, nonetheless, yet another riveting example of the great body of work you seem to accumulate here so effortlessly. You should know that our Director has reserved a special shelf in his own office for the display of the specimens you have previously submitted to the Institution, and the entire staff speculates daily on what you will happen upon next in your digs at the site you have discovered in your back yard.

We eagerly anticipate your trip to our nation's capital that you proposed in your last letter, and several of us are pressing the Director to pay for it. We are particularly interested in hearing you expand on your theories surrounding the "trans-positating fillifitation of ferrous ions in a structural matrix" that makes the excellent juvenile Tyrannosaurus rex femur you recently discovered take on the deceptive appearance of a rusty 9-mm Sears Craftsman automotive crescent wrench.

Signed, Harvey Rowe; Curator, Antiquities.

Mr. Mom

Earlier this year, the British weekly *New Society* ran an article stating that a man engaged in the world's first human male pregnancy after having an embryo implanted in his abdomen.

New Society reasoned, that the egg was fertilized in vitro and implanted into the male's abdominal cavity. The embryo attached itself to a major organ, and the man had to undergo hormone injections. The child will be delivered by caesarian section. The child will also be male, or else the necessary hormone injections would effectively castrate the male host.

The dangers of such a course of action are tremendous. Although some women have successfully given birth to children conceived outside the womb, ectopic pregnancies are quite dangerous, and nearly all ectopic embryos are removed soon after diagnosis. For a man to carry a child to term in such a manner will be a high risk, especially since the placenta will have to be left to decay inside the man's body after he gives "birth," as its removal would result in major hemorrhaging.

Small Village

If we could shrink the earth's population to a village of precisely 100 people, with all the existing human ratios remaining the same, it would look something like this:

70 would be non-white, and 30 would be white.

There would be 57 Asians, 21 Europeans 14 from the Western Hemisphere, both north and south, and 8 Africans.

52 would be female, and 48 would be male...yes, more chicks for me.

70 would be non-Christian 30 would be Christian.

89 would be heterosexual, and 11 would be homosexual.

6 people would possess 59% of the entire world's wealth, and all 6 would be from the United States.

80 people would live in substandard housing.

70 would be unable to read.

50 would suffer from malnutrition.

1 would be near death, and 1 would be near birth.

1 would have a college education, and only 1 person would own a computer.

The concept of "a billion."

A billion is a difficult number to comprehend. However, when that figure is put into perspective, it is much easier to understand:

A billion seconds ago it was 1959.

A billion minutes ago Jesus was alive.

A billion hours ago our ancestors were living in the Stone Age.

A billion dollars ago, at the rate Washington spends it, was only 8 hours and 20 minutes.

The Lurking Menace Of Frothing Soda

Tapping the side of a soda can will prevent its contents from foaming over when you open it.

A shaken soda can will spew foam at us when it's opened, so we're quick to embrace a bit of "secret knowledge" that promises to put us back in charge of things and keep the lurking menace of frothing soda at bay.

The fizz gets into carbonated drinks through a process involving the forcing of carbon dioxide and water together under pressure. An unopened can of pop is almost bubble-free because the high pressure maintained inside the container forces the carbon dioxide to stay incorporated in the liquid around it. When you open the can, you reduce the pressure — bubbles of gas quickly form in the liquid, grow, and rise to the surface, where the carbon dioxide is released into the surrounding air.

Shaking a can of soda will a create a zillion little bubbles as the agitation unbinds the carbonation from the solution; the more bubbles there are, the more carbon dioxide is looking to break loose at the first opportunity. Thus, when you open a just-shaken can, it's foam city.

Tapping the can will scare the carbon dioxide into staying inside, and frighten the bubbles into collapsing back into the solution. The tapping process loosens collected bubbles from wherever they've adhered to the inside of the can and cause them to rise to the top of the solution, thereby lessening the amount of "stuff" they expel when the can is opened.

Attack Of The Frozen Chicken

The following tales of space exploration finally answer the age old question, "Why are all the instruments seeking intelligent life pointed away from the earth?"

Alien Warning

In the Nevada desert, NASA was doing a test run for a future Mars expedition. On the second day of the test, a passing group of local Native Americans stopped to watch the strange goings-on. A NASA official spotted them and went over to talk to them. He explained that the work was in preparation for an expedition to explore Mars. The eldest of the locals considered this, and then asked if they could send a message for any life that might be on the planet. Amused by the unusual request, the NASA official agreed, and took a message that the Native American had written in his own language back to the base headquarters. Several NASA officials looked at the message, but none of them could translate it. A few years later, an expert on Native American languages came across the message and translated it.

It read, "Watch out for these people, they come to take your land!"

Asteroid Balloons

A man from Texas was obsessed that the world was going to end in any number of ways. As far as he was concerned it was just a matter of what got us first from a long list that ran from alien invasion to the impact of a giant meteorite. One day he was listening to radio signals from outer space when he spotted a shower of asteroids land in his backyard. The asteroids were bright green, and the man, worried that they were radioactive, retreated to his specially-built underground bunker and radioed for help. Eventually, the police turned up to investigate, only to discover that the luminous, radioactive asteroids were in fact green balloons from a nearby fair.

Attack Of The Frozen Chicken

Scientists at NASA have developed a gun for the purpose of launching dead chickens. It is used to shoot dead chickens at the windshield of airline jets, military jets, and the space shuttle, at each vehicle's maximum traveling velocity. The idea being, that it would simulate the frequent incidents of collisions with airborne fowl, and therefore determine if the windshields are strong enough to endure high-speed bird strikes.

British engineers, upon hearing of the gun, were eager to test it on the windshields of their new high-speed trains. However, upon firing the gun, the engineers watched in shock as the chicken shattered the windshield, smashed through the control console, snapped the engineer's backrest in two, and embedded itself into the back wall of the cabin.

Horrified and puzzled, the engineers sent NASA the results of the experiment, along with the designs of the windshield, and asked the NASA scientists for any suggestions.

The NASA scientists sent back a brief response: "Thaw the chicken."

"Extra-Terrestrial Exposure Law"

If the government has no knowledge of aliens, then why does Title 14, Section 1211 of the Code of Federal

Regulations, which was implemented on July 16, 1969, make it illegal for US citizens to have any contact with extraterrestrials or their vehicles?

On the same day that Apollo 11 was launched from Kennedy Space Center, the United States adopted Title 14, Section 1211 of the Code of Federal Regulations since known as the "Extra-Terrestrial Exposure Law."

The purpose of Title 14, Section 1211 of the CFR was to "make it illegal for U.S. citizens to have any contact with extraterrestrials or their vehicles"; the law allowed the government to prevent the possibility of biological contamination from pathogens carried to Earth by men and objects returning from space by enforcing a quarantine on any people, plant or animal life, or other material that had "touched directly or come within the atmospheric envelope of any other celestial body.

Did You Know? *During the space race back in the 1960's, NASA was faced with a major problem. The astronauts needed a pen that would write in the vacuum of space. NASA went to work. At a cost of $1.5 million they developed the "Astronaut Pen". It enjoyed minor success on the commercial market. The Russians were faced with the same dilemma. They used a pencil.*

Fruit Trees That Bear Real Meat

"If you build a better mousetrap, the world will beat a path to your door," or so they say.

Advances in technology are constantly intruding into our everday lives, and with these advancements of ingenuity comes a strange new set of humorous legends.

Expanding Underwear

A commuter in Tokyo, Japan caused mayhem on the subway when he accidentally triggered his newly-patented invention - a pair of self-inflating rubber underpants. They were created to serve as a lifesaver in times of flood or when lost at sea. Unfortunately they were designed to grow to over 30 times their uninflated size, and did so when the man set them off while rummaging around inside a pocket in an attempt to find a mint. This occurred during the rush hour and commuters on the already overcrowded train were crushed against the doors when it became clear that there was nowhere to hide from the expanding underwear. When asked why he was wearing the pneumatic knickers on a train, the man replied that his greatest fear in life was to be caught in a severe flood in case it caused him to be late for work. A fellow passenger saved the day in the end by puncturing the pants with a pencil.

Inflatable Bra

A young woman, paranoid about the smallness of her breasts, was delighted when she came across an inflatable bra that she could "blow up to any size desired". The woman bought the bra, and was exstatic that she no longer had to worry about her pirate's dream (a sunken chest). When a friend invited her to a party, she decided that would be the perfect opportunity to try them out. At the party, the woman spotted a handsome man in the corner, and decided that she was going to get to know him at all costs. However, as she was about to approach him, she noticed that the man was chatting to a rather buxom woman. The young woman retreated to the bathroom and inflated her bra until she was satisfied that her breasts looked bigger than the other woman's. She then approached the man and immediately attracted his attention away from the other woman. The man eventually asked her if she wanted to dance, and she readily agreed. However, the music suddenly increased in tempo and as the man took her in his arms, her bra exploded. The woman fled the party in tears.

Invisible Hole

The engineering department of a defense plant in Syracuse, New York, has been experimenting with steel wire, drawing it out very fine. They finally produced a piece of 120-gauge wire that was practically invisible. The boys were proud — so proud, in fact, that they cut off a strand and sent it to a rival defense plant farther upstate.

"This is just to show you what we are doing in Syracuse," they wrote.

Weeks went by, until a package arrived at the Syracuse plant. The scientists opened it with great care. Inside was a steel block; mounted on the block were two steel standards, and strung between them was the same piece of 120-gauge wire. At one end of the block was mounted a small microscope delicately focused on a certain spot on the wire. One by one the engineers placed an eye to the microscope and examined in silence the work of their rivals, who had bored, in the wire, a rather handsome little hole!

Man-Made Diamonds

In May 2003, LifeGem, a company based in Los Angeles, announced that it had developed a process whereby cremated remains could be rendered into synthetic diamonds. According to the company, the process involves choice pickings from the dearly departed, then subjecting the remains to lots of heat and high pressure. It takes about four months to complete.

LifeGem describes the process to render its "created diamonds" with how industrial diamonds are made, which is subjecting graphite to extremely high heat and pressure. Synthetic, or man-made, diamonds have been manufactured from carbon since the mid-1950s, when General Electric Company developed the process for making small diamonds for industrial uses. In the mid-1990s, gemstone-quality synthetics began to appear.

Could cremains, which are simply a mixed bag of elements be used as the raw material for fashioning synthetic diamonds?

According to Keith Pomeier, a chemistry professor at Northwestern University said, "There's no reason the process shouldn't work."

Ava Bloom, a chemistry professor at DePaul University in Chicago, maintains that it is feasible to make a "reasonably high-quality diamond" from the carbon in a cremated human.

Kenneth Delahey, head of LifeGem Memorials, claims that their diamonds are not just "reasonably high-quality", but are of the same quality you find at "Tiffany's."

Meat Trees

Researchers in Manchester, England have developed genetically engineered fruit trees that bear real meat. Finally, news vegetarians can really sink their teeth into.

Fruit from the new Meat Trees, developed by British scientists using gene-splicing technology, closely resembles ordinary grapefruit. But when you peel the large fruit open, inside is fresh beef.

"Our trees may sound like something out of a science fiction movie, but it's really a simple, down-to-earth idea whose time has come," declared Dr. Bif Tartar, director of agricultural bioengineering research for the UltraModAgri Group, which created the amazing trees. "Vegetarians have been complaining for years that despite their moral convictions against consuming meat, they still crave the flavor of a good steak once in a while. Now they can have their cake and eat it too."

What's The Racat?

Anyone who understands the joys of rabbit ownership will know that despite their incredible cuteness, they are not the most affectionate or exciting of creatures. Currently, a company in South America is offering to sell a new hybrid animal which they claim, combines the finest qualities of the rabbit and the cat. Male rabbits are famed for their willingness to attempt sex with any female creature regardless of species, and by a strange coincidence, rabbits and cats share the same number of chromosomes and a remarkably similar gestation period. Allied to this is the fact that female cats will quite happily raise the young of almost any species as one of their own. All these factors have combined to help animal breeders develop a brand new species of pet called a "racat". Although some breeders are pushing for the far more attractive name of "cabbit". The "racat" can be ordered from most large pet stores but may take a little while to arrive due to the almost legendarily laid-back nature of both cats and rabbits.

"If GM had kept up with the technology like the computer industry has, we would all be driving $25.00 cars that get 1,000 miles to the gallon."

Computers are not only the primary means by which rumors and other pieces of misinformation are spread, but they have become an integral part of our daily lives --so much so-- we have become dependant on them.

Microsoft Haiku

In Japan, they have replaced the impersonal and unhelpful Microsoft Error messages with Haiku poetry messages.
Haiku poetry has strict construction rules.
Each poem has only three lines, 17 syllables: five syllables in the first line, seven in the second, and five in the third.

Haiku poetry is used to communicate a timeless message often achieving a wistful, yearning and powerful insight through extreme brevity — the essence of Zen. Here are a few samples of the new Microsft Haiku Error messages:

Program aborting:
Close all that you have worked on.
You ask far too much.

Your file was so big.
It might be very useful.
But now it is gone.

The Web site you seek
Cannot be located, but
Countless more exist.

Chaos reigns within.
Reflect, repent, and reboot.
Order shall return.

Windows NT crashed.

I am the Blue Screen of Death.
No one hears your screams.

Replacement of Mouse Balls

BM field service memo details the procedure for replacing mouse balls.

If a mouse fails to operate or should it perform erratically, it may need a ball replacement. Mouse balls are now available as Field Replacement Units. Because of the delicate nature of this procedure, replacement of mouse balls should only be attempted by properly trained personnel.

Before proceeding, determine the type of mouse balls by examining the underside of the mouse. Domestic balls will be larger and harder than foreign balls. Ball removal procedures differ depending upon the manufacturer of the mouse. Foreign balls can be replaced using the pop off method. Domestic balls are replaced by using the twist off method. Mouse balls are not usually static sensitive. However, excessive handling can result in sudden discharge. Upon completion of ball replacement, the mouse may be used immediately.

It is recommended that each person have a pair of spare balls for maintaining optimum customer satisfaction. Any customer missing his balls should contact the local personnel in charge of removing and replacing these necessary items.

A customer without properly working balls is an unhappy customer.

The iLoo

Microsoft Corporation is bringing Internet access to the portable toilet.

The iLoo, developed by Microsoft's MSN division, will be a standard portable toilet, or "loo," as the Brits so quaintly call it. It will be equipped with a wireless keyboard and an extensible, height-adjustable plasma screen located directly in front of the seated user.

MSN plans to install an external "Hotmail station" on the outside of the MSN iLoo so people can do something useful while they queue. This will include a waterproof keyboard and plasma screen enabling users to surf the Internet while waiting.

MSN says it's in talks with toilet-paper makers to produce special paper imprinted with URLs that users may not have tried.

Tracy Blacher, the MSN marketing manager said, "The Internet's so much a part of everyday life, that surfing on the loo was the next logical and natural step. People used to reach for a book or magazine when they were on the loo, but now they'll be logging on! It's exciting to think that the smallest room can now be the gateway to the massive virtual world."

The Microsoft Car

At Comdex, a computer expo, Bill Gates reportedly compared the computer industry with the auto industry stating, "If GM had kept up with the technology like the computer industry has, we would all be driving $25.00 cars that get 1,000 miles to the gallon."

In response to Bill's comments, General Motors president, Mr. Welch issued a press release stating, If GM had developed technology like Microsoft...

1. We would all be driving cars that crashed twice a day, for no reason.

2. Every time they repainted the lines on the road, you would have to buy a new car.

3. Occasionally, executing a manoeuver such as a left-turn would cause your car to shut down and refuse to restart, and you would have to reinstall the engine.

4. When your car died on the freeway for no reason, you would just accept it, restart and drive on.

5. Only one person at a time could use the car, unless you bought 'Car95' or 'CarNT', and then added more seats.

6. Apple would make a car powered by the sun, reliable, five times as fast, and twice as easy to drive, but would run on only five per cent of the roads.

7. Oil, water temperature and alternator warning lights would be replaced by a single 'general car default' warning light.

8. New seats would force every-one to have the same size butt.

9. The airbag would say 'Are you sure?' before going off.

10. Occasionally, for no reason, your car would lock you out and refuse to let you in until you simultaneously lifted the door handle, turned the key, and grabbed the radio antenna.

11. GM would require all car buyers to also purchase a deluxe set of road maps from Rand-McNally, even though they neither need nor want them, and trying to delete this option would immediately cause the car's performance to diminish by 50 per cent or more. Moreover, GM would become a target for investigation by the Justice Department.

12. Each time GM introduced a new model, car buyers would have to learn how to drive all over again because none of the controls would operate in the same manner as the old car, and;

13. You would press the 'start' button to shut off the engine.

"Sir, the answer to that question is so simple that I will let my chauffeur, who is sitting in the back, answer it for me."

Despite their great scientific achievements, plenty of tales surround those who conferred the greatest benefit on mankind. Even the diligent inventor, or most brilliant of minds still find their way into folklore. Some of these stories are quite amusing, and a few have achieved legendary status.

Nobody's Fool

When Albert Einstein was making the rounds of the speaker's circuit, he usually found himself eagerly longing to get back to his laboratory work. One night as they were driving to yet another rubber-chicken dinner, Einstein mentioned to his chauffeur, a man who somewhat resembled Einstein in looks and manner, that he was tired of speechmaking.

"I have an idea, boss," said the chauffeur. "I've heard you give this speech so many times. I'll bet I could give it for you." Einstein laughed loudly and said, "Why not? Let's do it!"

When they arrived at the dinner, Einstein donned the chauffeur's cap and jacket and sat in the back of the

197

room. The chauffeur gave a beautiful rendition of Einstein's speech and even answered a few questions expertly.

Then a supremely pompous professor asked an extremely esoteric question about anti-matter formation, digressing here and there to let everyone in the audience know that he was nobody's fool.

Without missing a beat, the chauffeur fixed the professor with a steely stare and said, "Sir, the answer to that question is so simple that I will let my chauffeur, who is sitting in the back, answer it for me."

Did You Know? *Thomas Crapper is an elusive figure. Most people familiar with his name know him as a celebrated figure in Victorian England, an ingenious plumber who invented the modern flush toilet. He originally called his invention the "valveless water-waste preventer" and later changed it to "the automatic syphon flushing tank."*

You Do The Math

The renowned Nobel Prize is the legacy of Swedish chemist, inventor, and industrialist Alfred Nobel, whose 1895 will specified that most of his fortune be set aside to establish a fund for the awarding of five annual prizes in the fields specified by Nobel: physics, chemistry, medicine, literature and peace. The prizes were to be awarded "to those who, during the preceding year, conferred the greatest benefit on mankind."

A prize for a sixth category, economics, was added by the Bank of Sweden beginning in 1969. The first Nobel Prizes were distributed on 10 December 1901, the fifth anniversary of Nobel's death.

In the century since the Nobel Foundation was established, many have speculated on the reasons why Alfred Nobel did not provide for a prize to be awarded for achievement in the field of mathematics.

Surely an eminent man of science such as Alfred Nobel could not simply have forgotten about mathematics, so he must have had a good reason for omitting it. It was later discovered that Alfred Nobel deliberately avoided establishing a prize for mathematics out of vindictiveness because a prominent Swedish mathematician was carrying on an affair with his wife.

Did You Know? *The brassiere was invented by Otto Titzling. Titzling came to invent the item while living in a New York boardinghouse in 1912. One of his neighbors was a buxom opera singer named Swanhilda Olafson, and the structural engineering problems she presented inspired Titzling to create a contraption to uphold this lady friends ample bosom.*

chapterthirteen

"My wife kisses my balls for good luck."

--Arnold Palmer

poorsports

Over the last few decades sports has become America's premiere past-time. In fact, sporting events have now transcended their status as mere athletic contests to become a great national celebration on par with many political and state holidays.

. . . .

"I will never forgive you for making us move to Philadelphia!"

During SuperBowl, there is a two-week build-up of massive media coverage leading into a day of partying, overeating, drinking, wagering, and the anti-climax of a football game itself. As we should expect, a sport of such tremendous national importance has engendered its own unique set of legends, legends that express a number of our national values. Football legends usually involve numbers and a sense of enormity. The idea of big numbers, of being bigger than other people, is very American.

"Massive Toilet Use Havoc" Phenomenon

During Super Bowl Sundays, sewage systems of major cities have broken due to the tremendous number of toilets being flushed simultaneously during halftime. The havoc wreaked is due to the widespread simultaneous toilet flushing after the popular broadcast event. Toilet use during breaks in this large-audience program is certainly much higher than average, because millions of people will sit through the entire three-to-four-hour Super Bowl program, and although it features almost as much advertising time as actual football action, there are still those who steadfastly refuse to miss even a few seconds of the program and wait until the very end of the multi-hour event to heed nature's call.

"Super Bowl Indicator"

Want to know if the bulls or bears will be rampaging through the stock market this year? Look to the Super Bowl for the answer because a seemingly startling correlation appears to exist between who wins the big game and how the market will perform in the upcoming year. According to the "Super Bowl Indicator," stock market performance is predicted by the winner of the Super Bowl. If a team from the American Football Conference, or AFC is triumphant, it foreshadows a down market. But if a team from the the National Football Conference, or NFC wins the Super Bowl, it means dust off your red cape, because the bulls are coming.

Super Guacamole Sunday

Thanks to the influence of our Hispanic countrymen and neighbors, we've become a guacamole-loving nation. And Super Bowl Sunday, like other important celebrations, has a strong association with food, particularly snack foods such as potato and corn chips that cry out for something yummy to dip them in.

Super Bowl Sunday is also Super Guacamole Sunday, and naturally, it is the time of year when sales of avocados, the primary ingredient in guacamole, skyrocket. Sales of avacados shoot up within a three week period of Super Bowl Sunday.

Super Bowl Sunday accounts for about 67% of annual avocados sales.

According to the California Avocado Commission, that 67% is about 14 million pounds of avocados — that's a lot of avocados. Even Cinco de Mayo celebrations pale in comparison with only 8 million pounds sold annually.

Did You Know? *Before Super Bowl XXII, a reporter asked Washington Redskins QB Doug Williams, "How long have you been a black quarterback?"*

The Abuse Bowl

A news conference was called in the site of the forthcoming Super Bowl game, by a coalition of women's groups.

At the news conference reporters were informed that significant anecdotal evidence suggested that Super Bowl Sunday was "the biggest day of the year for violence against women."

Prior to the conference, there had been reports of increases as high as 40 percent in calls for help from victims that day. At the conference, Heather Marshall of the California Women's Law Center cited a study done at Virginia's Old Dominion University three years before, saying that it found police reports of beatings and hospital admissions in northern Virginia rose 40 percent after games won by the Redskins during the 1988-89 season.

The presence of Michele Redding at the conference, a representative of a media "watchdog" group called "Fairness and Accuracy in Reporting" (FAIR), lent credibility to the cause.

At about this time a very large media mailing was sent warning at-risk women, "Don't remain at home with your husband during the Superbowl."

The idea that sports fans are prone to attack wives or girlfriends on that climactic day persuaded many men as well. Maybe it should be refered to as the "Abuse Bowl."

The Philadelphia Eagle

The coach had put together the perfect team for the Philadelphia Eagles. The only thing that was missing was a good quarterback. He had scouted all the colleges and even the Canadian and European Leagues, but he couldn't find a quarterback who could ensure a Super Bowl win.

Then one night while watching CNN he saw a war-zone scene in Afghanistan. In one corner of the background, he spotted a young Afghan Muslim soldier with a truly incredible arm. He threw a hand-grenade straight into a 15th story window 100 yards away. KABOOM! He threw another hand-grenade 75 yards away, right into a chimney. KA-BLOOEY! Then he threw another at a passing car going 90 mph. BULLS-EYE!

"I've got to get this guy!" Coach said to himself. "He has the perfect arm!"

So, he brings him to the States and teaches him the great game of football. And the Eagles go on to win the Super Bowl. The young Afghan is hailed as the great hero of football, and when the coach asks him what he wants, all the young man wants is to call his mother.

"Mom," he says into the phone, "I just won the Super Bowl!"

"I don't want to talk to you," the old Muslim woman says. "You deserted us. You are not my son!"

"I don't think you understand, Mother," the young man pleads. "I've won the greatest sporting event in the world. I'm here among thousands of my adoring fans."

"No! Let me tell you!" his mother retorts. "At this very moment, there are gunshots all around us. The neighborhood is a pile of rubble. Your two brothers were beaten within an inch of their lives last week, and I have to keep your sister in the house so she doesn't get raped!"

The old lady pauses, and then tearfully says, "I will never forgive you for making us move to Philadelphia!

"Florida is going to win the World Series in 1997, yeah right!"

For a century now, baseball has been the essential American ritual. There are numerous plays, musicals, films, books, and television programs that have melded humor with the sport of baseball, so it comes as no surprise that the American national pastime remains the quintessential sport in the folklore arena.

Elevated Encounter

In the early '80s, a group of white, female tourists visiting New York City were joined in an elevator by a black man with a large dog in tow.

As the elevator doors closed, the man firmly commanded his dog to "Sit," at which point the timorous ladies – assuming they were being mugged – sat.

The man apologized profusely even though he had done nothing wrong and explained that the order was meant for the dog. Embarrassed, the women brushed themselves off and explained they were from out of town. One of the ladies asked nervously if the man could suggest a good restaurant nearby. He did so, then departed. After dining at the restaurant, the women were presented with a check marked "Paid in full." The waiter told them their meal had been paid for by baseball star Reggie Jackson – the man they had met on the elevator.

"Florida is going to win the World Series in 1997, yeah right!"

If any of you remember the movie "Back to the Future II" you may recall that Biff goes to the future and steals a Sports Almanac, where in turn he goes back to the past to give it to young Biff. As we all know Young Biff was able to become very wealthy by betting on games where he already knew the final score.

In an obscure line you hear young Biff say, "Florida is going to win the World Series in 1997, yeah right".

This movie came out in 1987, ten years before the Marlins did actually win the world series. And what's really weird is that Florida didn't even have a baseball team in 1987. The Marlins didn't even exist at the time.

Pennies For Your Thoughts

A player (who shall remain nameless) for the Toronto Blue Jays was suspended for five days by Warren Giles, the National League president, and fined $100. He wasn't too happy about it, and neither was the general manager. But there was nothing they could do.

So the Blue Jay owed the National League $100 and decided that the next time the Jays were in Cincinnati he would pay his debt in person. He went to a bank and got $100 worth of rolled up pennies, emptied them out, then put all the loose coins in a sack, and delivered them to Mr. Giles's office at the league headquarters in Carew Tower. He dumped the sack on his secretary's desk, she gave me a little smile, and he took off in a hurry. He was pretty proud of myself when he headed back to his hotel room, but he wasn't there long before the phone rang. It was Mr. Giles's secretary.

"Mr. Giles would like to see you," she said.

So he went back to the office and had a conversation with Mr. Giles. He told the Blue Jay to be careful about the way he was pitching.

The Jay responded in kind, "I am not about to change my philosophy of keeping batters off the plate." The conversation was very amiable.

"And by the way," Mr. Giles added, "I want you to take those pennies of yours and roll them up for me."

Fortunately, he had the paper rolls back in his room. He took the sack back to the hotel, and sat there for hours, putting the pennies in their containers, cursing all the way. Thank God he saved those containers or he would still be back in that Cincinnati hotel, rolling up $100 worth of pennies.

The Streak

Actor Kevin Costner was caught in bed with the wife of Orioles infielder Cal Ripken Jr. in August 1997, forcing the Orioles to cancel a game so that the distraught Ripken's consecutive-game streak would not be in jeopardy.

Cal Ripken, Jr. allowed actor Kevin Costner to stay at his house, following the wrap of "For Love of the Game". One morning, Ripken left for Camden Yards to play in a game. Somewhere between his home and the stadium, Cal realised that he had left something back at his house, and turned back to retrieve it.

Upon arriving at his home, he found Kevin Costner in bed with his wife. Cal then proceeded to beat Costner, to the point that he was unable to make any public appearances for a time. Cal then called the Orioles, and told them he wouldn't be coming in to play that day.

Upon hearing this, the owner reminded Cal about his streak, telling him the streak would end if he didn't play that day.

Cal told him it was impossible for him to come in, so there went the streak. Reportedly, the owner told him not to worry, and that he would take care of it.

That night, the game was cancelled due to "electrical failure" with some lights on the field. However, everything else, including the hotels and restaurants that were part of Camden Yards, worked perfectly. The next day, the lights were fixed, and Cal was able to play, streak intact.

"They'll put a man on the moon before he hits a home run."

In 1963, The Giants manager made a remark about his feeble-hitting pitcher Gaylord Perry.

He remarked, "They'll put a man on the moon before he hits a home run."

On July 20, 1969, Perry would collect his first, and only home run, minutes after Apollo 11's lunar module touched down on the Moon, and Neil Armstrong set foot on the moon.

"Picabo, I.C.U."

Every four years the world is awash with jokes regarding the Olympics. Afterall, the Olympics are where legends are made.

Did You Know? *Prior to the World Championships in Rome, Ben Johnson was asked whether he would prefer a gold medal or a world record. He said that he would prefer a gold medal because, "No one can ever take it away from me."*

I'm Winning For Two

In an issue of *Report* magazine, "Brave New World", columnist Celeste McGovern wrote of a gruesome method of blood doping used by some female athletes to boost athletic performance. Since enhancing drugs and even regular blood doping can be identified by regulators, the pregnancy-abortion scheme, while officially banned, is virtually impossible to stop.

Monica Pignano, director of research at the Washington pro-life group Life Dynamics is quoted by Report magazine quoting a European sports medicine expert, "Now that drug testing is routine, pregnancy is becoming the favourite way of getting an edge on the competition."

One Russian athlete told a reporter that as long ago as the '70s, gymnasts as young as 14 were ordered to sleep with their coaches to get pregnant -- and then abort. The procedure is so well known it has made it to the textbooks. LifeSite found the method described in a textbook in physiology by Dr. Erik Paulev of the Department of Medical Physiology, University of Copenhagen.

Professor Paulev wrote that pregnancy increases muscle strength in female athletes. "Female top athletes - just following the time when they gave birth to their first child - have set several world records. Of course, this is acceptable as a natural and unintended event. However, in some countries female athletes have become pregnant for 2-3 months, in order to improve their performance just after the abortion."

"Picabo, I.C.U."

The famous Olympic skier Picabo Street, is not just an athlete, she is also a nurse who currently works in the Intensive Care Unit (I.C.U.) of a large metropolitan hospital.

Although a fine nurse, Picabo is not permitted to answer the telephone because too much confusion ensues when she answers the phone and says, "Picabo, I.C.U."

"I'll bet that flutters your putter."

The game of golf is mentioned much earlier in folklore than any other sport. It's appeal is attributable to a societal shift in the nature of who now plays the game. Women take as many trips around the links as do their male counterparts, as a result, golf has grown to be a pastime enjoyed by both sexes, allowing legends to run rampant through the fairway.

Did You Know? *On October 25th, The New Zealand Dominion Sunday Times reported that Golfer Elaine Johnson was heard yelling, "I'll take the 2-stroke penalty, but I'll be damned if I play it where it lies," after her shot ricoheted off a tree into her bra.*

I'll Drink To That

How many of you golfers know why full-length golf courses have 18 holes, and not 20, or 10 or an even dozen?

In 1858, during a discussion among the club's membership board at St. Andrews one of the members pointed out that it takes exactly 18 shots to polish off a fifth of Scotch. By limiting himself to only one shot of Scotch per hole, the Scot figured a round of golf was finished when the Scotch ran out.

I'll drink to that.

Did You Know? *During a Tonight Show appearance, Arnold Palmer was asked by Johnny Carson if he had any good-luck rituals. The golfer replied, "Yes, my wife kisses my balls." To which Carson quipped, "I'll bet that flutters your putter."*

Poor Sport

A golfing fanatic was so furious after playing a losing shot that he threw his new bag of clubs into a nearby lake and stormed off. However, the other golfers weren't at all surprised, when five minutes later, he returned red-faced. He took off his shoes, rolled up his trousers and waded into the lake. No one was too surprised at these second thoughts, it was clearly an expensive set of clubs he'd hurled into the water. After rumbling around for a while the bedraggled golfer fished out the golf bag, but to the amazement of the bystanders, he merely unzipped a pocket, took out a set of car keys, flung the set of clubs back into the water and stormed off again.

Did You Know? *The word 'golf' is an acronym formed from "gentlemen only; ladies forbidden."*

chapterfourteen

"I love my cigar too, but I take it out of my mouth once in a while."

--Grouch Marx

popularculture

Pop culture has become a springboard for numerous legends, and no medium has had more of an impact on 20th century culture than motion picture. People have made careers out of endlessly analyzing and debating the meanings, styles, themes and techniques of filmmakers. While these films are earnestly dissected and studied, the actors and actresses who star in movies live their public lives in fishbowls.

Television has made its own mark in 20th century culture. If you add up the countless hours spent infront of the television it would equal more than half your life. So it's possible television did a better job raising you than your parents. We've seen and heard outrageous things on and about television, but most of them can't compare to the outrageous things we think we've seen or heard on television.

Commercial radio also played a tremendous role in popular culture. It was the first technological breakthrough that finally allowed people to experience live news events and entertainment right in our own homes -- shared moments with millions of fellow listeners. Radio's role in bringing us together has made it an enduring source for numerous legends.

And let's not forget about music. People have managed to generate some rather unusual stories regarding various pop artists and the music industry. Whether the focus is on the notorious musicians outrageous behavior both on and off stage, or about the music itself, like any other artistic endeavor, it's subject to interpretation.

. . . .

And The Oscar Goes To...

The types of legends that surround the filming industry are too numerous to categorize. The men and women who star in motion pictures lead heavily-scrutinized lives, so it's no wonder few people could prevent their private lives from becoming legend under those circumstances. But not all movie legends are about actors or films. There are many miscellaneous legends that have to do with other aspects of the film industry.

A Duck Fight Served In Black And White

In the 1988 the live action and animation film *"Who Framed Roger Rabbit"*, had Disney characters interacting with other famous cartoon characters from other studios such as Warner Bros. and MGM. One evening at the Ink and Paint Club, Disney's Donald Duck and Warners' Daffy Duck engage in a memorable piano duet. At one point the dialog between the two characters allegedly takes a nasty turn

Daffy says to Donald, "I've worked with a lot of wise-quackers, but you are dethpsicable!"

To which Donald replies, "God damn stupid nigger! I'm gonna WAAAAAAAAGH!!!"

And Daffy says, "This is the last time I work with someone with a speech impediment!"

"A horse! A horse! My kingdom for a horse!"

The Royal Exchange Theatre in Manchester, England, staged a production of William Shakespeare's play Richard III.

In the final act, the actor playing Richard III exclaims in a booming voice the famous line, "A horse! A horse! My kingdom for a horse!"

One evening, a man in the audience decided to comment, "Hey buddy, I've got a horse!"

There were a few giggles in the audience, when the actor replied, "I asked for a horse, not an ass!"

This quick ad-lib brought the house down and the production was an overwhelming success.

And The Oscar Goes To...

During the 1993 Academy Awards ceremony, the award for 1992's Best Supporting Actress had been mistakenly given to Marisa Tomei rather than the "real" winner, Vanessa Redgrave, because presenter Jack Palance called out the wrong name. Palance was unable to read the printing on the card, and became confused, and then arbitrarily announced Tomei as the winner because it fell last in the list of nominees and thus had not yet scrolled off the teleprompter screen.

I Give Siskel's Will Two Thumbs Up

The execution of the will of Gene Siskel, nationally known movie critic, was finally cleared through probate court after a few surprising requests. Siskel died of complications resulting from his May 1998 brain surgery. The bulk of his estate was, as expected, left to his wife and children. According to public records filed by in chancery court in Chicago, Gene Siskel asked that he be buried with his thumb pointing upward. The "Thumbs Up" was the Siskel-Ebert trademark, and has become a pop culture icon.

"I'm not surprised that Gene would request that," said partner Roger Ebert, "That's just the kind of guy he was."

Did You Know? *The horses in the Mel Brooks production, "Young Frankenstein" whined every time they heard the name of Frau Blucher, played by Cloris Leachman, because her name*

sounds like the German word for glue.

Keep It Clean

Urban garbage seems to be everywhere, except when you really need it.

A director was in Tornto filming a movie that ordered a massive pile of garbage to make Toronto look more like New York. But when the film crew came back from a coffee break, they found the trash had been cleaned up. Filming had to be halted while the director ordered more garbage. The incident was reported in the American magazine *Entertainment Weekly,* and the delighted city works commissioner proudly shows off copies at city meetings.

Penis Van Lesbian

A strikingly handsome young man walked into the office of a Hollywood agent with his resume and portfolio in hand. The agent reviewed the young man's slim resume and small portfolio with the care that was deserving of this fine young specimen.

"You have the obvious good looks and excellent demeanor of an actor," said the agent, "But tell me, have you had any roles that I might be aware of?"

"No sir, only the requisite high school and college plays," replied the handsome young man.

"I dare say I know the reason why, with a name like yours," the agent said.

"Sir?" inquired the handsome wannabe. "

"Your name. Penis Van Lesbian." exclaimed the agent. "That's not a name that will go far in Hollywood. I'd love to represent you, but you'll have to change your name."

"Sir," the handsome young man protested. "The Van Lesbian name was my father's, my grandfather's and his father's before him. We have carried this name for generations and I will not change it for Hollywood or any other reason."

"If you won't change your name, I cannot represent you," said the agent.

"Then I bid you farewell," said Penis Van Lesbian. "My name will not change." With that, Penis Van Lesbian left the agents office never to return.

Six years later, the Hollywood agent returned to his office after lunch with some producers and began shuffling through his mail. Mostly junk mail, trade journals, ect., all except for one letter. He opened the envelope and removed the letter. As he unfolded the fine linen paper, a check dropped from the folds and onto his desk. He looked at the check. It was for 50,000 dollars!

The letter stated, "Dear Sir. Several years ago, I entered your office determined to become an actor. You refused to represent me unless I changed my name. I objected, saying the Penis Van Lesbian name had been carried for generations and left your office. However, upon leaving, I reconsidered my hastiness and after considerable reflection, I decided to heed your advice and changed my name. Now I am a famous actor with many roles and known to millions worldwide. Having achieved this fame and fortune, it is often that I think back to my meeting with you and your insistence that I change my name. I owe you a debt of gratitude, so please accept this check with my humble thanks, because it was your idea which has brought me to such wealth and fame." The letter was signed, Dick Van Dyke.

Screen Test

Back in the 1930s, John Barrymore was one of the biggest things in Hollywood, and Carradine, a fine Shakespearean actor on Broadway, was seeking work in Hollywood. Somehow, Barrymore, an old friend of Carradine's was put in charge of his screen test at Twentieth-Century Fox.

"Not to worry, dear boy," said Barrymore. "I'll take good care of you."

Barrymore guided Carradine over to a vacant stage, where a cameraman and some lighting guys were waiting. He explained that the entire test would be done in pantomime.

"I want you to come out from behind this door," said Barrymore, "and you're to make the audience feel that you've just had the best feast of your life."

Carradine agreed and put on a helluva mime show, licking his lips, wiping them with his kerchief, patting his stomach, almost burping with contentment, smiling to himself, sighing with the rapture of it all.

"How did I do?" asked Carradine.

Barrymore cried out, "Cut! That was terrific."

"When do I get to see it?" asked Carradine.

"Tomorrow," said Barrymore."Come to the commissary at noon tomorrow. We'll take a look at it after lunch."

After lunch the next day, Barrymore corralled a half-dozen of the studio executives to take a look at Carradine. Carradine wondered why his friend was making such a big deal out of a simple, little, no-dialogue piece of celluloid. It all became clear when he looked up on the screen. After his marvelous mime, the camera cut back to the same door Carradine had come out of. Then came Barrymore, smiling and winking at the camera and zipping up his fly.

"She's in the attic!"

A director hired a young bit player who was very pretty, but a terrible actress. She was very ambitious and agreed that if she got some experience in the theater, it would help her career. Fortunately, she had a wealthy boyfriend who backed a road company of *"The Diary of Anne Frank"* just so she could play the leading role -- Anne Frank.

Before the opening in Chicago, Illinois, they had three weeks of intensive rehearsals, and everyday was more and more frustrating for the director. The actress was impossible. She couldn't remember her lines, her delivery was amateurish, and the more she rehearsed, the worse she got. The director was ready to quit the show, but she reassured the director that she was a poor rehearser.

"Believe me," she said, "When I face that opening-night audience, it'll all come together."

She invited the director who hired her for his film to the opening night, but he was not all that anxious to see her perform, and he had even less desire to be in Chicago in February.

As soon as the curtain went up she blew her opening lines, and her performance went downhill from then on. By the intermission the audience was totally fed up with her. Then, in the first scene in the second act, when the Nazi soldiers break into the home, overturning furniture and shouting, "Where is she? Where's Anne Frank?!"

The entire audience yelled back, "She's in the attic!"

Did You Know? *Donald Duck was once banned in a foreign country because he didn't wear any pants and cavorted with an unmarried female duck!*

Snow White And The Seven Symptoms

A friend of a friends grandfather had an important job on what was then the largest private construction project in the world: Walt Disney World".

Many of them blew off steam after work most days. One night he broke up a fight at a local bar between one of his friends and a fellow construction worker. The construction guy took off, so he asked his co-worker what the problem was.

He told how the construction worker said that Walt Disney had been a cocaine addict, and as a result, Walt Disney had invented Snow White and the Seven Dwarves. Snow White represented cocaine, and the seven dwarves were the symptoms of various stages of cocaine addiction: Bashful, Grumpy, Sleepy, Dopey, Sneezy, Happy, and Doc.

Did You Know? *"The Madness of King George" is the film adaptation of the Alan Bennett play "The Madness of George III". It seems the film's title was changed from "The Madness of George III" because the Brits figured American audiences would think it was a sequel and not go to see it, assuming they had missed "I" and "II."*

"Chachi" is Korean for "penis."

"When I watch TV and see those poor starving kids all over the world, I can't help but cry. I mean, I'd love to be skinny like that, but not with all those flies and death and stuff."

--Mariah Carey

Thanks to radio and television, we have been provided with a means to share common experiences in our lives. Although we grew up and lived thousands of miles apart, we still listened to and watched the same programs, knew the same actors, and actresses, and we could all recite the "Jolly Green Giant" theme. So ingrained in our consciousness are some of these radio and television "memories" that we vividly recall events that never even took place.

Baghdad Betty

Baghdad Betty, Iraq's English-language radio service is a product of the Iraqi propaganda machine. In a recent broadcast, demoralizing the US forces in the Saudi Desert, she took a credibility nosedive. While indulging in some mischievous bitchery she reported that the wives of US soldiers were committing adultery by sleeping with movie stars.

She reportedly said, "Why are you Americans here? Don't you know you will die in the desert? While you are here, your wives and girlfriends are dating American movie stars . . . like Tom Cruise, Paul Newman, Arnold Schwarzenegger and Bart Simpson."

I am sure the first three presented some cause for anxiety, but who initiated the deviant practice of molesting under-age, primary coloured cartoon characters?

Beauty and the Beast

A rather portly-built young man was approached on the street one day by a woman who appeared to be an exotic and rather beautiful belly dancer, complete with a jewel in her navel. This wasn't a regular experience for the man, known to his friends as 'Chubby', and he thought his luck was finally turning, particularly when the beautiful woman smiled at him.

As Chubby smiled and said, "Hello," he realised that the exotic lady was accompanied by a television crew.

"I'm from the local 5:00 news and we're doing a feature," said the beauty, "Would you like me to teach you to belly dance on live TV?" At which point, Chubby ran away in response.

Did You Know? *At a farewell party thrown after the filming of the final episode of "Green Acres", the cast and crew barbequed and ate the porcine actor who played Arnold Ziffel. Arnold The Pig was a valuable member of the cast. Just because he was a pig was no reason to eat him.*

Filling In The Broadcasts

A familiar plot employed in numerous television sitcom episodes is the plight of the hapless character who, having recently undergone some dental work, such as the installation of fillings or braces, begins to pick up radio broadcasts through his/her teeth.

In 1942, during the early days of American involvement in World War II, residents along the Pacific coast of California lived in dread fear of an imminent attack by the Japanese, especially after a Japanese submarine appeared off the coast of Santa Barbara on February 23, 1942. A Los Angeles woman who recently had several temporary lead fillings installed in her teeth, was driving home when she heard music, but when she reached down to turn the radio off, she noticed it wasn't on, but for some reason the music kept getting louder, at which point, she realised it was coming from her mouth.

Her mouth was humming and thumping with the drumbeat, and she thought she was losing her mind.

"What the hell was going on?" she thought to herself. Then the music started to subside. When she got home she went to bed, not sure if she should tell anybody what had happened because they might think she was crazy.

However, she decided to tell her husband, and when she recounted the story he laughingly told her that she was picking up radio broadcasts through her fillings, and that the same thing had happened to a friend of his. After that, nothing more happened.

A week later, she took a different route home from work, and all of a sudden, her mouth started jumping again. This time it wasn't music, it sounded more like Morse code. It started softly, and then de-de-de-de-de-de. As soon as it started fading, she stopped the car and started backing up until it was coming in a full strength DE-DE-DE-DE-DE-DE DE-DE-DE-DE! She got out of there real quick. But the next day she told the police about it, and they called the FBI, which led to the capture of a Japanese spy using an underground Japanese radio station. He was posing as somebody's gardener.

I Have The Equipment, And I Know How To Use It.

A female broadcaster and US Army Lieutenant General Reinwald were discussing the sponsoring of a Boy Scout Troop on his military installation over National Public Radio.

When the interviewer asked the Lieutenant what he was going to do with these young boys on their adventure holiday, he replied, "We're going to teach them climbing, canoeing, archery, and shooting."

"Shooting!" said the interviewer, "that seems a bit irresponsible."

"I don't see why, they'll be properly supervised on the range, and will be taught the proper range discipline before they even handle a firearm," said the Lieutenant.

"You have to admit that this is a terribly dangerous activity to be teaching children," rebutted the interviewer, "Afterall, you're equipping them to become violent killers."

The Lieutenant looked at the interveiwer and simply responded, "Well, you're equipped to be a prostitute, but you're not one, are you?" End of interview.

Did You Know? *A children's radio show host, thinking that his microphone had been turned off, wrapped up his broadcast one evening by inadvertently blurting out over the air, "There, that oughta hold the little bastards!"*

"Please Won't You Be My Victim!"

Fred Rogers served in the military as a Marine sniper. Some cynical folks may loathe to believe that the gentle, soft-spoken host of "Mr. Rogers' Neighborhood" was exactly what he seemed, but he wasn't. Mr. Rogers had 42 confirmed sniper kills in Korea, and served three tours of duty in 'Nam as a sniper and has been credited with kills in excess of 1500 meters." Fred Rogers was the number three Marine sniper in the Vietnam war. And one of the reasons he always wears long sleeve clothing is because his arms are covered in Marine tattoos.

Did You Know? What happens when you predict snow but don't get any? Well, there was a female news anchor who, the day after it was supposed to have snowed and didn't, turned to the weatherman and asked, "So Phil, where's that 8 inches you promised me last night?"

Randomly Selected

Do you remember the televisied quiz show version of "Scrabble"? Were the computer chose 9 letters at random, and the contestants then had thirty seconds in which to make the longest word as possible in that time?

Well, one evening on Primetime TV, the combination of letters that the system randomly selected, and brought up right at the start of the game on National Television spelled out the phrase "WACKMEOFF".

Did You Know? The first episode of Joanie Loves Chachi was the highest rated American program in the history of Korean television because "Chachi" is Korean for "penis."

Sergeant Kangaroo

One night on The Tonight Show with Johnny Carson, Lee Marvin was the guest.

Johnny said to Lee, "I'll bet a lot of people are unaware that you were a Marine in the initial landing at Iwo Jima, and that during the course of that action, you earned the Navy Cross and were severely wounded."

Lee Marvin's response was, "Yeah, I got shot square in the ass and they gave me the Cross for securing a hot spot about halfway up Mount Suribachi. The bad thing about getting shot up on a mountain is guys getting shot hauling you down. But at Iwo, I served under the bravest man I ever knew. We both got the Cross the same day, but what he did for his Cross made mine look cheap in comparison. The dumb bastard actually stood up on Red Beach and directed his troops to move forward to get the hell off the beach. That Sergeant and I have been life long friends."

"When they brought me off Suribachi I passed him as he lit a smoke and passed it to me lying on my belly on the gurney. "Where'd they get you Lee?" he asked. "Well Bob, they shot me in the ass and if you make it home before me, tell my Mom to sell the outhouse."

"Johnny, I swear, Sergeant Keeshan was the bravest man I ever knew!" I now know him as Bob Keeshan. You and the world know him as "Captain Kangaroo".

The Newly-Wed Game

If you're not in the know, The Newly-Wed Game was a popular TV game show hosted by Bob Eubanks, where the partner was asked questions about the other whilE they were out of earshot, and then the question was repeated to see if their answers matched.

The host was asking the groom all sorts of questions such as, "Which side of the bed does she sleep?" and "What's her most disgusting habit?" when he came to the final question, "Where's the most unusual place you've ever made whoopee with your wife?"

The groom started by laughingly replying that he had no intention of answering, until eventually, egged on by the baying audience, he replied, "In the back of my car."

A huge roar of approval went up as the bride was led back into the studio, to give her replies to the questions. The host went through all the questions again, and the wife was doing very well, everytime giving the same answer that her husband did.

However, when it came to the final question, "Where's the most unusual place you've ever made whoopee with your husband?"

The bride started shaking her head and muttering, "No way" as the crowd began to bay for a reply.

Eventually the groom lend over and gently took her by the arm saying "Don't worry honey, I already told them."

"You're sure?" she asked with a nervous expression.

"Of course, honey, I'm sure," he replied.

"Okay," she said. "If you're sure."

Then slowly, holding the microphone close to her chest, the bride announced to the studio and viewing audience, "Up the bum."

Did you know? *Mariah Carey was one of the first celebrities to comment on the death of the King of Jordan. Mariah told CNN, "I'm inconsolable at the present time. I was a very good friend of Jordan, he was probably the greatest basketball player this country had ever seen, we will never see his like again." When told by reporters that it was King Hussein of Jordan who had died and not Michael Jordan, Mariah was then led away by her security in a state of 'confusion.'*

You Bet Your Life

"You Bet Your Life" was a program that provided Groucho Marx with a career apart from his brothers and introduced him to a generation too young to remember him from his stage or film work.

The interview-quiz show, featuring the famous $100 bonus paid to any contestant who said the "secret word," debuted on radio and television beginning in 1950, and continued on TV only from 1956 through 1961 — all in all, an amazing fourteen-year run for a quiz show with a tiny budget, a plain set, and a small jackpot, even by 1950s standards.

The most infamous remark of Groucho's "*You Bet Your Life*" career occurred when he was interviewing a contestant with twenty-two children, which was reputedly the largest family in America at the time.

Groucho said, "Why do you have so many children? That's a big responsibility and a big burden."

"Well, because I love my children and I think that's our purpose here on Earth, and I love my husband," she replied.

To which Groucho replied, "I love my cigar too, but I take it out of my mouth once in a while."

"Hey look, Paul McCartney was in a band before Wings!"

Music has spawned several categories of related legends: tales about the people who make it, the media on which it is recorded, the packages that hold it, and stories about the music itself.

Boy Band

In New York City, Jive Records thinks they may have pulled another coup. On March 18th, 2004, they signed another boy band, hoping to tap into the elusive Over 65 demographic. The new band, "Heart Attack" is the latest chart topping success to hit America.

Their first single, "I Wanna Get In Your Depends" has already reached Number One at the Fairmont Retirement Home, in Boynton Beach, Florida.

The band's success so far, has been attributed to the members' ability to work together throughout the good times and the bad.

"We've been really lucky so far," says founding band member Bueford "B-Ho" Houston, 95. "We've had to replace our bad boy, three times, on account of them dying, but we're happy with our direction."

The group has plans of touring, but Johnson "J-Dog" Cornforth, 86, also known as the "cute one", is worried about how the fans will treat them.

"It's important for me to have my nap at 2:30 every afternoon," says Johnson. "If them groupies are rapping their canes on my hotel room door at all hours of the day, I won't get any rest, and I'll be cranky for the concert."

Gerald "G-Spot" Elmer, 91, also known as "the bad boy" is grateful for the encouragement from his family. His son recently granted him leave from the extended care facility to perform at the Boynton Beach Recreational Annex, earlier this year.

"G-Spot" reports, "It's important to realise your dreams. Me, I can't remember my dreams. But if I did, I'd sing about them."

The group's success is the biggest surprise. They released their debut album, "I Love You, But I've Forgotten Your Name" in late June, and would have reached platinum in their first week, had the album been available on vinyl.

Concert promoter and band manager Richard Cummings insists that "Heart Attack" aren't an overnight sensation.

"It's taken the better part of a century to nurture them into what they are today", adds Richard. "When you see them at the next Seniorpalooza, you'll realize what we're talking about, as long as we can schedule them to appear onstage before 3pm."

The other two band members, Scott "Scottie Too Hottie" Popalinski, 86, and Russell "Pimp Grandaddy" Jenkins, 91, both admitted that maintaining a single image is also important.

"Since we're all straight-up widows, we hope to project ourselves as being elusively available," says Russell. "But it's not just about the dames. It's about liquor and dames."

Their next concert appearance is tentatively scheduled for June 9th, at the 10th Annual Golden Acres Lawnbowling Tournament in Fort Lauderdale, Florida. Provided Scott "Scottie Too Hottie" Popalinski survives his replacement hip surgery.

"Buddy Holly and the Crickets."

The film "The Buddy Holly Story" depicts the name "The Crickets" being bestowed upon Buddy's group by zealous Buffalo disk jockey 'Madman' Mancuso, who, after having locked himself in the studio while he played "That'll Be the Day" over and over, tracked down Buddy for a phone interview. Upon learning from Buddy that one of the songs, the as-yet-unnamed group had recorded in Buddy's garage "had a cricket on it," so the DJ anointed them "Buddy Holly and the Crickets."

Death By Ham Sandwich

"Mama" Cass Elliot of The Mamas and the Papas death was caused by a heart attack. However, the true cause of death was not determined until an autopsy was performed a week later.

Dr. Sims, Cass Elliot's physician, and Gary Winston, a London coroner determined that Elliot had not in fact succumbed to a heart attack brought about by the effects of long-term obesity. Elliot had long been overweight, standing 5'5" and weighing 238 lbs., about twice the proper weight for a woman of her height and build, and although the prolonged effects of obesity and several crash diets had weakened her heart to the point of failure, a heart attack was not the cause of death.

Dr. Kenneth Sims, the pathologist who performed the autopsy on Elliot, found traces of food blocking her trachea.

Cass Elliot's physician stated, "She died as a result of choking on a ham sandwich while in bed, and from inhaling her own vomit."

Did you know? *Music mogul Phil Spector lost a lawsuit, and the guy he lost it to demanded the royalties to the next "Greatest Hits Album" as compensation. So Spector recorded a little ditty in which a man says the title over and over, and pressed up a couple of copies. Neat revenge.*

"Hey look, Paul McCartney was in a band before Wings!"

In Atlanta, Georgia, a man in his mid-forties was made to feel truly old one day when he was browsing in a local record store. Looking through the rock section for a rare James Taylor track, he saw a young boy hold up a copy of The Beatles album "Let It Be".

He was even more shocked when he heard a young man comment to his friend, "Hey look, Paul McCartney was in a band before Wings!"

It's not easy being green

A sound engineer announced that he discovered that the sound quality on compact discs improved significantly if the thin outer edge of the CD was coated with a green marker pen. Music lovers were heartened by the news until they found out that the sound engineer was a green fanatic. The engineer had painted his entire house various shades of green, owned a green Volkswagen Beetle, and had previously declared that green M&Ms were known to have aphrodisiac qualities.

Did you know? *John Lennon deliberately chose the song title Lucy in the Sky with Diamonds because the initial letters of key words form the acrostic "LSD".*

Lost In Translation

Madonna was interviewed by a Hungarian magazine called "Blikk". The questions to Madonna were asked in Hungarian and then translated into English. Madonna's responses were then translated back into Hungarian. The interview was then published in Hungarian and, finally, translated back into English.

Blikk: Madonna, Budapest says hello with arms that are spread-eagled. Did you have a visit here that was agreeable? Are you in good odor? You are the biggest fan of our young people who hear your musical productions and like to move their bodies in response.

Madonna: Thank you for saying these compliments. Please stop with taking sensationalist photographs until I have removed my garments for all to see. (laughs). This is a joke I have made.

Blikk: Madonna, let's cut to toward the hunt. Are you a bold hussy-woman that feasts on men who are tops?

Madonna: Yes, this is certainly something that brings to the surface my longings. In America it is not considered to be mentally ill when a woman advances on her prey in a discotheque setting with hardy cocktails present. And there is a more normal attitude toward leather play-toys that also makes my day.

Blikk: Is this how you met Carlos, your love servant who is reputed? Did you know he was heaven-sent right off the stick? Or were you dating many other people in your bed at the same time?

Madonna: No, he was the only one I was dating in my bed then, so it is a scientific fact that the baby was made in my womb using him. But as regards those questions, enough! I am a woman and not a test-mouse! Carlos is an everyday person who is in the orbit of a star who is being muscle-trained by him, not a sex machine.

Blikk: May we talk about your other "baby," your movie, then? Please do not be denying that the similarities between you and the real Evita are grounded in basis. Power, money, tasty-food, Grammys -- all these elements are afoot.

Madonna: What is up in the air with you? Evita never was winning a Grammy!

Blikk: Perhaps not. But as to your film, in trying to bring your reputation along a rocky road, can you make people forget the bad explosions of Who's That Girl? and Shanghai Surprise?

Madonna: I am a tip-top starlet. That is the job that I am paid to do.

Blikk: OK. here's a question from left space. What was your book Slut about?

Madonna: It was called Sex, my book.

Blikk: Not in Hungary. Here it was called Slut. How did it come to publish? Were you lovemaking with a man-about-town printer? Do you prefer making suggestive literature to fast selling CD's?

Madonna: These are different facets to my career highway. I am preferring only to become respected all over the

215

map as a 100% artist.

Blikk: There is much interest in you from this geographical region, so I must ask this final questions. How many Hungarian men have you dated in bed? Are they No. 1? How are they comparing to Argentine men, who are famous for being tip-top as well?

Madonna: Well, to avoid aggravating global tension, I won't say. It's a tie (laughs). No, no, I am serious now. See here I am working like a canine all the way around the clock! I am too busy even to try the goulash the makes your country for the record books.

Blikk: Thank you for your candid chitchat.

Madonna: No problem, friend who is a girl.

Did you know? *Keith Richards' drug and alcohol addiction became the fodder upon which rock and roll legends were born. In order to cure "Keef's" heroin addiction, Richards flew to the Swiss chalet of an exclusive physician in Switzerland for a blood transfusion to completely replace the heroin-laced blood in his body with good clean blood.*

"Puff, The Magic Dragon"

"Puff, the Magic Dragon" is not a song about the innocence of childhood lost. It is what its writers have always claimed it to be: a song about marijuana. The poem that formed the basis of the song "Puff, the Magic Dragon" was written in 1959 by Leonard Lipton, a nineteen-year-old Cornell student, who while smoking pot, was inspired by an Ogden Nash rhyme about a "Really-O Truly-O Dragon," and, used a dragon as the central figure.

"Puff" was an obvious name for a song about smoking pot; little Jackie Paper's surname referred to rolling papers; "autumn mist" was either clouds of marijuana smoke or a drug-induced state, and the land of "Hanah Lee" was really the Hawaiian village of Hanalei, known for its particularly potent marijuana plants; and so on.

Rocker Misconception

Most people know about the rock stars reputation for trashing hotel rooms, but not many people know why. This story might explain their behaviour.

A famous rock star, who shall remain nameless, was resting up in his hotel room in LA after an exhausting world tour. All he wanted that night was some well-deserved rest and some peace and quiet, so after a long hot bath, the musician got into bed and attempted to get some sleep. However, his attempts at sleep were thwarted by a frantic buzzing sound.

Realising it was a fly, he rolled up a magazine and tried to swat it, but the tired man kept missing. Getting increasingly frustrated, he kept going after the fly, ignoring the fact that he was knocking over furniture and breaking ornaments. At one point, he lost his footing, and hit his head, knocking himself out.

The musician was revived an hour later by angry hotel staff, who assumed the rock star had got drunk and wrecked his room. In pursuit of the elusive fly, he had caused over five thousand dollars' worth of damage, and was banned from that particular hotel. He now takes a pet spider everywhere he goes.

How does Michael Jackson pick his nose? From a catalogue.

We see celebrities as caricatures, so we feel free to spread salacious rumors about their personal lives. People have even made careers out of the time-honoured tradition of "celebrity sex". We derive satisfaction by chuckling at the foibles of the privileged because we hold them at a higher moral standard than we hold ourselves. We live in a society where most of us don't even know the name of some of our neighbours or co-workers, but the faces and habits of celebrities are familair to everyone.

Behind Her All The Way

With the possible exception of that work in progress known as Michael Jackson's face, no celebrity body part in recent memory has achieved greater prominence than JLo's derriere. It is enthroned as an object of veneration on fan Websites. It has inspired a new trend in below-the-waist surgical implants. Gossip columnists have worn out thesaurius searching for superlatives to describe it such as,"ample," "deluxe," "abundant," "big". Salon magazine once devoted an entire essay to its cultural significance.

There's no getting around it, Jennifer Lopez's personal fame has very nearly been eclipsed by that of her own behind.

Nor is there any getting around the deluxe insurance policy she took out to protect her "ass-et". In 1999, tabloids on both sides of the Atlantic — *The Sun* in London and the *New York Post* — ran articles claiming that Jennifer Lopez had indemnified her body to the tune of $1 billion. Even though pound-for-pound the singer's breasts fetched a more generous appraisal than her hiney. $100 million per breast vs. $300 million for legs and buttocks combined. Word on the street soon had it that the "abundant butt" alone is now valued at a cool billion.

Hef Will Make A "Star" Out Of You.

Do you know what the small stars that appear on the Playboy cover are? A distribution code used to designate the advertising regions for different editions of the magazine? Wrong!!

The edition indicators used by *Playboy* were a code indicating how many times Hugh Hefner had slept with the current centerfold or, on the assumption that Hef *always* slept with the centerfolds, his personal rating of how good a bed partner the playmate was. The stars usually appeared inside the letter **'P'** on the cover but if the stars appeared on the outside, Hef had failed in his attempts to bed that month's featured playmate.

How does Michael Jackson pick his nose? From a catalogue.

The numerous plastic surgeries Michael Jackson has endured has not resulted in a less than striking change than the work done on his nose. It is said Michael Jackson has undergone rhinoplasty six times, on each occasion reducing and reshaping that facial feature drastically. Those who look upon plastic surgery with disapproval find vindication for their stance in the whisper that during a concert Jacko's nose finally

gave up the ghost when Michael Jackson's prosthetic nose fell off during his 30th anniversary TV special and because he had editing rights, it was edited out.

Did you know? *It was reported that police in Gary Indiana pulled over Janet Jackson in a routine traffic stop today. Ms. Jackson (if your nasty) was issued a ticket for having a headlight* *out.*

Spared Ribs

Women such as Cher, Elizabeth Taylor, Jane Fonda, Racquel Welch, Tori Spelling, Pamela Anderson, Gina Lollobrigida, Victoria's Secret model Stephanie Seymour, Kate Moss, and Britney Spears have all spared ribs to the goddess of vanity. Male rocker Marilyn Manson has also had ribs removed. In his case though, the procedure wasn't to reduce waist size; it was to facilitate oral self-gratification. I also heard Rosie O'Donnell once had four ribs put in . . . at Tony Roma's.

"What would you say to a little fuck?"

Harlan Ellison the infamous, and vertically challenged science fiction writer, in the days before he married his present fifth wife, who is his own size and with whom he is happy at last, could not resist going about with tall model types, all of them topping him by two or three feet.

One night on the town, Harlan approached one of these giraffe-like women, fixed her with his glittering eye, and said, "What would you say to a little fuck?"

The model just looked down at him and said, "I would say, 'Hello, little fuck.'"

chapterfifteen

"Give Little, Give Seldom, And Above All, Give Grudginly. Otherwise what could have been a proper marriage could become an orgy of sexual lust."

--Ruth Smythers; wife of Reverend L.D. Smythers Pastor of the Arcadian Methodist Church

sacredinstitution

Weddings and the subsequent carryings-on of newlyweds fascinate us. It's the beginning of a couple's life together as husband and wife; a turning point in each of the couples lives as they take their passage through the portal to married life. Marriage somehow reaffirms all that is right in the world.

The event itself also has a happy impact on the rest of society, because it is the celebration of a new family created out of what moments earlier were two independant entities. Considering the importance of the ceremony and the paternal interest we have in the newly married, it's no wonder so many nuptials and wedding stories have worked their way down the alter into lore.

· · · · · · · · · · · · · · · · · · ·

"Give Little, Give Seldom, And Above All, Give Grudingly."

Nearly every ordinary activity has minor superstitions attached to them, but nowadays the average person travels down lifes path unaware of these beliefs. That is, until somebody gets married.

"Give Little, Give Seldom, And Above All, Give Grudginly."

The following is instruction and advice for the young bride on the Conduct and Procedure of the Intimate and Personal Relationships of the Marriage State for the Greater Spiritual Sanctity of this Blessed Sacrament and the Glory of God. It was Written by Ruth Smythers beloved wife of The Reverend L.D. Smythers Pastor of the Arcadian Methodist Church of the Eastern Regional Conference. Published in the year of our Lord 1894.

To the sensitive young woman who has had the benefit of proper upbringing, the wedding day is, ironically, both the happiest and most terrifying day of her life. On the positive side, there is the wedding itself, in which the bride is the central attraction in a beautiful and inspiring ceremony, symbolizing her triumph in securing a male to provide for all her needs for the rest of her life. On the negative side, there is the wedding night, during which the bride must pay the piper, so to speak, by facing for the first time the terrible experience of sex.

At this point, let me concede one shocking truth. Some young women actually anticipate the wedding night ordeal with curiosity and pleasure! Beware such an attitude! A selfish and sensual husband can easily take advantage of such a bride. One cardinal rule of marriage should never be forgotten: Give Little, Give Seldom, And Above All, Give Grudginly. Otherwise what could have been a proper marriage could become an orgy of sexual lust.

On the other hand, the bride's terror need not be extreme. While sex is at best revolting and at worse rather painful, it has to be endured, and has been by women since the beginning of time, and is compensated for by the monogamous home and by the children produced through it.

It is useless, in most cases, for the bride to prevail upon the groom to forego the sexual initiation. While the ideal husband would be one who would approach his bride only at her request and only for the purpose of begetting offspring, such nobility and unselfishness cannot be expected from the average man.

Most men, if not denied, would demand sex almost everyday. The wise bride will permit a maximum of two brief sexual experiences weekly during the first months of marriage. As time goes by she should make every effort to reduce this frequency.

Feigned illness, sleepiness, and headaches are among the wife's best friends in this matter. Arguments, nagging, scolding, and bickering also prove very effective, if used in the late evening about an hour before the husband would normally commence his seduction.

Clever wives are ever on the alert for new and better methods of denying and discouraging the amorous overtures of the husband. A good wife should expect to have reduced sexual contacts to once a week by the end of the first year of marriage and to once a month by the end of the fifth year of marriage.

By their tenth anniversary many wives have managed to complete their child bearing and have achieved the ultimate goal of terminating all sexual contact with the husband. By this time she can depend upon his love for the children and social pressures to hold the husband in the home.

Just as she should be ever alert to keep the quantity of sex as low as possible, the wise bride will pay equal attention to limiting the kind and degree of sexual contacts. Most men are by nature rather perverted, and if given half a chance, would engage in quite a variety of the most revolting practices. These practices include among others performing the normal act in abnormal positions; mouthing the female body; and offering their own vile bodies to be mouthed in turn.

Nudity, talking about sex, reading stories about sex, viewing photographs and drawings depicting or suggesting sex are the obnoxious habits the male is likely to acquire if permitted.

A wise bride will make it her goal never to allow the husband to see her unclothed body, and never allow him to display his unclothed body to her. Sex, when it cannot be prevented, should be practiced only in total darkness. Many women have found it useful to have thick cotton nightgowns for themselves and pajamas for their husbands. These should be donned in separate rooms. They need not be removed during the sex act. Thus, a minimum of flesh is exposed.

Once the bride has donned her gown and turned off all the lights, she should lie quietly upon the bed and await her groom. When he comes groping into the room she should make no sound to guide him in her direction, lest he take this as a sign of encouragement. She should let him grope in the dark. There is always the hope that he will stumble and incur some slight injury which she can use as an excuse to deny him sexual access.

When he finds her, the wife should lie as still as possible. Bodily motion on her part could be interpreted as sexual excitement by the optimistic husband.

If he attempts to kiss her on the lips she should turn her head slightly so that the kiss falls harmlessly on her cheek instead. If he attempts to kiss her hand, she should make a fist. If he lifts her gown and attempts to kiss her anyplace else she should quickly pull the gown back in place, spring from the bed, and announce that nature calls her to the toilet. This will generally dampen his desire to kiss the forbidden territory.

If the husband attempts to seduce her with lascivious talk, the wise wife will suddenly remember some trivial non-sexual question to ask him. Once he answers she should keep the conversation going, no matter how frivolous it may seem at the time.

Eventually, the husband will learn that if he insists on having sexual contact, he must get on with it without amorous embellishment. The wise wife will allow him to pull the gown up no farther than the waist, and only permit him to open the front of his pajamas to make connection.

She will be absolutely silent or babble about her housework while he is huffing and puffing away. Above all, she will lie perfectly still and never under any circumstances grunt or groan while the act is in progress. As soon as the husband has completed the act, the wise wife will start nagging him about various minor tasks she wishes him to perform on the morrow. Many men obtain a major portion of their sexual satisfaction from the peaceful exhaustion immediately after the act is over. Thus the wife must insure that there is no peace in this period for him to enjoy. Otherwise, he might be encouraged to soon try for more.

One heartening factor for which the wife can be grateful is the fact that the husband's home, school, church, and social environment have been working together all through his life to instill in him a deep sense of guilt in regards to his sexual feelings, so that he comes to the marriage couch apologetically and filled with shame, already half cowed and subdued. The wise wife seizes upon this advantage and relentlessly pursues her goal first to limit, later to annihilate completely her husband's desire for sexual expression.

Robin Hood, Robin Hood, riding through the glen...

A friend of a friend took his girlfriend for a romantic evening, topped off with a visit to the cimena to see the blockbuster movie "Robin Hood: Prince Of Thieves". They loved the touching, and tender film, especially the smoochy theme song, "Everything I Do, I Do It For You" by Brian Adams.

Later the same night, as they listened to "their" song in a local pub, the boyfriend got down on one knee, proposed, and his paramour enthusiastically screamed yes.

Come the day of the wedding, the groom, waiting for his future wife to arrive at the church, had a word with the church organist. He asked the organist if he could play their song, the theme from Robin Hood, instead of the standard wedding march. The organist, a stickler for tradition, hesitantly agreed.

As the bride entered the hushed church, the organist struck up the Robin Hood theme as arranged. The only problem was he'd never heard of Bryan Adams song. Instead, he accompanied the bride's procession with the jaunty and highly inappropriate "Robin Hood, Robin Hood, riding through the glen" theme from the Sixties television series of the same name.

"How else was I supposed to pay for that damned wedding?"

A wedding, although serious and solemn, is supposed to be a happy and joyous occasion. The wedding ceremony itself is one of the most powerful representations of a couples hopes and dreams. So it is symbolically important that every aspect of the occasion be carefully planned down to the last detail. But no matter how perfect you plan for this special day, traumatic and embarrassing moments can still arise.

Birthday Tux

A bachelor party prank went terribly wrong when the best man slept through his alarm. Sadly, the groom-to-be made the mistake of passing out the previous night, allowing his friends to strip him and leave him handcuffed to the pulpit of the church he was to be married in.

The plan was that the best man would set his alarm and get to the church early enough to rescue the groom.

That was not to be... instead, the guests arrived at the appointed time only to find the groom waking up in a daze, completely naked. Covering his nudity with the priest's prayer book, the groom escaped to the vestry and put on a cassock.

Thankfully, the bride had a sense of humour, and declared, "At least, he got here on time".

Although the groom was dressed in an unorthodox manner, the marriage went ahead almost on time.

Broken Groom

A young man was out enjoying his bachelor party on the eve of his wedding, with the usual drunken mayhem. The groom drank so much that he blacked out, so as a prank, his best man, who just happened to be a male nurse, carried him to the hospital and had his left leg put in a cast. The next morning, he woke up in bed, hung over.

Immediately, he went into a panic about his leg. His best man told him he was lucky to have escaped from his fall with only a simple fracture of the left leg. The groom was forced to get married on crutches, and even spent the reception in plaster.

As the couple drove off to their honeymoon destination, the groom's friends decided it was time to tell him the truth. They phoned the hotel where the newlyweds were staying and left a message that his leg was not in fact broken.

Unfortunately, in order to prevent his friends from interfering with his honeymoon, the groom had given them the number to a different hotel.

Father of the Bride

In Lafayette, Louisiana, a wedding reception was tarnished when it was discovered that someone had been picking the pockets of several guests and stealing their wallets.

However, on returning from their honeymoon, the newlyweds invited their wedding party, including a few friends over to watch the wedding video. Halfway through the video, the husband's father jumped up, rewound the tape, and played it again.

"Aha!" he cried, "There's the thief!"

There on the video was the wife's father pinching somebody's wallet.

Red-faced, the father of the bride complained, "How else was I supposed to pay for that damned wedding?"

Insulting Priest

A bride and groom getting married in Edinburgh, Scotland were most surprised when the priest marrying them began to insult them and the wedding party. The priest called the groom "a stupid idiot with the intelligence of a monkey" before comparing the bride to an elephants arse.

In front of the stunned congregation, the priest then broke into a rendition of Madonnas "Like a Virgin" before turning around, lifting up his cassock and mooning the stunned couple.

The priest then smiled at the couple and said, "I'm a priest-o-gram courtesy of your best man. Good luck. May you have lots of furry, little children," and then ran off to be replaced by the somewhat embarrassed genuine priest.

No Wedding and a Funeral

Parties can be risky, but this experience would make any husband-to-be have second thoughts about holding a last bachelor celebration.

At a ski resort in Colorado, the stag party was in full, drunken swing when the participants took to the slopes for some night-time skiing. The so-called friends of the husband-to-be proceeded to tie him naked to a sled and send him flying down the slope. Unbeknown to them, the bride-to-be's father was enjoying a relaxing stroll at the bottom of that same slope.

Powerless to do anything other than shout, "Get out of the way!" the naked sleder failed to attract the attention of the man who was soon to become his father-in-law.

Instead, the sled rammed into the man, killing him instantly. The wedding was replaced by a funeral, and the marriage was unsurprisingly called off.

The Ladies Last Eye Full

For her hen-night treat, a bride-to-be went with some friends to see one of those raunchy male stripper acts.

The ladies were having a riot ogling the hunky fellas' bulging pecs. They were all getting over-excited, shrieking as the gyrating Adonises disrobed.

Apparently, the bride-to-be got a little tipsy and forced her way to the front of the stage to get a better view. Dancing in a frenzy, she was almost overcome when, at the climax of his act, one of the writhing hunks whipped off his dental floss G-string and flung it onto her face.

A couple of days later she was checking her complexion in the bathroom mirror when she noticed a spot near her eyelid. The blemish was a little stressing; especially with the wedding, and wanting to look her very best for the photographs.

Over the next few days, she tried every kind of cream, but the spot just got larger and larger, until she was driven to visit the doctor.

The quack took one look, and informed the girl that he'd have to operate immediately. She had a pubic louse living in her face.

The Wedding March Went Grate

A couple was getting married in a church in Paris, France. The groom was waiting at the pulpit and hundreds of guests were anxiously awaiting the bride's arrival.

Eventually, the organist began playing "The Wedding March" and all the guests stood up.

The first bridesmaid entered the church, but on her second step down the aisle, she got the heel of her shoe stuck in a grate in the floor. The usher next to her, tried to pull out the shoe, only to pick up the entire grate with it. To save any embarrassment, he took the grate with him.

Unfortunately, the bride, resplendent in her gown and veil, had not noticed, and as she glided down the aisle, she fell down the hole the grate had uncovered.

"Those breasts are lethal weapons."

In New Jersey, a fun-filled bachelor party at a strip club turned deadly when the 28-year-old groom-to-be who was enjoying the attentions of a well-endowed stripper, suffocated while his face was buried in her breasts.

Police said the mind-boggling drama unfolded, while Barry Delaney was attending his bachelor party at the Eager Beaver strip club, which had been rented out for the private affair.

According to investigators, Delaney was enjoying a lap dance when disaster struck. One of the strippers, Pussy Willows, got too into her performance and suffocated the man between her 72-DD breasts.

Witnesses said that Delaney had his fair share of beer, but didn't seem out-of-control.

Friends of Barry Delaney said, "When the song, "I'm Too Sexy" began to play, he became excited and began to dance on the tabletop, hooting and hollering like an idiot."

Miss Willows, apparently pleased to see someone enjoying her choice in music, moved in closer.

When Delaney took his seat, she began giving him a lap dance, shaking her breasts in his face. The more she shook, the deeper Delaney got lost in her cleavage.

"Barry was having so much fun," partygoer Kevin Gilmore said. "We all thought he loved being in that chick's chest. Who could have known that when he was waving his hands around, he was signaling for help?"

Cheering onlookers eventually realised that Delaney was no longer moving, and pulled him from between Miss Willows breasts.

Now Delaney's family is suing Pussy Willows and the Eager Beaver for wrongful death.

Delaney's father, Gerald, won't specify the amount they are suing for, but claims that it isn't about the money.

"Those breasts are lethal weapons," he told reporters. "The Eager Beaver should not have allowed Pussy Willows to have her bust enhanced to the size that she did, and we hope that by filing this lawsuit, we can send a message to other strippers: keep your bra size within a reasonable range."

Pussy Willows made a statement through her attorneys, "I thought he liked it in there."

The Eager Beaver declined comment.

"Oh my God! What the hell is he doing here? He's supposed to be on his honeymoon in Banff this weekend!"

Lets pretend for a moment the bride and groom manage to make it through their wedding unscathed, they still have the honeymoon and the beginning of married life, which provide ample opportunities for things to go awry.

Day Trip

A group of young men from Calgary, Alberta, Canada went on a day trip to the resort town of Banff, Alberta. They spent most of the day seeing all the sights and trying out the ski slopes, and then found a bar in which to get a few drinks before returning home.

In the bar, they befriended a man who looked like he'd had a few too many drinks. The near-drunk was glad to have an audience and told the group of daytrippers joke after joke before finally passing out.

Unsure what to do, one of the group searched the man's pockets and eventually found his home address in his wallet. Seeing that the man was also from Calgary, the young men decided to do him a favour and take him home with them. Back in Calgary, one of the group volunteered to take the man home, and on reaching the address knocked on the door.

The woman who answered was startled to see the man and said, "Oh my God! What the hell is he doing here? He's supposed to be on his honeymoon in Banff this weekend!"

"Keep It In The Family"

A friend of a friend has been engaged for almost a year, and will be getting married next month. His fiancee's mother is not only very attractive but really great and understanding. She is putting the entire wedding together and invited him to her place to go over the invitation list, because it had grown a bit beyond what they had expected.

When he got to her place they reviewed the list and trimmed it down to just under a hundred people, then she floored him with an odd request. She explained that in a month he would be a married man and before that happens, she wanted to have sex with him.

Then she just stood up, walked to her bedroom and on her way said, "You know where the front door is if you want to leave."

He stood there for about five minutes and finally decided exactly how to deal with this situation, and headed straight out the front door.

There, leaning against his car was her husband, his father-in-law to be, smiling. He explained that they just wanted to be sure he was a good kid and would be true to their little girl. He shook his hand and congratulated him on passing their little test.

But know he isn't to sure whether or not he should tell his fiancee what her parents did, and that he thought their "little test" was asinine and insulting to his character. Personally, I think he should keep the whole thing to himself including the fact that the real reason he was walking out to his car was to get a condom.

The Best Man For The Job

A bride and a groom are at their wedding reception, and everything is going perfectly, until the groom stood up to give a toast. He thanked all the guests for coming and for the stack of presents on the table, then thanked the father of the bride for the beautiful reception.

He then went on to tell the guests that he had a surprise for all of them. He instructed them to look under their chairs. Which they did, where they found a picture taped to the bottom of each seat.

The guests were shocked and horrified to see it was a picture of the bride and the best man having sex!

The groom then stated he had a feeling they were having an affair and hired an investigator who took the photo.

225

He then looked at the father of the bride and said, "Thank you for the $30,000 sit-down dinner and party, but I'm out of here." And he walked out.

He filed for an annulment the following Monday.

Did You Know? *Wives mark their territory using fabric softener. I never knew what that stuff was for until I noticed women coming up to me, sniffing, then saying under their breath, "Married!" and walked away. You can take off the ring, but it's hard to get that April fresh scent out of your clothes.*

Wedding Ring Around The Toilet

A newly married man got drunk at a nightclub after a hard week at the office. Just before the nightclub was about to close, the man ran to the toilet to throw up, and in the process lost his wedding ring down the toilet. His attempts to retrieve it ended in disaster when his arm got stuck in the U-bend. His cries for help went unheard. The staff assumed the man had left and closed up the nightclub. The man had to spend the whole night with his arm stuck down the toilet soaking in his own vomit until cleaners found him the next day, and helped him get his wedding ring back. As soon as he got home, the man's wife was so disgusted at the sight and smell of him, she threw her wedding ring at him and demanded a divorce.

chaptersixteen

<u>**Disclaimer: Must be 18 years of age to read this chapter**</u>

"Oral sex? You want oral sex? You'll get oral sex when the kid next door walks on the moon!"

--Mrs. Gorsky; Apollo Astronaut Neil Armstrong's next door neighbour

sexrated

Sex is a subject of the utmost importance to us, yet we are extremely reluctant to talk about it. Sex is a biological urge: it's nature's way of ensuring we reproduce. Sex is what seperates us from the animals (unless you are mountain folk) because humans link the acts of sexual intercourse with notions of love and romance. We made monogamy and sexual fidelity moral standards, we've created taboos that have long prevented open discussion of sexual matters, and thanks to science we have even been successful in controlling the mechanisms of reproduction.

Just talking about sex can be embarrassing enough; but getting caught in the act is perhaps our most supreme humiliation. A favorite pasttime of ours is to gossip about the sex lives of our friends and neighbors, and even more fascinated by the sexual practices of the rich and famous. We relish in the moral tales about unfaithful partners who are caught in their transgressions and meet revenge at the hands of angry mates, and we love the poetic justice that awaits those who dare to engage in illicit sex. We have fantasies about love potions that will turn unattainble objects of our desire into willing and eager sexual partners. But the legends don't stop with the act of intercourse itself: the mysteries of reproduction have spawned legions of misinformation and old wives' tales, so it's not surprising that sex legends are an extremely fertile crop in the field of contemporary folklore.

I hope you get a chuckle out of (and maybe even learn a thing or two from) the many sex-related legends to be found here.

. . . .

Borgasims

Aphrodisiacs are magical potions used by the love lorn to obtain the ojects of their desire. But they are also powerful drugs used by the unscrupulous to seduce unwilling partners. Consequently, rumors and legends about the existence and effects of aphrodisiacs are plentiful. Here are a few *sex*amples.

Borgasims

Recently it was discovered that doctors prescribed an anti-depressant drug that was found to have an unexpected side effect: the patients had an orgasm each time they yawned.

The drug "clomipramine" usually elevates mood, and boosts physical activity an appetite. However, the *Canadian Journal of Psychiatry* reported that four patients on the drug had orgasms while yawning.

"There is a small subset of people who have been affected this way," commented Dr. Albert Allan, a London GP who has prescribed the drug. "I understand they find this side effect quite pleasant."

One woman who took "clomipramine" told researchers it cured her depression, but she wanted to go on taking it because of its peculiar properties. She found she could experience an orgasm even by deliberate yawning. And a man who had also taken the pills said he was "highly satisfied" with the drug's usefulness.

Around five percent of "clomipramine" users reported the side effect, though for most people the drug inhibits the ability to reach orgasm. The *New Scientist* says that the users of this drug have been comparing notes on the Internet and speculating on its unusual consequences: people who experience it, would presumably seek out the most boring person they could find at parties.

Did You Know? *Men and women are different in the morning. Men wake up aroused in the morning. Men can't help it. We just wake up and we want you. Women are thinking, "How can he want me the way I look in the morning?" Well, it's because men can't see you. We have a genetic defect that prevents a male from having blood flow anywhere near their optic nerves.*

Rendered Helpless

Men need to be more alert and cautious when getting a drink offer from a woman. There is a new drug that is in liquid form. The drug is being used by female sex predators at parties and bars to induce male victims to have sex with them. The shocking news is that the drug is available virtually everywhere!

It goes by the street name, "beer."

All women have to do is buy a "beer" or two for almost any guy and then simply ask the guy home for no-strings-attached sex. Men are rendered literally helpless against such tactics.

Secret Blowjob Goddess Society

My roommate came home one day and told me about an interesting conversation he had with the top sales weasel at his company. She came into his office and noticed he had a box of Altoids on his desk.

For those of you not familiar with Altoids, they are these obnoxiously strong peppermints made in England. Anyway, as soon as she saw them, she burst into laughter. Turns out she had recently had an affair with a guy who called her and left her an incredibly steamy voice mail message after a sexual encounter. He went on and on about what an amazing blow job goddess she was, and how he'd never be the same again, etc.

She was kind of puzzled, thinking, "What did I do to this guy that was so different from my regular technique?"

She eventually figured it out: she's a smoker, and before getting intimate with the guy, she had gone to the bathroom to "freshen up", and not having a toothbrush, she crunched on about four Altoids and then got busy. According to my roommate, apparently things went amazingly.

So she passed this little tidbit on to another female sales weasel at the company, who immediately tried it out on her fiancee.

Apparently this guy had never been into oral sex, but liked the mint sensation so much that he asked her to stop and chew another Altoid mid-blow job. He is now a fellatio gourmet.

My roommate says this news has been going around his office, and having a box of Altoids on your desk is now like being part of the Secret Blowjob Goddess Society. It's the equivalent of having the hottest car or coolest computer. News spread like crazy among the females, who all went out to lunch, stopping at Walmart to buy a box of Altoids (they range about $2 for 100, so I've heard) and their partners across the city are getting one hell of a corporate blow job. As far as company-wide morale boosting events, it doesn't get much better. Some of the men found out about the "Altoid Aphrodisiac" — they went out after work to buy them for their wives. They strategized on how to get their wives to eat them.

For what it's worth — it really does work! It leaves a lasting tingle that is quite exquisite.

Dough..nuts

Awe, the penis -- the object of pride, envy, and hilarity. Without comment we view it in classic works of art all the time, but whenever we catch a glimpse of it in any other circumstance, we can't help but snicker like schoolchildren. What is so funny about this male organ? Perhaps the fact that every single man on earth has his own personal name for it (such as, the admiral). Or maybe the following legends of phallic humor will provide some clues.

"Bang, bang, you're dead!"

A young man had just begun his first year at UCLA, and was sharing a house with several other students. One day, the student was in a hurry to get ready to go out, so he left a couple of the friends with whom he shared the house chatting in his room, while he went to have a shower.

After his shower, he still heard voices in his room, so he decided to surprise his friends by whipping off his towel, kicking open the door, with penis in hand, he began leaping dramatically into the room shouting, "Bang, bang, you're dead!"

Unfortunately, the voices did not belong to his fellow students, but rather, his girlfriend and her parents who had made a surprise visit.

Dough..nuts

A college fraternity house full of males had a raucous party one Friday, that lasted all night, preventing the college girls next door to get even a wink of sleep. The next morning, they posted an angry letter to their noisy neighbours.

That afternoon, the girls received a huge box of doughnuts with a note saying, "Were very sorry for keeping you up all night and we would like to invite you to come over tonight for a drink."

The girls, pacified by the boys' apology, ate the doughnuts happily and then got dressed up for the evening party. When the girls arrived, the boys plied them with drinks and begged their forgiveness. One of the girls, returning from the bathroom, decided to have a look at the boys' bedrooms. She was looking around one room when she came across a large photo of the boys, naked with big grins on their faces.

229

However, on closer inspection she noticed to her horror, that hanging on each boy's penis was a doughnut.

Handle With Care

Following a compulsory class on the dissection of a human corpse, a group of students decided to have a bit of fun, so when no-one was looking, they removed the corpse's penis, placed it in a plastic bag and made off with it. That night, at the university's student bar, they planned their little practical joke, and went down to the mens room to wait for other drunken students to come in to relieve themselves.

Eventually, a likely candidate came in. The prankster went to a urinal, pretended to take a leak, and suddenly began screaming as if he were in agony, while brandishing the corpse penis. The medical students took turns performing this testicular trick during the course of the evening, and as a result it was understood that several male students began to handle their penises with great care when using the toilet.

Did You Know? *A wife from Minneapolis, Minnesota found out her husband had several affairs during their 25 years of marriage, and vowed to put a stop to his philandering ways. One night, when her husband came home drunk and passed out on the couch, she took a tube of Superglue and stuck her husband's penis to his leg.*

"Happy" Encounter

A butcher from Lancaster, Ohio had a reputation for shocking people by sticking a salami in his trousers and exposing it. When his victim commented on the exposed protrusion, the butcher would then take out a cleaver and lop off the tip. However, the joke went too far one day when he spotted a female friend he hadn't seen for years.

Too his delight, he popped an extra large salami down his trousers, and leaving the tip sticking out, the butcher approached his friend who commented, "My God, you must be pleased to see me, you're huge!"

Whereupon, the butcher replied, "Sorry, I have no control over it."

He took out his cleaver and lopped off the tip. His friend promptly had a heart attack, and her husband successfully sued the butcher for several hundred thousand dollars.

Hung Like A Cucumber

After a man passed out on the dance floor of a discotheque in Los Angeles, California, he was rushed to the emergency room of a local hospital. The physician who examined the unconscious patient discovered that the man had a cucumber wedged into the crotch of his ultra-tight pants, placed there to make him appear to be extremely well-hung. The cucumber had pressed against blood vessels in the man's leg, cutting off the circulation, causing him to faint.

Put Another Penis On The Barbie!

One summer weekend, a group of Football-loving students at the University of Manitoba decided to celebrate a victory by having a barbecue. There was plenty to drink, and in no time, the students were singing and vomiting all over the place. One student, particularly worse for wear, was feeling hungry and decided to put some more sausages on the barbecue.

However, he was so intoxicated, instead of opening a package of sausages, he pulled out his penis and laid it on the barbecue. Five minutes later, he was found turning it every which way with a spatula, seemingly oblivious to the pain, and was whisked off to the Emergency Room.

Turkey Neck

In Great Falls, Montana, two kids with nothing better to do decided to play a trick on an elderly man who tended to fell asleep every evening sitting on a rocking chair on his front porch. The kids found a turkey neck and waited until the old man nodded off. Once the man feel asleep, they crept up and carefully placed the turkey neck in the zipper of the old man's trousers, then hid behind a bush to watch what happened.

Too their surprise, a neighbourhood cat took an interest in the turkey neck and pounced on the old man. The old man woke up startled to see the cat nibbling on what he thought was his pecker. The poor old man fainted with shock and the mischievous kids laughed all the way home.

Under The Blanket

An elderly gentleman visited a predominantly female hairdresser to get his hair cut. The man sat in the seat covered with the large nylon cloaks they give you to keep your clothes clean. While cutting his hair, the attractive young female hairdresser noticed that her client was staring curiously at her in the mirror. Not only that but his hand was making some very suspicious and oscillating motions under the cover at his groin.

The hairdresser screamed, "Pervert!" and smacked him over the head with her hairdryer.

At which point the cloak fell, to reveal that the customer was merely cleaning his glasses.

"When I'm assessing income tax."

A friend had landed his first big role as an opera singer, even if it was a Gilbert and Sullivan show. It had been a struggle for him to find anything prestigious before because his memory was so bad.

But in this case his voice was sufficiently good — a lovely rounded bass — to warrant the producer giving him a chance to prove he could cope. The role was that of the famous Tax Collector, and as a concession, the stage director allowed the singer to have a crib sheet positioned in the pit to remind him of his words.

On opening night, the bass crooner paid more than the standard number of visits to the toilet facilities, but his voice was in good shape. On cue, he strolled confidently onstage and positioned himself in front of his idiot board. The band struck up his theme, and a deep, rich timbre filled the theatre.

Sadly, hazards lie in wait for the unwary. The words of the song go, "My stately pen is never lax. When I'm assessing income tax".

Unfortunately, the mischievous scamp felt-tipped the words on to the card, and neglected to leave a space between 'pen' and 'is', and the nervous artiste simply sang, "My stately penis never lax. When I'm assessing income tax".

This brought a royal flush to his cheeks — and raising a few eyebrows among the genteel ladies in the boxes.

His mistress was equally shocked when she saw her husband, naked on the bed inside.

Adultery is one of many sexual activities that violates our social mores. When you commit adultery you don't break the law, you break a commandment. The many humorous legends devised about adultery are our way of expressing tacit disapproval of marriage partners who fail to "forsake all others."

The lesson of the following legends are clear: Don't cheat, because you won't get away with it. No matter how well you try to cover your tracks, or how completely you think you're deceiving your partner, you will get caught.

Dangling Evidence

The groom-to-be swore to his fiance that he wasn't going to engage in any shenanigans with the stripper at his bachelor party, but then came the drinks, the striptease, and the howling from his friends.

After a while, he found himself alone in a dark hotel bedroom and in good professional hands. The stripper went down on him and apparently did the condom trick, which involves a condom hidden in her mouth and slyly unrolling it a bit onto him while working away.

When he returned home from the bachelor party, his fiancée was wide awake. As he was explaining how the bachelor party was just like any other get-together, no big deal, he got undressed and removed his pants to reveal . . . yes, the dangling evidence.

Mr. Fix It!

A wife, unhappy in her marriage, seduced the repairman who fixed her television set. They were having frantic sex in the kitchen when she heard her husband's car pull into the driveway. With little time to spare, the woman bundled the repairman into the grand piano in the lounge, and pretended to dust when her husband entered. The wife did all she could to get her husband out of the room, but he just collapsed on the sofa and demanded a drink.

A few drinks later, the wife had still been unable to persuade her husband to leave the room Suddenly, the door bell rang. Several friends had turned up to say hello. The husband was delighted, and opened a special bottle of wine just for the occasion. Knowing the husband to be a good piano player, the friends asked him to play, and he enthusiastically relented.

On opening up the grand piano, the husband was shocked to see the repairman bunched up over the strings. Not wanting to made a scene, he told his friends that the strings were broken and he wouldn't be able to play. The repairman was forced to stay hidden in the piano until the last of the guests had left, at which point, the husband "tuned" him ruthlessly.

The Last Resort

A man from Texas, after months on a waiting list, finally managed to secure a room for a weekend getaway at a five star oceanview resort. Instead of taking his wife, he took his secretary, telling his wife he was going away on business.

The secret lovers were having an intimate moment when they heard music playing loudly in the next suite. After a while, it began to annoy the man, and he told his mistress that he was going to put a stop to it. The woman, anxious that he might get hurt, accompanied him.

The man knocked abruptly on the door, and nearly died when his wife opened it. His mistress was equally shocked when she saw her husband, naked on the bed inside. While the women proceeded to scream at each other, the men ended up fighting until neighbouring vacationers came and broke up the altercation.

The next morning, the married couples each went their separate ways, and as a result of their behaviour, they were banned from ever returning to the resort.

The Privacy Act

A husband discovered his wife was having an affair with a colleague from work. He realised that in order to get a divorce, he would need evidence of her infidelity and decided the best way was to record the couple in the act.

One evening when he knew his wife was out with her "colleague", the man broke into the colleague's apartment and hid under the bed, armed with a tape recorder. Not long after, he heard the couple enter the apartment with lots of breathless activity, and the frantic removal of clothes before his wife and her lover jumped into bed.

Unfortunately, the husband was not counting on their love making to be so vigorous, and before he knew it, the bed was slamming into him repeatedly. The poor husband, forced to emerge from under the bed, tried to sneak out, but he fainted from the blows to the head, landing right on top of the dynamic couple.

The husband got his divorce, but on the grounds of his wife's evidence that he caused her unprecedented mental abuse by not giving her any privacy.

Wrong Place At The Right Time

A young English man was talking to a colleague in a pub and explained how frustrated he was because he couldn't seem to meet any women.

His colleague, who was married, told him that he knew just the place and explained that at Seven Oaks, there were dozens of young wives waiting for husbands who were out in the city with their secretaries.

The following Friday, the young man took the train to Seven Oaks after work. However, on arriving at Orpington, he noticed lots of pretty women waiting, and decided that he might as well try his luck there. He hung around and eventually found the courage to ask an attractive blonde if she would like to go for a drink. He was pleasantly surprised when she said she'd be delighted.

They went to a pub and were getting on famously, when the woman exclaimed, "Oh, no, it's my husband!"

The woman's husband stormed up to their table and said to his wife, "How could you? After all we've been through!"

The husband then turned to the young man and said, "As for you...I said Seven Oaks, not Orpington!"

"I would've jumped in sooner but you seemed to really be enjoying yourself."

We humans are extremely reluctant to talk about sex, and the thought of being watched by others while "in the act" is profoundly disturbing and embarrassing. Sex is the most private and intimate activity we engage in, so the fear of being observed in the bedroom is our greatest violation of our personal privacy; the stories below are expressive of that fear.

"Come and get it while it's clean!"

There was a Baptist couple who were really important people in the church. It was the woman's birthday and her husband had planned a surprise party for her. While she was upstairs taking her shower that night, the

233

minister and the rest of the church people were led in by the husband and hid behind the chairs in the living room.

His wife, upon finishing her shower, walked down the stairs and stood naked at the bottom and hollered to her husband, "Come and get it while it's clean!"

Don't Be Late For Your Hand Job Interview.

My friend's younger brother went out with a woman, which is surprising because he still lives at home, so it was a big deal for him. His mother was dead against him going out that evening because he had an interview for a new job first thing in the morning. However, he went out promising that he would be back early.

He and the woman went out for a drink, then danced at a local club before she invited him back to her place for "coffee." After the usual drinking coffee and listening to Barry White, they ended up in bed for more dancing: the horizontal polka.

They both had a fantastic raunchy time. However, by this time it was now about 3:00am, so he announced, "I have to go home. I've gotta work in the morning."

The woman took him to the front door of her apartment. As they're walking through the main room, she noticed her panties lying on the floor.

"Here," she said giving them to him, "Take these to remind you of me."

He stuffed them in his pocket and left, promising to phone.

He woke up at 7:00am in the morning feeling like shit. However, he got the normal morning stiffy, and started thinking of the night before, which made him even more 'inflamed'.

Then remembering the womans panties in his pocket, he took them out and began sniffing them. The memories came flooding back, so he decided to have a quick hand job, but wanting to have both hands free, he put the panties over his head so that the waist band was positioned over his nose. Although, this obscured his eyes, he continued on enjoying a pretty satisfactory hand job.

After a short rest, he took the panties off his head so he could find a Kleenex. However, he noticed a cup of coffee, and two slices of toast on his bed side table.

It turns out, his mother had come in and brought him his breakfast so he wouldn't miss his important interview.

Everything Is Gravy!

My co-worker Derek invited his mother over for dinner. During the meal, his mother couldn't help but notice how beautiful Derek's roommate Laura was. She had long been suspicious of a relationship between Derek and his roommate, and this only made her more curious.

Over the course of the evening, while watching the two interact, she started to wonder if there was more between Derek and Laura than met the eye.

Reading his mother's thoughts, Derek volunteered, "I know what you're thinking, but Laura and I are just roommates."

About a week later, Laura came to Derek and said, "Ever since your mother came to dinner, I can't find my beautiful silver gravy ladle. You don't suppose she took it, do you?"

Derek replied, "Well, I doubt it, but I'll call her and ask, just to be sure."

So he sat down and phoned his mother. He got the answering machine, so he left a message, "Mom, I'm not saying you 'did' take a gravy ladle from my house, and I'm not saying you 'did not' take the gravy ladle. But it has been missing ever since you were here for dinner."

A few hours later, Derek received a message on his answering machine from his mother which stated, "Derek, I'm not saying that you 'do' sleep with Laura, and I'm not saying that you 'do not' sleep with Laura. But if she was sleeping in her own bed, she would have found the gravy ladle by now."

For Lover's Only

A couple spent a romantic weekend at a hotel in a room that was well-equipped for lovers. It featured a hot spa, a television with access to porno films, as well as a large canopied bed, complete with vibrating mattress. The couple had a fantastic time indulging in all kinds of sexual experimentation, and they decided this hotel would be a great place for their honeymoon later that year.

A few months later the couple was marrried, and like they planned, drove to the hotel, looking forward to another fun-filled weekend. This time around, they stayed in an even plusher suite with panoramic views across the city, a huge bath and all the other luxuries of their previous room.

There was also a VCR and several video tapes with titles such as, "Sex Toy Story 2", "Inspect-her Gadget", and "Saving Ryan's Privates". After a long soak in the hot tub, they relaxed in the luxurious bed and put on a tape. They were getting turned on by the films, when suddenly the bride shrieked.

There, in full colour, but with a dubbed soundtrack, were the two of them in a series of compromising poses caught during their previous stay in the hotel by a hidden camera.

Great Melons

In Boston, Massachusetts a man was so disgruntled at the price of watermelon in his local supermarket that he decided to stage a formal protest.

When the supermarket was particularly busy, the disgruntled customer took the manager at gunpoint, and ordered him to have sex with each and every watermelon one after another. Customers watched in shock as the manager complied. After the manager had penetrated every watermelon, the security guard jumped on the gun-totting man and wrestled him to the ground.

The humiliated manager shouted, "What took you so damn long?"

The security guard just shrugged his shoulders and said, "I would've jumped in sooner but you seemed to really be enjoying yourself ."

Happy Campers

A couple set out on a camping trip with their children and a new pop-up tent trailer. After arriving at the campsite, they spent the better part of the afternoon setting up the tent. Knowing they wouldn't be able to use of the bed at night, because the whole family would be sleeping together, the couple decided they'd like to make a little romantic use of it, so they sent their children down to the lake to play. The couple entered the tent and proceed to make love.

Unfortunately, the tent-trailer unit wasn't set up properly, and it soon collapsed from the couple's "activity," exposing them to all the other campers at the site.

The couple hurriedly packed up the tent, grabbed their children, and departed.

"Sorry, I thought you were the man I lost my virginity to."

Partners who end up in bed with each other by mistake are a common occurance in folklore. These tales often concern punishment of someone who has committed a sexual "no-no", such as the person of power who uses their position to extort sexual favors, or the spouse who mistrusts his or her mate's faithfulness without just cause, or just simply a case of mistaken identity.

Chatroom Rendezvous

A young woman had been single for so long that she decided to try out a virtual sex chatline on her computer.

Calling herself "Bootylicious" she discovered that it was more than enjoyable. After a few weeks trying out various chatlines, she found someone called "Cyberthug" and got thoroughly turned on by their virtual intercourse.

Their chats became more and more regular and in time they were turning each other on every night. After nearly a year of frantic cybersex, they both agreed that they were finally ready to meet, and arranged to meet up at a suitable rendezvous in a hotel. A little nervous but very excited, Bootylicious arrived at the hotel earlier than arranged so that she could prepare a romantic atmosphere in their suite. She placed candles all around the bed and scattered rose petals around the room before undressing and lying on the bed in anticipation of Cyberthug's imminent arrival.

Soon after, there was a knock on the door. "Is that you, Cyberthug?" asked Bootylicious.

After receiving the sought-after affirmative answer, she panted, "Come in, come in!"

Cyberthug walked in to see Bootylicious sprawled naked on the bed, but when their eyes met, it wasn't lust, but horror on their minds.

Bootylicious was Cyberthug's daughter!

Give Him The Old "How's Your Father!"

One Sunday after morning church service, a man stayed to help his local priest tidy the church gardens.

When they had finished, he invited the priest over for dinner, and the clergyman accepted. The priest, who was feeling somewhat dirty after the work, asked if he might have a shower before the meal, and naturally, the man agreed.

His wife, meanwhile, had been cooking dinner and gone upstairs to tidy herself up. Hearing the shower running and finding the bathroom door unlocked, she assumed that it was her husband using the shower, so without a second though she entered the room.

While applying her make-up, she fantasized aloud about what she planned to do to her husband after dinner, describing in detail how his cross-dressing turned her on, and how excited she was about the bondage gear they had just bought. Fully made up, she reached through the shower curtain and gave the bather's penis a friendly pat before going back downstairs.

The wife was startled when she spotted her husband in an armchair watching television, and fainted when he told her that he was waiting to have dinner once the priest had finished his shower.

In Disguise

A married couple were invited to a fancy New Year's Eve costume party. The wife organised the costumes for her and her husband, but on the night of the party, she developed a terrible migraine. She talked her husband into going, so he put on his devil's costume and went out to celebrate, while his wife rested in bed.

An hour later, the wife's migraine subsided and she decided to join her husband at the party. She also realised that he had not seen her costume yet, and figured she could surprise him. Dressed in her Catwoman outfit, she arrived at the party, and spotted her husband in his devil's costume. She noticed he was somewhat enamoured by a Marilyn Monroe lookalike, with whom he appeared to be flirting outrageously.

Seeing "Marilyn Monroe" leave her husband's side, the wife decided to test his fidelity firsthand and greeted him, with a sexy meow. After a few dances, the husband took her outside, and keeping their masks on, they made love.

Afterwards, the wife rushed home and climbed into bed. When her husband returned, she asked him how the night went.

Somewhat drunk, he replied, "It was really boring without you there, so I lent my costume to your brother and watched videos all night. But it seemed like your brother had a good time though."

Love At First Site

A man met a woman at a bar one night, and although she was taller and more heavily-built than him, he fell completely in love. A few days after their first meeting, he asked her to marry him and was overjoyed when she agreed.

The next day, they ran off to Las Vegas, visited a wedding chapel, made their vows and booked into a hotel for their honeymoon.

However, the man was somewhat disappointed when his bride emerged from the bathroom wearing a chunky pair of pyjamas, promptly got into bed, turned out the light and gruffly said goodnight.

The couple returned to the man's home the next day, but night after night he was let down by his beloved. After a few days of this, the exasperated man begged his wife to sleep with him, but to no avail.

Days went by and the man became more and more desperate, until one night his wife couldn't take any more of his whining and shouted at him, "Look, you stupid idiot, I'm a friggin' man, okay?"

More Than He Paid For

A Canadian man on a business trip in Amsterdam, decided to spend an evening off looking around the red-light district. The man cruised around the area for a while, enjoying the window displays, until he spotted a tall, slim, blonde beauty and decided he could not resist her charms.

Signalling to the woman, he entered her building through the door at the side where an older woman greeted him before guiding him to a room with a bed in it. The man was relieved when the older woman told him that the blonde woman would be right with him, but explained that it would be better to sort the money out now. The man paid her, and made himself comfortable on the bed.

Eventually, the blonde woman entered, began caressing her customer before stripping him, and then undressed herself. She was fondling him when the man suddenly cried out, grabbed his clothes and ran. He noticed that he was about to make love to a hermaphrodite when he reached down only to realise he was getting more than he paid for.

Stranger On The Bus

In Los Angeles, Calfornia a woman was on the bus when she thought she recognised a man sitting a few seats in front of her.

"Hello Brian," she called.

But the man didn't turn around. She called out several more times, but the man still failed to turn around. Finally, with everybody else on the bus looking at her, she went over and tapped the man on the shoulder.

"Brian," she began, but stopped when the man turned around.

Realising that she didn't know the man after all, she said, "Sorry, I thought you were the man I lost my virginity to," and red-faced, she got off the bus.

You Sure Unclogged His Pipe

A helpful husband started to fix a leak under the kitchen sink one weekend while his wife left to go out shopping. Upon her return she noticed two legs sticking out from under the sink, so she bent down, carefully unzipped the jeans and started to give him a blow job. Suddenly there was a loud bang. It turned out that the husband had given up trying to fix the leak and had called a plumber in. The plumber had been so surprised that he sat bolt upright and knocked himself out on the sink.

"The Anal Sex and Fetish Perversion Company"

Watching pornography breaks so many taboo's, that is why we are fascinated by these images. It allows us to watch people having sex. Sex, we're taught, is a private matter between two loving people...blah...blah..blah. So it is incredibly naughty to observe others in this act, either by watching a video or through the camera of our mind as we read an explicit book. It's a sneaky vice, and best of all, no one knows we're getting our kicks this way! As always, the discovery of the seamy truth about others play a major role in the enjoyment aspect of these legends.

Embarrassing Purchase

The LAPD have been unable to recommend a prosecution for the following scam:

A company took out a newspaper advertisement claiming to be able to supply imported hard core pornographic videos. Since their prices seemed reasonable, people began placing orders and making payments via cheque.

After several weeks, the company wrote back explaining that under the present law they were unable to supply the materials, and do not wish to be prosecuted. So they return their customers' money in the form of a company cheque. However, due to the name of the company, few people ever bother to present these to their banks.

The name of the company was: "The Anal Sex and Fetish Perversion Company".

The Smiles Matched

A young woman who wrote out a check at a clothes store in Marina del Rey several years ago was asked by the clerk to see her driver's license, she explained apologetically that her wallet had been stolen. But, she added, she did have one form of ID.

"I was the May centerfold in Playboy magazine," she told the clerk. "I have the centerfold here in my purse if you want to see it."

She took it out, and the smiles matched. Restores your faith in humanity, doesn't it?

"Three Women Do It."

A teenage criminal on the run, was browsing in a bookshop when he came across a section in the back full of X-rated porn videos.

Feeling mischievous, he bought a video with a title that roughly translated meant, "Three Women Do It".

Walking home, excited by the thought of watching the video, the boy spotted a police car parked near his house. In a panic, the boy fled in the opposite direction, and hid in an abandoned mill.

After a few days, the boy, fed up with eating pieces of stale grain, couldn't take it any more, and went to the nearest police station to turn himself in.

Proffering the video for the police sergeant's inspection, The sergeant started laughing and said, "Son, buying porn videos is not illegal. I can't arrest you for this."

The boy couldn't believe his ears, and on finding out that the police had parked outside his house because of a burglary nearby, he ran home to play the video.

However, his relief turned to utter disappointment when the video turned out to be about three 40-year-old women talking about leaving their respective husbands to become nuns.

Did You Know? *A sex line caller complained to Trading Standards after dialling a 900 number from an advertisement entitled 'Hear Me Moan'. The caller was played a tape of a woman nagging her husband for failing to do jobs around the house. Consumer Watchdogs in Dorset refused to look into the complaint, saying, "He got what he deserved."*

Video From Home

During Operation Desert Storm, an American soldier based in Iraq received a package from home.

Instead of a letter, it contained a video with the message, "To my loving husband. Hope you and your buddies enjoy this." It was signed, "Your loving wife."

One evening, with a bit of wrangling, the man finally gained access to a VCR, and invited his colleagues along to watch the film. As he and his friends had hoped, it turned out to be an amateur porno film. The star was a young woman who, to the delight of the soldiers, was wearing an Iraqi combat uniform complete with a mask that covered her head and face. Except, for the holes that exposed her eyes, nose and mouth.

As the film progressed, the woman removed all her clothing except the balaclava and proceeded to have energetic sex in a wide variety of positions with several young men. As the film neared the end, the woman sat up and finally removed the balaclava.

Looking straight into the camera, she demanded, "Will you give me a divorce now, you asshole?"

The soldier broke down as he recognised his wife on film.

The money will be used to train them for new positions in hotels.

Although prostitution has engendered some of the world's oldest legends, here is a much more contemporary sampling of stories involving the worlds oldest profession.

License To Thrill

Two pretty, earnest young school teachers went to Mexico for the summer break. They avoided all the tourist places, desiring only the real flavor of Mexico. Arriving in a highly favored little inland city, they set out to explore.

Coming to a street mellifluously named the "Avenue of the Beautiful Springs and the Waterfall and the Bridge That Is Music in Stone", they turned into it, only to be pounced upon by the local law enforcement and haled off to the police station.

There the captain explained that their offense was trespassing on the red-light district. There was a fine of 300 pesos for any girl caught without a license on the "Avenue of the Beautiful Springs and the Waterfall and the Bridge That Is Music in Stone."

The girls protested that they were simply sightseeing and had no idea of muscling in, but the captain said the fine remained. Then he had an inspiration.

"The fine is 300 pesos, but the license costs only 25. Why don't you apply for licenses?" he asked.

The girls thought this was a fine idea. For the Mexican equivalent of $5 each, they received handsomly engraved documents giving them access to solicate sex on the "Avenue of the Beautiful Springs and the Waterfall and the Bridge That Is Music in Stone."

Did You Know? *The city of Brussels paid 200,000 Pounds to Save Prostitutes. The money will not be going directly into the prostitutes' pocket, but will be used to encourage them to lead a better life. The money will be used to train them for "new positions" in hotels.*

Money Well Wasted

A man traveled to Montreal, Quebec on business from another part of the country. He checked into the Holiday Inn and arranged to have a hooker sent to his room. A few minutes later, a knock came on his door. He open it to find his own daughter, who was a student at the local university. Presumably, she found her allowance to be insufficient, probably due to the fact that her father was spending all his money on prostitutes.

"Then let this be on your conscience, you cheating bitch!"

"Heaven has no rage like love to hatred turned,
Nor hell a fury like a woman scorned."

-- William Congreve, The Mourning Bride

The betrayal of lovers and spouses have inspired some truly inventive forms of revenge.

Plugged In Both Ways

My sister heard from a friend who had an impeccable source at the local hospital that one of the town's chiropractors had been admitted to the emergency ward with severe burns to his anus. It turns out he was having an affair with one of his clients, and their taste in sex ran towards the kinky, bondage. The wife discovered the two in 'flagrante delecto' with the husband tied to the bed. The mistress who was pretty good at tying knots fled, and the chiropractor was left prostrate. The wife was so upset that she took her hair curler and plugged it in both ways, if you catch my drift.

Plummet To The Alter

A skydiving fanatic introduced his girlfriend to his hobby and she took to it immediately. She loved both the adrenaline rush and the fact that they were sharing the experience. Soon, they were both going skydiving every weekend.

One weekend the man decided to propose to his girlfriend during a jump. So, once their parachutes had opened and they were sailing towards the ground, he took a ring from his pocket and asked her to marry him.

His girlfriend replied, "Sorry honey, I can't marry you. I'm sleeping with your brother."

Before she could say anything more, the man snapped off his parachute and yelled at her, "Then let this be on your conscience, you cheating bitch!" and plummeted to his death.

The girlfriend was shattered, especially since she was only joking and actually loved the man.

Uncontrollable Bodily Functions

A bunch of my co-workers went out one Friday night and drank tons of beer. Dean was the only one able to reel in a fine young lass, and brought her home for a night cap.

However, he was so drunk, that he ended up puking on his date while doing it doggy style. When he got done puking he passed out. We found the results the next morning when we went to pick him up for breakfast. He was laying on the floor in his own vomit with a big pile of shit on his chest.

241

The used underwear had supposedly been worn by schoolgirls, and were being sold for the equivalent of US $50 a piece.

Do we want our friends, neighbors, and co-workers to know the details of our sex lives? Do we want them observing us in the act? How embarrassing, then, when they catch us engaging in some rather kinky sexual practices (*mine involves a jar of pickles, six female circus midgets, and a mechanical bull, but that is a whole other story and a whole lot more therapy*).

Good Grip

A woman came into a Neurologist office with bloody holes all over her face, some deep and some shallow. There was a uniqueness to the pattern on her face, so the doctor asked what happened, especially since she was in the office for a different medical reason.

The woman told the story that she was performing oral sex on her boyfriend when she had a seizure. The seizure caused the woman's mouth to clamp down, and her jaw to lock shut on the man's penis. The man tried everything to get the woman to let up, pulling, hitting, etc. His agony was so strong that he grabbed for the nearest object, which happened to be a fork, and continuously jabbed the woman's face.

Finally, I guess her seizure subsided and she let go, but was left with a bleeding face and half of her boyfriend's penis.

Kinky Neighbourhood Spiderman

A friend of a co-worker was worried when she hadn't seen her neighbours for a couple of days. Their car was in the driveway, but their newspapers were piling up outside the door. So she ran over to the house and knocked on the door, but there was no reply, so she listened at the door and could hear faint sounds of groaning.

She rushed back home and phoned the Police, who duly arrived and broke the door down. They searched the ground floor and found nothing. But when they went upstairs, they heard moaning coming from behind the main bedroom door.

The police burst in to find the woman, wearing a maid's outfit, tied and gagged on the bed.

They hurridly untied her, and she started sobbing, "My husband, he's in the wardrobe".

Thinking that the husband had been killed, the police opened the wardrobe to find the husband, dressed in a Spiderman outfit crumpled at the bottom of the wardrobe with a broken leg.

It transpired that the couple had been playing a "sexual game." He pretended to be Spiderman and would jump off the top of the wardrobe and save his wife, or should I say "The damsel in distress".

However, the roof of the wardrobe had collapsed and he'd been stuck in the wardrobe for two days.

Non-Smoking Carriage

The commuter train to downtown Toronto was so packed that the commuters and travellers were squashed next to each other on the seats and in the aisles of the carriages. A young couple in one corner seemed to be more packed still, and about 15 minutes into the journey it became apparent that they were actually having sex. Men with bowler hats and umbrellas pretended not to notice, young women giggled, old men and women muttered quietly, while others averted their eyes, but none said a word or tried to put a stop to this display of exhibitionism.

A few minutes and some stifled gasps later, the couple reached their "destination" so to speak, tidied up their clothes and relaxed. It was only when both the young man and young lady lit up a cigarette that they sparked a reaction.

One polite gentleman leaned towards them and said, "Excuse me, but this is a nonsmoking carriage."

Did You Know? *In Japan in 1993 previously-worn panties were being offered for sale in vending machines. The used underwear had supposedly been worn by schoolgirls, and were being sold for the equivalent of US $50 a piece.*

Sins of The Flesh

A priest from Virginia was sickened by the sex and violence portrayed on television. He claimed it lead to sins of the flesh rather than enlightenment, and decided to make a point at his next Sunday service.

He brought a variety of sex toys to the church and explained to his startled congregation the uses of each before burning them in a bin. After he showed the congregation a condom, a dildo, sexy lingerie and a porn video, he threw them into the bin, poured gasoline over them and set them on fire.

Thinking that the sermon was over, people began to leave, but the priest barked, "I'm not finished yet. This last item is totally contemptible in the eyes of the Lord!"

He pulled out a rubber blow up doll and blew it up to its full size. The congregation stared in disbelief as their priest espoused the doll's despicable and sinful nature. The priest stuffed the rubber doll into the burning bin where it exploded, throwing up pieces of hot latex all over the church and the astonished congregation.

Stain Of Love

A young teenage couple was having sex at the girl's parents' place, in the living room. Soon they engaged in sodomy.

For some reason, maybe she was nervous because her parents might come home any minute, or maybe it was the first time she experienced sodomy, whatever the reason, when the boy came out after having ejaculated, the disaster occured.

You guessed it...a big smelly shit on the carpet.

Suddenly, the youths heard the girls' parents pulling into the driveway. They managed to get dressed just in time, and rushed to the bedroom where they took innocent poses. Suddenly they heard the girl's father screaming. Thank God they had a dog.

Through The Teeth, Down The Gums, Look Out Stomach, Here He Cums...

A not-so-bright couple, growing up in one of those tiny backroad towns in Alabama, had been married two years, and ran a gas station on the main highway. Business had been surprisingly good, so they decided the woman would stop taking the contraceptive pill and try for a baby.

After a year of trying, there was no sign of a baby. The couple was confused, because they ate healthy, and even tried having sex in different positions, at different times of the day. They could not understand why a baby hadn't been conceived, so they decided to visit a doctor, the nearest one being in a town 50 miles away. The doctor asked them the relevant questions and examined each of them in turn.

However, on examining the woman, he asked her, "How exactly do you have sex?"

The woman was too embarrassed to answer, but her husband readily replied,"Come on Doctor, you know! Like everyone else! I put my "thing" in her mouth and go for it!"

Did you know? *A woman from Albany, New York, had the misfortune to be playing with a vibrator when it got stuck and had to go to hospital to have it removed. As if that wasn't embarrassing enough, she had promised to go on a blind double-date with a friend of hers the next night, and who should her blind date be? Why, the doctor who had to remove the vibrator, of course!*

"Wholly Self-Gratifying Ends"

A man was plastering the wall of his lounge when he inadvertently made a hole in the wall. For some strange reason, the man decided to use the hole for wholly self-gratifying means, possibly because he hadn't had sex in over a year.

Smearing the edges with grease, he was just reaching climax when a deep thrust caused him to burst through the wall. On the other side, an octogenarian grandmother was engrossed in her soap operas when she spotted what looked like a snake on the wallpaper. The man ended up in hospital after the grandmother smashed his manhood with a bible in a bid to squash a dangerous snake.

Those Southerners Are Known For Pumpin' The Kin!!

Our attitudes towards sex and sexuality have become much more liberal and open in recent decades. However, there are still subjects that children and adolescents often find somewhat frightening and mysterious. It's common knowledge that youngsters express their uncertain feelings towards sexual matters by circulating stories involving sexual escapades which contain a high "gross out" factor. Just as little boys and girls avoid dealing with each other by declaring the other gender to have "cooties", older children keep the subject of sex at arm's length by associating it with unsavory tales involving combinations of food, insects, animals, self-mutilation, and masturbation. These tales usually end with someone who has engaged in sex losing either his or her life or genitalia.

"Inflate your tires, but hide your bicycle pump where it cannot tempt you."

The government is cracking down on a disgusting new craze called "Pumping".

A spokesman for Cedar Sinai hospital told reporters, "If this perversion catches on, it will destroy the cream of America's manhood."

He was speaking after the remains of 13-year-old Charles Fieber had been rushed into the hospital's emergency room.

"Most 'Pumpers' use a standard bicycle pump," he explained, "inserting the nozzle far up their rectum, giving themselves a rush of air, creating a momentary high. This act is a sin against God."

Charles took it further still. He started using a two-cylinder foot pump, but even that wasn't exciting enough for him, and he boasted to friends that he was going to try the compressed air hose at a nearby gasoline station. They dared him to do it, so under the cover of darkness, he snuck in.

Not realising how powerful the machine was, he inserted the tube deep into his rectum, and placed a coin in the slot. As a result, he died virtually instantly, but passers by were still in shock. One woman thought she was watching a twilight firework display, and started clapping.

"We still haven't located all of Mr. Fieber," say police authorities. "When that quantity of air interacted with the gas in his system, he nearly exploded. It was like an atom bomb went off or something."

"Pumping is the devil's pastime, and we must all say no to Satan," concluded the hospital spokesperson. "By all means, inflate your tires, but hide your bicycle pump where it cannot tempt you."

She Lobster Mind, But Flounder Children!

One morning around 4:30am 24-year old Anna Gibson of Kittery Maine, woke up with a painful need to urinate. At first she thought it might be diarrhea, but when she stood up out of bed, she realized that it was urinary pain, which is a similar feeling of having diarrhea (just out the wrong hole).

She wobbled to the toilet and upon sitting down, her vagina erupted into the most horrific messy farting noise you could possibly imagine. For the next few minutes, in paralyzing pain, Ms. Gibson continued to push and squirt out of her vagina a burning tide of wretch and filth, while gripping the sides of the toilet, white-knuckled. She was screaming so out of control, that the neighbors called the police.

When medics arrived they found Ms. Gibson unconscious lying on the floor of her bathroom wearing nothing but her bathrobe. Running down her leg, was a stream of a brownish green "syrup like substance". The medic had to transfer her to a stretcher, so he grabbed her left leg, which was bent crossing her other leg, to straighten her out. When he lifted her left leg to straighten her body out, he exposed her vagina at which point a creature, no larger than the tip of a finger wormed its way out of her genitals and landed on the floor with a wet popping sound. Shocked, the medic stared at the creature that was lying on the tile bathroom floor in a casing of mucous. It was a tiny mud shrimp and it sat there on the cold floor gasping for water, while flipping itself back and forth. The horrified medic turned to the toilet feeling the nausea setting in. When he put his face down into the toilet to puke what he saw was so horrific that to this day he cannot look into a toilet without convulsing.

The entire toilet bowl was boiling with baby brown mud shrimp flipping and splashing at a furious pace.

You think that is disgusting? Here is how it happened:

Ms. Gidson official death was the result of a combination of shock and severe head trauma. She stood up over the toilet in pain, and when she saw what she had done, she went into shock and fell, smashing her head on the toilet and then on the floor. It is believed by medical police that on two nights before the accident she had purchased a live lobster at a fish market. While lying in a tub, she gently inserted the creature's tail into her vagina to derive pleasure. At that point, she held a lighter under the creature's face causing it to flip its tail in a violent snapping motion.

The medics found a lesbian XXX video in the VCR with the TV was positioned on a table in front of the tub. The lobster was found in the kitchen garbage can wrapped in a paper bag. Traces of Ms. Gibson's DNA were found on the lobster, along with pubic hairs that had wedged themselves between the lobster tail joints. The lobster's face was lightly burned with the same fuel used in lighters. The lobster's digestive track and colon were found to be full of mud shrimp egg casings. Doctors believe that the lobster had eaten them (they are common in the water at fish markets and are usually harmlessly boiled to death) and the lobster had crapped them out into Ms. Gibson's "no-no special place" when she was torturing it.

Maine mud shrimp only take two days to gestate and Ms. Gibson was only four days away from getting her period. Doctors believe that at that point of her menstrual cycle, her womb was the perfect PH balance to grow these mud shrimp, which are a much larger version of the popular "Sea Monkey" pets sold throughout the US. Over night the eggs hatched and the mud shrimp began doubling in size every ten minutes.

You can imagine the pain she was in when she woke up that morning and gave birth to well over 1,000 mud shrimp in her toilet.

Those Southerners Are Known For Pumpin' The Kin!!

Police arrested Jeff Skandeberg, a 25-year old white male, resident of Mountain Home, Arkansas in a pumpkin patch at 12:00am one Friday night.

Skandeberg was charged with lewd and lascivious behavior, public indecency, and public intoxication at the County courthouse on the following Monday.

The suspect allegedly stated that as he was passing a pumpkin patch, and decided to stop.

"You know, a pumpkin is soft and squishy inside, and there was no one around for miles. At least I thought there wasn't." He stated in a phone interview from the County courthouse jail.

Skandeberg went on to state that he pulled over to the side of the road, picked out a pumpkin that he felt was appropriate to his purposes, cut a hole in it, and proceeded to satisfy his alleged "need."

"I guess I was just really into it!" he commented with evident embarrassment.

In the process, Skandeberg apparently failed to notice the police car approaching and was unaware of his audience until officer Susan Turner approached him.

"It was an unusual situation, that's for sure." Said officer Turner. "I walked up to Mr. Skandeberg and he was just working away at this pumpkin."

Officer Turner went on to describe, "I just approached him and said, "Excuse me sir, but do you realise that you are screwing a pumpkin?" He got really surprised, as you'd expect, and then looked me straight in the eye and said, "A pumpkin? Damn... is it midnight already?"

"To Boldly Go Where No Gerbil Has Gone Before."

When you look at all the proclivities known to man, beastiality is the one that falls farthest outside our sexual morals. So it is to be expected that we would create numerous legends (most often involving a gerbil) to scorn those who dare engage in outerspecies intercourse.

Of Beast And Man

A 65-year-old man lent his video camera to a friend so he could film a wedding. A few weeks later, the friend had a showing of the film he made. The newlyweds, their parents, grandparents and various friends including

246

the camera owner, all turned up to watch the film. Everybody seemed delighted with the film, and as it drew to an end, they all talked excitedly about what they had seen. All of a sudden the chattering stopped and there was dead silence. The old man, wondering what had happened, looked around to see himself on the television performing sexual acts with his neighbours dog.

"To Boldly Go Where No Gerbil Has Gone Before."

"Lighting the match was my big mistake. But I was only trying to retrieve the gerbil," Dandy Randy Douglas told bemused doctors in the Severe Burns Unit of Chicago City Hospital.

Dandy Randy, and his homosexual partner Cotton Del Rio, had been admitted for emergency treatment after a felching session had gone seriously wrong.

"I pushed a cardboard tube up his rectum and slipped "Bitches", our gerbil in," Dandy Randy explained. "As usual, Cotton shouted out 'Smackdown', my cue that he'd had enough. I tried to retrieve Bitches but he wouldn't come out, so I peered into the tube and struck a match, thinking the light might attract him."

A hush came over the crowd at a press conference when hospital spokesman, Dr. Marion Braun described what happened next.

"The match ignited a pocket of intestinal gas and a flame shot out the tubing, igniting Mr. Douglas hair and severely burning his face." explained Dr. Braun, "It also set fire to the gerbil's fur and whiskers which in turn ignited a larger pocket of gas further up the intestine, propelling the rodent out like a cannonball."

Dandy Randy suffered second degree burns and a broken nose from the impact of the gerbil, while Cotton suffered first and second degree burns to his anus and lower intestinal tract.

The Peanut Butter Solution

My co-workers friend Mason worked during the day and his fiance Wendy worked at night. They would get lonely without anyone else around and decided to get a dog. Mason loved that dog and always took him out to the park to run, to go hunting, and even snuck the dog peanut butter.

But for some reason, despite Mason's affection, the dog just seemed to like Wendy better, which really pissed Mason off.

One day, as per usual the usual routine, Mason put the dog in the basement before he left for work so he wouldn't destroy the house before Wendy got home from her day. Mason ran out the door, but remembering that he had promised his buddy at work could borrow his golf clubs for the weekend, Mason ran back into the house and edged into the basement to retrieve his clubs, shutting the door behind him so the dog wouldn't bolt.

While he was getting his clubs, he heard Wendy open the door and call out, "Baby, you down there? I missed you!"

He was just about to answer when the dog leaped up and nearly knocked him over. When he got back on his feet and looked up the basement stairs, he found, to his horror, Wendy at the top of the stairs buck naked with peanut butter smeared all over her crotch.

Mason filed for divorce.

"Why Does Sperm Taste So Salty Then?"

It's not quite as embarrassing as getting caught in the act, but can still be disheartening to discover eavesdroppers have been listening in on our private conversations about our sexual matters. However, when we are on the eavesdropping end, such matters can be quite amusing.

Family Affair

A saleman and a banker had been commuting to work together for a number of years and formed as strong a bond as one can get in such a situation.

One day, the banker boarded the train looking like he was on the verge of tears. With some probing, he revealed that his wife had left him. Eager to cheer him up, the salesman invited him for dinner that evening.

That night, joining the salesman, his wife and daughter for dinner, the banker began to cheer up, and became a frequent visitor to the household. A few weeks later, the salesman came across a letter in his daughters bag. The letter proposed a passionate liaison with the banker. Furious, the salesman told his daughter that he would not permit her to see the banker, but the daughter told him where to go, and stormed off in defiance.

A week later, the saleman confronted the banker and said, "Look, you have to stop seeing her. It's driving us all apart."

To which the banker coldly replied, "Stop seeing who? Your daughter or your wife?"

Free Sperm Sample

"A guy walked into a sperm donor bank wearing a ski mask and holding a gun. He goes up to the nurse and demanded her to open the sperm bank vault.

She said "But sir, its just a sperm bank!"

"I don't care, open it now!!!" he replied.

So she opened the door to the vault and inside were all the sperm samples.

The guy then stated "Take one of those sperm samples and drink it!"

She looked at him and said, "But, they are sperm samples!"

"Do it!".the crook yelled.

So the nurse sucked it back.

"That one there, drink that one as well." he demanded.

So the nurse drank that one as well.

Finally after four or five samples the man took off his ski mask and said, "See honey - its not that hard."

"Good Luck, Mr. Gorsky."

When Apollo Mission Astronaut Neil Armstrong first walked on the moon, he not only gave his famous

"One small step for man. One giant leap for mankind" statement, but it was followed by several remarks, including the usual COM traffic between him, the other astronauts, and Mission Control.

Before he re-entered the lander, he made the enigmatic remark, "Good luck, Mr. Gorsky."

Many people at NASA thought it was a casual remark concerning some rival Soviet Cosmonaut. However, upon checking, they found there was no Gorsky in either the Russian or American space programs.

Over the years, many people and reporters have questioned him as to what the "Good luck, Mr. Gorsky" statement meant. On July 5, in Tampa Bay, Florida while answering questions following a speech, a reporter brought up the 26- year-old question to Armstrong. He finally responded. It seems that Mr. Gorsky had died, so Armstrong felt he could answer the question.

When Neil was a kid, he enjoyed playing baseball with his brother in the backyard. One afternoon his brother hit a fly ball, which landed in front of his neighbors' bedroom window. The neighbors were Mr. and Mrs. Gorksy.

As he leaned down to pick up the ball, he heard Mrs. Gorsky shouting at Mr. Gorsky, "Oral sex? You want oral sex? You'll get oral sex when the kid next door walks on the moon!"

Multi-Tasking

A friend of a friend was all geared up for a night in front of the television to watch hockey, and have a couple of beers while his girlfriend Joanne was still away.

Suddenly he got a text message from Cindy his friends ex, which stated, "I'm coming over because I need to see you."

So she shows up, and they get chatting about all sorts of stuff when they start to kiss and fondle each other. Next thing you know he is sitting in the arm chair with a beer in one hand, remote in the other, hockey on the box, and Cindy on her knees. Then the phone rings and it's Joanne who got bored waiting for her flight at the airport.

So now he's got beer, Cindy sucking and Joanne chatting to him on the phone. When Cindy stops sucking, she looks up at him, then winks and whispers, "Say hello to Joanne for me." Then gets back to the job in hand, so to speak.

I am not sure if he is the luckiest man on earth, or the worst boyfriend in the world.

"Nobody slept with mommy while you were away this time!"

Several years ago, a friend of a friend was returning home from a trip just when a storm hit, with crashing thunder and severe lightning. As he entered his bedroom around 2 am, he found his two children in bed with his wife, Jane, apparently scared by the loud storm. He resigned myself to sleep in the guest bedroom that night.

The next day, he talked to the children, and explained that it was okay to sleep with mom when the storm was bad, but when he was expected home, don't sleep with mom that night.

The children said, "Okay."

After his next trip several weeks later, Jane and the children picked him up in the terminal at the appointed time. Since the plane was late, everyone had come into the terminal to wait for his plane's arrival, along with hundreds of other folks waiting for their arriving passengers.

As he entered the waiting area, his son saw him, and came running shouting, "Hi, Dad! I've got some good news!"

As he waved back, he said loudly, "What's the good news?"

"Nobody slept with mommy while you were away this time!" his son shouted.

The airport became very quiet, as everyone in the waiting area looked at the boy, then turned to him, and then searched the rest of the area to see if they could figure out exactly who his mom was!

The Lady Is A Tramp

The following is a reply by a women with eleven kids on aChild Support Agency form in the section for listing details regarding the father. This lady was quite the entertainment engineer.

Regarding the identity of the fathers of my children. Regarding my twins, child A was fathered by Richard Shaw. I am unsure as to the identity of the father of child B, but I believe that he was conceived on the same night.

As to the identity of the father of my son Christian, I was being sick out of a window when taken unexpectedly from behind. I can provide you with a list of names of men that I think were at the party if this helps.

I do not know the name of the father of my little Anna. She was conceived at a party where I had unprotected sex with a man I met that night. I do remember that the sex was so good that I fainted. If you do manage to track down the father of Anna can you send me his phone number? Thanks.

I don't know the identity of the father of my daughter Monica, but he drives a BMW that now has a hole made by my stiletto heel in one of the door panels. Perhaps you can contact BMW service stations in this area and see if he's had it replaced.

I have never had sex with a man regarding my son Jesus. I am awaiting a letter from the Pope confirming that my son's conception was immaculate and that he is Christ risen again.

I cannot tell you the name of my daughter Lilith's dad as he informed me that to do so would blow his cover and that would have cataclysmic implications for the British economy. I am torn between doing right by you and right by my country. Please advise.

I do not know who fathered of my son Mark because all squeegy kids look the same to me.

Darren Filman is the father of my daughter Stephanie. If you do catch up with him can you ask him what he did with my Aerosmith CDs?

From the dates it seems that my daughter Caroline was conceived at Disney World -- maybe it really is the Magic Kingdom.

So much about the night my youngest son, Raine is a blur. The only thing that I remember for sure is that Martha Stewart did a programme about eggs earlier in the evening. If I'd have stayed in and watched more TV rather than going to a party, my eggs might have remained unfertilised.

Toddler Tale

While in line at the bank one afternoon, a toddler decided to release some pent-up energy and ran amok. The mother was finally able to grab hold of the child after receiving looks of disgust and annoyance from other patrons. The mother told her that if she did not start behaving right now, she would be punished.

To the amusement of the bank patrons, the little girl looked the mother right in the eye and said in a voice just as threatening, "If you don't let me go right now, I will tell Grandma that I saw you kissing Daddy's pee-pee last night!"

"Why Does Sperm Taste So Salty Then?"

A teacher was lecturing to her biology class about the human reproductive system. At one point, she mentioned that fructose, a complex sugar, is a major component of sperm.

On hearing this, a puzzled student raised his hand and innocently asked, "Why does sperm taste so salty then?"

All the other students burst out laughing.

Realising the implication of what he had just said, the young man addressed the class, "Well, I was going to come out soon anyway. Hey, everybody, I'm gay and I'm proud."

Satisfied with the effect of his proclamation, he stood up and walked out, leaving everybody gasping.

"You bitch, you've never given me a blow job!"

We are reluctant to discuss the subject of unmarried, underage youngsters engaging in sex. This taboo that has been long-held by society has led to the creation of a group of improbable legends regarding teenage sexual activity.

Birthday Surprise

A teenager returned home on his birthday after an unpleasant day at school where everyone seemed to go out of their way to ignore him.

Although he wondered if his family and friends might have been setting him up for a surprise, arriving home he was greeted as normal. When his parents told him they were going out, he realised they had forgotten.

Lonely and a little sad, the boy telephoned his girlfriend to see if she could join him, but she declined his invitation, stating that she was busy. Irritated at the cold response, especially on this day of all days, he called up his ex-girlfriend, who willingly came over, where soon after things became steamy, and they moved the action upstairs to his bedroom.

Ten minutes later, the phone rang and the boy, now naked, ran downstairs to answer it, eagerly followed by his naked ex-girlfriend. The call was from his mother, who said she had forgotten to hang up the clothes in the laundry room, and asked him if he would do it. He agreed, and taking the girl on his back, went into the laundry room to sort out the washing.

As he turned on the light there was a shout of "Surprise!" and he saw both his parents, a collection of his school friends and his girlfriend.

His mother, seeing her son and his ex-girlfriend naked, stammered quietly, "Here's your present," as she handed him a cellular phone.

Sex Bracelets

Youngsters signal sexual availability with jelly bracelets.

Sex Bracelets are back - and kids are using them with out their parents knowing what they are doing. Jelly bracelet fashion accessories have been around since the 80's. But instead of a fashion statement, they may be making a statement about your kid's sex life. These bendable pieces of colored rubber have become a sexual code to many teens. Here's a common breakdown:

Yellow signifies hugging.

Purple represents kissing.

Red means a lap dance.

Blue means oral sex; and

Black is full out intercourse.

Also, in a game called "snap", if a boy breaks a jelly bracelet off a girl's wrist, he gets a sexual coupon for that act.

It's become such a problem in some middle schools in the Southern states that districts started banning the bracelets. If your daughter is wearing one of these bracelets, it may be cause for concern.

Surprise For Mother

A woman was feeling ill one day and left work early. When she arrived home, she caught her teenage daughter having sex with her boyfriend on the floor in the front room.

After admonishing her daughter the mother lectured her about the use of contraceptives and asked her if her boyfriend used condoms. The daughter, angry at being told off, replied that she had been using her mother's contraceptive pills for the last two months.

The mother, now worried, said that she hadn't noticed any pills missing. The daughter replied smugly that she had been replacing the pills she took with tic tacs.

A week later, the mother discovered that she was pregnant.

You Blew It With Me!!

A teacher told her biology class about the common types of bacteria found in saliva. Frustrated by her students' apparent lack of interest, she told them they were about to undertake an experiment. After showing them pictures of what they could expect to find, he asked the students to take scrapings from inside their mouths and view them under the microscope.

A female student examined her sample, but was unable to identify a particular type of cell, so she asked the teacher to have a look. The teacher took a look through the students microscope and then exclaimed, "Well, I never, that's a human sperm cell".

Immediately, a male student who everyone knew as the girl's long-term boyfriend, shouted at the girl, "You bitch, you've never given me a blow job!"

The girl broke down in tears and ran out of the room.

"You're a bit old to believe in Father Christmas, aren't you?"

There is a long held discrimination against homosexuality. Many stories have been created that portray homosexuals as abominations -- deviants who engage in sexual practises, and sexual predators who force themselves on unwilling participants.

Father Christmas

A man decided he was going to throw himself off a bridge. His wife left him, he lost his job and he owed thousands of dollars to the bank.

Just as he finished his prayers and closed his eyes, ready to jump, Father Christmas tapped him on the shoulder, "Are you okay?"

The man explained why he was so miserable, and again, prepared himself to jump.

"Stop!" shouted Father Christmas. "I will grant you three wishes if you can do me a favour."

The man replied, "Would you really? That would be wonderful. Thank you."

Father Christmas granted him his three wishes, and as a result the man decided not to jump after all.

For his three wishes he asked that his wife would come back to him and beg for his forgiveness, his boss would beg him to return and give him a $20,000 pay rise, and all his debts would be cleared.

"Oh, thank you!" the man said. "What is it that you want me to do for you?"

Father Christmas told the man to drop his pants and bend over. After a somewhat rough sex session, Father Christmas asked the man how old he was.

"Thirty-six," replied the man.

"You're a bit old to believe in Father Christmas, aren't you?" laughed the jolly, fat homosexual.

Headaches and a Sore Rectum

A Stanford University student sharing a room with a fellow student, had been suffering from headaches and a sore rectum for quite some time, so he paid a visit to the doctor, who prescribed a hemorrhoid cream.

A week later, the student was still suffering the same problems, but another visit to the doctor proved useless.

One night, the student ran out of toothpaste and looked in his roommate's cupboard to see if his roommate had some that he could borrow.

On looking through the cupboard, the student was surprised to find a bottle of chloroform and some Vaseline. Later, the student questioned his roommate, who eventually admitted that he was a homosexual and had thought that drugging him was the only way to relieve his sexual frustration.

Surprisingly, the student came around to the idea, and the two roommates have since embarked on a long and loving relationship.

Just A Little Gay

A gay couple decided to take a weekend holiday by the oceanside. They stayed at a small hotel owned by a middle-aged woman who had recently been widowed.

Before long, it became obvious to one of the men, who was not entirely gay, that she was quite interested in him, so when his partner suggested going for a walk, he declined the offer, explaining that he was tired. As he expected, his partner went for a walk on his own, at which point, the man made his move on the woman. They had very passionate sex for several hours, but after their brief liaison, it was never repeated and it remained a secret. In what he considered a cunning move, the man gave the widow his partner's name pretending it was his own.

However, three years later the partner received a letter from a lawyer informing him that the widow had died, and that she left him the hotel and all her savings. Along with the lawyers letter was another letter, this time from the woman, describing in great detail their "afternoon of unbridled passion" which she asserted, she would not forget until the day she died.

chapterseventeen

"I will be voting Republican this year
because the democrats left a bad taste in her mouth."

--Monica Lewinsky

strangebedfellows

Politics is supposed to be the second oldest profession. I have come to realise that it bears a close resemblance to the first.

In all seriousness, politics is the art or science of governing, especially the governing of a political entity, such as a nation, and the administration and control of its internal and external affairs.

There is a complex love-hate relationship between us and politics. We expect the government to protect our interests, yet they don't want to see themselves held accountable to it.

The men and women who have the pivotal role in leading our country, also lead the most heavily-scrutinized lives of anyone in the world. Even with all the power politicians hold it still isn't enough to prevent their actions from becoming legend.

. . . .

A slight tax increase costs you two hundred dollars, and a substantial tax cut saves you thirty cents.

"In this world nothing is certain but death and taxes."
--Benjamin Franklin

The subject of death is covered elsewhere in the book; so here I present a small section about taxes.

Did You Know? *A slight tax increase costs you two hundred dollars, and a substantial tax cut saves you thirty cents.*

Fair Share

How Taxes Work . . .

There is a very simple way to understand the tax laws. Let's put tax cuts in terms everyone can understand. Suppose that every day, ten men go out for dinner. The bill for all ten comes to $100. If they paid their bill the way we pay our taxes, it would go something like this:

The first four men — the poorest — would pay nothing; the fifth would pay $1, the sixth would pay $3, the seventh $7, the eighth $12, the ninth $18, and the tenth man — the richest — would pay $59.

That's what they decided to do. The ten men ate dinner in the restaurant every day and seemed quite happy with the arrangement — until one day, the owner threw them a curve.

"Since you are all such good customers," he said, "I'm going to reduce the cost of your daily meal by $20."

So now dinner for the ten men only cost $80.00. The group still wanted to pay their bill the way they paid there taxes. So the first four men were unaffected. They would still eat for free. But what about the other six — the paying customers? How could they divvy up the $20 windfall so that everyone would get his "fair share?"

The six men realised that $20 divided by six is $3.33. But if they subtracted that from everybody's share, Then the fifth man and the sixth man would end up being paid to eat their meal. So the restaurant owner suggested that it would be fair to reduce each man's bill by roughly the same amount, and he proceeded to work out the amounts each should pay.

And so the fifth man paid nothing, the sixth pitched in $2, the seventh paid $5, the eighth paid $9, the ninth paid $12, leaving the tenth man with a bill of $52 instead of his earlier $59. Each of the six was better off than before. And the first four continued to eat for free.

But once outside the restaurant, the men began to compare their savings. "I only got a dollar out of the $20," declared the sixth man who pointed to the tenth. "But he got $7!"

"Yeah, that's right," exclaimed the fifth man, "I only saved a dollar, too . . . It's unfair that he got seven times more than me!".

"That's true!" shouted the seventh man, "Why should he get $7 back when I got only $2? The wealthy get all the breaks!"

"Wait a minute," yelled the first four men in unison, "We didn't get anything at all. The system exploits the poor!"

The nine men surrounded the tenth and beat him up. The next night he didn't show up for dinner, so the nine sat down and ate without him. But when it came time to pay the bill, they discovered, a little late what was very important. They were fifty-two dollars short of paying the bill! Imagine that!

And that, boys and girls, journalists and college instructors, is how the tax system works. The people who pay the highest taxes get the most benefit from a tax reduction. Tax them too much, attack them for being wealthy, and they just may not show up at the table anymore.

Where would that leave the rest?

Unfortunately, most taxing authorities anywhere cannot seem to grasp this rather straightforward logic!

Did You Know? *Albert Haddock, an englishman in the 19th century got mad at the local tax collector over his bill and conceived a most ingenious idea for getting even. In payment of income tax, he made out a cheque on a cow and led it to the office of the Collector of Taxes.*

"I am a jelly doughnut."

We all love the pithy quote, the clever put-down, the scintillating turn of phrase. We store them away in our mental jewelry box, waiting for just the right occasion to decorate a conversation with their sparkle. What we often don't realise is that many of these glittering linguistic gems are not the real thing, but mere costume jewelry.

Arrange The Meeting

In a recent interview, General Norman Schwartzkopf was asked if he though there was room for forgiveness toward the people who had harbored and abetted the terrorists who perpetrated the 9/11 attacks on America.

In classic Schwartzkopt fashion his answer was simply, "I believe that forgiving them is God's function. Our job is simply to arrange the meeting."

Bush and John 3:16

The Lord has a way of revealing those of us who really know him, and those that don't!!!

Recently President Bush gave a big speech last week about how his faith is so "important" to him. In this attempt to convince the American people that we should consider him for president, he announced that his favorite Bible verse is John 16:3.

Of course the speech writer meant John 3:16, but nobody in the Bush camp was familiar enough with scripture to catch the error. And do you know what John 16:3 says?

John 16:3 says; *"And they will do this because they have not known the Father nor Me".*

The Holy Spirit works in strange ways. Pass it on.

Did You Know? *In the Atlanta Journal-Constitution's "The Vent," a number of well-respected Surgeons were quoted saying politicians are the easiest people in the world to operate on. They have no guts, no heart, no spine, and their heads and rear ends are interchangeable.*

Dying Wish

Madeline B. Ashbula, 88, passed away on February 23, 2004, under the loving care of the nursing aides of Heritage Manor of Atlanta, Georgia. She was a native of Lexington, Kentucky. She was a retired Vice President of the International Life Insurance Company of Atlanta, Georgia. Her husband, William M. Ashbula predeceased her. She is survived by her two daughters, Alisha DoWors and her live-in boyfriend, Richard, of Atlantic City, New

Jersey, and Marlena Kovaks and her husband, Stacey Kovaks, of Lexington, Kentucky. Three sisters, three grandchildren and two great grandchildren, also survive her. Funeral services were held in Atlanta, Georgia.

Memorial gifts may be made to any organization that seeks the removal of President George W. Bush from office.

Did You Know? *John F. Kennedy made a major German language blunder in his famous "Ich bin ein Berliner" speech in Berlin, Germany. What he should have said was, "Ich bin Berliner", meaning "I am a citizen of Berlin!" What JFK said was, "Ich bin ein Berliner!" which really means "I am a jelly doughnut." A "Berliner" is in fact a type of jelly doughnut made in Berlin.*

"How much do you charge for mowing a lawn, my good man?"

Thurgood Marshall, the first Black member of the Supreme Court, was mowing the lawn at his posh residence in a Washington suburb when a car stopped in the street.

The woman driving the car noted a Black man mowing a lawn and called out, "How much do you charge for mowing a lawn, my good man?"

Marshall hesitated, and the woman said, "Well, what does the lady of the house pay you?"

And Marshall said, "She doesn't pay me anything, ma'am. She just lets me sleep with her every night."

"I Hope Your All Republicans."

Ronald Reagan was awake and alert when he was wheeled into the emergency room at George Washington University Hospital after an assassination attempt.

However, A couple of days after the assassination attempt, a head nurse in the George Washington University Emergency Room claimed that Reagan was not at all that awake and alert.

When they wheeled the president in, he looked up at the doctors and nurses and said, "I hope you're all Republicans".

Did You Know? *When Lyndon Johnson was running for congress he was quoted calling his opponent a "pig fucker." Lyndon's campaign manager said, "Lyndon, you know he doesn't do that!" Johnson replied, "I know that, but I want to make him deny it."*

"Hold on! You're not going to fire any cattle guards until you give them six months' retraining!"

Some of us foolishly expect that those folks in the political world have our best interest at heart, and always know what they're doing. Not always!

"All Wet"

On February 10, 2004, Defense Secretary Donald Rumsfeld told Senator Edward M. Kennedy that he was "all wet" when the Senator alleged that the Bush administration lied about Iraq's weapons of mass destruction to justify going to war.

The verbal clash came during Mr. Rumsfeld's testimony at a Senate Armed Services Committee hearing probing the state of pre-war intelligence.

Senator Kennedy began his questioning of the Defense Secretary by saying, "Don't you think some members of the Bush administration should be held legally accountable for the lies they told about Iraqi weapons, and the subsequent cover-up?"

"First, with all due respect Senator Kennedy, you're all wet," commented Mr. Rumsfeld. "The administration has not lied or covered up. However, in general, I do believe that when a man commits a crime he should face the bar of justice. He should not be allowed to serve in positions of power in our government, and be hailed as a leader, when the question of his guilt remains unresolved, if you know what I mean."

Did You Know? *When Stevie Wonder sat down at the keyboard center stage for "Dubya's" inauguration, President Bush, who was sitting in the front row got very excited, and started to smile and wave at the music icon. Mr. Bush was insulted when Mr. Wonder did not respond.*

A number of amazing coincidences can be found between the assassinations of Abraham Lincoln and John F. Kennedy.

Abraham Lincoln was elected to Congress in 1846.

John F. Kennedy was elected to Congress in 1946.

Abraham Lincoln was elected President in 1860.

John F. Kennedy was elected President in 1960.

The names Lincoln and Kennedy each contain seven letters.

Both were particularly concerned with civil rights.

Both wives lost their children while living in the White House.

Both Presidents were shot on a Friday. Both were shot in the head.

Lincoln's secretary, Kennedy, warned him not to go to the theatre.

Kennedy's secretary, Lincoln, warned him not to go to Dallas.

Both were assassinated by Southerners.

Both were succeeded by Southerners.

Both successors were named Johnson.

Andrew Johnson, who succeeded Lincoln, was born in 1808.

Lyndon Johnson, who succeeded Kennedy, was born in 1908.

John Wilkes Booth was born in 1839. Lee Harvey Oswald was born in 1939.

Both assassins were known by their three names.

Both names are comprised of fifteen letters

Booth ran from the theater and was caught in a warehouse.

Oswald ran from a warehouse and was caught in a theater.

Booth and Oswald were assassinated before their trials.

In The Nixon Of Time

Richard Nixon's San Clemente retreat is located on the beautiful coastline of southern California. It was his sanctuary — very private, very secure. The usually withdrawn former president would relax there, indulging in the ordinary pleasures non-presidents take for granted. Often in the evenings he'd go for a swim in the ocean alone, preferring the setting sun as his only company to anything that might remind him of past days, both triumphant and bitter. However, this habit of solitude was almost his undoing.

On one occasion he was caught unaware by a big swell and was losing the battle to keep from going under, when two surfers who'd been trespassing on his property came to his rescue. The sputtering man was pulled from the waves by the two brave surfers. Once safely recovered on shore, Nixon promised to grant each of them anything within his power to give as his way of showing gratitude.

The one lad asked that the beach be opened to the public so that all could enjoy it.

"Granted," said Nixon.

The other boy made a seemingly strange request: upon his death, he wanted to be buried in Arlington National Cemetery.

Puzzled, the former President agreed to see to this. "But why?" he asked. "Why that of all things?"

The lad lowered his head in shame. "Because when my father finds out I saved Richard Nixon, he's gonna kill me."

Moral Turpitude

The current U.S. Congress includes several dozen members who have committed various crimes and other acts of moral turpitude;

29 members of Congress have been accused of spousal abuse.

7 have been arrested for fraud.

19 have been accused of writing bad checks.

117 have bankrupted at least two businesses.

3 have been arrested for assault.

71 have credit reports so bad they can't qualify for a credit card.

14 have been arrested on drug-related charges.

8 have been arrested for shoplifting.

21 are current defendants in lawsuits.

And in 1998 alone, 84 were stopped for drunk driving, but released after they claimed Congressional immunity.

These are the People who make Laws that we must obey? Your tax dollars at work!

Tackling Crime

A US congressman was interviewed live on the television news. The central aspect of the interview focused around the success the government had been in tackling crime. He was especially proud of the fact that violent street robberies were at an all-time low. On leaving the television station, the congressman went to his car parked outside. Suddenly, a man jumped out of the shadows and held him at gunpoint. The congressman lost his wallet, his watch and his car, but best of all, the thief also stole his clothes. The humiliated congressman had to go back inside the television station completely naked, only to be spotted by the reporter who had just interviewed him. Five minutes later, the congressman gave a somewhat less confident interview.

Did You Know? *When you rearrange the letters in, PRESIDENT CLINTON OF THE USA, with no letters left over and using each letter only once it can spell out: HE FINDS INTERNS TO COPULATE.*

These People Are Running The Country

For those who have never traveled to the great West, cattle guards are horizontal steel rails placed at fence openings on highways to prevent cattle from crossing. For some reason the bovines will not step on the guards, probably because they fear getting their feet caught between the rails. We need to make that clear in order for everyone to appreciate the following true story.

President Clinton, angry at Colorado's response to the grazing-fee increase, decided to strike back.

After a bit of study, he called in Bruce Babbitt and said, "There are 100,000 cattle guards in Colorado. That's way too many. Fire half of them."

Babbitt did as he was told. But before he could carry out the order, Pat Schroeder called Clinton.

"Hold on!", she said. "You're not going to fire any cattle guards until you give them six months' retraining!"

The Big Smoke

In England, "National No Smoking Day" can provide people with an excuse to act in outrageous ways, such as, dousing anyone caught smoking with a bucket of cold water.

In Argentina, things have been known to become even more extreme. A masked man calling himself "The Big Smoke" chose "No Smoking Day" to terrorise smokers in Buenos Aires by forcing anyone he catches smoking, at gunpoint, to eat the entire pack of cigarettes. As each victim chews and gags on a mouthful of tobacco, "The Big Smoke" takes the opportunity to preach about the hazards of smoking, and the dangers of passive smoking. Although some victims say they would give up smoking, most appear to be desperate for a smoke after their ordeal. Government officials have consistently denied rumours that "The Big Smoke" is employed by them.

Did You Know? *If you go to Google.com and type in the phrase, "miserable failure" (excluding the quotes) then hit the "I'm Feeling Lucky" button, it will bring up the website of President George W. Bush.*

What's The Chicken Scoup?

One day, President Coolidge and the first lady were visiting a government farm. Soon after their arrival they were taken off on separate tours. When Mrs. Coolidge passed the chicken pens she paused to ask the man in charge if the rooster copulates more than once each day.

"Dozens of times," was the reply. "Please tell that to the President," Mrs. Coolidge requested.

When the President passed the pens and was told about the roosters, he asked, "Same hen every time?"

"Oh no, Mr. President,", said the farmer, "A different one each time."

The President nodded slowly, then said, "Tell that to Mrs. Coolidge."

"Lincoln, Navy One, 12,500 lbs, I have the balls!"

Myths are important symbols of cultural unity, and perhaps no myths are more important in the modern era than the military myths that establish our national heritage and tell us where we came from as well as who we are.

War is perilous, and opportunities for calamity abound, leaves the military an open target for folklore.

A Whale Of An Enemy

Despite the big advance in technology in recent decades, laughable mistakes can still be made.

For several months, the Swedish Navy had been convinced that foreign submarines were operating in Swedish waters. Despite a strongly worded speech by the Foreign Minister at a United Nations Conference, no government would admit to using submarines in Swedish territorial seas. Incensed, the Vice Admiral decided enough was enough and launched a massive naval operation to uncover the offenders. After weeks of extensive searching filled with long days spent tracking sound waves around the Baltic Sea, it was concluded that the culprits were not submarines, but a school of whales that had taken a liking to the area. Even so, the Vice Admiral is still convinced that foreign vessels had been violating Swedish waters.

Divert Your Course

A transcript from a radio conversation between a US naval ship and Canadian authorites off the coast of Newfoundland was released by the Chief of Naval Operations on October 10, 1995.

Americans: "Please divert your course 15 degrees to the North to avoid a collision."

Canadians: "Recommend you divert your course 15 degrees to the South to avoid a collision."

Americans: "This is the captain of a US Navy ship. I say again, divert your course."

Canadians: "No, I say again, you divert your course."

Americans: "This is the aircraft carrier USS Abraham Lincoln, the second largest ship in the United States' Atlantic Fleet." We are accompanied by three destroyers, three cruisers and numerous support vessels. I demand that you change your course 15 degrees north. That's one-five degrees north, or counter measures will be undertaken to ensure the safety of this ship."

Canadians: "This is a lighthouse. Your call."

Help Wanted

The CIA had an opening for an assassin. After all the background checks, interviews, and testing were done, there were three finalists, two men and a woman.

For the final test, the CIA agents took one of the men to a large metal door and handed him a gun.

"We must know that you will follow your instructions, no matter what the circumstances", explained the agent, "Inside this room, you will find your wife sitting in a chair. Kill her!"

The man replied, "You can't be serious. I could never shoot my wife."

The agent said, "Then you're not the right man for this job. Take your wife and go home."

The second man was given the same instructions. He took the gun and went into the room. All was quiet for about five minutes. Then the man came out with tears in his eyes. "I tried, but I can't kill my wife."

The agent said, "You don't have what it takes. Take your wife and go home."

Finally, it was the woman's turn. She was given instructions to kill her husband. She took the gun and went into the room. Shots were heard, one shot after another. They heard screaming, crashing, banging on the walls. After a few minutes, all was quiet. The door opened slowly and there stood the woman. She wiped the sweat from her row.

"This gun is loaded with blanks," she said. "I had to beat him to death with the chair."

"If we have so many dead, how many can there be of the enemy?"

During the late medieval years in Hungary, the city of Paks was just a little village, which today is a small city boasting Hungary's single nuclear plant. In the past, the village had trouble with a neighboring village. They kept sending their cows to graze on Paks land, and vice-versa.

One day a foreigner attacked the Paks herdsman, beat him badly, and confiscated his cows. But this was not just any herdsman, it was the son of the mayor. The people of Paks took up arms - or rather, work tools they could wield as arms. The result was a small battle between the two villages, in which dozen of peasants bit the dust.

The brave Paks army retreated in defeat.

The mayor of Paks, undaunted, ordered his men to fabricate a cannon to blast the enemy to smithereens. It was easier to order it than to do so, as they did not have the necessary tools and materials to build a cannon.

"No matter," said the wise mayor, "Chop a tree down, and create the cannon from its trunk!"

During the night the people of Paks created the first wooden cannon in history, ready for deployment. They towed it up a nearby hill, and the entire village gathered around to watch the victory.

The Gunmaster loaded the cannon with gunpowder, put a large rock projectile in the barrel, pointed the weapon towards the enemy village and fired it.

Twenty people near the cannon died, and many others were seriously wounded.

However the mayor survived, and immediately issued a victory message for his people, saying, "If we have so many dead, how many can there be of the enemy?"

"Lincoln, Navy One, 12,500 lbs, I have the balls!"

One of my co-workers old Navy buddies stationed on the carrier Abraham Lincoln explained briefly the procedure of a plane approaching a carrier for landing.

The pilot is asked by the air controller to "call the ball". In naval aviation lingo "call the ball" is a visual aid used on carriers to let pilots know if they are on the proper glide slope to land on the deck. The part that moves up and down depending on how you're doing on the glide slope looks like a ball or "meat ball". The fact that you have a visual on the approach aid dictates a call to the roller on the ship.

He was on the Abraham Lincoln when President George W. Bush made an approach to the aircraft carrier. The standard response from the pilot of the plane carrying the President should have been "Lincoln, Navy One, 12,500 lbs, Roger Ball", which means, I have the ball in sight and I am on glide path. For a safe landing, the weight is given for setting the correct braking tension of the arresting gear cables.

Instead, "Navy One" while on final approach for trap aboard CVN Abraham Lincoln, the President made the radio call, "Lincoln, Navy One, 12,500 lbs, I have the balls!"

His call brought down the house on the carrier. No wonder the military appreciates and likes the man!

Non-traditional Means

A despondent trainee soldier facing disciplinary action decided to take his life.

However, instead of using a rifle on the range or a more traditional means, the soldier tied an electrical cord of a floor buffer around his neck, then threw it out the second story window. Unfortunately, the hapless soldier did not meet his maker, instead, he met the CO and Army Psychiatrists when the buffer shattered into pieces on the ground below because the cord was about a story too long. The soldier was discharged and had to pay for the buffer.

Did You Know? *France is demanding that all American soldiers buried over there be dug up and removed from their land. You know, the ones that died in World War II freeing that country? It was in all the news — "They want our dead out of their country." Worst of all, they sent a note to the government saying, "Come and pick up your trash."*

Perfect Escorts

President Lyndon B. Johnson had a reputation for calling on military agencies and demanding special services for his family. He once called the Marine Basic School in Quantico, Virginia informing them that he was hosting a formal get-together at the White House, and he requested the presence of two tall and good-looking Lieutenants to serve as escorts for his daughters, and they need to be there at six o'clock sharp.

As you know LBJ was a southerner and a Texan so he made it very clear that the escorts were not Mexican. The next night, at six o'clock, Mrs. Johnson answered the knock at the door, and sure enough, there were two tall, good-looking Marine Lieutenants standing at attention.

"We're here to escort your daughters, ma'am," said one Lieutenant.

"But you're both black," replied the first lady. "There must be some mistake."

"No, ma'am," the other Lieutenant spoke up, "Captain Rodriguez never makes mistakes."

Riverboat Whoopin'

In the past few years the scourge of the casino riverboat has been an increasingly significant presence on the Ohio River. The Ohio River borders the Commonwealth of Kentucky; and the siren song of payola issuing from the discordant calliopes of these gambling vessels has led thousands of Kentucky citizens to vast disappointment and woe. No good can come to the citizens of Kentucky hypnotized from the siren song issuing from these casino riverboats, the engines of which are fired by the hard-earned dollars lost from Kentucky citizens.

Therefore, a resolution by the House of Representatives of the General Assembly of the Commonwealth of Kentucky is encouraging the purchase and vigorous use of the USS Louisville 688 VLS Class submarine.

This encourages the formation of the Kentucky Navy and subsequently immediately encourages the purchase and armament of one particularly effective submarine, namely, the USS Louisville 688 VLS Class Submarine, to patrol the portion of the Ohio River under the jurisdiction of the Commonwealth to engage and destroy any casino riverboats that the submarine may encounter.

Notification will be given to the casino riverboat consulate of this impending whoopin' so that they may remove their casino vessels to friendlier waters.

Toy Soldiers

The M-16, a rapid-fire, 5.56 mm assault rifle carried by thousands of American soldiers during the Vietnam War, grew out of efforts to develop a replacement for the standard M-1 Carbine used during World War II.

The M-16 was constructed using plastics and alloys, a much smaller and lighter weapon than its predecessors, one that fit in with the developing Vietnam-era strategy of sacrificing accuracy in favor of more easily-carried weapons with rapid rates of fire and high muzzle velocities (i.e., "spray" fire).

Hundreds of thousands of M-16s were supplied to US troops in the mid-1960s as US Army made the M-16 their standard rifle.

After the gun was introduced in Veitnam, soldiers noticed a familiar company logo embossed on the handgrip, and started complaining. Later shipments arrived without the imprint "Made by Mattel", but the grips were still manufactured by the company.

Did You Know? *The sexual prowess of soldiers always diminished after returning home from the war, because the miltary put saltpeter (potassium nitrate) into the tea/coffee', and eggs of soldiers to reduce randiness while in combat. The military did not want a certain "joint" to get stiff when it wasn't supposed to. If you are a soldier, you should spot saltpeter right away. It gives the eggs a greenish tint, almost camoflauge like.*

Wooden Decoy

A German "airfield" built in occupied Holland was constructed with meticulous care, and made almost entirely of wood. There were wooden hangers, oil tanks, gun emplacements, trucks, and aircrafts.

The Germans took so long in building their wooden decoy that Allied photo experts had more than enough time to observe and report it. The day finally came when the decoy was finished, down to the last wooden plank. Then early the following morning a lone RAF plane crossed the Channel, came in low, circled the field once, and dropped a large wooden bomb.

Osama Bin Laden has underdeveloped genitals.

A 1654 Nostradamus prediction said World War III would begin with the fall of "two brothers," a reference to the destroyed World Trade Center towers.

"In the City of God there will be a great thunder. Two brothers torn apart by Chaos. While the fortress endures, the great leader will succumb. The third big war will begin when the big city is burning."

--Nostradamus 1654

Here is a humorous collection of various rumors to come out after the September 11 terrorist attack on the United States of America.

Cave-Life Is Good

The Military found a memo on a dead Iraqi soldier that had been written by Osama Bin Laden addressing his "cavemates" regarding "cave-life".

Hi guys. We've all been putting in long hours but we've really come together as a group and I love that. Big shout out to Omar for putting up the poster that says, "There is no I in team" as well as the one that says "Hang In There, Baby." That cat is hilarious. However, while we are fighting a jihad, we can't forget to take care of the cave. And frankly I have a few concerns.

First of all, while it's good to be concerned about cruise missiles, we should be even more concerned about the scorpions in the cave. Hey, you don't want to be stung and neither do I, so we need to sweep the cave daily. I've posted a sign-up sheet near the main cave opening.

Second, it's not often I make a video address, but when I do, I'm trying to scare the most powerful country on earth, okay? That means that while we're taping, please do not ride your razor scooter in the background. Just while we're taping. Thanks.

Third point, and this is a touchy one. As you know, by edict, we're not supposed to shave our beards. But I need everyone to just think hygiene, especially after mealtime. We're all in this together.

Fourth, the food situation; I bought a box of junior mints recently, and clearly wrote "Osama" on the front, and put it on the top shelf. Today, my junior mints were gone. Consideration. That's all I'm saying.

Finally, we've heard that there may be American soldiers in disguise trying to infiltrate our ranks. I want to set up patrols to look for them. First patrol will be Omar, Muhammed, Abdul, Akbar, and Richard Smith.

The memo was signed, Death to all infidels, Love Osama!

Department of Homeland Security Alert

Department of Homeland Security has just been notified that there have been 6 suspected terrorists working out of your office. Five of the six have been apprehended: Bin Sleepin, Bin Loafin, Bin Goofin, Bin Lunchin and Bin Drinkin have been taken into custody.

Agents are advising that they could not find the terrorist fitting the description of the sixth cell member, Bin

Workin. Security is confident that anyone who looks like he's Bin Workin will be very easy to spot.

You are obviously not a suspect at this time.

"Private" Security

The advice given to Americans to stock up on duct tape and plastic has sparked a lawsuit which has been filed against Tom Ridge, the Department of Homeland Security and President George W. Bush.

Cameron Sobey, the owner of Sobey Construction in Burbank, California, has filed a lawsuit claiming emotional distress, personal injury and sexual disfunction after he wrapped his "privates" in duct tape to protect them from a biological attack.

"After watching Mr. Ridge on television advising us to stock up on duct tape and plastic, I went to the local Wal-Mart and bought $100 worth of duct tape to protect myself", Sobey said. "When I got home, I taped up my windows and doors. After I did that I realised if survivors like myself are going to reproduce and populate the Earth after a biological attack, we have to protect our privates as well."

Sobey claimed in his lawsuit that he wrapped his "privates" in duct tape as test of Homeland Security. When he tried to remove the tape, Sobey injured himself when the tape began peeling off skin and body hair. After calling an ambulance, Sobey was taken to the hospital where the doctors and nurses laughed at him.

"I told the doctors and nurses at the hospital if they laughed, I would file a lawsuit against them and the hospital. They laughed anyways and now I have another lawsuit pending" Sobey said with tears streaming down his face. "They went out their way to make me look like a fool. Once I saw the doctors scalpel go toward my privates, I totally lost it and blacked out".

Also named in the lawsuit is the President of the United States, George W. Bush.

"President Bush is just as liable for injury to my reproductive future because he hired Mr. Ridge to run the Department of Homeland Security and Mr. Ridge gave the nation bad advice. They also made me look like a fool." Sobey sobbed.

Did You Know? *Osama Bin Laden has underdeveloped genitals because of a medical accident that happened to him as a baby. Supposedly, while he was going to school in Chicago, he started dating an American girl who laughed at him before they had sex and ever since then, he has become bitter toward Americans.*

7/11

Everyone knows that terrorists are around and obviously planning something big. What the FBI and CIA won't tell people is that there is a major conspiracy afoot which could affect all people in the USA.

Everyone is familair with the 7-Eleven convenience store chain. They are on every corner, in every city and small town in North America. Anyone who has shopped in a 7-Eleven knows that they are owned predominantly by people of middle-eastern origin; in fact, the parent company of the franchise, 7-Eleven Limited Partnership is owned by a group with ties to Osama bin Laden.

The year is undetemrined, but the day, July 11th (7/11), every single 7-Eleven store has been instructed to unleash attacks on their surrounding neighborhoods. This includes, toilet papering peoples homes, throwing eggs at windows, placing shit in brown paper bags on doorsteps, blowing up the stores themselves, and possibly using 'dirty' nuclear bombs as well as conventional explosives as an outright assault on the American people. This will cause a major disruption in all major American cities. So keep your eyes open if you live near a 7-Eleven.

Sometimes you have to stand up for what you believe you're not sure about.

People always ask me why I don't vote. I simply respond, "No matter who I vote for, a politican always wins."

You know those shows where people call in and vote on different issues? Did you ever notice there's always like 20% "I don't know". It costs 90 cents to call up and vote, and they're voting "I don't know."

A man says to his wife, "Honey, I feel very strongly about this issue. Give me the phone." Then says into the phone, "I don't know!" Hangs up, and looks proud.

Sometimes you have to stand up for what you believe you're not sure about.

I am dedicating the following tales to the "I don't know voters"; the ones that call up phone sex girls for $3.00 a minute and say, "I'm not in the mood."

Our Little Monica Is All Grown Up

On her 30th birthday Monica was interviewed on CNN's Larry King Live. It seems like only yesterday she was crawling around the White House on her hands and knees.

The central aspect of the discussion focused around the upcoming presidential election. Monica told Larry she will be voting Republican this year because the democrats left a bad taste in her mouth.

The interview quickly changed to her miraculous Jenny Craig weight-loss. When Larry asked her how she lost the weight, Monica simply replied, "I've learned not to put things in my mouth that are bad for me."

Presidential Election Announcement

Due to an anticipated voter turnout much larger than originally expected, the polling facilities may not be able to handle the load all at once.

Therefore, Republicans and Independents are requested to vote on Tuesday, November 7.

The Democrats will vote on Wednesday, November 8.

This is minor change is to make sure that nobody gets left out and everything will run smoothly.

Did You Know? *A bridegroom in Dharol village in India, Himachal Pradesh walked out in the middle of his wedding to vote. One ritual done with, he returned and completed the other. As one wag put it, the diligent groom may not have wanted to waste his last chance to make a choice of his own.*

Patron Saint Of Disputed Elections

Prior to the farce that was the U.S. Presidential election of 2000, very few knew what the little bits of paper punched from a ballot were called, and no one much cared.

The situation surrounding the balloting in Florida changed all that, overnight. The electorate found itself in a world where talk of 'chads' was all the rage, with the significance of dimpled, hanging, and pregnant ones hotly disputed.

An unfamiliar word no one had much noticed was now on everyone's lips. 'Chad' was fast on its way to becoming the word of the year.

The media quickly picked up the slack with a history of its etymology when ordinary dictionaries failed to provide much illumination.

Somewhere in the furor, someone noticed there had once been a Catholic saint of the same name, and a hasty perusal of the details of his life appeared to link him to a disputed election, which kicked in the irony afterburners. It didn't take long for statements of, "St. Chad is the patron saint of disputed elections."

Right To Vote

It is the 21st Century, and in this century 2007 is a significant year to Black America.

Did you know that their right to vote will expire in the year 2007?

Seriously! The Voters Rights Act signed in 1965 by Lyndon B. Johnson was just an ACT. It was not made a law.

In 1982 Ronald Reagan amended the Voters Rights Act for only another 25 years. Which means that in the year 2007 they could lose the right to vote!

Does anyone realise that African Americans are the only group of people who still require permission under the United States Constitution to vote?!

In the year 2007 Congress will once again convene to decide whether or not Blacks should retain the right to vote. In order for this to be passed, 38 states will have to approve an extension.

Not only should the extension be approved, but this Act must be made a law. Their right to vote should no longer be up for discussion, review or evaluation.

Who..bert Humphrey?

Back when Hubert Humphrey was active in politics, he and his campaign manager took a few days for a fishing trip in Minnesota.

While they were in a small town, a bus-load of tourists pulled in. The manager suggested that this was a good opportunity to impress a few voters and that he should go on the bus, "pump them up" a bit, and shake everybody's hand. This sounded good so the manager got on the bus. However instead of introducing his candidate, he pretended to be the mayor welcoming everybody to town.

Then looking towards Humphrey he said, "I guess I should mention that we have a guy here who thinks he's Hubert Humphrey, and he does look and talk an awful lot like Hubert Humphrey. But he's a harmless fellow and we kind of like him, so we'd appreciate it if you would just kind of be nice to him."

After Humphrey shook their hands he commented on how strangely they acted.

The only thing French's mustard has in common with France is that they are both yellow.

I dedicate the following tales to the people who's anti-war slogan is "No War For Oil." It might be time to drop the signs and sue your school district for allowing you to slip through the cracks and robbing you of the education you deserve.

Did You Know? *As you may have seen on the news, earlier this year there was an anti-Bush protest in Portland, Oregon that got violent. As the police beat and arrested the protesters, people yelled, "Bad cop! No donut!"*

"Dick Tator"

Back on April 23, 2002 in Kuwait City 2003, Iraqi dictator Saddam Hussein was caught with his pants down -- literally. A shocking 1968 porn film surfaced, exposing the flamboyant strongman performing raunchy homosexual acts!

The image quality of the grainy 16mm film, uncovered by the Kuwaiti secret police, was poor -- but experts who've taken a close look at the hairy-chested actor are "100 percent certain" it is a younger, trimmer Saddam.

"There is no doubt in my mind that this is Saddam -- there's no mistaking those eyes and that distinctive nose," declared Hussein biographer Sadiq al-Sabah, who's seen the eye-popping footage first-hand.

It may be hard to believe that a man who now leads one of the most powerful nations in the Middle East once acted in porn movies, but to anyone familiar with how reckless and sexually promiscuous

Saddam was in his youth, this will come as no surprise. It's also a known fact that the young, desperate soldier did anything for money.

"Saddam has appeared in more than 85 of these films under a variety of stage names, most frequently "Dick Tator", revealed the researcher.

Did You Know? *The President has asked that we unite for a common cause. Since the hard line Islamic people cannot stand nudity, and consider it a sin to see a naked woman that is not their wife, all women should run out of their house naked to help weed out the terrorists.*

Massa-shoot-us!

The Massachusetts quarter is one of the coins honoring the state's admision into the union. The depiction represents the minutemen who fired the first shots of the revolutionary war and has been used by the State of Massachusetts as a state symbol.

Recently, President Bush signed an executive order forcing the treasury department to recall all 25 million commemorative quarters and issue ones more appropriate to the history of Massachusetts, after Senator Charles Schumer suffered personal humiliation and was injured as a result of the release of the Massachusetts commemorative quarter.

Senator Schumer was elevated to the Senate from the House of Representatives chiefly because of his unyielding stance for reasonable gun control legislation. Senator Schumer was drinking in an upscale Georgetown watering hole with Senator of Massachusetts, Ted Kennedy.

According to police reports, Senator Kennedy was idly flipping a quarter, which just happened to be the newest release. The quarter landed unnoticed in Senator Schumer's glass.

As Senator Schumer lifted the glass to take a sip, he spied in the bottom, an image of a man with a gun. The Senator was so frightened by this he dropped the glass and dove under the table. Senator Kennedy seeing this, and believing Senator Schumer had a waitress down there, dove on top of him causing minor injuries.

Nothing In Common

The makers of French's Mustard made a recent statement claiming, "We at the French's Company wish to put an end to statements that our product is manufactured in France. There is no relationship, nor has there ever been a relationship, between our mustard and the country of France. Our mustard is manufactured in Rochester, New York. The only thing we have in common with France is that we are both yellow".

Did You Know? *It was reported on February 12, 2004 that severe earthquakes have occurred in 10 different locations in France. The severity was measured in excess of 10 on the Richter Scale. The cause was 56,681 American soldiers buried in French soil who died in their youth to liberate a country which is guilty of shameful unspeakable behavior in the 21st century, rolling over in their graves.*

The advances of women achieving equality throughout the world ...

Several years before the Gulf War, Barbara Walters did a story on gender roles in Kuwait. She noted then that women customarily walked about 10 feet behind their husbands. However, when she recently returned to Kuwait she observed that the men now walked several yards behind their wives.

Ms. Walters approached one of the women and said, "This is extraordinary. Can you tell the free world just what enabled women here to achieve this reversal of roles?"

"Landmines," said the Kuwaiti woman.

Did You Know? *Even if you are anti-war, you are still an "infidel" and bin Laden wants you dead, too.*

The Perfect Plan For Peace

Here's the plan:

1) The US will apologize to the world for our "interference" in their affairs, past &present. You know, Hitler, Mussolini and the rest of them 'good old boys'. We will never "interfere" again.

2) We will withdraw our troops from all over the world, starting with Germany, South Korea and the Philippines. They don't want us there. We would station troops at our borders. No more sneaking through holes in the fence.

3) All illegal aliens have 90 days to get their affairs together and leave. We'll give them a free trip home. After 90 days the remainder will be gathered up and deported immediately, regardless of who or where they are. France would welcome them.

4) All future visitors will be thoroughly checked and limited to 90 days unless given a special permit. No one from a terrorist nation would be allowed in. If you don't like it there, change it yourself, don't hide here. Asylum would not ever be available to anyone. We don't need any more cab drivers.

5) No "students" over age 21. The older ones are the bombers. If they don't attend classes, they get a "D" and it's back home baby.

6) The US will make a strong effort to become self sufficient energy wise. This will include developing non-polluting sources of energy but will require a temporary drilling of oil in the Alaskan wilderness. The caribou will have to cope for a while.

7) Offer Saudi Arabia and other oil producing countries $10 a barrel for their oil. If they don't like it, we go someplace else.

8) If there is a famine or other natural catastrophe in the world, we will not "interfere". They can pray to Allah or whomever, for seeds, rain, cement or whatever they need. Besides most of what we give them is stolen or given to the army. The people who need it most get very little, if any anyway.

9) Ship the UN Headquarters to an island some place. We don't need the spies and fair weather friends here. Besides, it would make a good homeless shelter or lockup for illegal aliens.

10) All Americans must go to charm and beauty school. That way, no one can call us "Ugly Americans" any longer.

11) The Statue of Liberty is no longer going to say, "Give me your poor, your tired, your huddled masses." Instead, she's going to have a baseball bat and she's yelling, "You want a piece of me?"

Now, ain't that a winner of a plan ??

"The problem with the French is that they don't have a word for entrepreneur."

As a politician, part of your job is to maintain a strong relationship with a variety of cultures from all over the globe, so it's no surprise that tales about foreign affairs find a ready audience.

"Axis of Just as Evil"

Bitter after being snubbed for membership in the "Axis of Evil," Libya, China, and Syria announced earlier this month they had formed the "Axis of Just as Evil," which they said will be way more evil than that stupid Iran-Iraq-North Korea axis, that President Bush warned of in his State of the Union address.

However, Axis of Evil members immediately dismissed the new axis as having, for starters, a really dumb name.

"Right. They are Just as Evil, in their dreams!" declared North Korean leader Kim Jong-il. "Everybody knows we're the best evils, best at being evil. We're just the best."

Diplomats from Syria denied rumors that they were jealous over being excluded, although they conceded they did ask if they could join the Axis of Evil, but Syrian President Bashar al-Assad was told it was full.

"Axis of Weasels."

U.S. Secretary Defense Donald Rumsfeld apologized for referring to France and Germany as an "Axis of Weasels."

The Defense Secretary said he was out of bounds with the comments.

"I'm sorry about that Axis of Weasels remark," said Rumsfeld. "I didn't mean to dredge up the history France and Germany share of pathetic compliance with ruthless dictators."

"I should have known better than to remind people that these two nations, which live in freedom thanks only to the righteous might of America, Britain and their allies, that these nations are morally and politically bankrupt, and have failed to learn the lessons of history," he said. "The Axis of Weasels was an inappropriate thing to say. I really should not have called them the Axis of Weasels. I think it's the 'Weasels' part that was most offensive, and when I said that France and Germany formed an Axis of Weasels. Of course, I'm very sorry."

Did You Know? *In the British press in July 2002, President Bush, Britain's Prime Minister Tony Blair, and France's President Jacques Chirac were discussing economics, and in particular, the decline of the French economy. "The problem with the French," Bush afterwards confided in Blair, "is that they don't have a word for entrepreneur."*

"Neil"

The British are wizards of pomp and ceremony. Even innocent bystanders and spectators sometimes feel themselves involuntarily caught up in and reacting to the drama of the moment, though they may know little or nothing of the ritual itself. Parliament's equivalent of the U.S. Speaker of the House is called the "Keeper of the Woolsack," who wears resplendent gold-and-scarlet robes topped with a ceremonial wig. At one time the office was held by a Sir Quentin Hogg, Lord Hailsham.

After Parliament adjourned, Lord Hailsham strode into the corridor, passed an American tour group, when he spotted an old friend, the Honorable Neil Marten, an MP with whom he wished to speak.

"Neil," Lord Hailsham called out.

Then followed by an embarrassing silence, all the tourists obediently fell to their knees.

"Royal Flatulence"

At Heathrow Airport in England, a 300-foot red carpet was stretched out to Air Force One and President Bush strode to a warm but dignified handshake from Queen Elizabeth II. They rode in a silver 1934 Bentley to the edge of central London where they boarded an open 17th century coach hitched to six magnificent white horses.

As they rode toward Buckingham Palace, each looking to their side and waving to

the thousands of cheering Brits lining the streets, all was going well, and was a glorious display of pageantry and dignity. Suddenly the scene was shattered when the right rear horse let rip the most horrendous, earth-shattering, eye-smarting blast of flatulence, and the coach immediately filled with noxious fumes.

Uncomfortable, but maintaining control, the two dignitaries did their best to ignore the whole incident, but the Queen decided that was a ridiculous manner with which to handle a most embarrassing situation.

So she turned to President Bush and explained, "Mr. President, please accept my regrets. I'm sure you understand that there are some things even a Queen cannot control."

George W., ever the Texas gentleman, replied, "Your Majesty, please don't give the matter another thought. You know, if you hadn't said something I would have assumed it was one of the horses."

Still Queen

A British army officer returned to London after spending 10 years in various corners of the world. At a fashionable cocktail party he suddenly found himself with an attractive woman whose face seemed familiar. Feeling that he knew her from somewhere, he asked how her father was. "My father is dead," she replied.

"Oh, terribly sorry," the man said.

Then, still groping for a clue, "How's your brother?"

"I don't have a brother," the woman said. "Just my sister."

"Of course, how stupid of me," the officer replied.

Feeling he was now getting on the right track he asked. "How *is* your sister?"

"Fine," said the attractive woman. "Still Queen."

chaptereighteen

"I asked for ice, but this is ridiculous."

--Multi-millionaire John Jacob Astor; passenger aboard the HMS Titanic

touristtrap

It is when we take on the role of tourist we are at our most vulnerable. When we aren't being cheated by unscrupulous travel agents and tour guides who may not have our best interests at heart.

We have to worry about all the discomforts, dangers, and pitfalls of our chosen mode of travel.

Making our way through unfamiliar territory and places where we may not speak the language or understand the local customs can be disastrous.

And who knows what lurks beneath those souvenirs we innocently cart home from abroad.

. . . .

"I asked for ice, but this is ridiculous."

Human dealings are fraught with the potential for things to go wrong, and when you factor the role of tourist into the equation, that potential grows. Failure to properly understand the customs or cultures, or plan for eventualities can lead to hilarious results that usually victimize the hapless traveller.

"Apart from that, no news I can think of."

A rich American man was picked up by his chauffeur at the airport after a long business trip. The man asked his chauffeur what had been happening in his absence.

"Well sir!" said the chauffeur, "I'm afraid your dog died after she ate some burnt horseflesh.

"Burnt horseflesh?" asked the man.

"Yes, the stables burnt down after your mansion was consumed by fire," replied the chauffeur.

"Fire?" exclaimed the man.

"Yes, sir," the chauffeur replied hesitantly, "The fire was caused from candles around the coffin of your dear mother, who died of a heart attack when she found out her husband, your stepfather ran off with your wife."

Uncomfortable with the silence that followed, the chauffeur added, "Apart from that, no news I can think of."

Daddy Deadest

Two sisters from Houston, Texas, took their elderly father for a holiday in Mexico. However, a few days into their trip the father suffered a heart attack and died. Distraught and not thinking straight, the two sisters decided to try to take the body back themselves on the train, so that he could be buried in Texas.

They propped their father up in their compartment to make it look like he was just sleeping. After a few hours, the train stopped at a small town, so the sisters got off to get something to eat and freshen up. They left their dead father on the train wrapped in a blanket, confident that no-one would touch him. The sisters spent so long looking for a place to eat that they lost track of time and just about missed their train.

Panting, they finally returned to their compartment, but were shocked to discover that not only had a couple of drunken men taken over their compartment, but their father was nowhere to be seen. One sister, deciding to be blunt, told the men about their dead father.

The drunken man turned to his companion, and laughing said, "He was already dead. Thank goodness for that. I was so drunk, I accidentally dropped my suitcase on him and thought I killed him, so we threw him out the window a few miles back."

Exposed Tan

Vacation time was sun-tan time as far as Janie, an admirably proportioned flight attendant, was concerned, and she spent almost all of her day on the roof of her hotel soaking up the warm sun's rays.

She wore a bathing suit the first day, but on the second, she decided that since no one could see her way up there, she slipped out of it for an overall tan. She'd hardly begun when she suddenly heard someone running up the stairs. Lying on her stomach, she pulling a towel over her derriere, and she continued to recline as before.

"Excuse me, miss," said the flustered little assistant manager of the hotel, out of breath from running up the stairs. "The Hotel Plaza doesn't mind your sunning on the roof, but we would very much appreciate your wearing your bathing suit as you did yesterday."

"What difference does it make?" Janie asked rather coldly. "No one can see me up here and besides, I'm covered with a towel."

"Not exactly," said the embarrassed man, "You're lying on the dining room skylight."

Last Stop

A couple was on a dream vacation on the Orient Express from Moscow to London. Early one morning, the man was woken up when the train came to a sudden halt.

Unable to get back to sleep, he went to use the bathroom, but found it was occupied, so feeling desperate, the man went to use the bathroom on the next carriage.

After using the bathroom, he went to return to his carriage, but was horrified to discover that the train had left the carriage he was on behind.

Unfortunately, the train company decided to leave the carriage behind because there were no longer any passengers in it. The poor man was stranded half-dressed in Leipzig while his wife was on her way to London.

Did You Know? *Multi-millionaire passenger John Jacob Astor made an archly humorous quip when the Titanic struck an iceberg. Astor said, standing at the bar after the collision, "I asked for ice, but this is ridiculous."*

New Chambermaid

An elderly lady went on a week's holiday to a resort in the Rocky Mountains.

Arriving at the resort, she came across a toilet brush on the floor, and picked it up to hand to the receptionist.

Before she could say anything, the receptionist told her to clean the toilets on each floor. The old lady tried to explain who she was, but the receptionist was most insistent, and the old lady didn't like to say no to people.

With two sets on each of the six floors, and being a perfectionist, it took the old lady a good three and ahalf hours to scrub down all the toilets. With the job done, she returned to the reception only to be reprimanded for taking so long, and was told to tidy up the rooms on the top floor.

It was only when the old lady asked if she could see her room first, and unpack her bags, that the receptionist realised she was actually a paying guest and not the new chambermaid.

"So, how'd you break your arm?"

A friend of a friend just got back from a holiday ski trip to Utah. He said conditions were perfect. 12 below, no feeling in the toes, basic numbness all over, one of those "tell me when we're having fun" kind of days.

One of the women in his group complained to her husband that she was in dire need of a restroom. He told her not to worry, that he was sure there was relief waiting at the top of the lift in the form of a powder room for female skiers in distress. He was wrong, of course, and the pain grew.

With time running out, the woman weighed her options.

Her husband, picking up on the intensity of the pain, suggested that since she was wearing an all-white ski outfit, she should go off in the woods. No one would even notice, he assured her. The white will provide more than adequate camouflage. So she headed for the tree line, began disrobing and proceeded to do her thing.

When parked on the side of a slope there is a right way and wrong way to set up your skis so you don't move. Well, she had them positioned the wrong way.

Steep slopes are not forgiving, even during embarrassing moments. Without warning, the woman found herself skiing backward, out-of-control, racing through the trees, somehow missing all of them, and into another slope. Her derriere and the reverse side were still bare, her pants down around her knees, and she was picking up speed all the while.

She continued on backwards, totally out-of-control, creating an unusual vista for the other skiers.

The woman skied back under the lift and finally collided violently with a pylon. The bad news was that she broke her arm and was unable to pull up her ski pants. At long last her husband arrived, and put an end to her nudie show, then went to the base of the mountain and summoned the ski patrol, who transported her to a hospital.

In the emergency room she was regrouping when a man with an obviously broken leg was put in the bed next to hers.

Making small talk, she asked, "So. how'd you break your leg?"

"It was the darndest thing you ever saw," he said. "I was riding up this ski lift, and suddenly I couldn't believe my eyes. There was this crazy woman skiing backward out-of-control down the mountain with her bare bottom hanging out of her clothes and pants down around her knees. I leaned over to get a better look and I guess I didn't realise how far I'd moved and fell out of the lift...so, how'd you break your arm?"

The Smarts and The Stupids

Two families - we'll call them the Smarts and the Stupids, met on a train to London, England.

The fathers of the two families started to talk to one another, and it soon became apparent that the Smarts had bought only one ticket between them for the journey.

Shortly before the ticket inspector came round, the Smarts headed off to the toilet.

After collecting the Stupids tickets, the inspector banged on the door of the toilet and shouted, "Tickets, please."

A single hand emerged, complete with ticket, and the inspector, having satisfied himself that all was well with the world, clipped the proffered ticket and carried on down the train.

The Stupids were deeply impressed by this feat of cunning, and in the course of the rest of the journey they arranged to meet the Smarts for the trip home.

Sure enough, on the journey home the two families met again, only this time the Stupids had bought just the one ticket, and the Smarts hadn't purchased any this time.

Just as the Smarts were beginning to explain how they were going to get around the problem, the ticket inspector was spotted heading their way.

The Stupids rushed into the toilet, and a short while later there was a knock at the door.

"Tickets, please" said Mr. Smart, before pocketing the Stupids ticket and joining his family in another toilet.

"Is it possible to see England from Canada, because they look so close on the map."

These following tales demonstrate that not everyone who arranges our means of travel has our best interests at heart, but equally demanding is the clueless tourist who can make any travel agent's life hell.

An American boaster in Paris

An American man on holiday in Paris decided to hire a personal tour guide to help him look around the city.

278

The tour guide first took his client to the cathedral in Montmartre where the tourist asked him how long the cathedral took to build, to which the reply was, "About ten years".

The American retorted, "Gee, in America, we would have had this up in ten months!"

The next attractions were the Arc De Triomphe, Notre-Dame and the Louvre, and at each place the American asked the same question, and then retorted with a boast of how quickly the monument would have been built in America.

When they arrived at the Eiffel Tower, the American asked the guide, "Wow, what is that?"

Tthe exasperated man replied flatly, "I have no idea, it certainly wasn't here yesterday".

"Florida is a very thin state!"

A man called his travel agent, furious about his Florida package. The agent asked what was wrong with the vacation in Orlando. He said he was expecting an ocean-view room. The agent tried to explain that was not possible, because Orlando is in the middle of the state.

He replied, "Don't lie to me. I looked on the map, and Florida is a very thin state!"

Did You Know? *A travel agent got a call from a lawyers wife who asked, "Is it possible to see England from Canada?" The agent said, "No." The wife replied, "But they look so close on the map."*

Painted Lake

An American woman on holiday in New Zealand was staying in a hotel by a lake that was famous for its bright blue colour. She was sitting outside on the terrace of the hotel bar, gazing out over the blue lake, when the waiter brought her a glass of beer, so she asked him how the lake became such a rich blue colour.

The waiter, bored of being asked the same question throughout the summer, told her that every year at the end of summer the lake is drained and the bottom is painted blue. The tourist seemed to accept this explanation, so the waiter laughed to himself and thought no more of the conversation.

Towards the end of the summer, he was surprised to see the same woman at the hotel again.

As he took her order he made polite conversation, in which he stated that she must really like the hotel.

She replied, "Oh yes, and I just had to come back and see the painting of the lake bottom".

"What Trip To Paris?"

Unlike their American and Italian counterparts who would have been rather more worldly-wise, the marketing department of one English travel company managed to annoy a significant section of its customers.

To promote a service to Paris, frequent travellers in business class were made a special offer: "Every fourth trip, their spouses could travel with them to the City of Romance for free".

The campaign was a great success. That was until the marketing department phoned the spouses of the customers who had participated in the scheme to ask about the service and about their impressions of the promotion.

Many of the unsuspecting women promptly replied, "What trip to Paris?"

"I was told my flight number is 823, but none of these darn planes have numbers on them."

Oh, the joys of airline travel: the gourmet meal, and the hundreds of impatient travellers crowded into an enclosed space for hours on end with no stretching room in sight. It's no wonder almost anything can happen under such conditions of confinement.

A Good Pilot Is Always Prepared

A friend of a friend was on a flight that was delayed, so they settled down to wait. Three hours passed, and they were finally told the plane was now ready to board. Air Jamaica bought many of its planes second-hand from other airlines. The mid-sized jet was dirty, ancient, and was clearly one that no one else had wanted.

Inside, the passengers settled into the seats with 80 or 90 other passengers and waited...and waited.

Finally, the pilot's voice came over he loudspeaker. "We're all ready to go ladies and gentlemen. However, we've been waiting for the copilot, and he still hasn't arrived. Since we've already waited so long, we're just going to be flying without a copilot today."

There was a nervous buzz through the cabin.

He continued, "If any of you feel uncomfortable with this, feel free to disembark now and Air Jamaica will put you on the next available flight."

Then the pilot paused, and continued "Unfortunately, we are not sure when that will be. But rest assured, I have flown this route hundreds of times, we have clear blue skies, and there are no foreseeable problems."

Not one passenger, doubtful as they might have been, wanted to wait any longer for a plane that may or may not materialize, so they stayed onboard for the one-hour flight.

Once the aircraft reached cruising altitude, the pilot came on the loudspeaker again, "Ladies and gentlemen. I am going to use the bathroom. I have put the plane on auto-pilot and everything will be fine. I just don't want you to worry."

That said, he came out of the cockpit, fastened the door open using a rubber band to a hook on the wall. Then he went to the bathroom.

Suddenly, they hit a patch of turbulence. Nothing much, the cabin just shook a little for a moment. But the rubber band snapped off with a loud 'ping!' and went sailing down the aisle. The door promptly swung shut. A moment later, the pilot came out of the bathroom. When he saw the closed door, he stopped cold. The passengers watched him from the back and wondered what was wrong. The stewardess came running up, and together they both tried to open the door. But it wouldn't budge.

It slowly dawned on them that their pilot was locked out of the cockpit. Cockpit doors lock automatically from the inside to prevent terrorists from entering. Without a copilot, there was no one to open the door from the inside. By now, the rest of the passengers had become aware of the problem, and watched the pilot, horrified. What would he do?

After a moment of contemplation, the pilot hurried to the back of the plane. He returned holding a huge axe. Without ceremony, he proceeded to chop down the cockpit door. The passengers were rooted to their seats as they watched him.

Once he managed to chop a hole in the door, he reached inside, unlocked the door, and let himself back in.

Then he came on the loudspeaker, his voice a little shaken, "Ah, ladies and gentlemen, we just had a little problem there, but everything is fine now. We have plans to cover every eventuality, even pilots getting locked out of their cockpits. So relax and enjoy the rest of the flight!"

"Are You Gay?"

An airplane employee whose last name was "Gay" boarded a plane using his company pass. He saw that his assigned seat was occupied so he took a vacant seat nearby.

Unfortunately, another flight was canceled and the flight attendants were told that they had to remove nonpaying passengers so that the ticketed passengers could board.

A flight attendant came down the aisle and asked the occupant of Mr. Gay's seat, "Are you Gay?"

The man looked surprised, but he replied, "Well, yes I am."

"Then you'll have to get off the plane," the attendant said.

Overhearing this conversation, Mr. Gay spoke up, saying, "No, I am Gay. I am the one who will have to get off."

Immediately, two men sitting nearby jumped up and yelled, "Well, we're gay too. And there's no way in hell we are getting off this plane."

Did You Know? *A New Hampshire Congresswoman asked for an aisle seat so that her hair wouldn't get messed up by sitting next to the window.*

Capetown, Massachusetts?

A political candidate's staff member wanted to go to Capetown.

The agent started to explain the length of the flight and the passport information when the staffer interrupted her with, "I'm not trying to make you look stupid, but Capetown is in Massachusetts."

Without trying to make her look like the stupid one, the agent calmly explained, "Cape Cod is in Massachusetts, Capetown is in Africa."

Compressed Air

A airplane passenger gave bottom marks to an airline after getting sealed to a toilet seat for more than two hours during a trans-Atlantic flight. The American woman used the toilet, but pushed the flush button before standing up.

To her horror, she realised that the powerful vacuum action had got her in its grip. Her body was sealed to the seat so firmly that it took airport technicians to free her.

Destination Fat

A New York politician called and asked, "Do airlines put your physical description on your bag so they know who's luggage belongs to who?"

The agent replied, "No, why do you ask?"

She replied, "Well, when I checked in with the airline, they put a tag on my luggage that said "FAT", and I'm overweight; I think that is very rude."

After putting her on hold for a minute while the agent looked into it, he came back and explained that the city code for Fresno, CA is "FAT", and that the airline was just putting a destination tag on her luggage.

Did You Know? *An Illinois woman called her travel agent and said, "How is it possible that my flight from Detroit left at 8:20am and I got into Chicago at 8:33am?" The agent tried to explain that Michigan was an hour ahead of Illinois, but she could not understand the concept of time zones. Finally, the agent told her the plane went really, really really fast, and she bought that.*

"Don't forget the coffee!"

A friend of my coworker was one of the lucky passengers on board an American Airlines flight to Boston during the recent hurricane "Bob". The captain did his best to skirt the edge of the storm, but it was a pretty rough ride just the same - rough enough that the flight attendants were ordered to strap themselves into their seats for about half an hour. Many of the passengers were putting the little plastic-lined bags in their seat pockets to good use, when the turbulence finally abated.

The flight attendants unbuckled themselves, and the captain's voice came on over the intercom, "Well, ladies and gentleman, that was quite some ride, wasn't it? But we came through it just fine, the way we always do, and I'm happy to report that it looks like the remainder of our trip should be much calmer. On behalf of myself and today's flight crew, I'd like to thank you very much for your calmness and cooperation, and extend our best wishes for a pleasant stay in Boston."

After a short pause and several clicks, "Jesus Christ!! That was one hell of a ride. Boy, I sure could use a strong cup of coffee and a blow job, right about now!"

As a stricken stewardess dashed up the aisle to the cabin to inform the captain that his intercom was still on, one of the passengers called out, "Don't forget the coffee!"

Elite Member

On a recent flight, CEO Gord Bune had pre-boarded the aircraft and was sitting on the flight deck chatting with the Captain and First Officer. He left the flight deck just before pushback to take his assigned First Class seat.

A OnePass Platinum Elite member boarded the flight furious that he had not been upgraded. Seeing several First Class seats open, he began to argue with the flight attendant over why he had not been upgraded.

The flight attendant said she would get a gate agent to look into the matter, but the Elite member began swearing at her profusely.

Mr. Bune was on his way back from the cockpit when this occurred, and intervened, asking, "Can I help somehow?"

The passenger said, "Who the f*** are you?"

"I'm the CEO of this company," Gord replied. "May I see your ticket, sir?"

The passenger gave his ticket to Gord, who saw a total fare of just under six hundred dollars. He then pulled out his billfold and peeled off six $100 bills, placing them in the man's hand. And then he tore the ticket up.

"Now," Gord said, "you get the f*** off my airplane!"

The flight attendant could barely contain herself.

"Fast. Neat. Average."

A co-worker of a friend of a friend told him how to get a free visit to the cockpit during a flight.

He said write "fast, neat, average" on a piece of paper and ask an attendant to give it to the pilot.

On May 7, 2004, this friend was a passenger on a Chicago-bound American TransAir plane departing from Ronald Reagan National Airport in Washington, D.C.

Remembering what his co-worker said, he handed a note reading "Fast. Neat. Average." to a flight attendant and asked her to deliver it to the pilot.

The pilot, puzzled by the note and suspicious of the passenger's motive in sending it to him, contacted airport police and headed the aircraft back to the gate. He was taken off the plane and detained for questioning, while the flight departed without him.

Airport police took him into custody, but after several hours of questioning and background checks he was released.

He told Airport security the message on his note had just been a misunderstanding. He thought it would get him a visit to the cockpit.

It turns out, "Fast. Neat. Average." is a code used by Air Force Cadets, and can only be understood by an Air Force pilot. The American Trans Air pilot did not have military experience.

"Fast. Neat. Average" is used by cadets at their table in Mitchell Hall to report on the quality of food and service.

The real intent is to use it as a training aide to teach fourth classman how to fill out an Air Force form: a black pen, within the space given, how to make corrections on a form using a single line and initials, how to properly make comments, including negative ones on an official form, and how to follow procedures in a short period of time under pressure.

"Fast. Neat. Average" actually means the meal and service were fine: fast (service), neat (server's appearance), average (portion size).

Did You Know? *A travel agent just got off the phone with a man who asked, "How do I know which plane to get on?" The agent asked him what exactly he meant, to which he replied, "I was told my flight number is 823, but none of these darn planes have numbers on them."*

Flight Safety Misinformation

On a flight to San Francisco from Seattle the flight attendant reading the flight safety information had the whole plane looking at her with a "what the hell?" expression on their faces.

Before takeoff the flight attendant said:

Hello and welcome to Alaska flight 438 to San Francisco. If you're going to San Francisco, you're in the right place. If you're not going to San Francisco, you're about to have a really long evening.

We'd like to tell you now about some important safety features of this aircraft. The most important safety feature we have aboard this plane is, The Flight Attendants.

Please look at one now. There are 5 exits aboard this plane, 2 at the front, 2 over the wings, and one out the plane's rear end. If you're seated in one of the exit rows, please do not store your bags by your feet. That would be a really bad idea. Please take a moment and look around and find the nearest exit. Count the rows of seats between you and the exit.

In the event that the need arises to find one, trust me, you'll be glad you did. We have pretty blinking lights on the floor that will blink in the direction of the exits. White ones along the normal rows, and pretty red ones at the exit rows. In the event of a loss of cabin pressure these baggy things will drop down over your head. You stick it over your nose and mouth like the flight attendant is doing now. The bag won't inflate, but there's oxygen there, I promise.

If you are sitting next to a small child, or someone who is acting like a small child, please do us all a favor and put on your mask first. If you are traveling with two or more children, please take a moment now to decide which one is your favorite. Help that one first, and then work your way down.

In the seat pocket in front of you is a pamphlet about the safety features of this plane. I usually use it as a fan when I'm having my own personal summer. It makes a very good fan. It also has pretty pictures. Please take it out and play with it now.

Please take a moment now to make sure your seat belts are fastened low and tight about your waist. To fasten the belt, insert the metal tab into the buckle. To release, it's a pulley thing — not a pushy thing like you're car cuz you're in an airplane, hello!

There is no smoking in the cabin on this flight. There is also no smoking in the lavatories. If we see smoke coming from the lavatories, we will assume you are on fire and put you out. This is a free service we provide.

There are two smoking sections on this flight, one outside each wing exit. We do have a movie in the smoking sections tonight, hold on, let me check what it is . . . Oh here it is, the movie tonight is "Ishtar!"

In a moment we will be turning off the cabin lights, and it's going to get really dark, really fast. If you're afraid of the dark, now would be a good time to reach up and press the yellow button. The yellow button turns on your reading light. Please don't press the orange button unless you absolutely have to. The orange button is your seat ejection button.

We're glad to have you with us on board this flight. Thank you for choosing Alaska Air, and giving us your business and your money. If there's anything we can do to make you more comfortable, please don't hesitate to ask. If you all weren't strapped down you would have given me a standing ovation wouldn't you?

After Landing the flight attendant came back on the speaker and said:

Welcome to the San Francisco International Airport. Sorry about the bumpy landing. It's not the captain's fault. It's not the co-pilot's fault. It's the Asphalt.

Please remain seated until the plane is parked at the gate. At no time in history has a passenger beaten a plane to the gate. So please don't even try. Please be careful opening the overhead bins because shift happens.

"I wonder what happens when I press this button."

A few years ago a plane flying across the Gulf of Mexico crashed, killing all 182 passengers.

Investigators were mystified as to the cause of the accident because it had passed a thorough inspection before takeoff, the pilots had not reported any problems, and there had been no distress calls.

Further investigations revealed nothing and rumours about the plane being another casualty of the Bermuda Triangle propagated.

However, some months later, the plane's black box was discovered washed up on a Mexican beach.

Investigators listened to the recordings, and heard the last words that the pilot spoke, "I wonder what happens when I press this button."

They have yet to find out which button the pilot pressed.

Lifetime Passes

A child born in-flight is awarded free air transport on that airline for the rest of his life. This unwritten rule is whispered as the reason airlines restrict the travel plans of expectant women. After all, if you don't allow the ladies to fly when they're getting close to their time, you never need worry about providing lifetime passes to their kids, right?

Did You Know? *People who fear flying will be happy to know it is the safest form of travel, and more people are killed every year by donkeys than by airplane crashes. Yes, contrary to what we may think, a slow, clumsy, primitive mode of transportation is actually more dangerous, or at least kills more people than air travel.*

Seeing Eye Pilot

My co-worker was flying from San Francisco to Los Angeles. By the time they took off, there had been a 45-minute delay and everybody on board was pissed off.

Unexpectedly, they stopped in Sacramento on the way. The flight attendant explained that there would be another 45-minute delay, and if anybody wanted to get off the aircraft, they would reboard in 30 minutes. Everybody got off the plane except one gentleman who was blind. My co-worker noticed as he walked by that the blind man had flown before because his Seeing Eye dog lay quietly underneath the seats in front of him throughout the entire flight.

He could also tell he had flown this very flight before because the pilot approached him and, calling him by name, said, "Herb, we're in Sacramento for about an hour. Would you like to get off and stretch your legs?"

Herb replied, "No thanks, but maybe my dog would like to stretch his legs."

All the people in the gate area came to a completely quiet standstill when they looked up and saw the pilot walk off the plane with a Seeing Eye dog! The pilot was even wearing sunglasses. People scattered. in a panic to change planes, or possibly change airlines!

Did You Know? *An Aide for a Bush cabinet member once called and asked if they could rent a car in Dallas. When the agent pulled up the reservation, he noticed they only had a 1-hour layover in Dallas. When the agent asked him why he wanted to rent a car, he said, "I heard Dallas was a big airport, and we will need a car to drive between the gates to save time."*

Wait In Line

In Denver, the United Airlines gate agent was confronted with a passenger who probably deserved to fly as cargo.

During the final days of Denver's old Stapleton airport, a crowded United flight was cancelled, and there was only one agent rebooking a long line of inconvenienced travelers.

Suddenly an angry passenger pushed his way to the desk, slapped his ticket down on the counter and said, "I have to be on this flight and it has to be first class."

The agent replied, "I'm sorry sir. I'll be happy to try to help you, but I've got to help these folks first, and I'm sure we'll be able to work something out."

But the passenger was not impressed. He asked loudly, so that the passengers behind him could hear, "Do you have any idea who I am?"

Without hesitating, the gate agent smiled and grabbed her public address microphone.

"May I have your attention please?" she began, her voice bellowing throughout the terminal. "We have a passenger here at the gate who does not know who he is. If anyone can help him find his identity, please come to Gate 21."

With the folks behind him in line laughing hysterically, the man glared at the United agent, gritted his teeth and yelled, "Screw you!"

Without flinching, she smiled and said, "I'm sorry, sir, but you'll have to stand in line for that too."

"Why do you think the manager owns a pig and why in God's name, if he did, do you think he would want to have sex with it?"

Modern travel has allowed us to come in contact with a variety of cultures from all over the world. Although people are alike wherever our travels lead us, there are still differences in customs and pronunciation that can lead to amusing and potentially embarrassing situations.

Did You Know? *An American family returned home from a vacation in New Zealand with a neat Aboriginal-made elongated wooden bowl, which they used for party snacks. Then one day an anthropologically better-informed visitor pointed out that the two little holes in the side were* *for a waistband and while it was indeed used for parties where it came from, namely corroborees, it was meant to hold only two nuts.*

Foreign Airfairs

A friend of a friend was taking a flight on Bodrum Airlines, a foreign airline. The instructions on the passenger ticket were garbled as only non-English speakers can.

You do not get rezarvation with Bodrum Airlines.

You can not give back your ticket, but, if you annonce us before 24 hours your depart that you cannot fly you can use your ticket with in one year. After passing one year, you can not fly with your ticket.

You have to pay extra price if your baggece more than 10 kg. if aircraft baggece cappacity is avalleble. Lost baggece insurance is Twenty Thawzent doll hairs.

Ticket price for 0-2 year ache babys are 10% of normal price.

You have to get in touch with contuar befe 30 mitutes of the departure, atherwine you don't get on the board and you don't have any rights for justice.

Your ticket cann't bu used if you be late or you miss departure time.

If someone gets ticket by doing tricky, Bodrum Airlines has rezerved the rights that there is no must to give a permation that passenger gets on the board.

Bodrum Airlines is able to carry all passengers and baggeces but if any unusual things happen the can pany can change schadule or find another aircraft or company.

Bodrum Airlines is not able to cary out flight schadule if an unusual thinks take place like bed weather, notam, float, fire, eath queke, war, gone of elefricity, natural disaster, etc.

Each passangere has ensurance of Twenty five milyon.

Pragnent and sick people have to have doctor's permetion that they can get on the board.

Do not allawe to drink alcaol and smoke cigarets on board.

"May I lick your buttocks?"

A prankster has stirred up trouble by publishing a Japanese-to-English phrase book with incorrect definitions for every phrase!

Now thousands of Japanese tourists who've painstakingly studied the bogus dictionary in preparation for trips to America are arriving on Japanese shores only to encounter blank stares, hysterical laughter and even brutal beatings as soon as they open their mouths.

"The man who compiled this dictionary clearly went out of his way to wreak havoc," said New York hotel concierge Stella Morse, who arranges tours for many VIP guests from Japan. "For example, when the Japanese think they're asking: "Can you direct me to the rest room?" the book actually has them saying, "Excuse me, may I lick your buttocks?"

Morny. Rune-sore-bees

The exchange between an English-speaking traveller and a member of the hotel staff in a Far East hotel was recorded in the "Far-East Economic Review" about five years ago. It is really hard to fathom.

Room Service: Morny. Rune-sore-bees.

Hotel Guest: Oh, sorry. I thought I dialed Room Service.

Room Service: Rye, rune-sore-bees. Morny. Djewish to odor sunteen?

Hotel Guest: Uh... yes. I'd like some bacon and eggs.

Room Service: Ow July den?

Hotel Guest: What?

Room Service: Aches. Ow July den? Pry, boy, pooch...?

Hotel Guest: Oh, the eggs! How do I like them? Sorry. Scrambled please.

Room Service: Ow July dee baycome? Crease?

Hotel Guest: Crisp will be fine.

Room Service: Hokay. An Santos?

Hotel Guest: What?

Room Service: Santos. July Santos?

Hotel Guest: Ugh. I don't know... I don't think so.

Room Service: No. Judo one toes?

Hotel Guest: Look, I feel really bad about this, but I don't know what "judo one toes" means. I'm sorry.

Room Service: Toes! Toes! Why djew Don Juan toes? Ow bow eenglish mopping we bother?

Hotel Guest: English muffin! I've got it! You were saying toast! Fine. An English muffin will be fine.

Room Service: We bother?

Hotel Guest: No. Just put the bother on the side.

Room Service: Wad?

Hotel Guest: I'm sorry. I meant butter. Butter on the side.

Room Service: Copy?

Hotel Guest: I feel terrible about this but...

Room Service: Copy. Copy, tea, mill...

Hotel Guest: Coffee! Yes, coffee please. And that's all.

Room Service: One Minnie. Ass rune torino fee, strangle aches, crease baycome, tossy cenglish mopping we bother honey sigh, and copy. Rye?

Hotel Guest: Whatever you say.

Room Service: Hokay. Tendjewberrymud.

Hotel Guest: You're welcome.

Spanish Incuisine

An American couple planned to go to Spain for a two-week holiday and sought the advice of a friend who was always showing off his language skills and bragging about all the countries he had been to.

He gave them tips on where they should go, and on where to stay. He also taught them a few key phrases in Spanish. After arriving in Spain, the couple took a room in a hotel and then went out for some authentic cuisine. After finally selecting a restaurant, the man decided to try out the Spanish phrases their friend had taught them.

When he asked the waiter for the menu, the waiter just stared at him before running off and coming back with the manager. The man repeated the same phrase to the manager. Again, the response was startled stares, before they ran off and came back with the chef.

The chef asked the man in English, "Why do you think the manager owns a pig and why in God's name, if he did, do you think he would want to have sex with it?"